KISSING FROGS

Liz was sitting under the huge umbrella, wearing more make-up than usual. Her scent overpowered the jasmine and basil in the pots. She raised an eyebrow at Luc's dusty dishevelment. 'You do look hot and bothered.'

'Do I?' A teapot, glasses and a jug of Pimms stood on the table, along with the filo parcels and some olives.

'Some Pimms?'

'Thank . . .' Luc followed Liz's gaze across the swimming pool and realised the offer was directed elsewhere. Gasping, she almost dropped her sketchbook.

'Lucasta, Count von Retzen. Count, Lucasta James. Lucasta's been sketching,' added Liz hastily, as if this might excuse Luc's tattiness. 'Anywhere nice?'

Luc heard nothing. The world might have been exploding into a million pieces around her and she wouldn't have noticed.

No longer hidden behind dark glasses, the eyes were lapis lazuli blue.

Also by Sarah Ingham

Parallel Turns

About the author

A former journalist, Sarah Ingham now writes full-time. *Kissing Frogs* is her second novel.

Her first novel, *Parallel Turns,* was published by Hodder & Stoughton in 1999:

'Even the snow-laden atmosphere does nothing to cool the passions in this steamy story of sex, snowploughing and chalet girls' *Marie Claire*

'A very well-written romp with more twists and turns than an off-piste run' *Ms London*

Kissing Frogs

Sarah Ingham

CORONET BOOKS
Hodder & Stoughton

Copyright © 2000 by Sarah Ingham

The right of Sarah Ingham to be identified as the Author of
the Work has been asserted by her in accordance with the
Copyright, Designs and Patents Act 1988.

First published in Great Britain in 2000
by Hodder and Stoughton
A division of Hodder Headline
First published in paperback in 2000
by Hodder and Stoughton

A Coronet Paperback

10 9 8 7 6 5 4 3 2 1

British Library Cataloguing in Publication Data.
A catalogue record for this title is available
from the British Library.

ISBN 0 340 74844 3

Printed and bound in Great Britain by
Mackays of Chatham PLC, Chatham, Kent

Hodder and Stoughton
A division of Hodder Headline
338 Euston Road
London NW1 3BH

Chapter One

Luc James's pulse was going nuclear as the Customs officer rummaged through her bag. The sweat trickling down her back had nothing to do with the sauna-like heat in Athens airport.

'Here we go, here we go, here we go-oh.' Soccer fans were swarming through the hall, Union Jacks draped round their shoulders. They had been on the same four-hour flight, travelling to watch a friendly.

'He should be testing them for rabies,' said Ella Parr, pointedly looking at her watch.

Eyes fixed on her bag, Luc silently willed Ella to shut up and not draw attention to herself. Ella popped her chewing-gum and continued to gaze blithely round the hall. The officer pulled out a plastic bag containing a battered pair of espadrilles. He pulled a face. Certain he'd sniffed, Luc was mortified.

'Strip-search these two.' A fan went past, riding on top of a baggage trolley wheeled by three friends. He swigged from a vodka bottle. 'They'd love it.'

Luc blushed crimson in horror at the thought. With her red face, pounding heart and stress sweat, she could have been in a marathon, running from a posse of the local drugs squad. Fortunately, the Customs man ignored the fan's advice and continued to rummage through her bag. Any minute he'd ask Ella to open her backpack, lying on the trolley like an unexploded bomb. He held a pair of knickers up to the light.

'Clean, I hope,' muttered Ella. 'What's the Greek for fur coat and no knickers?'

Luc glared at her. Ella looked as cool as if she'd just stepped out of a fridge.

Any minute now they could be arrested for possession. If they weren't, she was going to be arrested for murder. Ella's murder. How could Ella have been so stupid as to take such a huge risk? She'd mentioned it when they were waiting by the baggage carousel, as casually as if she had packed some sunscreen. 'A bag of the Caribbean's finest and we're not talking bananas.' Luc had begged her to go and flush it down the loo, but Ella had shrugged, saying Greek porridge might be interesting.

Yawning loudly, Ella pushed her long blonde fringe out of her eyes. Luc knew that expression of bored, blank innocence; it was the same one Ella had worn that day they'd been caught bunking off double physics and going into the betting shop. Ella had said they were only trying to raise a few extra pennies for the African Mission, that term's charity. 'Passing on the Good News,' she'd told a highly sceptical Sister Paul.

As the Customs officer delved deeper into her bag, Luc felt the word 'guilty' tattooed across her forehead, branding her for life like her imminent criminal record. She wanted to demand to speak to the British consul there and then, get it over with. The sooner they were arrested, the sooner they'd be eating Greek porridge and the sooner she'd be home. Why hadn't she stayed there?

'Hey, blondie. Ginge!' cried a Geordie amongst a group of passing fans. He waved a sweating cheese baguette at Ella before stuffing it down his shorts. 'Fancy a nibble?'

'You should be quarantined.' Ella turned away in fury. 'Why pick on us instead of those creeps? We'll miss our ferry.' She glared at the Customs man, who hastily dropped Luc's washbag and motioned they were free to go.

The arrivals hall was chaotic. French air traffic controllers

2

had just begun a work to rule. 'Delayed' clattered up next to all incoming flights on the arrivals board. A groan went up among those waiting. The local garbage men were on strike and litter spewed out of bins.

Seeing the Geordie sharing the baguette with his friends, Ella turned the trolley 180 degrees and bolted in the opposite direction. 'I need a drink.'

'And I need a holiday, not an audition for *Midnight Express*,' hissed Luc. She clutched the trolley for support, her trembling legs threatening to buckle under her.

'That was Turkey.' Ella opened her bottle of duty-free bourbon. She swigged and coughed. 'Close.'

Luc snatched the bottle, her hands shaking.

It was already four o'clock. Outside, the temperature was in the nineties, the light blinding after the gloom inside the terminal. Buildings shimmered in the heat as if they were about to melt. Cars, taxis and coaches blasted their horns, their exhaust fumes rivalling the smell of kerosene. A helicopter swung into the air and disappeared south towards the cool of the Aegean.

They headed for a metal-roofed bus shelter. Reaching inside her battered bag for her guidebook, Luc wondered why she'd packed three sweaters along with most of her other just-in-case stuff. Well named. For the next ten days that was exactly where it would stay.

'It's so hot.' Ella fanned herself with the sickbag that they'd played noughts and crosses on during the flight, when she hadn't been reading the *Financial Times* or making sculptures out of the inedible food. The flight attendant hadn't been impressed by her mashed-potato snowman.

Luc treble-checked her guidebook for the bus which would take them across Athens to Piraeus. 'Number Forty. Goes via Constitution Square. And hold on to that sickbag.' She still felt queasy at the thought of the risk Ella had run.

'You could've improved your cooking by baking me cakes

with files in them.' Ella shrugged. 'Does Delia Smith have a recipe? She doesn't run to hash cookies. Ben checked.'

'Ben would.' Luc thumbed the guidebook, scanned some lines and squeaked. ' "On no account even think about drugs. The Greek Government has begun a major initiative to combat . . . cracking down . . . Draconian . . ." Oh God.'

'I'd have been carted off, not you. And even if you had, it would've been a change. That's what you want, isn't it? Change? Some adventure?'

Luc was tempted to hit her over the head with the guidebook. 'A Greek Cell Block H isn't quite what I had in mind.'

During the wait for the bus, they practised the Greek phrases in the back of the book. 'Please. *Pa-ra-kalo. Para-kalo. Paraka-lo.*' Then they tried to fathom the alphabet, before examining the money.

'Gorgeous.' Ella peered at the chiselled face of Apollo on a 1,000-drachma note. 'Wonder if they still make Greeks like him? *Parakalo* God, they do.'

The excitement of being somewhere new hit them as the bus started its journey towards the centre of Athens. They were disconcerted not to see the columns of the Parthenon immediately, but even the dreary warehouses seemed to be more exotic than those on the way to Heathrow. The giant hoardings were a novelty because of the strange lettering. All they'd worked out so far was that a P was an R.

Back in London, they had decided to head straight for the islands. Living in one city, they wanted to avoid another. Ella said cities were for long weekends in February. Now they'd arrived, Luc felt a pang of guilt about not exploring Athens. Her sense of skiving off was reinforced by chapter after chapter in the guidebook devoted to the Acropolis and Museum of Byzantine Art and the Archaeology Museum.

'Perhaps we should do some sightseeing.' She tried to muster some enthusiasm about visiting the landmarks of the birthplace of Western civilisation, but felt drained just reading about them. Outside the window, Athens was on a slow boil in the heat of the relentless sun.

'We could always come back next week.' Ella gazed up and up at the columns of the Parthenon, sounding doubtful.

'The cradle of democracy,' Luc read from her book.

'And a very long, hot walk. Are there any sherpas?'

As the bus went further into the heart of Athens, it slowed to a crawl and stopped. The traffic was solid. Tree-lined boulevards were flanked by dark stone buildings, their porticos and balconies decorated with Art Nouveau motifs. Cool and elegant, they were slightly forbidding, as if they had exotic secrets to keep.

'Constitution Square,' said Luc, gazing out. 'That must be the Parliament building.' Fronted by a vast courtyard, it ran the length of the square. 'The Grande Bretagne. "In 1944, Churchill negotiated Greek independence . . ."'

'There's McDonalds.' Ella cut short the history lesson.

The bus moved off, only to stop again a few minutes later beside a tiny patch of open ground. Railings guarded two crumbling Doric columns. A woman in a business suit was talking into her mobile. '"My name is Ozymandias, king of kings",' quoted Ella. '"Look on my works, ye mighty, and despair."'

Nervous about missing the ferry, they became twitchy, looking at their watches more frequently. Luc read out that the local taxis were among the cheapest in Europe, which didn't calm their nerves. They hadn't expected to see TV aerials and neon and Marks and Spencer and traffic jams. 'Apparently there's been a port at Piraeus for three thousand years.'

'About how long this bus is going to take to get there.'

The port was huge. Getting off the bus, they were both overwhelmed by the bustle. Cargoes were being unloaded, forklifts threatened to topple over. Lorries and taxis were hooting, directed by officials blowing shrill whistles. Hundreds of back-packers milled around, shrieking gulls swooped overhead. Like floating multi-storey car-parks, five ferries were moored around the horseshoe-shaped quayside.

'Which boat? Where do we get a ticket?' Squinting in the glare, Ella looked round helplessly. The heat was brain scrambling, making it impossible to think. A foghorn boom echoed off the warehouses.

'Which boat to Praxos?' Luc called out to a goatee-bearded blond carrying a guitar. He ignored her. 'Praxos? Praxos?' Every passer-by ignored her.

'Eanie, meanie,' cried Ella in despair, gazing from one ferry to the next. They didn't have time to get it wrong. 'Why didn't we get a taxi?'

'Ask over there?' suggested Luc, pointing at a booking office. 'Run.'

'That's the ferry,' shouted Ella over another foghorn boom. A sign hooked to the quayside railings said Eos, Thira, Mathi, Praxos. A scooter beeped and swerved to avoid her. As they dodged through the remaining throng who were boarding, Luc's heavy bag banged against her shin.

A metallic voice came over a loudspeaker. It switched to English, ordering anyone not sailing to disembark immediately. Ella barged her way to the front of the crowd and asked a uniformed crewman where they could get a ticket. He pointed to a shed in the distance. Ella swore. 'Come on,' she shouted at Luc.

They scrambled into the booking office. 'Praxos. Tickets?' panted Luc at the clerk, her *parakalos* forgotten. The few stragglers were boarding.

'One way?'

They looked at one another blankly. 'One way,' said Ella, her voice staccato with anxiety. 'Let's just get on board. Worry about it later.'

As the computer printed out their tickets agonisingly slowly, they glanced over their shoulders, anxious they'd be left behind. Luc handed over a wad of drachma. Without bothering to count it, she snatched up her change and sprinted after Ella across the quayside.

They made it. Just.

'Are we going to end up in Calais?' asked Ella, climbing the steps to the passenger deck. Their hearts sank. They could've been on a cross-Channel ferry. A dismal cross-Channel ferry. In a vast lounge area, people had already staked out their territory by putting their luggage on the seats. Food was being unpacked and children settled. Dozens of people were queuing at the bar.

Ella looked at the purple and mauve swirly carpet and shuddered. 'Where's that sickbag?'

Luc surveyed the scene, her heart as heavy as her bag. The lounge was stuffy and smelt of old cooking fat. Three babies were bawling.

Back in London, they had pictured something more romantic. A large old fishing boat, perhaps, wooden-decked, where they'd lie on steamer chairs and watch the sun set and then the stars appear. There'd be a few other passengers, charming fogey classicists who'd tell them about Homer and Plato. Ella wanted to read Byron by the light of the moon, which would shimmer like mercury on the inky water.

'Deck?' suggested Luc.

They climbed another two flights of metal stairs on to the open deck. It was covered with moulded plastic orange seats. The ferry was just leaving the murky-brown harbour, heading for the open sea. Black smoke belched from its funnel as it cut through the almost waveless water. They stood against the rail and watched as the warehouses and cranes became more toy-like, as Piraeus gradually turned into a child's model of a port. The hubbub grew hushed. The sea was flat calm, the sun had a gentler brightness, the breeze was warm. Finally Athens was nothing more than a backcloth, so still it was painted, rather than a smoggy, hilly city of teeming millions.

For the first time that day, Luc allowed herself to relax.

*

When Ella had suggested they go to Greece, Luc had offered to collect some brochures from the travel agent, an offer Ella had scorned.

'What for? It's simple. All we need is a flight to Athens, then we jump on a ferry and head for one of the islands. We can stay up on deck, sleep under the stars.'

'But where will we stay?'

'We'll find something when we get there. Easy peasy. It's June. Lowest of the low season.'

'But we could waste loads of time. I can only afford ten days. Surely a package would be more practical?' Luc had known she sounded feeble, but Ella was someone who got lost on the Circle Line. What would happen in Greece?

'You want that sort of holiday?' Ella had grown exasperated. 'Met at the airport by some clipboard in a red skirt and matching scarf, shepherded on to a coach, then dumped in a building-site hotel and sold tours and ouzo nights for a week? Forget it.'

'But . . .'

'But nothing. For the past month you've done nothing but complain about how dull you've become. Package holiday? Shall I buy you a pair of knitting needles?'

Luc took another lungful of the Aegean air and gazed down into the blue, blue water. The tensions that had built up within her were beginning to drift away like the smoke from the funnel. The bus journey had been nerve-racking as they'd wondered if they'd make the ferry in time. Then before that, at the airport. If they'd been caught . . . Her guidebook warned of at least a year in gaol for possession of even the smallest amounts of grass. When she had made Ella read the passage as the bus passed the Olympic Stadium, Ella had laughed.

'You can't be cold.' Ella noticed her shiver. 'I'm going to find some ice.'

She had tied up her hair. From afar, in her ankle-length floral frock, she could have been going to a 1930s tea dance. But with the rose tattoo on her arm and the diamond stud in her snub nose, the doormen wouldn't have let her in.

'At least we can watch the sun set and go to sleep under the stars.' Ella returned with two plastic beakers and some ice from the bar. 'Drink?'

'Perhaps we should've brought some food,' said Luc.

'Like what? Eccles cakes?'

Seventy-something Dolly Tilling, their only neighbour in the Mews not earning telephone numbers, always took Eccles cakes on her little journeys to ward off constipation. Her last little journey had been to Ulan Bator on the Trans-Siberian Express. Luc and Ella had looked after her cats, Trotsky and Lenin, named to irritate the two po-faced American bankers at number twelve.

'There's a restaurant downstairs,' added Ella. 'We're on a boat, so there's bound to be some nice fish.'

They sipped their drinks in silence, looking out at the distant coastline of ochre hills. As Athens melted away, Luc was filled with an intoxicating sense of space and freedom. It was the first time in months she had seen a natural landscape, somewhere empty of buildings, devoid of the man-made. A few people came up on deck but kept well away from them, perhaps wanting to enjoy a similar illusion of solitude.

The sky began to glow pink and gold as the ferry rounded Cape Sounion.

'Look.' Ella clutched Luc's arm in delight. At the top of a steep, rocky hillside was a ruin of columns.

' "The Temple of Poseidon built during the fifth century BC, a landmark since then for boats sailing between Piraeus and the islands," ' quoted Luc from her guidebook. ' "Almost half of its thirty-four original columns remain. Byron recorded his visit in 1810 by carving his name in one of them." '

'Wish we could stop.' Ella rummaged in her backpack and brought out her Byron anthology.

'Why there and not the Parthenon?'

'The site, the sea, the view . . . It's more, more . . . Greece.' Awestruck, silent, they gazed and gazed at the silhouette of columns. Their minds were giddy with history. All the history that had come between then and that moment centuries ago when slaves had levelled the earth on the hilltop. From Socrates to satellites, from Plato to NATO, from the *Iliad* to the Internet.

Luc made her way down the steep steps to get some more ice. All the seats that lined the corridors to the bars and restaurants were taken. Why would anyone want to sit indoors on such a wonderful evening? She met eyes and smiled, something she avoided doing in London. Walking back, she saw a sign saying cabins.

Back up on deck, it was suddenly far colder than it had been ten minutes before. Rubbing away the goosebumps on her arms, she sat down, then almost sprang up again in alarm. 'We can't,' she hissed. 'Someone will smell it.'

'Tambourine as well as those knitting needles?' sighed Ella, lighting her pipe.

A bit later, they were stretched out on the deck. Heads resting on their bags, beatific smiles lit their faces. On the western horizon, the low smoky clouds appeared to be forming another land mass.

'Longest sunset I've ever, ever seen,' murmured Luc.

'Bit kitsch,' said Ella, after what seemed about twenty minutes.

'What?' Luc struggled to regain control of her drifting mind.

'More Norman Rockwell than Turner,' said Ella, after what seemed another twenty minutes.

'What?' Luc's tongue was as numb as her brain.

'Remember Annabelle Turner? School. Cross between Stalin and Pol Pot.'

'Who?' Everything seemed so far away, her voice was distant

as if it belonged to someone else. Luc yelped, panicked paranoia entering her bloodstream. As if she'd been injected with adrenaline, she lurched up.

'She reported us for smoking. Not here now, is she?'

An ear-shattering trumpet blast came over the PA, followed by an announcement in Greek. The ferry was approaching land. As the sky in the east turned blue-black, the deck lights had been switched on. It was about as romantic as being on the perimeter fence of a prison.

'I'm starving,' said Ella.

Luc was getting cold. She delved in her bag for a sweater. 'Let's eat.'

Lugging their stuff, they made their way below, both feeling dazed, as if they were walking through water. Passengers were sprawled out on the seats in the passageways. Despite all the to-ing and fro-ing around them, some were asleep. 'This isn't right,' said Ella as they found themselves back in the migraine carpet lounge for the third time.

Luc looked round helplessly. Two men, short sleeves showing off the black pelts on their forearms, stared up from their game of backgammon. One tugged at his hair, pointed at Luc and gave a low wolf whistle. Embarrassed, she turned away.

'Drawing attention to yourself again,' sighed Ella.

'It's not my fault,' hissed Luc. 'Wish I had the guts to get a crew-cut.' With her long cinnamon-coloured hair, white skin and lime-peel eyes, she hadn't changed much since school, where she'd been known as eeky freaky. Then Ella had arrived, taken one look and cried, 'Flaming June.' Luc had been mystified until Ella had pulled out her book on the Pre-Raphaelites, saying she could have been Leighton's model.

'Restaurant,' Ella pointed at the sign. 'Let's concentrate.'

They followed the signs, but could have followed their noses as the smell of frying grew stronger. Despite imagining they'd spend ten days living off salads dressed with aromatic olive oil, both of them yearned for chips. With HP sauce. After struggling to open the double doors, they stumbled into the restaurant. People were queuing at the self-service counter, plates laden with steaming chicken. Luc's mouth watered. She was famished.

An epauletted white-shirted man came up to them, shaking his head and saying something. They looked at him blankly. 'Eeenglish?' He sighed impatiently. 'Shut. Close-ed. Feeneeshed.'

Gazing at the chicken and salivating, Ella was horrorstruck. 'You can't be.'

'We're hungry,' whimpered Luc. 'Starving.'

He smiled triumphantly. 'Bar. Upstairs. Sandweeeches. Peeza. Here, close-ed. Too late.'

They plodded back upstairs to the bar. Some passengers were gathering up their possessions, the ferry was approaching Eos. Ella and Luc scarcely gave it a glance, they were too hungry to care. At the bar counter, a ghetto blaster was turned on full volume. A mournful woman's voice sounded like a cat being strangled to the sound of a bouzouki.

'Toasted sandwich?' said Luc, looking at the cellophane-wrapped white bread without much enthusiasm.

'Two,' cried Ella, struggling to make herself heard above the cat strangling. 'And some cookies. And some water.' The barman took their money without a smile and put the sandwiches in the microwave. 'What a rip-off. It's almost as much as the ticket.'

They went back on deck to bag some orange seats before the new arrivals boarded. The prison perimeter lights made everyone look pasty. The migraine carpet would've tasted better than the cottonwool bread, the processed cheese and the soggy tomato.

Slightly revived after one and a half packets of chocolate chip cookies, and feeling more together as the effects of the grass wore off, they decided to sort out a cabin. The deck was not only unromantic, but freezing.

There was an information desk opposite the purser's office. Their faces fell as they realised that sitting behind it was the same officer who had ordered them out of the restaurant.

'*Kala* er . . .' said Luc brightly. What was good evening?

'Yes?' He didn't bother to glance up from the pile of papers in front of him.

'We'd like two beds, berths,' said Ella. '*Parakalo.*'

'Yes.' He started adding up some figures on his calculator.

'Two berths,' repeated Ella, when he had written down a figure at the bottom of a ledger sheet.

'I know, mees.'

'This is the right place to ask?' said Luc.

'Yes.' He put aside his papers and smiled. 'Impossible. All booked.'

'What?'

'Fully booked. You are too late. Again. First restaurant. Now beds.'

Ella's expression suddenly had the appeal of a lost Labrador puppy. 'You must have something.'

'Please check,' wheedled Luc. 'Please.'

'Meeses, there is nothing. Now go away and stop wasting my times and your times.'

Ella suddenly became more Rottweiler than Labrador. 'Listen, I know there's something and you know there's something. If I were the Greek prime minister you'd be able to find it. And you'd have let us get something proper to eat. Sandwich? I've eaten better dog food . . .'

'Ella,' hissed Luc. People were staring.

'Wasting all our times.' He made a shooing motion. 'Go aways.'

An older officer arrived at Luc's elbow and spoke rapidly to his colleague while Ella fumed in silence. The second man smiled at Luc. 'I am very sorry, lady. Right now, there is nothing. Come back at midnight when we have left Thira. Maybe then, we have something for you.'

'That would be wonderful.' Luc smiled gratefully. 'Thank you.'

'Oscar for that damsel in distress act?' muttered Ella.

At half past midnight, they were huddled together up on deck. Under their frocks, they were both wearing leggings and two T-shirts, with two sweaters on top. The bundles of clothes made them look like the present halfway through a game of pass-the-parcel. Despite all their layers, their teeth were chattering.

'Only another seven hours to go.' Sighing, Ella looked at her watch.

'Any more cookies?'

'Last one. Should've brought some Eccles cakes. More bourbon?'

'Here.' Luc passed the bottle, now well over half empty.

'Told you to undo the buttons on your skirt.'

'Would've been done for indecent exposure.'

Before Luc had gone down to see the older officer at midnight, Ella had made her brush her hair and put on some lipstick. 'Say we're journalists writing a tour guide and that we've got friends in very high places in the EU. Friends that organise subsidies for olive oil growers. And if that doesn't work, start weeping.'

Luc had tried half-heartedly, but with zero result. A million sorrys, beautiful *kyria*, but nothing.

Scores more passengers had boarded at Eos and Thira. The ferry now resembled a refugee ship, evacuating fleeing hordes from a war zone. The new arrivals had stampeded into the lounge looking for seats or immediately staked out their floor space in the corridors, hunkering down inside their sleeping-bags. The decks looked as if a massacre had taken place.

Stepping round the prostrate bodies as she returned to the open deck, Luc realised why there was such a desperate scramble for space. A bitter wind had blown up.

Ella swigged again, which stopped her teeth chattering. 'We'll know for next time. Water, food . . .'

'Sleeping-bags.' Luc glanced around at the sleeping backpackers. Snug inside their Force Fours, they had inflatable ground mats and woolly hats. They had looked at Ella and Luc with smug contempt, like expert Do-it-Yourselfers meeting someone whose shelves had just collapsed.

Ella shook her watch to check it was working and picked up her anthology. 'Lucky for Greece, Byron didn't have to doss down on an overnight ferry.' She sniffed. As she fumbled in her backpack, half the clothes she was using as a blanket fell on to the deck.

'That's not a tissue,' warned Luc as Ella was about to blow her nose.

'Dollars. Must've been in here since New Orleans.' She suddenly smiled. 'We've tried reason, we've tried charm, we've tried being pathetic. And failed. Bribery?'

Cheered up, Ella sauntered off. Luc took another swig of bourbon, then emptied the few remaining crumbs of the cookie packet into her mouth. She was resigned to not getting a berth, but Ella hated being thwarted. She had to get her own way. If there had been a cabin, she would've insisted on staying up on deck all night. Luc tried to settle herself more comfortably in the seat and not to think about the comforts of an organised package holiday.

Was she right to trust Ella's optimism that they'd find somewhere to stay? Supposing they had nine nights of sleeping rough? Just like school, being with Ella was a hurdy-gurdy ride at the funfair. Sometimes Luc was exhilarated, sometimes she was downright scared, sometimes she wondered why she'd joined the ride in the first place.

Nothing much had changed since school a decade earlier, ever since the fifteen-year-old Ella had turned up in the middle of one term with all the glamour of someone who'd been expelled.

'Luke?' Ella had been puzzled.

'Short for Lucasta,' explained Sarah, who until then had been Luc's best friend.

'Oh, like Lovelace's heroine,' said Ella, causing an intake of breath. She'd stared back at the blank faces. 'Lovelace. As in Richard Lovelace. The poet.' Had Ella muttered 'dummies'? 'Civil warrior, on the Royalist side, although that must've been a let-down. Charles the First was so wet. Some of his poems were to Lucasta. He would not have loved her so much loved he not honour more. But he had a thing for Althea and Elinda as well, not to mention Chloris, but that was really about the joys of masturb—' The lesson had been cut short by the arrival of Sister Paul.

At school, Ella had tested the limits of authority. She still did. Six months ago, she'd been banned from driving. Again. She had refused to be breathalysed, telling the police that their road-block was a denial of her civil liberties. They'd warned her that with her previous drink-drive conviction, she'd automatically be banned. Ella said she'd take the risk. Ella had lost. Ella had bought a bicycle.

Since then, she'd become anti-car, which had resulted in her being arrested for causing an affray during an anti-bypass build-ing protest in Berkshire. Ella had featured on the early evening news being dragged from a tree. Liz, her half-sister, had seen the bulletin. She'd been on the phone immediately, saying she'd never live down the disgrace.

'Please? A light?'

Startled, Luc glanced up. All she could make out was a pony-tail, combat pants and a huge sweater. She handed over Ella's lighter.

'Zippo. Snap. Mine's run out.' He cupped his hand round the flame. The flickering light showed up amazing cheekbones. His accent was strange, vaguely German. 'Aren't you cold? Or does the bourbon warm you up?'

'Not really.' Luc grew flustered, realising how bad it looked.

She was wrapped up like a tramp and nursing a bottle of Jack Daniels. The best-looking man she'd seen all year had found her auditioning for the starring role in *Edna the Inebriate Woman*.

'English?'

'Yes. You?'

'Dutch. Where are you headed?'

'Praxos. And you?'

'Antipraxos. Less spoilt. You should go. How long are you in Greece?'

'Only ten days,' Luc sighed. 'I've got to go back to work.'

'In London? What do you do?'

'Temping at the moment. Secretarial stuff.' She didn't want to think about her depressing lack of career. 'And you?'

'Photographer. News. No weddings, no portraits, no fashion.' He smiled.

'In Holland?'

'Sometimes. Just got back from Namibia.'

'Oh,' said Luc, immediately feeling small-town. He was a reminder that there was a whole world out there, places to go, people to meet.

'Travelling alone?'

Luc shook her head. 'With a girlfriend. She's trying to sort us out somewhere to sleep. Bribery this time. Nothing else has worked.'

He laughed, showing off beautiful teeth. 'You couldn't persuade them? I'm surprised.'

A figure was advancing towards them. Wearing immaculately pressed chinos, polished deckshoes and a polo shirt, he had a cashmere sweater knotted round his shoulders. About fifty, he was short, with cropped iron-grey hair. Among the scruffy backpackers, he was as out of place as a Valentino ballgown.

'Hans. Are we playing hide and seek?' The voice was port drinker's American, rich and smooth and bass.

'I wanted a smoke.'

'Naughty. We're trying to quit.' He glanced round in distaste.

'I've seen better refugee camps. Making friends? And you are . . .?'

'Luc. Luc James.'

'Michel Duveen. English? I thought everyone in England was at Ascot this week.' He looked her up and down. 'Perhaps not. Friday last year. Such a disappointment. Half the Enclosure could've been in K-Mart. Still, Glyndebourne made up for it. So much gorgeous fun.'

'I've never been,' said Luc.

'Really?' It had eighteen syllables and he looked at her like Lady Bracknell confronted by news of the handbag. Dismissing her, he turned to Hans. 'Time for our picnic. Georgos did the chicken beautifully and I've got the barman in that squalid little lounge to pop the wine in his freezer. These Greeks are so accommodating.'

Father and son? Uncle and nephew? Friends? As Luc glanced from one to the other, her heart sank.

'*On y va?*' The American raised his eyebrows. She suspected they were slightly plucked.

Hans got to his feet. 'Thanks for the light. Good luck, eh?' Each of his rangey strides was matched by two fussy steps.

Holding a grey blanket in triumph, Ella chucked another packet of cookies into Luc's lap and sat down. 'I've just seen the most gorgeous man.'

'Hans the Dutch photographer.'

'Hans-some is as hans-some does. And he definitely does. How do you know?'

Luc explained.

'Who said smoking was an anti-social habit?' demanded Ella. 'Is he coming back?'

'Forget it,' said Luc.

'Why? Girlfriend lurking?'

'Worse.'

'How much worse? Wife? Not . . .?' Ella's jaw dropped.

'Typical, isn't it?' Luc grimaced. 'So, bribery failed?'

'They just laughed. Impressed by our persistence though. The older one found me a blanket and a shot of Metaxa.' She munched happily. 'By the way, he's got the hots for you.'

Luc groaned.

The night wore on, the ferry headed due south. Huddled under the blanket, fortified by the remains of the bourbon and three packets of cookies, they gave up trying to sleep in the backside-numbing bucket seats. 'Could be worse,' said Ella at two-thirty, breaking into another packet of duty-free cigarettes. She'd switched from Byron to Jackie Collins.

It was worse below decks. The air was stifling. The lounge's migraine carpet was strewn with bodies like the aftermath of a cult mass suicide. The only people awake were Nintendo addicts and a few swarthy men, prowling around with a predatory gleam in their eyes. Despite being strangled for hours, the cat was still in full ear-bleeding voice.

Standing beside the rail, Luc gazed up into the night sky, wishing the prison perimeter lights would fuse. She hadn't seen the stars properly for months.

'Wish I knew more than the Plough,' said Ella. 'Should've brought an astral map.'

'Look,' gasped Luc, filled with a magical pleasure. She clutched Ella's arm in delight. 'A shooting star.'

'It's a satellite.'

'What?'

'Sorry. It's probably beaming down shopping channels.'

And the moon had been conquered for Americans to play golf on. It was vaguely depressing. Luc wished they hadn't bothered.

Trying to get comfortable and keep warm, they pulled the blanket more tightly around them. Luc got out her guidebook and studied the map. When the Creator had finished making the Earth, He had a handful of dust left over and threw it, forming the hundreds of islands off the Greek mainland. 'Where's Liz?'

'Ia.' Ella frowned, not looking up. 'Their villa sounds great. Of course, Liz swanked on about how she'd got a deal. Timid the Twit said to drop in on them if we were passing.'

'Oh?'

'I pointed out we'd be hundreds of miles away, so there wasn't much chance.'

'Nice of them to offer though,' suggested Luc.

'Tim offered. I could picture Liz squirming in horror. Thank God we weren't on the same flight.'

'She's not that bad.'

'You don't have to suffer her.' Ella almost ripped the page. 'She didn't try and get you put into care. She probably got the phone exorcised after I hung up. And she didn't say thank you for her birthday present.'

'Surprised?' Ella had tracked down a copy of the saccharine *Sisters, Such Devoted Sisters* and sent it to Liz after another of their rows. Luc was wistful. 'Nice to have a sister.'

'Half-sister,' snapped Ella.

The stars were still visible, but the sky on the eastern horizon was turning from black to charcoal. The ferry was edging closer to a rocky coastline. The air was different, carrying the musty scent of olive groves.

At six o'clock, three ear-shattering whistles came over the loudspeakers followed by a voice saying the ferry would shortly be arriving in Mathi.

The backpackers raised their heads from their sleeping bags, staring round bug-eyed and disoriented. Blinded by the early morning sunshine, they swapped their woolly hats for sunglasses. They seemed so grumpy at being woken up that Luc and Ella were glad not to have bothered going to sleep.

Luc leaned over the rail watching hundreds of people troop down on to the quayside. She was itchy-eyed with tiredness. The scene was as frenetic as Piraeus. Diesel fumes filled the air from the line of lorries and buses and taxis which snaked round the hairpin bends on the mountainside, waiting to enter the port. Ugly concrete warehouses lined the road, giant hoardings defaced the hillside, which was topped by a massive radio mast.

Expecting a quaint fishing village, it was a disappointment.

'Manage to sleep?' Hans the Dutchman stood beside her, in wraparound shades and dark stubble.

Luc shook her head. Suddenly aware that she hadn't brushed her teeth and got rid of yesterday's breath, her mouth was clamped tight shut. Mortified he'd caught her in her Michelin Man layers of clothes and crusted make-up, she could've thrown herself into the sea. 'Bribery failed.'

'Lucky. The cabins are shit. Do something nice with the money you've saved. Did you watch the sun rise? Yes? So you've got a good memory as well.'

As he smiled, Luc reminded herself that he was so far out of bounds he could've been back in Namibia. On the quayside a taxi driver was leaping out of his cab, yelling 'Malaka' at a moped rider.

'Thank God we brought our own.' Ella arrived back, clutching a roll of loo paper. 'Otherwise, drip dry . . .' She blushed scarlet when she realised who was standing beside Luc.

Ten minutes later the ferry began the final leg of the journey. After catching sight of Mathi, Ella was apprehensive about what Praxos would be like. Few passengers had remained on board.

'Less people, less action, more expensive,' said Hans, which didn't sound encouraging. It sounded even less promising when he added that Michel knew it well.

'Michel knows what well?' The bass voice rang out. 'Poisoning ourselves again?' He tut-tutted at Hans's cigarette and glanced at the loo roll in alarm. 'We don't have a cold, do we? My dear, aren't you hot?' Fanning himself with his Panama, he frowned at Luc's layers.

'Not really.' Luc immediately felt the sweat break out on her nose.

'They were on deck all night,' explained Hans.

'My dears, how ghastly for you.' The American brushed imaginary flecks from his crisp pink shirt. 'All those cretinous backpackers. Bovine or ovine? I can never decide.'

'It was romantic.' Ella was defensive. 'Wasn't it, Luc? Watching the stars, reading Byron . . .'

'Byron?' A slightly plucked eyebrow was raised in the direction of Ella's backpack. 'I didn't realise *Hollywood Wives* was part of his œuvre. Hans, we'd better run along. Are you girls staying on Praxos? Try Yannis's on the harbour. Tell him I sent you and I'll be looking in on our way back.'

As the ferry docked in Praxos, Luc and Ella clutched one another in euphoric delight.

Nature had carved a perfect half-moon harbour out of the steep hills, which were covered with white cuboid houses like tumbling dice. Behind a fortress sea wall was a three-sided quay. Dozens of yachts and fishing boats were moored in the mirror-blue water. Shops and restaurants flagged the cobblestoned waterfront. A maze of narrow passageways led off it, too narrow for cars, too steep for mopeds. In the centre of the quayside was a white clock-tower. Its delicate carved stonework seemed to have been made of lace.

Few people were about. Led by a small boy, a donkey laden with panniers of water melons disappeared up into one of the narrow lanes.

Overjoyed, Luc and Ella almost ran down the gangplank. Wanting to get their bearings, suddenly daunted by the thought of trekking around searching for a room, they decided to have some breakfast.

They found a blue-awninged café next to the clock-tower halfway round the quayside, almost at the water's edge. They ordered omelettes and coffee. The smell of new bread from the bakery next door made them even hungrier. They felt the early morning sun on their backs as their itchy eyes took in a hundred new images.

Luc got out her guidebook. 'Praxos . . . Praxos . . . "The tiny flower island." That's true.' Bougainvillaea and jasmine tumbled down balconies and whitewashed walls, geraniums grew from brightly painted tins nailed beside doorways. ' "Certainly beautiful, but limited," ' continued Luc. ' "Not much to do. Expensive compared to neighbouring islands, the picturesque port with its clock-tower is filled with chi-chi jewellery shops and eateries, including Kostas, loved by mega-rich yachties . . ." Kostas. That's here.'

'Mega-rich yachties?' Ella glanced at two leather-faced local fishermen sitting at the next table, tiny cups of coffee in front of them. 'How reliable is that guide? Anything about where to stay?'

Luc scanned the lines. Having fretted most of the night that they'd find nothing, she was almost resigned to kipping down on the quayside. 'Mentions Yannis's. Overlooks the waterfront, rooms with balconies, some of the best on Praxos. Wonderful courtyard.' Her face fell. 'Unlikely to get in unless booked in advance.'

'We can try.'

'Mathi. "Ugly port, avoid the package-tour gulags, head straight for the beaches around Pelekas, the hippy hang-out. Pulsates with sex, drugs and rock and roll till five a.m. . . ." '

'Home from home,' said Ella.

They devoured the omelettes and bread, watching the waterfront come to life. Crews were breakfasting on decks, shop shutters were opening, cargoes were unloaded on to handcarts before being wheeled away up one of the tiny lanes.

'*Kali mera.*' The well-fed man sitting behind his desk peered over his half-moon spectacles, a cigarette holder clamped between his teeth. Busy with paperwork, he seemed displeased by the interruption.

The office was cool after their search for Yannis's round the steep lanes and passageways behind the quay. Outside, it was getting hotter by the second. Scarcely able to lift her bag, Luc had suggested that they go into one of the scores of other places offering rooms. Ella had refused to give up.

'*Kali mera*,' said Ella. '*Milete Anglia?*'

'A little. You want a tour?' A wrinkled monkey hand motioned they should sit.

'Are you Yannis?' She slung down her backpack.

'No. His uncle. Yannis busy. You want to change money?'

'Later,' Ella assured him quickly. 'Actually, we'd like a room.'

'We are very busy. Have you booked?'

Luc's heart sank. Ella made sure she was hiding her tattoo and widened her brown eyes in appeal. 'A simple room, somewhere safe.'

'Safe?' He seemed offended. 'Praxos very safe. No troubles here. Not like Mathi.'

'Good.' Ella smiled. 'You understand that travelling alone we must be very careful.'

'I understand.' Yannis's uncle got up and switched on a kettle on top of the filing cabinet. His gut hung over his waistband.

'A nice, simple, safe room.' Ella pressed on. 'With a balcony perhaps.'

Luc rolled her eyes. She no longer cared where they slept, she was so weary she could have dossed down in the lane.

He raised his eyebrow. 'Very busy.' Eyes transfixed with supplication, Ella gazed at him and deliberately crossed her legs, exposing acres of thigh. 'Very busy.' They held their breath as he began turning pages of a ledger, glancing at Ella's legs. As he shook his head, Luc's spirits plummeted still further. Imagining another long trek round looking for somewhere else, she felt even more exhausted. Why hadn't they booked a package?

'How do you know Yannis?' he asked, puffing on his holder.

'We don't,' said Luc. 'But an American friend of ours, Michel Duveen, told us to come here.' Would his name carry weight?

He shrugged. 'We have many Americans . . .' Eyes on the pages, he shook his head. 'Very busy.' Luc began to panic that there would be nowhere else on the whole of Praxos. Why hadn't she booked a package? Why had she listened to Ella?

'Room five.' He was holding out a key. 'How many days you stay?'

Luc was about to speak, but Ella cut in. 'We'd like to see it first.' She was adamant.

Scowling, he shrugged. 'Left, through a green door and then up the stairs. You can leave your bags.'

Luc hesitated. Could he be trusted?

'Come on,' said Ella.

Just up the tiny lane opposite a photo shop, a peeling pistachio-coloured door was set into a white wall. It opened on to a stone-flagged courtyard shaded by a trellised vine. A secret garden. Lemon and fig trees fought for space, jasmine spilled out of urns and purple bougainvillaea poured down the walls and the railings of the first-floor balcony, reached by a wrought-iron staircase.

They climbed the steps, then walked round the balcony to room five. It was so simple it could've been a cell. Whitewashed and L-shaped, it had two beds, a small table and a lamp. There was a shower behind a door to the left. In the entrance was a tiny stove and recessed shelves for their clothes. The only decoration was a poster of a white cupola against a blue-black sea.

The sun was trying to break in through the shutter slats on the far wall, casting stripy shadows. Luc pulled open the shutters and smiled in delight as she stepped out on to the balcony. It overlooked the sparkling waterfront. To the left was the clock-tower, to the right the sea. It was perfect.

Ella looked at Luc. 'I know we've got a room with a view, but must you dress like something out of the film?'

'I'm not getting burnt.' Cursing her colouring, Luc had doused herself in block-out before putting on an ankle-length skirt, a long-sleeved shirt and a huge straw hat.

'Where's your parasol?'

'Where's the rest of your shorts?'

Over her bikini, Ella was wearing a singlet and cut-off jeans that showed off her long legs and half her backside.

It was almost midday. After filling in forms and handing over their passports to Yannis's uncle, they'd showered, set the alarm and caught up on a few hours' sleep. Now they were eager to explore and get to the beach at Agios Agathas. It could be reached, according to the guidebook, by a bus that circled the island.

'Up,' said Yannis's uncle, when Luc asked directions to the bus stop. 'Left side of the clock-tower, then up, up, up. Hot, hot, hot.'

Three tethered donkeys, their coats grey and mangy, huddled together in the shade of the clock-tower wall trying to escape the relentless sun and ninety-degree heat. Few people were about and many of the shops were closing. The boats moored round the quayside were as still as if they'd been photographed.

They went round the quayside and began walking up a narrow passageway, their senses bombarded. The cobblestones under their feet had been worn smooth over the decades. Dazzling light bounced off the white walls, doors opened on to dark, cool interiors. Shops, houses, workshops were jumbled side by side. A baby's cry, music, a radio programme could be heard behind the closed shutters. Flowers splashed the white with colour. The air was thick with the scent of jasmine.

Their steps grew shorter and slower, more laboured. They reached a tiny square, a walnut tree at its centre. 'My clogs are getting squelchy,' panted Ella, squinting in the glare. 'Dinner there this evening?' Just beyond was a restaurant in a garden, similar to their courtyard, the tables shaded by trellising. She scowled at two men eyeing her and tried to adjust her shorts which had ridden up.

Luc fanned herself with her hat. Trying to pretend to herself that she wasn't so unfit, she kept her mouth shut and consciously breathed through her nose. Which was sweating. She hadn't realised they had climbed so high. Looking back, the flat roofs of the town were like steps leading back to the quayside and the deeper blue of the open sea. The clock-tower had shrunk to miniature.

About ten minutes later, the whitewashed buildings began to get further apart, the surroundings more neglected. Scrubby patches of land were fenced off by link-wire, chickens pecked at the dusty ground. Up ahead, a moped roared past.

'Finally,' gasped Ella. 'Bus?' she called across to a middle-aged couple standing beside a blue pole at the roadside.

'*Ja. Zehn Minuten,*' called back the man. 'Ten minutes.'

Deeply tanned, they had silver nose protectors attached to their sunglasses. She wore a bikini, a fuchsia sarong and a paunch emphasised by a silver chain round her waist. Under his sandals, his beige socks came halfway up his varicose-veined calves.

'You've got to get up very early to beat them to the porno vids,' muttered Ella.

'Sssh,' hissed Luc. Opposite was a three-storey concrete hotel, swimming costumes drying across the balcony railings. Even in the sunshine, it was bleak. The only view was of the gritty road and a scrubby olive grove. Tour operator stickers were plastered over the dingy entrance. Luc knew that if they'd taken a package, they would've been staying there. 'We're so lucky.'

'Aren't we?'

'The bus,' said the German woman unnecessarily, as it pulled up.

Every hour and a half the bus made a circular tour of the island, past Agios Agathas and Ermioni, before returning to the top of the town. It then went round the other way. The driver made unscheduled halts when hailed by locals, but tourists were ignored.

'Best way to see Praxos,' quoted Luc from the guidebook. 'Only locals can have cars here.'

'Are you trying to get a blue badge or something?' said Ella, peering out of the window. Like on school trips, she had gone straight to the back seat, like on school trips she had lit up. A few more people got on. Suddenly the driver looked back down the aisle and yelled something in Greek.

'No smoking,' called the German smugly, a few seats in front. 'Can't you read?'

'No,' snapped Ella. 'Away from school that day.' She began humming the *Dambusters'* theme tune.

The bus bounced across pot-holes and climbed steadily higher, lumbering past dusty olive groves and crumbling stone walls and a few villas behind iron gates. It was forced to stop as a herd of goats were shepherded across the road by a ragamuffin boy. Somewhere, hidden up among the parched hillsides, was a monastery at the highest point on the island. Below, through a tangle of pine forest, was the sea. Turquoise over sand, blue-black above rocks, it glinted white-gold in the sun.

The driver turned down a rutted track and halted beside a taverna. 'Agios Agathas.'

The beach was about a quarter of a mile wide and fringed by woods. A few boats were moored to a jetty at one end. Luc and Ella headed the opposite way. Trekking across the burning sand to some rocks, they felt like Lawrence of Arabia.

'Or one of his camels,' said Ella. 'It's so hot.'

Dumping their stuff, they tore off their clothes and ran into the water.

Luc let the sun dry her off for five minutes before she pulled her mat into the shade of the rocks, cursing her colouring.

'Be pale and interesting,' consoled Ella.

'Interesting people go to exotic places and get brown. I look like I've spent a rainy week in Cleethorpes.' Luc put on more block-out.

'Hardly. Think damsels, think Flaming June, think La Belle Dame Sans Merci. Think knights in shining Armani palely loitering and slaying dragons.'

Luc picked up her cinnamon-coloured plait of hair and glared at it. 'Knights don't exist.'

'Quentin? He's in line for a baronetcy, so he's a sort of knight. Stop being so picky.'

'Quentin? He's barely a man. He's an estate agent.'

'He wasn't that bad. Though by his age, he should've heard of Clearasil.' Ella unhooked her bikini top. 'You shouldn't have led him on.'

'I didn't.' Luc was indignant. 'I thought he was a friend. I didn't expect him to pounce and declare undying love in the kitchen department of Peter Jones.' She shuddered. 'Not in the middle of choosing a dustbin.'

Quentin, yet another mistake. All she'd done was have dinner with him a few times. He was nice enough; cheerful and good-natured, even if he thought that letting off fire extinguishers and putting whoopie cushions on the passenger seat of his Golf were the Himalayas of amusement. He ate steak and kidney, lamb cutlets and cottage pie. Sushi was like the French, not to be trusted. He could talk for hours about rugby and the Conservative Party.

Quentin joined Jamie, Patrick and George. They wore the same stripy shirts and loved their black Labradors, Lords cricket ground and Stilton more than they'd ever love any woman. 'Odd sort of chaps, women,' Patrick had once told her.

Ella had encouraged her to break away from serial Sloanes and introduced her to Tas's mates. Deciding Hackney squats were as unappealing as Fulham terraces, Luc had wondered if she should join a convent. The celibacy vow wouldn't have been a problem, she'd managed six months.

She sighed and retied her plait. Her love life was at best bread and butter pudding, at worst famine. A famine to Ella's feast. Luc was starving but she wanted honeydew and nectar, not stodge. Ella had said Luc should stop looking for the big one. Luc, Ella believed, wanted the sonnets and the symphonies and the waves crashing on the beach before she'd even kiss a man.

Luc glanced up the beach, then frowned at Ella. 'Are you sure . . .?'

'What's wrong?' Ella pulled a face. 'Luc, everyone's topless. Except you. The prude. Make the most of them before they go south.'

The afternoon ebbed away as they swam, read and people-watched. Despite Luc's warnings to be careful, Ella insisted on lying out in the glare of the sun, when she wasn't disappearing up the beach to buy beers and bottles of water and slices of watermelon.

'Ice cream?' asked Ella, after managing five minutes of being still.

Luc watched her stride away, long-legged and broad-shouldered. She was far taller than most of the local men, an Amazon to Luc's waif.

Ella needed constant novelty, whereas Luc was content just to sit in the shade, feel the breeze on her body and watch the waves. She marvelled at how only two days before she'd been stuck in a pet food firm's grotty office in Clerkenwell. Whoever said marketing was interesting had never had to type a report on Budgie's Betta Bites or do hours of photocopying and filing. It had been her worst assignment in fourteen months of temping.

'Here.' Ella chucked a Cornetto.

Luc hesitated, seeing a million calories going straight to her hips. 'I shouldn't.' As she'd come out of the water, she'd felt less like Ursula Andress in *Dr No* than a pagan fertility symbol, all big stomach, huge bum and fat thighs.

'Get some tits.' Ella munched on the cone and stared at the horizon. 'We need a boat. That's how the best coves are reached apparently. Wonder if we should go to Mykonos? More to do there.'

'We've only just got here.'

'Um.' Ella frowned.

'Let's give it a chance.' Luc sighed. Back in London, Ella had insisted that she wanted to chill out. She'd been adamant that she wanted lazy days and restful nights. Praxos was idyllic and they'd secured one of the best rooms on the island, well within Luc's budget. To Ella, budget meant Budget and was something that the Chancellor of the Exchequer had to worry about.

Determined to get a tan as fast as possible, Ella ignored Luc's warnings that she was turning a bit pink. At a quarter to six they shook the sand from their stuff, folded up their beach mats and headed towards the taverna.

The bus was far busier on its return journey. Two black-clad crones sat in front of them, chattering loudly. Every word seemed as unfamiliar as Chinese.

'I think *ne* means yes,' whispered Luc.

'What?' Ella scowled at the German man who was staring at her chest which bounced under her singlet as the bus hit another pot-hole. 'Just because Frau Cow's are resting on her knees.'

The bus was overtaken on a hill by a teenager on a moped, whose engine sounded like a mosquito. A few people boarded at Ermioni, a fishing hamlet round the coast. The road climbed still higher, giving a view of the whole island, tiny compared to the endless sea.

The first thing that Ella had packed was a corkscrew. After the bus dropped them at the top of the town outside the gulag hotel, they ambled back through the maze of lanes, stopping to buy a bottle of ice-cold white wine and some pistachios.

While Ella showered, Luc sat out on the balcony. She sipped, gazing down at the quayside. Yachts were entering the harbour to moor for the night. The bars and restaurants were starting to fill up. The stone on the clock-tower glowed gold in the setting sun.

Ella arrived, leaving a trail of wet yeti footprints behind her. She was vaguely covered up in a small towel. 'I can't get rid of the sand. It's really sticky and itchy.' She turned round and pulled up her mane of hair. Between her wriggling shoulder blades, her skin was an angry lobster red.

'That's not sand. You're burnt.'

'I can't be . . . Don't look so bloody smug.'

'Your face is a bit pink too.' Luc giggled.

Ella glowered at her. 'That's from the shower.'

'Hang on.' Luc got up and fetched her aftersun. 'Not here,' she hissed nervously, as Ella tried to reach round and the towel slipped. Two men were staring up from the quayside. 'With your back, we don't need a red light. Get inside.'

'Where's the adaptor?' asked Ella, hairdryer in hand, when Luc emerged from her shower.

'You've got it, haven't you?'

'No.'

They stared at one another in dismay.

'Nine whole bad hair days?' Ella sounded as if the end of the world was nigh.

'I'll get one tomorrow. By then it should be dry.' Luc looked accusingly at her dripping mass. Without a dryer, her hair had the allure of a rusty Brillo pad. The top would be plastered to her scalp then the frizz started at ear level. On a good day she was like Crystal Tips; a bad, an ungroomed Shetland. Ella, similarly suffering, had once tried ironing hers, which had led to a horrible smell of singeing and an osteopath's bill.

Ella purposefully stubbed out her cigarette. 'Now I know why people have Swiss Army knives.'

'I am not, not, not having a number one cut.' Luc grew alarmed.

''Course you're not,' Ella tutted. 'Corkscrew?' Frowning in concentration, she attacked the plug screws with its metal tip. 'Shit. Where's my tweezers?' She brandished the two bare wires at Luc. 'Done it.'

'So?'

'So everything's standard in Europe now. We must be on the same wattage or voltage or whatever. Where's a socket? Pass me the matches, will you?'

'Ella, don't. You'll get electrocuted.'

Ignoring Luc, Ella stuck the bare wires into the wall socket, securing them with bits of match. 'Here goes.' Luc was beginning to back towards the balcony when a whirring filled the room. 'Done it.' Ella smiled in triumph. 'Brush, please.'

'Brill . . .' Luc was cut off by a sudden flash of light, a bang, then the smell of burning.

'Fuck.' Ella dropped the smoking hairdryer.

Outside, doors were being opened and voices raised in consternation. Luc darted out on to the courtyard balcony. 'Congratulations. The whole building has fused.'

Dressed, but with damp hair, they crept out of their room and down the wrought-iron staircase into the courtyard. In a hallway, torch in hand, cigarette holder between his teeth, Yannis's uncle was examining a fuse box. He spotted them as they tried to sidle past. '*Kali spera*, misses.'

They froze, bracing themselves, certain that they'd be ordered to leave.

'*Kali spera*,' said Ella brightly. Luc knew her expression. Fair cop guv resignation. It was exactly the same look she'd had when they'd been caught coming out of a pub by Sister Joseph. It had been towards the end of Ella's first term. In those two months Luc had smoked her first joint, drunk her first Margarita, had her first ever detention and then her first bad report, which said she'd become strangely unsettled.

'Yous knows how this happened?'

Luc held her breath, her mind going blank.

'Don't know much about electricity,' hedged Ella. 'Away from school that day.'

'No worries. Be fixed soonest. Very sorrys, enjoy your evening.'

Relieved, they almost sprinted into the lane. Neither could remember where the garden restaurant lay in the maze of alleyways. Suddenly famished, unable to think straight they headed back to Kostas, where they'd had breakfast.

'It's not very adventurous,' said Luc as they strolled round the quayside. Lights were coming on, the water shimmered in the setting sun. Fishermen were arranging their nets before casting off for the night, old ladies sat on benches eating ice cream and watching the world go by.

'Who cares?' said Ella, slowing down in front of a jeweller's window. 'We've got loads of nights left.'

Kostas was packed. They were given a table right in the centre. The air buzzed with chatter and laughter, hummed with well-being. Music came from a bar three doors along. They revelled in the atmosphere, delighted to be outside on a balmy summer's evening with a view of the yachts and an ever-changing parade of passers-by.

'Yum.' Ella's eyes followed a silver platter of fish being set down on a neighbouring table. 'Yes?' She was taken aback when the waiter told her to go and pick some. At the counter, they peered at the line of mullet, the scales iridescent, black eyes staring.

'I feel like a Roman emperor giving the thumbs-down to a gladiator,' said Luc.

'They've already had it. Small, aren't they? Two each?'

Luc was put off having dolmades when Ella said they reminded her of condoms and opted for a Greek salad. The crumbly white feta was covered in herbs and sweet olive oil. Ella had some octopus. Wolfing down bread and knocking back white wine, they sat in contented silence.

*

'*Signome. Excusez-moi, mademoiselle.*'

Trying to fillet the mullet, Luc failed to realise that the voice was directed at her. She shifted her chair without looking up, allowing the man to squeeze past. A few minutes later, the same voice repeated an apologetic '*Pardon*'.

Luc scraped her chair round, but not far enough. 'Sorry.' She glanced up to find a pair of black eyes giving her a quick but thorough up-and-down appraisal. The Frenchman was in his mid- to late forties, his grey and black hair tied back in a ponytail. Luc had always associated this with ad execs way past their sell-by dates, yet this man seemed a stranger to a cushy, expense accounts existence. Squat, muscly, tanned, he seemed the out-of-doors type, as if he were used to handling horses, perhaps.

'*Merci. Karisto.*' His black moustache emphasised his hooked nose. He returned to his table. Three other men were sitting around it, beer bottles and packets of Gauloises and Gitanes piled up in front of them.

'I'm whacked.' Ella yawned. 'God, that could feed an African village for a week.'

Luc turned round, following her gaze. Waiters were setting down plate after plate of octopus, kalamari, kebabs, tzatziki and hoummos. The bottles and cigarette packets were being moved like chess pieces by the four. Wine was poured, the Frenchman tasted it, winced then laughed. Suddenly his black eyes were on Luc's. Hastily she looked away.

Ella poured out the remains of the wine as the clock-tower bell struck ten. 'It's still early. Hope I haven't got sunstroke.'

Their sleepless night, dinner, being somewhere strange were all catching up. Luc felt drowsy after a day in the sun and fresh air. It was different from her usual drained collapse-into-bed weariness after a day of London working and living. Her quiet dreaminess was at odds with the animated crowds strolling round the quayside, peering at the yachts and cruisers. 'Shall we get the bill?'

Glancing round for a waiter, Luc realised the Frenchman was

staring at her while picking his teeth. She felt awkward, as if he had X-ray vision and knew the colour of her knickers. He smiled lazily and said something to the man opposite him, who turned round.

Luc did a double-take. Ella gasped.

'Mine,' breathed Ella, just loud enough for Luc to hear, a heartbeat before Luc said it.

His eyes were topaz, huge, such a pale green they were almost striped with yellow. His blond hair was bleached by the sun, which seemed to be his smile. Despite the short dreadlocks, the singlet, the bangles round his sinewy wrists, he could've been a model for a classical statue, carved to show the heart-breaking perfection of the gods.

Apollo had come to life.

Chapter Two

———— >◦◦◦< ————

At nine o'clock the following morning, Luc went shopping. Usually a chore, it had a novel charm in the early morning sunshine. Instead of grey pavements, roads and cars, there were smooth cobblestones, sparkling water and boats. She skirted three sides of the quay and watched the fishermen gut their catch, chucking waste into the harbour water. Gulls shrieking overhead swooped down. On the yachts, crews were having breakfast and scrubbing decks. There was a smell of diesel, a chug, chug, chug and a gurgle of water as a cruiser's engine ticked over.

Yannis's was directly opposite, the other side of the harbour. Luc slowed down, enjoying feeling the sun on her back, trying to work out exactly which was their room. As if someone had slapped her, her musing was cut short by a horrible scraping noise behind her.

Luc turned round as Apollo flashed past her on a skateboard.

'*Bonjour*.' He glanced behind him, grinned at her and waved, his dreads bouncing in the sunlight, his huge stripy eyes hidden by wraparound sunglasses.

At that moment the sun seemed to shine more brightly. '*Bon . . .*'

He was already halfway to the clock-tower. His baggy board-shorts were faded, his sneakers were threadbare, but his white

T-shirt was pristine, with something printed across the back. Suddenly he flipped the board up into the air, jumped off and made a running catch.

Humming, grinning to herself, Luc ambled on round the quay until she was opposite the clock-tower. As she and Ella left the restaurant the night before, they had both felt slightly let down that Apollo was far more interested in filleting a snapper than bothering to glance again in their direction. Ella had suggested with a dispirited sigh that perhaps the four were gay.

Luc peered over the stone wall at the open sea. It had been ages since she'd had the time to stop and stare. Which poem? Ella would know. She'd probably know the whole of it off by heart.

There was a statue of a woman further ahead at the end of the quay. Not a goddess, but a woman in the long skirts of the nineteenth century. A merchant's wife? Luc sauntered on, smiling shyly as the fishermen in their boats wished her *kali mera*.

Her humming stopped as she caught her breath, the statue forgotten. The white yacht was as long as a tennis court. Its graceful, elegant lines made every other boat in the harbour look like a tub. Enchanted, Luc crept closer, as if drawn by a magnet. A French tricolor was hanging near the stern. Up beyond the gangplank two men in pristine white T-shirts were scrubbing the deck. Printed on their backs was *Les Voiles Blanches*.

'Breakfast? Star.' Coming on to the balcony, Ella peeled back her mascara-clogged eyes and squinted in the sunshine.

Luc had gone to the bakery and the cavernous supermarket, buying fresh bread, coffee, eggs and some watermelon. The bougainvillaea and hibiscus she'd picked in the courtyard were in a glass of water on the table.

Watermelon juice dribbled down Ella's huge Baci da Roma T-shirt. She peered across at the clock-tower. 'Ten? Still, it's only eight in London.' Her brown eyes widened. 'Look at that yacht. It's ginormous.'

'*Les Voiles Blanches.*'

'French? Do you think . . .?' Luc nodded. Ella squinted harder. 'Apollo? Wish we had some binoculars. Now I know why all the nice girls love a sailor.'

They lingered over breakfast, watching the comings and goings round the quayside. The sun rose higher, its light and heat becoming more intense. As Ella read Byron, Luc picked up her guidebook. Like finally putting a face to a long-heard name, she could identify the places mentioned.

'We can walk to Agios Agathas. Via the monastery.'

'Walk?' Ella sounded alarmed. 'How far?'

'Six, seven miles. Through the woods. It would be different.'

'So would getting dysentery.'

Luc gave up and went inside to get her sketchpad. She tried to become absorbed in studying the clock-tower, but her eyes kept wandering in the opposite direction towards the French yacht. Ella occasionally glanced up from her book, her gaze mirroring Luc's. They looked round as the balcony doors in the neighbouring room were flung open.

'Ohmigod. Marce. Will you just take a look at this view?'

'Wow. Neat. Hi there. Early lunch?' Taken aback, Ella and Luc smiled their hellos. 'Marcie Vale. And this is my friend Sherry Ryan.' They each had about three hundred perfect teeth in determined jaws. They were tanned and blonde and fully made-up, their shorts and singlets showing off gym-worked muscles. Even their toes looked trained. Ella and Luc introduced themselves.

'You guys English?' said Sherry. 'From London? Great. We're out of Columbus, Ohio. Been here long?'

'Arrived yesterday,' said Ella, lighting up.

'We're heading to London in early fall.' Marcie frowned at the cigarette. 'Planning to hang out in Rome and Paris first, catch the Matisse show, then up to Edinboro for the festival. You guys know Bellini?'

'The drink?' asked Ella.

'The artists, Ellen,' corrected Sherry. 'We're making a study.'

'Oh. How long have you been travelling?'

'About a month.' Marcie fanned the air, as if she feared that the smoke would waft across the ten-foot gap. 'Like we started in Athens and went to Istanbul, hoping to bus it to Moss-cow. But the guys there. Additoode. You know.'

'Addi . . .?' said Ella.

'I mean, we are talking medieval. What's with these Turks? Haghia Sophia and the Blue Mosque were kinda awesome.'

'Great,' agreed Sherry. 'But Turkey was a pain, so we hoofed it to Prague. You guys seen Prague?'

'Is it on the Circle Line?' asked Ella.

Luc shot her a look. 'It's supposed to be beautiful.'

'You guys don't know?' Sherry sounded amazed. 'Pity. I mean, it's like, wow. Don't you just love Baroque?'

'The politico-religious dynamic is fascinating,' said Marcie.

'Prefer Rococo, don't we, Luc?' Ella smiled.

Luc gave her a quizzical look. 'So, how long are you planning to stay here?'

'Going to take in the beach for a few days.' Sherry showed off her teeth. 'Chill out, go running. Is the drinking water safe here? Say, Ellen, what's that you're reading? Byron? Brave. You can handle his additoode towards women? Hostel.'

'Hostel?' Ella was bemused. 'Backpackers' hostel? Oh hoss-tile. God, no. Wish I could walk in beauty like the night. And I'd part from him with sorrow and tears.'

Marcie and Sherry exchanged glances. 'I mean,' Marcie flashed her teeth, 'don't we as women have a dooty to ask ourselves if this sort of lideradure is relevant or valid in today's . . .'

'Sorry, but we really ought to be getting ready,' cut in Luc, seeing Ella's eyes flash. 'Nice to meet you.'

'Have a nice day.' The Americans smiled, showing off their prodigious teeth. 'See you guys around.'

'Not if we see you first,' muttered Ella in the safety of the bedroom.

'Come on,' said Luc. 'What's the difference between Baroque and Rococo?'

'Don't have a clue.' Ella shrugged. 'They inspired this huge desire in me to pick my nose and eat the bogeys.'

On the way up through the town to the bus stop, they stopped and bought a mask and snorkel. With their towels and mats and cards and Travel Scrabble and sunscreen and bottles of water they felt like two of the mangy donkeys. Wearing baggy Chinese trousers, Ella attracted far less attention than she had the day before. Although she wouldn't admit it, her back was still painful and the rest of her too pink to take any chances.

The bus driver recognised them and pointed at the no smoking sign as Ella handed over some drachma. '*Ne?*'

'*Ne, ne, ne,*' said Ella impatiently. 'Understood. *Endaxi.*' The guidebook had described it as a catch-all phrase, meaning no problem.

'*Endaxi,* eh?' He laughed and said something as the engine roared to life.

Luc peered out of the window at the concrete Paradise Inn, with its view of the bus stop and scrub. Once again she was delighted that they hadn't opted for a package.

They decided to go to Ermioni, the fishing village they'd passed through the day before. The guidebook promised a sheltered bay and a taverna. A few minutes after the bus left Agios Agathas and was rounding a bend high above the sea, they spotted a deserted beach far below through a gap in the woods. With its turquoise water and pale, pale sand it was postcard perfect.

'Wish we had a boat.' Luc smiled, thinking how glorious it

would be if she and Apollo were like the owl and the pussycat, sailing away for a year and a day on *Les Voiles Blanches*.

'We can walk,' said Ella, spotting a dirt track leading off the road, down through some scrub to the trees. 'Take a picnic.'

The beach at Ermioni was a few minutes from the bus stop. Battered fishing boats were tied to a small stone jetty. A white jeep was parked outside the taverna, a simple wooden shack with four tables outside, sheltered by trellising. Apart from a couple shaking the sand off their mats, the beach was deserted.

As they stood admiring the water, the couple walked towards them. He was wearing the briefest of trunks and heavy gold chains round his neck and wrist, which caught the sun as he talked into his mobile. His companion tottered across the sand beside him in her gold wedged sandals. Her hair was almost the same canary-yellow as her bikini. As they passed Ella and Luc, they stared at them coldly from behind their sunglasses.

'Do you reckon she's by the hour?' muttered Ella.

'Sssh.'

'Just love that ankle chain. Darwin was right.' Ella shuddered, gazing at the man's hairy back. 'We are descended from the apes. Yuk. Still, matches her roots.' She watched them climb into the jeep. 'Must be local. Shall we go by those rocks? Shade for your whitest shade of pale skin.'

Time melted away as they swam and swapped the snorkel. The glass-clear water was sometimes bath-warm, in patches Arctic cold. Ella floated like a starfish. Shoals of black minnows swam towards her, only to about-turn at the slightest movement.

The sun beat down relentlessly. Ella joined Luc in the shade. Faces sheltered by their hats, they sat reading and staring at the waves. They let the warm breeze dry them, leaving behind a salt crust on their skin. The T-shirts they'd both been swimming in, much to the amusement of some fishermen at the taverna, were spread out on the rocks beside them. As Luc rubbed more Factor 1,000 into her arms, London's congested claustrophobia and Budgie's Betta Bites seemed a lifetime ago. The waves were like a metronome, slowing down her heart-rate and her thoughts, inducing a wonderful restfulness.

Ella was already halfway through a Mary Renault, but had also bought a book of Greek myths. Luc flicked through the pages, wishing she could be more like Artemis the huntress and less like a passive nymph who got turned into a tree.

Some teenagers arrived on their scooters, raced into the waves and began a noisy game of water polo. Ella looked up, then glanced at her watch. 'It's really two o'clock?'

They hopped across the baking sand to the taverna. Apart from the fishermen, they were the only customers.

'*Yassas.*' An ancient crone stepped out from behind the beaded curtain.

'*Parakalo.* Beer?' said Luc hesitantly. 'Two?'

The woman looked at them blankly.

'Beer,' repeated Ella.

'Ah, *birra. Due.*' Smiling, she shuffled back inside.

'We must learn some Greek,' said Luc, feeling ashamed. 'Should've bought a tape or something. *Karisto.*'

Two bottles were set down along with a plate of plump olives. '*Poli zesti.*' The crone fanned herself with her hand and pointed up at the sun, saying something about helios. '*Poli zesti.*'

Luc immediately thought of parrots and putting the kettle on.

'*Poli. Poli.*' Ella caught on. 'Very. A lot. Much. Multi. Very hot. *Poli zesti.*' She smiled at the crone. 'Like polygamy.'

'Or polytechnic,' said Luc. 'Funny how your mind works.'

They played rummy while they sipped their beers and nibbled at a Greek salad and bread. It was too hot to eat much. Feeling woozy after draining their third bottle, they were bewildered to find that more than an hour had slipped away. The rocks that had been sheltering them had disappeared beneath the water.

'The sea, the sea,' said Ella, gazing at the blue horizon. 'Bet they've gone. Sailed away into the sunlight.'

*

'What day is it?' asked Ella, as they walked past the chain-link fence and the pecking chickens. 'There's dinner.'

'Friday. Better send some postcards soon.'

They ambled down the passageways, orienteering themselves by the glimpses at the clock-tower far below. Outside every house were hanging baskets, even old drums of olive oil had been painted and planted with geraniums. Passers-by smiled and wished them *kali spera*.

'A whole week left. Bliss.' Ella peered at some cream cotton jerseys hanging outside a shop. 'Even you might go back with a tan. A whole ten minutes, today, was it?'

'Fat chance.' Luc sighed. 'Who knows, I might be glad when I'm fifty. When you're a leathery old prune.'

'If I reach fifty, 'said Ella sombrely.

' 'Course you will.'

'Janie didn't. You go on.' Screwing up her face, Ella stared at her dusty clogs. Janie, her mother, had died when Ella was seventeen. The cancer had been swift and cruel. Luc went on. At times like this, Ella wanted to be alone, hating any show of pity. A sympathetic arm would be shoved away. Luc understood the best thing she could say and do was nothing.

'They're still here.'

Coming out of the shower, Luc found Ella out on the balcony. Her eyes were slightly red and swollen, but her spirits restored. A bottle of wine and a bowl of pistachios were on the table. She was peering into a hand-mirror and covering her face with thick white cream. 'Greek yoghurt,' she announced, dabbing again and licking her finger. 'Yum. Alternative aftersun.'

'Who told you that?'

Ella shrugged. 'Read it somewhere. Supposed to be brilliant for the skin. Go on.' She held out the pot.

'Now what?' asked Luc, studying her death-mask reflection.

'You let it dry, then wash it off.' Ella squinted across the harbour. '*Oo ah, France est là*.' She began humming the *Marseillaise*. 'Shit we've forgotten about the adaptor. Is that Apollo? Oh God.' She crouched down as if avoiding snipers. 'Let's hope they haven't got a telescope.'

The dried yoghurt cracked around Luc's nose. She sniffed. 'Yuk. Sour milk. Ella . . .'

'You're imagining things.'

'I'm not. Cheesy sour milk with yellowy bits floating in it.'

'Cleopatra had baths in asses' milk . . .'

'I feel sick.' Shrieking, Luc raced Ella to the bathroom. 'You'd never make a beautician,' she said, washing her face. Ella had once tried to pierce their ears with a pair of compasses sterilised by a bunsen burner flame in the school's chemistry lab. 'I can still smell it.'

Ella rinsed her nose ring under the tap. 'Makes you wonder why Mark Antony bothered.'

The clock struck the half-hour. Halyard clips rang out like wind chimes as they tapped metal masts. A cruiser chugged into its berth. The low call of voices and laughter was joined by the eee-orr of a donkey. Water lapped against the harbour wall. Just as Luc opened up her sketchpad, thinking how restful it all was, she was interrupted by the saccharine voice of Karen Carpenter.

'Won't you bring me a letter, the sooner the better, Mr Postman . . .' rang out of a tape machine on the Americans' balcony table.

Luc glared. Where were Marcie and Sherry? She tried to think beautiful thoughts by concentrating on the view, but then Barry Manilow launched into his full-throated 'Mandy'. She was tempted to throw her espadrille at him.

'Hi there, Lou.' Sherry waved across. 'Good day?'

Luc was about to reply but heard a howl of outrage from Ella, coming out of the shower. 'What a fucking racket. It's making my ears bleed.'

Luc froze and pressed on hurriedly. 'Did you play frisbee?'

Sherry shook her head. 'We ran out of time. Visited the church, took in the museum. Cute place. Some interesting artefacts.' Luc had read about the museum, but hadn't dreamt of actually visiting it. 'Explored a bit. Did some shopping for dinner, washed clothes, you know. Say, Lou, do the guys here bother you? Their additoode is like, prehistoric. All that staring.'

'Oh.' Luc was at a loss. 'I'm sorry.'

'We felt visually raped.'

Taken aback, Luc poured herself another glass of wine. She wondered how the Americans had been dressed. As Ella had said on the bus coming back, the local women looked as if they were going to church in Athens. She'd vowed not to be as blatant as she had the day before.

In the background, Neil Diamond had taken over from Barry Manilow. Wearing just a towel, Ella stormed on to the balcony. 'Call that mus—' Catching sight of Sherry, she took a deep breath and smiled sweetly. 'Nice day? Please don't think I'm being hostel or confrontational, but would it be possible to have a more tranquil music situation? It's having a negative positive impact on my personal space. You see, this is the time for my meditation.'

'Sure, Ellen.' Sherry turned round.

As 'Sweet Caroline' died away, a whirring of a hairdryer could be heard. Luc and Ella looked at one another, horrorstruck. Having been so scathing, neither felt it right to ask a favour. Consciences struggled with vanity. The contest was short. Vanity won. Hands down.

The Americans refused the offer of a glass of wine as if they'd been offered Class A drugs. Neither touched alcohol, because it interfered with their training. No, they weren't training for anything, they just hit the gym back home. Like every day.

'Pity they don't develop some taste in music along with their abs and their lats,' said Ella, breaking off a huge hunk of bread and dipping it in hoummos swimming in olive oil. They were at the garden restaurant near the fig tree square. Tiny cats prowled round. A tanned dark-haired couple were being led to the neighbouring table.

'They've already been to the museum,' said Luc.

'What museum?'

'Exactly. All we've done is hit the beach and worry about hairdryers. Perhaps I should start running.'

Ella shuddered. 'Have more sex. It's the equivalent of a three-mile jog.'

'Really? I must've pulled a hamstring or something.' Luc sighed. 'While you're winning marathons.'

'Ginger whinger.' Ella pulled a face. 'You're too fussy. You want the sonnets and the symphonies . . .'

'And the waves crashing on the beach. I know, I know.'

'Anyway, what about Patrick? He called the other day.'

'His mother. He had a mother like the psycho in *Psycho* had a mother.' Luc shivered. 'What a disaster that night was.'

'Another one you led on, trollop.'

'Trollop?' shrieked Luc, then glanced nervously at the couple. The man was ordering in Greek. 'Your bed is more like a trampoline. Hussy.'

'Hussy? At least I use my room. What about the time I found you on the sofa with Jamie?'

'We were playing cards. He was teaching me . . .'

'Stud poker. We know. Well named in Jamie's case.'

'Nothing happened. Nothing much, anyway. We had a lot of tequila and things just got out of hand.'

'In hand I think, unless my eyesight's going.'

Luc ssshed her. 'That was a year ago now.'

The waiter came to remove their plates. Catching him gazing at Ella's cleavage, Luc felt even more anaemic and decidedly unalluring in comparison. Already getting tanned, Ella exuded vitality, sexy earthiness. Luc knew the long black pinafore was a mistake, emphasising her paleness.

47

'Stop fretting,' ordered Ella. 'You're full beautiful, a faery's child.'

Luc scowled. 'I feel about twelve in this dress.' A tiny grey cat started mewling as it wove in and out of the table legs. Thinking it was starving because it was so small, Ella offered it a pellet of bread which was examined and disdainfully refused. The man at the next table threw it a piece of squid, which it gobbled down before disappearing up a fig tree. 'Reminds me of Jamie,' said Luc. 'Gets fed and runs away.'

'Ungrateful,' the man boomed in pure Home Counties. Luc and Ella blushed scarlet. 'Give me dogs any day.'

'Nice couple,' said Ella later, as they sat outside the bar on the quayside. The Metaxa tasted almost chocolatey. They'd got chatting to the pair, who were spending two weeks island hopping on a small yacht. Mooring somewhere different every night, they spent the day sailing, anchoring in coves at lunchtime.

Jon, an Army major, had said Praxos and Hydra were the nicest places they'd visited so far. 'But if you get the chance, go to Ia. Head straight for the old port.'

'Beautiful,' agreed his doctor wife, Jane. 'You'll be able to find yourselves rich husbands there. Your own, I hope, not someone elses.'

Luc felt the brandy warming her throat as it trickled down. She'd been enchanted by the idea of idyllic, deserted beaches reached only by boat. 'We should learn to sail.'

'Or get to know someone with a yacht.'

A waiter suddenly set down two more glasses of brandy. 'These must be for someone else.' Luc was puzzled. 'We haven't ordered them.'

'No mistakes. From the mens there. With their comp, compli, how you say? Compliments.'

They turned round. Ella smiled. 'What was I saying about a yacht?'

Luc watched Ella walk over to the Frenchmen's table and was struck by her smiling confidence, which contrasted with her own sudden feelings of reserve. Only three of them were there. The pony tail was now standing up, taking Ella's hand and bowing over it with old-fashioned gallantry. He introduced her to Apollo and the third man.

'Are we joining them?' mouthed Ella looking back, eyebrows raised.

Chairs were already being rearranged. Luc rebelled at the men's assumption that she'd come running. She knew people around were watching with curiosity and was embarrassed to be thought of as an easy pick-up.

'Come on,' urged Ella.

'Please.' Apollo grinned. As his topaz eyes met hers, Luc's reluctance vanished. His smile was like a lighthouse, guiding her to where she ought to be. She got to her feet.

'And this is Lucasta. Luc,' said Ella. 'Luc, Henri. Henri, Luc.'

'*Enchantée, mademoiselle*.' As Henri's black eyes gave her the once-over, he took her hand and bowed. 'It is mademoiselle, I hope. Not madame?'

'Mademoiselle,' said Luc, wishing he'd let go. 'Thank you for the drink.'

'My pleasure.' His hand still clasping hers, he turned to the other two. 'Now, may I introduce Bertrand?' Luc returned a shy smile from a crew-cut with spectacles. 'And Yannick. I was very jealous this morning because he saw you and I did not.'

Taken aback by the thought that she'd been talked about, trying not to cringe at Henri's touch, Luc grew even more flustered when Apollo grinned. Although older than she'd thought, late rather than early twenties, he was even more dazzling close up. His smile was so warm it could've ripened nectarines in February. The sun-bleached dreadlocks, so at odds with his classical bone structure, added to his charm.

'Now, let's sit,' said Henri. 'You ladies, here and here.' He motioned they should be either side of him. Ella sat next to

Yannick and Luc was beside Bertrand. '*Santé*. Here's to engine trouble.'

'Engine trouble?' asked Ella.

'The yacht, she has problems. We have to wait for a part from Athens,' said Henri. 'But without the problems, we would've left and never met you.'

His eyes wandered over Luc, as if she were up for auction and he was thinking of making a bid. The black stare was so intense it made her claustrophobic. Gazing down at her drink, she asked how long it would take to fix.

'Bertrand, our mechanical genius, says less than a day.' Henri broke into French.

'*J'espére*.' Bertrand gave another shy smile. 'I'm sorry. My English is so bad.'

'Better than our French,' said Ella. 'It's a beautiful yacht. We've been admiring it from our balcony.'

'Thank you.' Henri gave a slight bow.

'Had her long?'

'You think I own her?' Henri smiled. 'No. I'm the skipper, these boys are my crew.'

'Oh.' Ella frowned. 'Who's the owner?'

Henri tut-tutted. 'No names. She is very discreet. Like her yacht, she is not so young, but still beautiful and elegant.'

'French?' asked Luc.

'French.'

'Is she nice?' Ella burst out laughing when Yannick and Bertrand exchanged rueful glances. 'So, that's a no. Difficult, then?'

Yannick smiled, the lines around his eyes crinkling. 'Madame has her way. There is no negotiation, no argument. *C'est fini*. Apart from my hair.' He tugged at his blond dreadlocks. 'She told me to get it cut or leave. I said, OK, I leave. She surrendered.'

Henri nodded. 'Madame is boss. She's fair, but she's boss.'

'How often do you see her?' asked Ella.

'Perhaps ten weeks a year.'

'No relaxation then,' said Yannick. 'But she is brave. In February, horrible storm off Guadaloupe. Mast broke. Huge waves. She remained calm, made us all food, coffee, stayed on watch all night.'

'Courage,' agreed Bertrand. 'Good sailor.'

'You sail to the Caribbean?' Ella's brown eyes widened.

'Every year,' said Henri. 'Madame comes to Martinique in January. Summer we're in the Mediterranean. St Tropez, Portofino . . .'

'And now Greece,' said Luc.

'First time. Madame might arrive, might not. We stand by. This week she decided at the last minute to go to Hascot for the 'orse races.'

Luc's mind reeled at the thought of the lives of the Croesus-rich. She had met people who were comfortably off, but never any who had ninety-foot yachts and a gang of crewmen on standby. 'Weren't there four of you yesterday?'

Henri nodded. 'Xavi is on board. The harbour master warned there might be problems with security. So, no fun for him tonight. No talking to beautiful English girls.' He raised his glass to Luc.

Blushing, she stiffened again. Yannick grinned at her, then offered Ella his tobacco. She rolled a cigarette with quick dexterity. '*Très bon*.' He was impressed. Smiling, she reached across for her lighter. 'And this?' He pointed at her tattoo.

'Long story.'

Bertrand leaned forward to have a closer look, then said something to Yannick. 'He asks if it was painful.'

'I was too drunk to notice.'

Grinning, Yannick translated.

'It's quite small and pretty.' Ella examined the rose. 'Just think if it had been a dragon or Tas.'

'Tas?' asked Yannick.

'Tas. Short for Tasmania, because he was so wild. The man at the time. He got me to do it. Like the tattoo, he was pretty and a pretty big mistake.'

Yannick turned to Luc. 'Where's yours?'

'A tattoo?' She felt herself melting under his smile. 'I don't have one. Too much of a coward.'

'Too sensible,' said Ella.

Sensible. Luc felt a pin-prick of resentment. Sensible as in sensible shoes, like the ugly brown lace-ups worn by the nuns at school. She wanted to be likened to a pair of beautiful, impractical Manolo Blahnik stilettoes.

'It would not suit her.' Henri sounded categoric. 'Luc is demure. This English rose doesn't need a rose tattoo. She's too pretty. You're pretty too, Ella, but different. Wilder.'

'Why thank you,' said Ella dryly. 'Now, can we get you a drink?'

'Absolutely not.' Henri sounded offended. 'We get the drinks.' There was no waiter in sight so he ordered Bertrand to the bar.

Ella turned to Yannick, asking him where he was from. Luc wished she could swap places with her. She knew she ought to be making an effort to talk to Henri but his intense black stare was stifling. Although they were sitting outside, she almost wanted to ask someone to open a window.

Henri was saying something as Yannick threw back his head and laughed. Luc ordered herself to be polite and concentrate, not worry about how well Ella was getting on with him. She wasn't going to think about saying 'mine' a heartbeat too late.

'What do you do?' repeated Henri.

'I temp.' Luc drained her Metaxa. 'As a secretary.'

'You don't enjoy it?'

'Not much. I thought it would give me freedom. In fact, it's just the same treadmill but in different places.' A treadmill of dismal dead ends like Budgie's Betta Bites. A treadmill requiring sensible shoes.

'What would you rather do?'

'I simply don't know.' She sighed forlornly. 'So, where are you sailing next?'

'Hydra. Then Ia, perhaps. Some Greek friends of Madame's own an island nearby. If you want a new job, come and work for me.'

Luc was taken aback. 'Doing what?'

'Crewman. Someone to sort out food, clean, hostess. Xavier is leaving us. We need a fourth.'

'I can't sail.'

'Then you learn.' He shrugged. '*Les Voiles Blanches* is much harder to capsize than those little dinghies you see on your horrible reservoirs. She's a beautiful yacht, you will suit her. Madame loves the English. Her second husband, Sir Richard, made her a very rich widow. You make a good vinaigrette?'

Luc nodded. Yannick was sipping some of Ella's Metaxa, wrinking up his perfectly straight nose.

'So you can be our cook,' continued Henri. 'No one cooks on board, except on the Atlantic. Madame hates cooking smells. She allows coffee and *œufs durs*. We eat hot food ashore. You see, simple job.'

'You really mean it . . .' He nodded. She could spend the summer sailing round the Mediterranean, visiting those idyllic coves that the English couple had described earlier, mooring in different ports, going ashore to buy provisions, Apollo teaching her to skateboard . . .

The black eyes lingered over her. 'We could have a nice time.'

As Luc crashed back to reality, Bertrand returned with the Metaxas and beers. Pleading tiredness, he said good night and headed off along the quayside. She wanted to tug his sleeve and yank him back.

'And then there were four.' Smiling at Yannick, Ella looked as if all her wishes had just been granted.

'So, Ella, are you an artist?' asked Henri.

'Piss artist, perhaps. No, I can't paint a wall. I'm about to be a student again.' She lit another cigarette.

'Studying?'

'History.'

As she explained that she was planning to study for a Master's, Luc's eyes met Yannick's. He was so easy; easy on the eye, easy to talk to, easy to fall for. If only they could all play musical chairs. But with her luck, she'd find herself out. Or sitting on Henri. He was asking how Ella would manage going back to living on a student's income.

She smiled enigmatically. 'I'll get by.'

As Ella bloomed under the topaz gaze and the warm smile, Luc felt herself wilting, shrivelling up. She was the dull little wallflower, put in the shade by Ella's laughter and vibrancy. Ella had found her place in the sun. And sitting a fraction too close, Henri was casting a horrible shadow.

Henri offered them another drink aboard *Les Voiles Blanches*, an offer Ella accepted eagerly. Despite all the Metaxas, Luc was stone-cold sober. She exaggerated a yawn. 'I really ought to get some sleep.'

Ella took no notice. 'The walk will wake you up.'

'I'm still quite tired . . .' She hoped Ella would get the message.

She didn't. 'Lukewarm . . .'

Luc hesitated, torn between her longing to see the yacht and her instincts to keep her distance from Henri, a distance which might narrow alarmingly on his territory. But, she reasoned, she wasn't going to be alone with him, there were four chaperones about. And she might never again get the chance to set foot on a ninety-foot yacht.

As they strolled round the quay, the lights shimmered on the inky-black water. Soft music and laughter came from the boats, where crews sat on deck having a last drink. Burning cigarette tips glowed red.

Up ahead with Henri, Ella was pointing to Yannis's, across

the water. Beside Yannick, Luc shyly returned his sweet, sweet smile.

'What's it like? Living on a boat?'

'The last two evenings, the best. Other times, hard. You're in a very confined space. No private? What's the word?'

'Privacy,' suggested Luc.

'*Oui*. No privacy. Have to be considerate, respect one another, think of others all the time. And we must obey the boss.' He nodded up to Henri. 'Great skipper. Great man. One of the best. He likes you.' Yannick gave her a sideways glance. 'A lot.' Luc squirmed a smile. 'But then, who doesn't?'

Startled, she caught her breath.

He reached across and gently re-arranged a lock of her hair. 'Unfortunately Henri is my boss.'

Luc returned the topaz gaze. She felt guilty, awkward. Ella had staked her claim to her place in the sun, she couldn't trespass on Ella's ground. 'Confined space. It must be hard.'

'You have to be very tidy. You're beautiful, aren't you?' Smiling down at her, he shrugged. 'But Henri is my boss. And I need a job.'

'Very tidy? Don't think Ella and I could cope.' She was almost gabbling. 'Last time someone came round, they asked if we'd been burgled.'

'You and Ella live together? In London? Whereabouts?'

'In Chelsea. Some of the snottier neighbours say Knightsbridge.'

He whistled. 'Nice area. Expensive though. Good rent?'

'Very good. I'm lucky. Ella's my landlady.'

'She is? Nice flat?'

'House. Ella calls it the Doll's House.'

'Ella owns a house?' Sounding bewildered, he glanced up ahead. 'But . . .'

Luc was used to the reaction. The American bankers who had just moved into the Mews had assumed the mud-splattered Ella was a squatter when she came back from Glastonbury the year before. Especially when they saw Tas, Ella's souvenir from that weekend. They'd called the police.

'Are you and Ella ever in France?' asked Yannick.

'Sometimes.'

'You'll have to come to St Tropez and visit us. When Madame is away. We have more time.'

'What did you do before?'

'Before *Les Voiles Blanches*? I was training for public administration. Civil Service, yes? Very straight. Suit. Short hair. Awe-full.' He shuddered. He watched Ella at the gangplank, slipping off her clogs. 'So Ella's . . .' Returning her wave, he left the question unasked.

The gangplank swayed slightly under their bare feet. As Luc stepped on deck, she thought she'd gone through the looking glass into a more beautiful, more enchanted world. The colours were brighter, the air sweeter. Like a velvet cloak, a magic wrapped itself around her.

'You see, Luc. You are at home,' said Henri. 'A tour?'

He led them below. Despite the low ceilings there was a sense of space. Plump cushions of navy and cream begged to be sat upon. Teak and brass shone as if an army of housemaids spent their lives polishing it. Henri opened doors to cabin after cabin. Bertrand was in one, reading Maigret, Xavier was fast asleep in another. Ella and Luc smiled in delight, unable to believe the luxury, the uncompromising excellence of design. The yacht was as groomed and glossy as interiors in magazines.

'My brother-in-law would love this,' said Ella, peering into the galley. 'Form following function. He's an architect. What a wonderful toy to play with.'

'A toy?' Henri sounded offended. 'This is an ocean-going yacht. As that, she is wonderful. That she is beautiful is secondary.'

Up on deck again, they settled on large navy cushions that covered two benches.

Yannick brought up a bottle of brandy and four glasses.

Henri sat next to Luc. She caught the sweet rose smell of his aftershave and saw a thin gold chain at the base of his throat. As he lit a cigarette, she realised that his hands were incredibly clean. She was surprised. Surely someone so masculine should bath in engine oil?

The moon was rising above the hillside, lights went out in the tumbling-dice houses. Although muted by distance, music could just be heard from one of the bars. Water lapped against the sides, the mooring ropes creaked. There was a constant, gentle rocking.

'Lovely to sleep here,' said Luc. 'So restful. Like a cradle.'

'Try it,' said Henri, giving her another black up and downer.

'Oh, I didn't mean . . .' Having melted away, her awkwardness returned.

'So,' cut in Ella. 'If I wanted a yacht like this for Christmas, how much would it cost?'

Henri shrugged. 'Millions. You'll need a very good job or a very rich boyfriend.'

'Perhaps Ella needs neither,' said Yannick, passing her his tobacco and papers.

Ella gave another enigmatic smile.

'Have you a rich boyfriend back home, Luc?' Henri offered her one of his Gitanes.

'No? Not a cigarette or a rich boyfriend? Any boyfriend?'

Luc wished she could fib, but couldn't. Ella and Yannick began talking about the stars. If Henri wanted a tête-à-tête, she must channel it on to more neutral ground.

Ella disappeared below. Luc got up and wandered over to the side, peering across the harbour to the clock-tower. Behind her Yannick and Henri broke into low fast French. Although she couldn't hear what they were saying, her intuition told her Henri was preparing to pounce.

She grimaced. Just her luck. Here she was on a beautiful yacht in one of the most romantic settings possible. There was even moonlight. All the ingredients were in place, including the gorgeous man. Sighing, she mooched towards the gangplank and stared out to the open sea beyond the wall.

'I think I'll go back,' she said flatly.

'What for?' Ella had combed her hair and put on more lipstick. She seemed to be floating on joy. 'Isn't this amazing? Isn't he heavenly?'

'Apollo.' Luc hoped her voice was neutral, instead of being filled with sour grapes. 'Ella, I don't want to . . .'

Suddenly Yannick appeared at Ella's side. 'You'll see better from up there. Less light. Come . . .'

Les Voiles Blanches rocked slightly as they disappeared up the deck towards the bow. Luc tried to concentrate on the statue and ignore the way her insides were being gnawed.

'You seem pensive,' called Henri.

'Just tired.' She tried to smile, her mouth seemed frozen.

'Well, come and sit then.' Henri patted the cushion beside him. 'I'm not going to bite you,' he added, laughing. 'We're friends, no?'

She walked across the deck as if it were a trip to the scaffold.

'Are you so nervous?' he asked, as she gingerly sat on the edge of the cushion. 'Or are you cold?'

Alarmed that he might offer to warm her up, Luc shook her head. 'I'm fine, thank you.' If only he'd stop looking at her so intensely.

'Thank you? You're very for-mall.'

'The English in me.' Her voice sounded strained. 'Formal, distant, reserved.' Unable to look him in the eye, she gazed up at the sky. She heard but ignored his murmur of *'Et trop belle'*.

'A little shyness is very feminine, very charming.'

'Very dull,' muttered Luc, stiffening as he took hold of her hand.

'You're cold. What beautiful fingers. Do you play the piano?'

'Not very well.' As if it belonged to someone else, she studied her hand lying inert between his snaking fingers. His warm touch wasn't unpleasant, but as she tried to ease away from it, his grip tightened slightly. She knew this was the moment to be assertive. 'Where's the North Star?'

Henri's right hand reached out behind her and began to massage her shoulder. 'Relax. I'm not hurting you, am I?'

'No. It's, er . . .'

'Well then. Don't be so silly. We're friends, no? It's companionable. That's an English word?'

'Yes.'

As his fingers kneaded her neck, Luc asked herself why she was so bloody polite. What was preventing her from saying take your hands off me, please. You're not bad-looking for someone almost fifty, you're not crass or stupid or smelly, but sorry, I simply don't fancy you.

To free herself, she reached forward for her brandy and a cigarette she didn't really want. She wanted it even less when he insisted on putting it in her mouth and lighting it for her.

She smoked without much enjoyment. Perhaps it would make her breath foul. Why hadn't she eaten a field of garlic and a sub-continent of curry for dinner? 'I think it's time . . .'

'It's early.' Henri pulled her to him, cradling her head on his shoulder so she got a view of his pale blue shirt, tanned hairy toes and the decking. 'Companionable? Yes?'

'Um.' Why was she such a limp wimp, unable to be straightforward? Why had she expected him to get the hint through her silence and body language rather than plain English? Or American? Marcie and Sherry were bound to have an off-pat speech for such a situation. They'd be assertive. And convincing. If she tried, this middle-aged Frenchman would simply laugh at her and say something about being friendly.

Why had she boarded his territory, accepted his brandy and then gone and sat beside him? Now she was almost lying in his arms, although her mind was screaming get me out of here. Luc realised that any brave Artemis-the-huntress side of her was obviously so dormant it was non-existent. Next she'd be turned into a tree.

She squeaked and went rigid as he suddenly took her face in both his hands and pulled her closer to him. He bent his head, ready to kiss her. If only she could be sick to order. Oh God . . .

A shout came up from the quayside. 'Anyones there? Monsieur le Capitaine. Anyones there?'

'*Merde*.' Letting go of Luc, Henri got up and strode towards the stern.

'Monsieur. Anyones awake?'

Following Henri, Luc saw an ageing hippy with a long, grey beard, waist-length grey hair and shorts. Had Z Z Top arrived on Praxos? 'The harbour master,' said Henri, waving down. '*Yassas*.'

'The parts. Flown into Mathi. Just arrived.'

'*Merci. Karisto*. Two minutes.' He turned round. 'Yannick. *Tout de suite*. Yannick.' Followed by a bewildered Ella, Yannick hurried up the deck. Henri ordered him to find Bertrand and Xavi.

'What's going on?' Ella's lipstick had disappeared.

'The engine parts are being delivered.' Feeling as light as air, Luc was almost skipping.

'I'm so sorry,' said Henri, once they were all on the quayside.

'Not as sorry as me.' Ella gazed longingly at Yannick, whose arm was round her shoulders.

'Tomorrow night we'll all have dinner. Yes?' Henri begged Luc.

Her heart sank. And sank even further when Ella nodded like a toy dog in the back of a car.

'Come here for drinks at around seven,' said Henri. 'Not before. We have to work. No distractions. Promise?' He frowned sternly at Ella and Yannick.

'Promise,' laughed Ella, squeezing Yannick's hand.

'*Au revoir*.' Pulling Luc towards him, Henri kissed her on both cheeks, murmuring something in French. '*A demain*.'

Chapter Three

Luc scowled into the shower-room mirror. Fizzing with energy, Ella was making breakfast and singing. Half an hour earlier, she'd jumped out of bed and raced down to the baker's.

'. . . I feel pretty, oh so pretty, I feel pretty and witty and gay . . .'

Luc felt ugly. There was a livid mosquito bite on her cheek and her eyes were red and puffy. She was porridge-brained from all the brandy and had woken up in the same mood in which she'd gone to sleep – morose.

Not even the view from the balcony, the blue, blue sky or breakfast laid out on the table could lift her spirits. Peering across the harbour, she could just make out Bertrand scrambling along the deck of *Les Voiles Blanches*.

'Thanks,' she mumbled, as Ella put a mug of coffee next to her sketchbook. She ripped out her half-completed sketch of the clock-tower. She'd completely misjudged the perspective. Not in the mood to talk, she picked up *Greek Myths* and turned to the index. Her eye fell on 'Paris, Judgement of'.

Ella began munching on a cheese pie. 'Tyropitta. Yum. Try one.'

'Later.' The crumbly white filling reminded Luc of the flabby state of her inner thighs, which that morning seemed especially unappealing. Knowing that Ella would pounce on any churlishness, she tried to inject some enthusiasm into her voice. 'What'll we do today?'

'Don't mind.' With a beaming smile, Ella stretched. 'Aren't we lucky? We've found the most perfect place and within two days we've been on the most beautiful boat in the whole of Greece.' Shading her eyes, she looked across to *Les Voiles Blanches*. 'Didn't you feel like a hundred million drachma walking aboard last night?'

'A hundred million,' agreed Luc flatly.

'So, come on. What about you and Henri?' On their walk back to the room, Ella had been too ecstatic to think about anything but Yannick. All she'd done was recount how he'd taken her to the bow, taught her about the stars and then kissed her. And how he was so gorgeous, those eyes, that face, that body . . . In her need to relive every second of her time with him, she'd failed to notice Luc's cool reticence.

'What about me and Henri?'

'Yannick says he's absolutely smitten.'

'Great.' Luc sighed heavily.

'What's wrong? He's very attractive, perfect older man material. He was a legionnaire.'

'As in the disease?' Luc scowled.

'The French Foreign Legion. He had incredible adventures in Chad and places. Made a Major, got loads of medals. Then he was a mercenary. Bet he's brilliant in bed.'

'I'm not going to find out.' Luc pulled a face. 'I don't fancy him.'

'You don't? Not a bit? Didn't you . . .?'

'No. He tried. Saved by the harbour master, thank God.'

'You've got a funny way of showing it.' Ella shrugged. 'Why say you wanted to sleep on board?'

'Look, all I meant was that it would be soothing. Like lying in a hammock or something. I can't see how you can say that I wanted to sleep with Henri. Because I don't. Not in a million years. OK?'

'Oh.' Taken aback, Ella frowned. She seemed apprehensive. 'What about dinner tonight?'

'What about it? You go.'

'I can't. Not on my own.'

'You won't be on your own. You've got Yannick.' Luc tried to ignore the stab of resentment which was twisting her guts.

'Hope so.' Joy lit up Ella's face. 'He won't think it was a huge, hideous mistake, will he? I don't know why you're so anti-Henri, I thought you liked the idea of an older man.'

'Not him.' Luc shuddered.

'He's very attractive, great muscles . . .'

'Ella, stop trying to sell him. I'm not buying. And I don't want to see him tonight.'

'Why not?'

'It's too much hassle. It was bad enough last night.'

'Come on, you can handle Henri. It's not as if you'll be alone with him. I don't see why you're making such a fuss.' Ella was losing her patience. 'It's not every day that you get an invitation to drinks on a fuck-off yacht. Just enjoy the swank and think, this time last week I was on a cattle-truck Tube train after a shite day's temping.'

'Thanks.' Luc picked up her book.

Ella stared out across to *Les Voiles Blanches*. 'Sorry. I thought you and Henri . . .' She chewed her lip. 'Listen, Luc, please come. If you're not there, Henri might decide to set sail into the sunset.'

'He won't.'

'I'll let you off this month's rent. Please come. I'll act as chaperone. Please. Have drinks, then dinner, then food poisoning. Please.'

'Mirror, mirror on the wall, who's the fairest of them all?'

In the tiny shower room, Luc examined the mosquito bite again. It was like a traffic light stuck on red. Perhaps it would stop Henri's advances.

She told herself to stop being such a tragedy and feel pleased for Ella. She and Ella were best friends, they had ten years of mutual experiences and shared memories. Very different, they complemented one another, Ella's wildness tempered by Luc's common sense, Luc's shyness feeding off Ella's confidence. Sometimes it was as if they were almost telepathic.

Men, including Yannick, came and went. Tas, Jamie, Bron the Beast, Ed, Johnny, Richie, even the non-events like Quentin and Patrick. How many frogs had been kissed between them over ten years? Ella went for men like Tas, the mavericks; while she herself found the clean-cut Jamies more appealing. Their taste was so different; the arty versus the hearty. Until now. Until they'd set eyes on Yannick and Ella had breathed 'mine', staking her claim a heartbeat before Luc had.

Like Paris, Yannick had judged. And preferred Ella.

Ella wasn't a rival. She was her best friend, had been ever since she'd arrived at school with dozens of books, a bag of grass and a fistful of attitude. She was an exotic feast compared to the carrot crunchers. Luc had been fascinated from the moment Ella had been caught in the maths class her second morning reading *Lady Chatterley* under the cover of her log tables. Desiccated, elderly Miss Bridstow had snatched up the book, then blushed scarlet catching sight of the title, before spluttering that to do anything in life, Ella would need qualifications.

'I'll get qualified, but I don't need differential equations to look like Julie Christie in *Darling*.'

Instead of going to Canada to visit her aunt and dislikeable new uncle, that Easter holiday Luc had gone to stay at Ella's. She'd thought she was in a kaleidoscope. With her straight blonde hair and eyes like melted chocolate, Janie Parr was like an older version of her daughter. The chaotic house was always full of people, drawn in by Janie's warmth, wonderful food and endless supplies of booze. It was half past ten when Luc had sat down to dinner that first night, along with an actor, a disgraced MP and a rat catcher who'd had his poetry published.

She pulled a face in the mirror, telling herself to accept Yannick's judgement with good grace. Jealousy was like a cancer of the soul. It destroyed the spirit and devoured friendships. Ever since the brandies had arrived at their table the night before, she had hated herself for seeing Ella as a rival. A more successful rival. If, on the walk from the bar to *Les Voiles Blanches*, Yannick had hinted that things might've been different, Ella must never know. Men came and went, but their friendship was sacred. Wasn't it?

Out on the balcony, alternately gazing at *Les Voiles Blanches* and reading, Ella was interrupted by Sherry and Marcie. The Americans were sipping hot water and lemon. They'd already been out jogging.

'Morning, Ellen.' Marcie looked askance at the remains of the tyropittas and the overflowing ashtray.

Mind torn between the plot and Yannick, Ella looked up. 'Morning.'

'More Byron?'

'Not today. More frisbee?'

'Oh, we're moving on,' said Sherry, pulling a face as she sipped. 'Say, are these lemons organic? Catching the six o'clock ferry. Hi, Lou. So, you guys are planning to stay for how long?'

'Another week perhaps,' said Luc, gazing across the sparkling water of the harbour. How could she have allowed stupid jealousy to blind her to the view? 'It's so beautiful.'

'Marcie and Sherry are leaving today,' explained Ella.

'So soon?'

'Like we'll walk to the beach via the monastery, then we'll have covered the possibilities here.' Marcie began a complicated hamstring stretch.

'Pretty spot,' said Sherry. 'Great if you want to veg on your butt, but like limiting if you're into culture.'

' "Whenever I hear the word culture, I reach for my gun",' quoted Ella in a murmur.

Luc suppressed a giggle. 'Where next?'

'Back to Athens.' Marcie straightened up. 'A must-see is the Museum of Byzantine Art.'

Ella settled her bag more comfortably on her shoulder. 'I feel like a pack-horse.'

It was far hotter. The sun seemed to sting their faces, each step up the hill to the bus stop was twice as much effort. They skirted the edges of walls, grateful for patches of shade, and felt sorry for the cats in their fur coats. Halfway up, they stopped and glugged back some water.

'I'm roasting.' Luc fanned herself with her hat. She could feel trickles of wet down her back.

Ella nodded, too hot to make the effort to speak.

Boarding the bus, they were surprised that every seat was taken. The still air reeked of garlic and stale sweat. Luc wondered if she also ponged, but, only too grateful to put down her lead-heavy bag, she didn't care. As the bus started, Ella was thrown backwards, almost landing on a baby being cradled in its mother's lap. It started to howl.

'I'm so sorry. *Signome*. God, why's it so packed?'

'It's Saturday,' exclaimed Luc.

As the bus meandered inland, a slight breeze blew in from the windows. Stooping, they craned their necks to get a view, while clutching the pole trying not to lose their balance as they hit various pot-holes. Ten minutes into the journey, a group of locals boarded, forcing everyone to squeeze even more closely together. It reminded Luc of the Tube in the rush-hour. Desperate for some more water, she was unable to move to reach down into her bag. She wished the baby would stop crying.

'That was horrible,' shuddered Ella, when they finally got off at Agios Agathas. The dusty track past the crowded taverna was baked to iron hardness. 'I should wring out these clothes.'

They halted, surveying the beach in disbelief. It was packed. Every few feet bodies lay stretched out in the sun. Noisy jet-skis were circling the bay sounding like giant mosquitoes. Boogie boxes were trying to outdo one another. A group were having a barbecue in the shade by the rocks. Even the water looked congested.

Ella was dismayed. 'Now what?'

'We could wait for the next bus and go to Ermioni,' suggested Luc. 'But that might be the same. It's the weekend.'

'No shade,' said Ella. 'We'll fry.'

'Taverna?'

Feeling like extras in *Beau Geste*, they retraced their steps to where dozens of people were queuing for a table. 'Shit. What are we going to do?' wailed Ella.

They tried to think, but the heat seemed to be lasering away their braincells.

'What about the beach we saw yesterday?' suggested Luc. 'A bit further up the road, down through the woods?'

'Brilliant. Anything's better than here. We'll get some more water.'

After buying two more extortionately priced bottles from the taverna, they set off. Dashed by the scene at the beach, their spirits rose with the thought they were doing something positive.

They walked uphill alongside a dusty olive grove set behind a crumbling stone wall. In the cloudless sky, the sun burned like a furnace. Mirage water was shimmering on the Tarmac up in the distance. The murmur of the sea could just be caught between the shrieks of the cicadas.

'How far?' Luc's sunglasses were slipping down her shiny nose.

'Just round this bend. I think.' Ella stopped for some water.

Both wondered if they shouldn't have stayed at Agios Agathas.

'Look.' Luc pointed, catching sight of the bay far below. Somehow the sand was bleached whiter, the sea was more turquoise than she remembered.

The glimpse of the beach gave them fresh energy. They reached the turning to the track which led to the woods, snaking its way down across the scrub-covered hillside. Much further than they expected, at least it was downhill.

They could feel the sweat on their scalps under their hats and their clothes were sticking to them. Ella began singing 'Mad Dogs and Englishmen', then broke off. 'We should've hired a moped.' The hot, dry air seemed to be singeing the inside of her nostrils.

'Or sailed.' Almost tripping on some scree, Luc suddenly saw the advantages of having Henri on hand. If not actually in hand.

After what seemed an age, they reached the edge of the woods. A derelict stone building, no larger than a hut, stood at the edge of a path. Its tiled roof had caved in, a few rafters were exposed.

Occasionally slipping and sliding, they followed the sandy path as it wove its way through the trees. The green tangle of branches overhead provided wonderful shade. Suddenly, the trees thinned out, the slope became more gentle and a perfect crescent of white sand stretched out before them.

Dumping their bags, stepping out of their shoes, tearing off their clothes, they ran to the water's edge.

'Worth it,' called Ella as she surfaced. The sea was idyllic, washing away the dust, the grime, the sweat. As they swam and floated, floated and swam, they were renewed. 'Worth every bloody, hot, awful step.'

They laid their mats in the shade of the trees, feeling like Robinson Crusoe before he saw Friday's footstep.

'Should've brought our eight records and a book,' said Ella, taking off her bikini top.

'And your luxury, Miss Parr?'

'Yannick.'

'He wouldn't be allowed.'

'*Les Voiles Blanches* to take me away then. I'd be useless on a desert island. No hairdryers.' Ella tried to drag a comb through her tangle. 'Oh God, what time are Marcie and Sherry leaving?'

Using her glasses as a mirror, Luc dabbed her face with block-out. 'Henri sort of offered me a job on board.'

'You're joking.'

Her mosquito bite stood out like a beacon. 'He was. Probably.'

'Supposing he wasn't? You should've said yes. I would. Just think, being paid to lie around on deck, living in luxury. Crossing the Atlantic . . .' Ella grew rapturous. 'Chance in a million.'

'Chances are I'd get very fit. Running up and down trying to escape Henri.' Luc grimaced. She shaded her eyes. Up the beach a backpacking hippy couple had just arrived, their hair bleached almost white by the sun.

'Henri's not that bad. Better than Quentin the zit.'

'That's not saying much.'

'Attractive, experienced, interesting . . .'

'I'm not interested.'

'OK.' Ella glugged her water. 'But if he offers you a job again tonight, take it. Just make it clear there are no strings.'

'Forget it. It's not asking, it's begging for trouble. I can hardly make my excuses and leave in the middle of the ocean. I'm not that good a swimmer.'

Having unhitched their backpacks, the couple stripped off and were wading into the sea. They waved. Ella waved back, then rummaged in her bag and fished out her Travel Scrabble. She picked out a tile. 'E. It's so hot.'

'D,' said Luc, grabbing six more.

'Flukey, Lukey. You know, there is such a thing as back for coffee which is just coffee.'

'In my experience, it usually back, fuck offee.'

'You just have to make it clear. Say you're not on the menu like the *petits fours*.'

Luc thought about having dinner with Henri later and scowled. 'I'd rather avoid situations like that in the first place.'

'Stop being such a victim.' Ella sighed.

'I'm not a victim, just useless at being assertive.'

'Well, you'd better learn. Otherwise you'll miss out. Aren't you glad you saw *Les Voiles Blanches*?'

'Well, yes. But . . .'

'But nothing. Men, including Henri, aren't predatory, unreasonable monsters. Honestly, sometimes I think you're stuck in Victorian times. Just like your clothes. What's that? You haven't got Scrabble, have you?'

'D. R. I. N. K. Twenty.' Luc drained her water bottle.

'D. O. P. E. Y. Eleven. That reminds me.' Delving into her bag, Ella brought out her pipe.

Soon it was hard to concentrate on the game. Even in the shade, the heat was relentless. Sauna-like, the air seemed too hot and dry to breathe properly. The hippy couple lay on the sand to dry off, but soon retired to the shelter of some rocks. Abandoning the game, Luc and Ella went for another swim. Their brains were scrambled, their bodies seemed not to belong to them. The waves that lapped over them were a distant sensation. Returning to their mats, lulled by the whisper of the sea and the call of the cicadas, they drifted off to sleep.

'Luc. Luc.' From far away, Luc heard her name being called. 'Wake up.'

Luc's eyelids seemed to be on fire, her head was throbbing. She sat up slowly. While they'd slept, the sun had moved round and they'd been in its full glare. It was almost four o'clock.

'Have some water.' Ella passed her their last bottle, now less than a third full. She squeezed her swollen eyes tight shut, massaging her temples.

'No.' Horrified, Luc examined her arms and legs. The skin was scarlet, as if she'd been boiled. Despite the heat coming off her like a scalding radiator, she shivered.

'Feel sick.' Ella adjusted her bikini bottoms. The white stripe on her hipbone showed up the seared pink of the rest of her. 'Let's go.'

Luc nodded, feeling too wretched to speak.

Slowly, painfully, they gathered up their stuff. It was agony putting their sand-covered clothes back on their salty burnt bodies. Their skin felt like it would split open with every movement.

The hippies had gone. The desert island solitude was disturbing. Both wished they had stayed among the crowds at Agios Agathas. Luc shivered again.

'Finish it.' Ella held out the water bottle. 'Less to carry. Should've brought some painkillers instead of all this junk.'

They began walking. The tops of their feet burnt, each step hurt. The roasting, tight skin on their legs protested. The path back up seemed almost vertical. They clambered over rocks and picked their way round gnarled tree roots, trying to avoid the razor-like gorse. Soon out of breath, they felt as if they had a pulse in their teeth and they were weeping sweat as it ran down into their eyes.

'At least it's not dark,' gasped Luc. She told herself she had absolutely nothing to be frightened of.

'Cold.' Ella shivered. 'And creepy.'

The woods seemed to be closing in on them like a green, dark tomb. The thick canopy of leaves shut out the sky and the sun. Jagged, twisting branches seemed to be reaching out to snatch them. The only noise was the rustle of the leaves and the cicadas. Each shriek built up to a higher-pitched scream of warning. Nature seemed to be warning them not to trespass again.

They pressed on, moving as fast as the steep terrain, their aching bodies and heavy bags allowed. Were unseen eyes watching them? Ordering herself not to be so irrational, Luc tried to calm her sudden panic.

'Don't know if I'd be glad to see someone or not,' said Ella up ahead.

'Wait.' Luc had to stop to empty a stone from her espadrille.

'Hurry.' Ella looked round, her face taut. A bird shot from the undergrowth, its call mocking her jump of alarm. Her heart pounded with fright. 'Shit.'

On their way down, they'd oriented themselves by their glimpses of the sea. As they struggled up the sandy path, there was no landmark to aim for. Nothing was ahead except the sinister green twilight of trees and undergrowth.

'This is the right way?' asked Luc, glancing round nervously.

'Better be,' said Ella.

They'd rarely felt so cut off from the world. If anything happened to them, who would know? Only the cicadas and a few birds.

'I feel like Little Red Riding Hood.'

'No wolves in Greece,' said Luc. 'Not on Praxos anyway.' Her insides were turning to ice water with the sense that once again they were being spied upon by those unseen eyes. Glancing back, adrenaline shooting through her, her pace quickened and she stumbled over a tree root.

'The hut,' called Ella.

'Thank God.' Luc moaned with relief.

'Scary, suddenly, isn't it?' Ella surveyed the delapidated building and shivered. It could once have been the gingerbread cottage where Hansel and Gretel were imprisoned to be fattened up for the oven. 'Come on, let's get to that road.'

They tried to hurry up the track, wanting to get as far as possible from the woods.

'How's your head?'

'Throbbing,' said Luc. 'Yours?'

'Same.'

They rounded a bend, only to realise the track snaked round

the hillside to another. They'd forgotten how far it was back to the road. Their steps slowed to almost nothing with the effort of going uphill. Luc looked down at her legs. Not only were they peony-puce, but there were red scratches from the gorse round her puffy ankles. Itchy heat bumps covered her arms.

Ella's pace grew more snail-like, the wearier and more despondent she became. Her ears strained to hear a mosquito scooter, a sign they were approaching the road. The cicadas seemed noisier, their shrieks filling the deserted, ochre hillside. 'Don't they ever shut up?'

Each new corner they turned only led to another long uphill stretch. The road seemed as real as the mirage water earlier.

Luc stopped again to empty the grit from her espadrilles. The strap on her lead-heavy bag was cutting into her burnt shoulder, her mouth was parched. The sun, though lower, was blinding her. 'Ella?'

She was bent over double. 'It's all right. Just a bit dizzy.'

'Just think of that nice long cool drink on *Les Voiles Blanches*.'

Ella smiled wanly, then, taking a deep breath, began to walk again.

They struggled on. Their heads hurt, their bodies hurt and they started to meander like drunks over the rutted track. Drained of energy, neither could think or walk straight. From out of nowhere, they heard the noise of an engine. A white jeep, its hood up, swept past them, kicking up dust.

'Ow. Bastard.' Some grit had landed in Ella's eye. Like Luc, she began to cough the dust from out of the back of her throat, making her even more thirsty. 'Probably that couple from the beach yesterday. Come on.'

Sighing, neither felt able to take another step. They rounded another bend, expecting to see the road. As her hopes were dashed, Luc tripped, falling on her hands. 'Shit.' She couldn't remember being so fed up. As she brushed the grit from her palms on her skirt, tears pricked her eyes. 'Shit. Shit. Shit.'

They heard an engine labouring. It was the jeep, on its return journey. 'Not quite a white charger, but it will do.' Ella stuck out her thumb, paying no attention to Luc's protests. 'They looked so horrid, bet they ignore us.' The jeep swept past. 'Told you.'

Luc was relieved. 'We shouldn't . . .'

Just as Ella was about to give the jeep the finger, the brakes were slammed on and it began to reverse, bouncing across the ruts. It stopped beside them.

The driver was the man with the mobile from the beach at Ermioni. He smiled at Ella, showing off gold back teeth. Sunglasses covered his eyes. With his bald head, pudgy face and thick lips, he looked like a frog wearing shades.

'English?' The stereo was playing the Eagles so loudly that he had to shout. 'You want lift?' While he said something in Greek, he gestured they should get in the other side.

'*Karisto*,' said Ella gratefully.

As they walked round, his passenger jumped out. '*Yassoo*.' He was bearded with wild black hair coming out from under a Yankees baseball cap. Shirtless, a gold medallion hung round his neck. A beer gut oozed over the top of his baggy shorts. '*Parakalo*.'

'Ella . . .' hissed Luc, hanging back.

'Stop fussing.'

The passenger pushed up the front seat and clambered inside, sitting behind the driver. After hesitating for a split second, Ella got in after him. With the roof up and the music blaring, the interior was claustrophobic.

Luc was closing the door when the jeep accelerated with a lurch. Alarmed, she thought she'd be thrown through the windscreen. 'If you could just take us to the road . . .' Bouncing up and down, the jeep sped along the rutted track. She braced her feet against the well in front of her and yanked at the seat-belt, wrapping it tight around her.

'You like Praxos?' yelled the driver, above the music. He smiled, gazing at her legs exposed by her wraparound skirt. 'How long you stay?'

Luc hastily adjusted her skirt. 'About a week.'

'You like Praxos boys?' asked the second man, his voice gravelly. As he spoke, the jeep was suddenly filled with the stench of alcohol. He said something in Greek.

Laughing maniacally, the driver put his foot down and they skidded round a bend, tyres screeching. Ella was thrown against the man in the back, Luc almost slid out of her seat on to the floor. As they came out of the bend, the jeep swung towards the edge of the track beside which was a drop of about thirty feet on to the gorse. They had the sickening realisation the driver had also been drinking.

'Can you slow down?' asked Luc. From being turned into a tree, she was going to end up wrapped round a tree. 'Slow down.'

They tore into another bend, wheels skidding. The jeep lurched, rocking left and right and left again, threatening to overturn. Luc was smashed against the side window, a kaleidoscope of trees, track and crumbling stone wall flashing past her eyes, laughter, music and the squealing engine deafening her.

'Stop,' yelled Ella, leaning forward.

'I love Engleesh girls,' said the man next to her.

'Stop.' Ella's voice was more panicked.

Laughing, the driver turned up the stereo.

'Engleesh girls love feely feely.'

'Let us out.' Panic and fear surged through Luc. Instinctively she fumbled for the door handle.

Still laughing, the driver suddenly grabbed her arm. Holding it as tight as a tourniquet, he pulled her towards him. 'Not leaving.' Luc yelped in pain.

'Bastard,' screamed Ella, trying to push the second man away from her. His fat fingers were under her skirt. 'Fuck off.'

'Engleesh girls love feely feely.'

While Luc tried to wrench herself free, the driver went into another bend as Ella, screaming and yelling, grappled with the man in the back seat. Squirming, twisting and shouting herself, Luc felt Ella kicking against her seat as she tried to fend off the man in the back, who roared in outrage as she pulled his hair.

'Bastard!' Ella let out an ear-shattering scream as the man slapped her and pushed her down on to the back seat, trying to clamber on top of her. 'Luc, help.'

Laughing as he peered into the mirror, the driver's grip tightened on Luc's arm, pressing into her burning skin. 'Yous likes. Engleesh girls likes.'

'Stop!' she screamed.

In the back the man grunted as Ella scratched his face and tried to knee him in the groin, then came a sound like a whip-crack as he slapped her. 'Help, Luc.' The jeep left the track and shot into the road. Luc saw a scooter swerve out of their path, heard its indignant hooting. '*Malaka,*' yelled the driver, hitting the brakes as Ella yelled for help.

A surge of blind rage went through Luc. She bit as hard as she could into the driver's hand, then smashed her fist into his pudgy jaw. As he let out a holler of rage, she wrenched at the steering wheel. The jeep veered violently left. The driver braked again and they went into a skid. As the low stone wall got nearer, Luc instinctively put her hands over her head and braced herself for the impact.

When it came, seconds later, they were all thrown forward and then back, like test-crash dummies. Luc felt the seat-belt cutting into her middle and Ella's attacker hitting her seat. The jeep ricocheted off the wall and the engine stopped.

As the rocking died away, Luc opened her eyes. Beside her, the driver was slumped over the steering wheel. 'Hotel California' was still playing on the stereo. From under the mangled bonnet, steam was hissing from the radiator. Her door had flown open.

'Ella?' Luc could only manage a whisper.

'Get m-m-m-me out of here, Luc. P-p-p-please.'

Hearing Ella's attacker groaning, Luc knew they must get away. She had to get out fast to free Ella, trapped in the back seat. Choking back her sobs, her fingers trembled on the seat-belt catch. As she lowered herself to the ground, blinded by tears, her legs almost collapsed beneath her.

'Fuck off, you b-b-bastard.' Ella pushed the man off her. Clutching his head, he put up no resistance.

'Here.' Luc held out her hand and tugged the sobbing Ella out of the jeep. Her T-shirt was bloodstained. 'Jesus.'

'His. The bastard. The bastards. They deserve to fucking die.' She stared at the two men, tears streaming down her face.

'Sssh.' Weeping, Luc put her arms around Ella and they clutched one another as if each were a lifebuoy. 'Let's get out of here. Bags. Need our bags.'

'Bloody things.' Sniffing, Ella tried to smile.

As Luc tugged Ella's bag from the back of the jeep, she met the man's eyes. They were blank, uncomprehending. He was obviously in shock too. Blood poured from his nose. Moaning, he muttered a plea in Greek. Luc ignored it. In the front, the driver was starting to come round. 'They'll live. Unfortunately.' The driver half opened his eyes, mumbling something. Fear shot through Luc. She grabbed her bag, then noticed his mobile phone lying on the floor. Snatching it up, she threw it as far as she could into the olive grove on the other side of the stone wall. 'Come on, Ella.'

Dazed, shaking and still crying, they stumbled down the hill as fast as they could. They had no idea where they were heading, all that mattered was getting away from the jeep.

'Jesus, Luc, that animal was about to rape me . . .'

'Wonder where the police station is?'

'What? Worry about it later,' pleaded Ella. 'Let's get back. I must have a shower. Please.'

Luc nodded, unable to face trekking around trying to track down the local police. There'd be hours of statements and bureaucratic form-filling. All she wanted to do was lie down. On the Tarmac. Right now. She looked back again. The jeep was nowhere in sight. Adrenaline had turbo-charged them.

'No shower.' Ella's teeth were chattering. 'Let's get to *Les Voiles Blanches*.'

Luc nodded, suddenly comforted. The yacht was sanctuary, Henri and the rest protectors.

'Stop it.' Ella pointed. The blue bus was labouring up the hill towards them, fumes pouring from its exhaust. They stood in the middle of the road, frantically waving their arms. It stopped with an angry hiss of its brakes.

The driver looked far from pleased as he opened the door. His displeasure turned to bewilderment at their dishevelled state.

'*Karisto.*' Ella brushed away her tears with the side of her hand. 'Two.' She sniffed.

They sat in silence, oblivious to the stares and gawps. Their fellow passengers wondered what had happened to the two tourists. Why were they crying and so dirty and dusty? Why was that T-shirt covered in blood? It was almost as interesting as Mr Theocropolous's accident. How he and his friend were unhurt no one knew. That flash car of his was a wreck. Why weren't they getting along to the doctor instead of poking among the olive groves?

Les Voiles Blanches had gone.

'What a vile end to a horrible day.' Ella sank on to her bed, bitter disappointment etched on her face. Her shoulders were slumped, she was utterly spent. Stiffness had made hobbling down through the town a torment. They had stopped at a tiny supermarket, where they'd each taken three painkillers, glugged back a litre of water and wolfed down some chocolate. 'Shit. Where's that bourbon?'

As she swung her legs off the bed, Ella peered down. Her thighs were a mass of bruises. 'Bastards. Red and black. My legs look like the anarchists' flag. God, your arm.'

'Arms. Matching pair.' Luc scowled. Her middle hurt from where the seatbelt had dug into her. 'Don't think I have whiplash. Lucky I didn't go through the windscreen.' She shivered.

'Here.' Ella passed her a bourbon and lit a cigarette with a shaking hand. 'Shit. Did I leave my brains at home or something? Why did we hitch?'

Luc had asked herself the same question dozens of times. 'Because of sunstroke and that trek through the woods and being told that Praxos was safe and . . .'

'Because these days a woman can do what she wants and go where she wants.' Ella sounded bitter. 'Sure we can.'

'Asking for a lift isn't asking to be attacked. It shouldn't be.'

'He was shorter than me, but he was so bloody strong. And he almost . . .' Ella shuddered. 'I must have a shower.'

Luc gazed up at the ceiling, unable to get the horror of the drive out of her mind. They could've been killed. If only they hadn't got into the jeep. If only they hadn't been so exhausted by the walk. If only they hadn't fallen asleep in the sun. If only they hadn't smoked that grass . . . Ella should never have brought it. If they'd been caught, they would be in gaol now. If only she hadn't allowed her instincts to be steam-rollered yet again by the force of Ella's personality . . .

'When did this arrive?'

Luc had drifted off for a few minutes. Shaking herself back into full consciousness, she saw Ella holding an envelope. 'Here. For you.'

Luc sat up and read the letter. It was headed *Les Voiles Blanches*, Saturday 4 p.m.

'Henri?' asked Ella. 'What does he say?'

' "My dear Luc. Unhappily our plans have changed and we leave Praxos. I hope our meeting is postponed not cancelled. I give you my address in St Tropez. Please write. Last night I dreamt of you. *Mille regrets. Au revoir.* Henri." ' She studied the italics. 'Beautiful handwriting.'

'Fuck the handwriting. Is there another letter in there? No?' screamed Ella. She screwed up her face. 'Shit. I'll never see him again. Suits you, doesn't it?'

Luc froze, wondering what Ella meant.

'Bitching all morning about meeting them again. Well, it's all right, you don't have to.'

'It's not.' Since the crash, the sense that *Les Voiles Blanches* and her four crew were close in the harbour had been the only comfort. That comfort had been ripped away. She and Ella were on their own. 'I'm going for a shower. We'll get ready, then we must go to the police.'

'Wish Marcie and Sherry hadn't left.'

'*Kali spera*.' A young couple were sitting under the trellised vine in the courtyard.

Ella gave a small nod, Luc mumbled back. Their mood was as sombre as their appearance. With their hair scraped back, no make-up and baggy clothes, Henri and Yannick would've walked straight past them.

'Typical,' sighed Ella. Yannis's uncle had gone, the office was shut for the night.

They limped into the narrow lane leading to the quayside. Luc's arms were prickly as if a million midges had bitten her.

'Blue beads are supposed to ward off evil,' said Ella, as they passed a jewellery shop. 'Should've bought some.'

The bars lining the quayside were filling up with customers drinking cloudy ouzo and watching the boats mooring. The carefree chatter and laughter seemed alien. Weighed down with baskets and suitcases, a donkey looked forlorn as he was led up the cobbled steps.

'I feel sick.' Ella grimaced. The smell of barbecued meat reminded her of her own roasted skin. 'Let's leave it.'

The harbour master with his patriarchal beard was hurrying towards them.

'*Signome*,' cried Luc. '*Signome. Milete Anglia?* Do you speak English?'

'A little.'

'Where can we find the police?'

'Tourist police? Near the tower.' He pointed. 'Behind the post office.'

The blue and white flag of Greece hung outside the tiny

police building. It was set back from the lane, behind a paved yard.

'Must we?' protested Ella.

'Yes.' Luc led the way and pushed the door open. The reception was minute, chill from air-conditioning. Posters pinned to the wall included an anti-drugs warning in English. Ella was reading it, when a blue-uniformed man appeared from the back room, a gun holster on his hip. She jumped guiltily.

'*Kali spera*. Do you speak English?' asked Luc. He was about forty, with curly hair, a large nose and wary eyes. He nodded. 'We want to report an attack.'

He raised his eyebrows slightly. 'Who was attacked?'

'We were. This afternoon.'

'On Praxos?' He sounded cautious.

'Yes. By two men in a white jeep.'

Frowning, he studied them. 'This way.'

The back office was immaculately tidy. The desk was clear apart from a telephone and a carafe of water. On the wall was a large-scale map of the island. In the corner, a fax machine was spewing out paper.

He got out a pad of paper. 'Your names. Where are you staying?'

Ten minutes later, Luc finished. He had listened without moving a muscle, without making any notes. Expecting sympathy, they were disconcerted by his calm matter-of-factness. 'Where was this beach?'

'A few kilometres from Agios Agathas,' said Ella. 'Down through some woods.'

He pointed at the map. 'Show me.'

'Er . . . here?' Luc's eyes glazed over, she was hopeless with maps. 'Or perhaps here. Ella?'

Ella frowned. 'If this is Agios Agathas, this must be the road. Is this the track? What's that there? The hut?'

'The electricity sub-station,' said the policeman.

'Oh. Not there then.' Ella smiled nervously.

He remained poker-faced. 'And when this car crashed, it was where?'

'Towards Agios Agathas,' said Luc hesitantly. 'When the bus picked us up we were going away from the jeep. So around here.' She gestured at the map. 'I think.'

'Sit down, please.' They sat. 'Let me be clear. You were walking, you don't know exactly where, at about four o'clock. This car stopped. Why? You know the driver?'

'No,' blurted out Ella. 'We were hitch-hiking.' She stuck out her thumb.

'Hitch-hiking? I see. You didn't explain that earlier.' He took a sip of water. 'Then you got in the back, you in the front. The car started. It went too fast. You became nervous and asked the driver to stop and let you out. You say the driver refused. You say the man in the back started to touch you. Then the car crashed. Tell me, what did you do after the crash?'

'We left,' said Luc.

He raised an eyebrow. 'You left. Despite the two men being hurt.'

'We were hurt too.' Luc pulled up her sleeve, showing off a huge black bruise. 'This is what he did to me.'

'This is not from the crash?'

'No.'

'You say he held on to you while driving the car?' Luc nodded emphatically. 'You're sure? And the man in the back did what?'

Ella blushed. 'He touched my breasts and my legs. Tried to pull off my clothes and then hit me. Here.' She touched her cheekbone.

'That's not from the crash?'

'No.'

'You say they were drunk, but you got into the car.'

'We didn't realise,' said Ella.

'If I said you pretended to be lost and these men offered you a lift today, I'd be wrong.' Ella and Luc glanced at one another, bewildered by his tone. 'If I said once you were in the car, you tried to steal their wallets, I'd be wrong. If I said once you were found out and threatened with the police, you tried to jump out of the car, I'd be wrong. If I said one of you then attacked the driver causing the crash, I'd be wrong.'

Luc and Ella gazed at him in appalled silence.

At Kostas, they studied the menu without enthusiasm.

'Two octopus, two souvlaki.' Luc couldn't be bothered to practise her ten words of Greek on the waiter. Dead-eyed, she stared at the harbour. The wine tasted bitter, the bread was hard to swallow.

'Scum,' spat Ella. 'Worked fast, didn't they?'

'They're not bringing charges against us?' Luc shook her head, then winced. Her body felt beaten up.

The water glinted orange and gold in the last of the evening sun. The yachts and fishing boats were rocking, gently tugging their mooring ropes. Laughter filled the warm air. Despite all the life around them, they felt as lonely as they had in the woods.

'Shit.' The red welt across Ella's cheekbone showed up vividly. 'Why isn't there a ferry?'

'Nothing we can do about it.' Luc dipped her napkin into the jug of water and pressed it on to her burning forehead. 'Only a night to get through.'

They gazed at the yachts, wishing they could leave at once. Praxos had lost its charm. Ella lit a cigarette. 'Earlier, when we found *Les Voiles Blanches* had gone, it wasn't Yannick I minded so much, it was being deserted. Abandoned.'

'I was hoping they'd say get your stuff and your passports, you're coming with us,' confessed Luc.

'Some feminists. So much for independence, taking care of ourselves. First sign of trouble, we want to swoon into a strong pair of manly arms.'

'Not necessarily Henri's.' Luc managed a small smile.

'Bet he'd love the chance to play the knight in shining armour. Rescue us and seek vengeance. He'd cut their dicks off and feed them to the nearest dog.'

'Ella,' protested Luc.

'It's justice, why object?' Ella eyed Luc. 'They would've raped us. And got away with it. Our word against theirs.'

'But . . .'

'There aren't any buts. Henri would've been on our side. Wish he was here.' She lit another cigarette, glancing around nervously. 'We're not being watched, are we? Or followed?'

Luc shivered. 'Nothing's going to happen here.'

'Isn't it?'

'Stop it,' ordered Luc, scanning the quayside.

Ella slumped further into her chair, a picture of despair and defeat. 'I'm so angry with myself for being scared and I'm pissed off with those two bastards for ruining our holiday.'

The waiter brought their souvlaki. Seeing their untouched octopus, he asked if everything was all right. 'No, it's far from all right, but it's not your fault,' snapped Ella. 'Bastards. Why should we let them get away with it? Perhaps we should tough it out.'

'We're not staying here.' A chill ran through Luc. 'We could bump into them anywhere. We're leaving. First thing. We'll be back home this time tomorrow.'

They only managed a few mouthfuls, but not wanting to be alone, lingered at the table until almost midnight.

Back in their room, Ella locked the door for the first time. She threw her blood-stained T-shirt into the waste basket and wished it was morning.

'Ella. Wake up. Ella.' Ella slowly unpeeled her eyes and was about to reach for the lamp, when Luc ordered her to leave it.

A vague glow came through the balcony shutters, otherwise

they were in darkness. Across the quayside, the bell tolled three.

'What's wrong?'

Heart racing, Luc put her mouth close to Ella's ear. 'There's someone outside. Listen.'

They both held their breath and strained their ears. Half a minute passed. The silence grew louder.

'Sssh,' repeated Luc, when Ella began to protest.

They froze. From the other side of the door, they heard a low murmur. A second voice said something in reply and chuckled. There was a jingle of metal against metal. Luc's hand gripped Ella's arm, fear and panic washing through her. A grating echoed round the darkness as a key was put into the lock and the door handle turned.

'Fire,' yelled Ella.

'Sorry for waking you up.' Fifteen minutes later, Ella was apologising to the young Greek couple who'd wished them *kali spera* earlier that evening.

'*Endaxi*. Anytime.' The man was wearing a Manchester United T-shirt and track pants. During the dash from his room, he'd seen two men sprinting across the courtyard and out into the lane. '*Perestika*. I'm sorry you leave with bad memories of Praxos.'

'Thank God you woke up.' Ella's teeth were chattering.

'Thank God you locked the door.' Luc was shaking as if she had a fever.

They spent the rest of the night out on the balcony trying to read, stiffening at any strange sound and glancing towards the door.

'*Kyrias*. Yous up early.' Yannis's uncle arrived outside the office at seven o'clock, cigarette holder wedged between his teeth. 'You're leaving?' He glanced at their bags. 'You can't. You said a week.' Unlocking the door, he ushered them into the office.

'We're leaving right now.' Ella was stony-faced. 'Someone tried to break into our room last night.'

He tut-tutted. 'Impossible. Yous dreaming.'

'Ask Mr Christaloudou in room four. He saw the two men.'

'He dreams too.'

'No he doesn't,' cut in Luc. 'Can you tell us what we owe and give us our passports?'

'And don't charge us for the extra nights,' said Ella. 'Thank you.'

He looked at them. They stared back. 'You arrive when?'

'Thursday.'

'Thursday. *Pempti*. Three nights . . .' He got out his calculator. After he'd put their money in the cash-box and locked it, he handed them their passports.

'Thank you,' said Ella. 'Is your nephew Yannis around?'

He waved his holder vaguely. 'Other side of the island.'

Luc picked up her bag. 'Does he drive a white jeep?'

The old man looked surprised. 'Yes. You've met him?'

'Oh yes,' said Ella. 'We've met him.'

Chapter Four

───◆◇◆───

Three hours later at Mathi's tiny airport, Ella handed over her credit card. It was a silvery colour with the name of an obscure but very smart bank in copperplate. Luc stared at it, as if for the first time. It was better than any passport to a stateless refugee. It bought Ella a lifetime of freedom and security.

A few minutes later they were dashing across the Tarmac to the propellered plane, the only one back to Athens that day. There was no time to put their bags in the hold. As they fastened their seat-belts, the engines came to life. The plane gathered a final burst of speed along the runway, then took off, soaring over a tomato farm, then the beach, and then the sea. They felt some of their troubles being thrown away like ballast.

'Close.' Relieved, Ella leaned her head against the seat back. 'We're like that couple in *Casablanca* winning our letters of transit playing roulette.' She gazed at the cobalt sea far below. 'Wish we hadn't paid for that room. His room.'

'He had our passports. We had no choice.' Luc tried to shift to a more comfortable position. Like Ella, she was as stiff as an old crow. Moving her head was agony, she had to turn her neck inch by inch.

Had the two really meant to break in, or were they just trying to scare them into leaving? Unable to sleep, they had puzzled until dawn about how the pair had known where to find them.

Had they watched them at the quayside restaurant, then followed them? Local gossip? As she suddenly remembered the grating in the lock, Luc had suggested the answer.

'It was so beautiful.' Ella sounded defeated. 'Why did those bastards have to spoil it?'

Arriving in Mathi, they realised how they'd almost taken Praxos for granted. After they'd got off the ferry, they'd leapt into a taxi and crossed the island to the airport. The dusty roads were filled with traffic, billboards advertised discos, parasailing and tours. The concrete hotels were Lubyankas, stickered with holiday company labels.

They hadn't realised that Athens had two airports. They were told to take a taxi to the second.

'So what'll we do when we're back?' said Ella, as they waited for a cab. 'You've given yourself a week off.'

Luc was engulfed by a deep gloom. 'God knows. Is Wimbledon starting? Perhaps I ought to call the Agency and see if there's any work.'

'We could drive to France or something. Correction. You can drive and I can navigate.'

'Liz has got your car,' said Luc. France was a bad idea; Ella got road rage sitting in the passenger seat.

'Lake District? Never been there. Could go fell walking.'

'After yesterday?' Luc sounded incredulous.

'Um, true. Well, what are we going to do?'

A taxi pulled up and took them on the short journey to the international airport. Ella grumbled that they could've walked. Inside the departures terminal it was icy cold because of the air-conditioning. As they pushed their trolley past a news kiosk, Luc caught sight of the English papers and dawdled to a stop. 'Washed Out' screamed a headline above a photograph of a car stuck in flood water. 'More Storms Forecast Say Weathermen'.

Ella was by the ticket counter. 'What do you mean, we can't change our flight?'

A pretty clerk with a shaggy perm shook her head. 'The terms of your ticket are clear, madam. This ticket is for Saturday. I'm sorry.'

'But this is an emergency. We must get back to London.' She turned to Luc. 'Bullshit bureaucracy . . .'

'Um?' Luc was staring at a poster of a dazzling white cupola against a backdrop of water the colour of lapis lazuli. It was identical to the one in their room on Praxos.

Ella sighed heavily. 'When's the next flight to London, are there seats and how much are two singles?'

The clerk said she'd check. She tapped into her computer.

'How much? What a rip off.' Ella was outraged. 'So if seats are available, why can't we just quietly change flights?'

The clerk was starting to lose patience. 'Because under the terms and conditions . . .'

'Oh for God's sake. Luc, what do you think? Luc?'

'Let's stay.' As the answer crystallised, some of her black gloom lifted.

'What?'

'Think about it.' Luc felt energy surging through her. 'We've had a vile twenty-four hours, we haven't slept, so we just want to hibernate. But tomorrow, back in London, we'll be hating ourselves for being so wet. So, we couldn't stay on Praxos, but there are thousands of other islands.'

'They could be like Mathi,' snapped Ella.

Luc pointed up at the poster. 'Where's that?'

'Santorini.' The clerk smiled. 'It's beautiful. Volcanic. Black sand. You can fly there in less than an hour.'

Luc hadn't budgeted for a flight. 'Are there ferries?'

'Yes, but it's a long journey.'

'How long?' asked Luc.

'Ten, twelve hours.'

They winced, unable to face another long ferry journey.

'Ia?' asked Ella. 'What about Ia?'

'Much closer. Different from Santorini, but as beautiful.

Greener. Full of flowers and pine trees. The air smells wonderful.'

'We can get a ferry from Piraeus?'

'Yes. Four, five hours. Or there's the *Flying Dolphin*. Ladies, if you want to get on this flight, I must know now.'

'What's the *Flying Dolphin*?' asked Luc.

'Catamaran. Very fast.'

'From Piraeus?'

'Nearby. Zia Marina. The flight will be boarding . . .'

'Zia?' repeated Ella. 'Zia Marina? Taxis will know it? Come on, Luc.'

The *Flying Dolphins* were like giant blue and sunflower-yellow beetles. During their hour-long wait at Zia's tranquil waterside, Ella went off to find a telephone, leaving Luc in the shade with their luggage.

'They were in.' Ella plonked herself down on the bench, handing Luc a bottle of water. 'Timid had just been to church. They'll meet us when we arrive and take us to the villa.'

'And?'

'And we're very welcome. We are. Don't worry. Miz sounded very friendly. Wonder if she's ill?'

Luc was uneasy. 'Are you sure they don't mind us crashing in on them?'

'More the merrier, probably glad of a contribution to the rent. There's another couple staying. Alex and Marina. He's Australian, some cricketing mate of Timid's. Journalist. She's Italian.' She glanced at Luc. 'It's only for a few days, give us a chance to get our breath back. Then we can go to Hydra. We can get a *Dolphin* from Ia. I've been efficient and checked.'

'They don't mind?'

''Course not,' said Ella blithely. 'Listen, I'll make a big effort. Promise. Swallow my pride, eat humble pie. Even if it does make me gag. Joke.' She smiled. 'Anyway, they've got no choice. We're family.'

The *Flying Dolphins* cost double the price of the ferry, but took less than half the time. The catamaran sounded like a jet and cut across the water like a torpedo. Luc and Ella went to the viewing platform at the stern. As Athens faded away far beyond the horizon, they got covered in salty spray.

'You can't say this hasn't been a change,' shouted Ella, hair whipping across the bruise on her cheekbone.

'It certainly hasn't been a rest.'

Luc was troubled. Was staying with Tim and Liz such a good idea? The last time she'd seen them was at a party at their beautiful minimalist house. A grown-ups' party, full of architects like Tim and interior designers like Liz, sipping Chilean chardonnay and having grown-up conversations on postmodern irony to the sound of Philip Glass.

Absolutely not included on the guest list were dozens of exuberant Kiwis, clutching tinnies. Luc and Ella had met two of them in a bar *en route*. Ella had mentioned the party and word had got round. Luc had hidden herself away in the garden trying not to cringe as Liz had stood sentry at the front door. More intimidating than any Maori warrior, almost dancing a haka in rage, Liz had sent them packing, threatening to call the police.

She had telephoned the next day. In a voice that would've soured milk, if there had been any in the fridge, she'd thanked Ella for ruining her evening.

Two hours later, the *Dolphin* docked at Ia's jetty. The town stretched out along the waterfront behind a white sea wall. Like souk traders offering up their wares, cafés, hotels and shops were jumbled together, all competing for custom. Carriages waited in the road, the dusty horses looking in need of a siesta. It was midafternoon, few people were about. There was no sign of Tim.

'Late. Typical,' sighed Ella, going off to get an ice cream.

The buildings were crumbling, whitewashed, set along a labyrinth of lanes, too narrow for cars. 'Blind Date Nite. All Spirits Half Price' said the sign outside a deserted café. The place next door offered Full English Brakfast and the World Famous Orgasmatron Coktale, as well as Big Screen Football Tonite Tonite Tonite. Everywhere were signs for tours, parasailing, windsurf, akomodations, happys hours.

Catching sight of more tour company stickers, Luc felt uncomfortable. Tourism was defacing all the delapidated prettiness. It was like seeing graffitied joke ears and a moustache on a poster of Ava Gardner.

'Let's get Liz to enter the karaoke competition,' said Ella. Luc giggled. 'I'll tell her that *World of Interiors* has said it's very now.'

'Welcome to Ia. So sorry I'm late.'

Beside all the muscly, tanned carriage drivers, Tim looked almost anaemic. His colour came from a million freckles. Although he was only in his mid-thirties, his once reddish hair was grey. His corkscrew curls matched his round silver spectacles. A white collarless shirt was tucked into baggy shorts that showed off his unremarkable legs. 'What a wonderful surprise to see you both.'

'And you.' Delighted, Ella hugged him.

Staring at them, he jumped as a horse whinnied behind him. 'Have you two been in the wars?' His kind face seemed hurt with worry.

'Ish. Where's Miz? Liz?' She corrected herself.

'Having a lie-down. One of her heads . . .' Liz was prone to headaches when she was under stress. 'Your carriage awaits. No, not one of these. A taxi. One of the few cars allowed on the island. Over there.' Noticing Luc wince as she picked up her bag, he seized it. 'Let me. What's happened?'

'Long story. Later.' Ella yawned. 'How's your karaoke?'

Tim looked apologetic. 'I'm afraid in a few years Ia will be completely spoilt. We tend to avoid this area at night. The noise from the discos is deafening.'

Despite the breeze coming through the open windows, the ramshackle old Mercedes taxi was as hot as a pizza oven. It followed a pot-holed road running beside the sea wall. Below, a tiny strip of beach was covered by roasting bodies. The cluster of cafés and bars gave way to houses and a tiny chapel. Flowers were everywhere, splashing whitewashed walls with pinks and reds and yellows and purples like Jackson Pollock's paintbrush.

The taxi climbed higher, away from the main town. At a large white church, the road forked. 'Wonderful, isn't it?' said Tim. 'Venetian influences. How was Praxos?'

'Stunning,' said Ella curtly. 'What's back there?'

'The old port. We're right at the top of this hill.'

After a few minutes, the taxi stopped at a pair of iron gates set in a high wall. A corner of a house could be seen behind a tangle of trees. It had its back to the road, as if shunning it. Lemon-coloured shutters shaded the windows. Tim led the way through a tiered garden, as cool and green as the bottom of a pond, to a heavy wooden door.

Before their eyes had got used to the dark of a hallway, they were dazzled by the light in a huge sun-drenched sitting room. A wall of windows overlooked a terrace and, far below, the azure sea.

Ella and Luc stepped out on to the terrace and gasped in delight. Dragonflies hovered above the sparkling water in the swimming pool. Terracotta pots were filled with herbs and jasmine.

'Quite something, isn't it?' said Tim. 'Lizzy found it through a client.'

'Surprise, surprise.' Liz surveyed their creased, dusty clothes and their battered, dusty luggage which was blocking her path. Dressed entirely in white, she was a walking advertisement for washing powder.

'Liz.' The half-sisters assessed one another, then pecked each other dutifully on the cheek. Liz hung back, restrained, as if Ella might smudge her. 'You're brown. Isn't she, Luc?'

'Very.' The tan was the only similarity between the half-sisters. Liz was angular, as hard-edged as the ends of her sleek brown bob. She only ever wore black or white. With her red-lipsticked chic, she was often assumed to be French. Ella had once bitched that as Liz's soul was pure Purley she should stick to Orlon cardies.

'Lovely place,' added Luc, immediately feeling she'd knocked thousands of pounds off its price.

'Um.' Liz gave a proprietorial glance around the terrace, which the luggage had untidied. 'Your face is dirty, Ella. And you're burnt, Luc. Let's show you to your room. You don't mind sharing, do you?'

'Shall I organise some tea?' offered Tim. 'Camomile, Lizzy? How's the head?'

'Better. Ginger, please.'

'Any chance of a beer?' asked Ella.

The villa was dark compared to the glare outside. In one corner of the sitting room was a rough stone staircase. Assuming they were about to go up, they were surprised when Liz took them through a cavernous kitchen into a gloomy passage. At the end was a spartan room with two single beds.

'Great, thank you,' said Luc with as much enthusiasm as she could muster.

'Don't force them.' Liz was watching Ella wrenching at the shutter latches.

'Done it.' The shutters covered a small window with a view of the gates and the road. Ella raised an eyebrow. 'The Presidential Suite.'

Liz ignored her. 'We'd better get the house rules clear from the start. Absolutely no smoking indoors. Towels aren't to be taken to the beach, use them to cover the upholstery, suntan oil is impossible to get out.'

'Fine.' Ella forced a smile.

'I called in a lot of favours to get this place so I don't expect half the island to be turning up here for a party.'

'Fine.'

'Your bathroom is next door. Keep it tidy.'

'Tea,' called Tim from the kitchen.

'I'll just unpack,' said Luc, beginning to wish they'd stayed away. She felt compelled to check. 'May I take a shower, please?'

Twenty minutes, some clean clothes and three painkillers later, Luc wandered back to the terrace. Ella sat at the edge of the pool, swigging beer from a bottle and dangling her feet in the water. Her creased flowery dress was rucked up over her knees, clogs and an ashtray were beside her.

Drinking tea, Liz and Tim were sitting at a large wooden table under a huge cream umbrella. Tim opened the beer which he'd kept in the shade and handed it to Luc. 'Still temping?' She nodded, then winced. 'Still hell?'

'Different sort of hell every few weeks at least. How's things with you?'

'So, so.'

'Any nice projects?'

'Something in Walsall.'

'Poland?' piped up Ella.

'Walsall, the Midlands,' corrected Liz, with a do-pay-attention sigh. 'And there's the Geneva house. In fact, we're waiting to hear from the client, so keep off the phone.'

Ella scowled into the water.

'Luc, whatever's wrong?' asked Tim, noticing her wince again.

'Er . . .' She hesitated, glancing at Ella, 'We had a bit of trouble . . .'

'What trouble?' Liz was sharp.

They were interrupted by voices. A door in the side wall opened. A couple arrived. Both were tanned to a coffee colour. She was wearing a red gingham bikini, with bougainvillaea in her mass of dark hair and plastic daisies covering her flip-flops. He looked more like her minder than a boyfriend, the impression highlighted by his build. He was so tall and broad that he seemed to block out the sun. Crew-cutted, his eyes hidden behind sunglasses, he seemed wary, as if on the look-out for kidnappers.

'Present for you, *cara*.' She was carrying an armful of flowers, which she put beside Liz. 'Ella and Luc, yes? Welcome to Ia.' Her smile was as warm as her brown eyes, her voice husky and theatrical, the rrrs rrrolled.

'Marina Jones and Alex Ireland.' Having made the introductions, Tim went off to get more drinks and a vase.

'Seesters?' Marina looked from Liz to Ella and back again. 'No.'

'Half-sisters,' they corrected her immediately.

'And Luc. As in the apostle? Bizarre for a girl.'

'Short for Lucasta,' explained Luc.

'Lucasta. Pretty name, eh, Alex?'

'Pretty pretentious.' He smiled.

'Oh, and Alexander isn't in New Zealand?' said Ella.

'It's just Alex. And I'm Australian, not a Kiwi.'

'An Aussie?' Ella feigned astonishment. 'Really?'

Liz began to arrange the flowers in a vase. 'What trouble?'

After Ella had finished the saga, there was a long pause. 'I knew there was something very wrong as soon as I saw you,' said Tim. 'Perhaps we should get you both to a doctor.'

Liz piled the empties on to the tray. 'How could you be so stupid as to hitch-hike?'

'We had sunstroke,' protested Ella.

'Well, you shouldn't be in the sun between eleven and three anyway. Especially you, Luc. We must call the police.'

'Good idea,' agreed Marina.

'What for?' Ella was alarmed. 'We've already been to the police.'

'You could've been killed. Attempted rape, assault, your room being broken into . . .'

'We've got no proof it was them. No one saw them. As for what happened in the jeep, they got their story in first.' Ella sighed. 'So there's no point.' Some of her ash blew into the pool.

'Mind your cigarette, can't you?' snapped Liz. 'Tim. Police. You'd better tidy yourself up, Ella.'

'I rather think it's up to the girls,' said Tim.

'I'd rather not,' said Luc.

'Let's just forget it,' pleaded Ella, then frowned. 'Anyway, what do you mean, tidy myself up?'

'You expect the police to be sympathetic if you go around looking like a bag lady?'

'Yes, frankly.'

'Don't be so naive. So get out of those scarecrow clothes, take that thing out of your nose and cover up that horrible tattoo.'

'What for? We're not, not, not going to the police.'

The sisters eyed one another. Luc prayed there wasn't going to be a row. Finally, Liz sighed. 'Very well. I hope you both learnt your lesson.'

' 'Itch-'iking is very dangerous.' Marina shivered.

'Dumb,' said Alex. 'You're not asking for it, you're begging for it.'

Kissing Marina's brown shoulder, Alex disappeared to their room to work. He was writing a book on agri-chemical industry and its effects on the environment and farmers. To Luc, it sounded unpromising, but Ella had seen the point immediately.

'On organo-phosphates and stuff?' she asked, shading her eyes and having to gaze up and up, he was so tall.

'And stuff. Yes,' he nodded. 'You'll buy it. You eat organic.'

'How can you tell?' she smiled.

'Your sort always do.'

'What sort?'

'Trustafarians.' He disappeared indoors.

Ella was open-mouthed, her eyes narrowing as she glared at Liz who was re-arranging a few of the flowers. Luc caught the look and froze. She was delighted when Ella took a deep breath and said she was off for a shower.

Tim was in the kitchen, mixing Pimms. Sitting beside Marina, Luc felt like a flat-chested sparrow sharing a perch with an exotic cockatiel. Marina's magnificent bosom spilled over the gingham. She'd loosened her hair and shaken out the bougainvillaea, so the dark curls tumbled down to her tiny waist. Luc couldn't help noticing the rolls of tummy fat that squidged over Marina's bikini bottoms. But brown fat never looked as bad.

'Horrible.' As if reading Luc's mind, Marina tugged at the roll. 'And this.' She plucked at her heavy thighs. 'Still, I can't imprison myself in a gym like Liz.' She tilted her face away from the low rays of the sun. 'More horrrible. Shows up all my wrinkles.'

'You haven't . . .' Actually, she had.

'Of course I have. I'm thirrrty-six. What? Ten years older than you?'

'Eleven.'

Smiling, Marina shrugged, examining her brown hands with their silver-varnished nails.

'You're married,' blurted out Luc. A huge emerald shone on her finger above a gold wedding ring. 'I didn't realise. How long?'

'Five years. Not to Alex.'

'Oh.'

She grinned. 'I gave my husband up for Lent and Lent carried on.'

Later, Ella and Luc sat at the terrace table, eating pistachios and drinking cold white wine. After their sleepless night and early start, neither felt like going out. The distance they'd covered that day seemed incredible, from Praxos to Mathi to Athens to Ia. The other four had gone down to the old port for dinner.

'Aussies aren't usually prickly,' said Ella. 'Wonder what Marina sees in him?'

A boat was far away on the horizon, its sails silhouetted against the sky.

'Tall, dark . . .' began Luc.

'Mouse, not dark. And you can hardly run your fingers

through a crew-cut. Good body though. Great job.'

A journalist, Alex's latest assignment had been out in a civil war-torn African state. When Ella had suggested the UN might be sent in, he'd raised an eyebrow over his beer bottle. 'And does this amazing insight of yours come from *Bunty* or *Twinkle*?'

Ella took a gulp of wine. 'Why couldn't Yannick play cricket? Then he'd be here now.'

Luc rolled her eyes. 'He's French. They don't.'

Ella stared out at the yacht. 'If only I could sail away for a year and a day with him.'

The sun seemed to be drowning itself in the sea. They could just hear the faint whoosh of waves turning on the beach far below, reached by a rocky path on the other side of the peach-tree wall.

They'd walked down to it before exploring the rest of the villa. The three upstairs rooms were airy and spacious, with mos-quito nets over the beds and views over the sea. 'Obviously we're well below the salt,' Ella had snapped, peering into the spare room's en-suite shower.

'A client of Tim's might be turning up,' retorted Liz icily, catching them. Luc had jumped, feeling like a trespasser. 'That's why you're downstairs.'

'Downstairs is great,' Luc had said. 'It's so nice that you've put up with us. I mean, put us up. I hope we're not imposing too much.'

Liz had stared into the mirror, checking her red lipstick. 'There's eggs and stuff in the fridge. Try not to make too much mess. Not you, Luc. Ella.'

Ella had very slowly breathed in and out through her nose, as if she were counting to ten.

When they cooked supper, Liz seemed to be hovering in the kitchen. Luc chopped up tomatoes, anxious about causing the minutest speck. The moment they'd finished their omelettes, she leaped to her feet to clear away and do the washing up.

*

The next morning Luc took a mug of coffee on to the terrace. Alex was already in the pool, pounding up and down doing a splashy, flashy butterfly. She sat under the umbrella, staring out at the sea and examining the bruise on her arm. After her fitful, broken sleep in the stuffy Presidential Suite, her brain was like porridge. Although her neck hurt less, her middle was still tight as if the seat-belt was continuing to cut her in half. Perhaps she should go to the doctor.

'Morning, Lucasta.' Alex finally stopped. Ignoring the steps, he hauled himself out. Luc registered the broadest shoulders she'd ever seen in her life, the most powerful biceps, a six-pack, then the fact that he was stark naked.

Water dripping off him, he nonchalantly picked up his towel and seemed to take an age to wrap it round his waist. 'Sleep well?'

Blushing scarlet, Luc averted her eyes and mumbled a reply.

'He has got the most amazing body,' said Ella. She and Luc were stretched out on the loungers under umbrellas beside the pool. 'Statue of David come to life. BSD?'

'Mad cow disease?'

'No, that's Miz. Big Swinging Dick?'

'I couldn't look.'

She had heard him tap-tapping away on his laptop by the open window up in the bedroom, until Marina had insisted he come into town with her and Liz. Interested in the local building techniques, Tim had gone to the old port where a house was being renovated. They all planned to hire mopeds and go to the other side of the island to have lunch at a beach-side taverna.

Neither Luc nor Ella could be bothered to leave the villa. Blanketed by the warmth, they closed their eyes behind their sunglasses and listened to the murmur of the sea and the call of the cicadas. The breeze carried the different scents, sometimes pine, then olives, then jasmine.

Luc began to sketch a terracotta pot of basil, but abandoned it. Occasionally they picked up their books, only to start snoozing. When they got too hot, they jumped into the pool, disturbing the dragonflies.

Luc knew she ought to prefer natural beauty to the man-made, the beach to the pool. But it was wonderful not to have to trek in the heat weighed down like a forlorn donkey, not to have to worry about sand and finding patches of shade. Or being attacked. The villa was so safe, so peaceful, particularly with Liz five miles away. She still felt exhausted.

'Bruises are fading,' said Ella, staring down at her thighs. 'It still looks pretty obscene though.' She leaped to her feet. 'Shit.'

Luc froze, adrenaline pumping through her.

A hunched old man had appeared from nowhere. He was Spiros the gardener, husband to Elena, who was indoors sweeping the terracotta-tiled floors. It took hours for their heart-rates to return to normal. At any unexpected sound, both glanced up, nervous.

'This is pathetic.' Ella was cross with herself. 'Why are we being such scaredy-cats?'

'Why do I feel so tired?' Luc yawned. Her guidebook said there was a fine example of an eighteenth century merchant's villa near the tiny chapel. Why weren't they more like Marcie and Sherry who would've ticked it off within twenty minutes of their arrival?

After their day of indolence, eating watermelon, playing Scrabble and reading, they wandered down the hill into the main town. Getting ready for the evening, Luc had been hurried out by the arrival of the others. Although friendly enough, Liz put her on edge. They arranged to meet up with them later at the old port.

Both felt like animals emerging from their lair after winter hibernation, curious, but apprehensive about what lay beyond the burrow. Retracing the taxi's route, they passed the white church, took the left-hand fork to the town and came to the tiny chapel on the waterfront road towards the jetty. The merchant's villa was closed for the day.

Deserted in the afternoon heat, the town's cafés and bars were now filling up. The Blind Date bar pounded out the current English number one above a hubbub of English voices. Two girls in tight crinkly micro dresses, dayglo drinks in hand, cocktail umbrellas behind their ears, giggled their way up into a horse-drawn carriage. An appreciative audience of waiting drivers got a flash of their knickers.

Luc and Ella drifted on, content just to sniff the air. The town was like a busier, flatter Praxos. Buildings were jumbled together higgledy-piggledy, greenery and flowers covered every balcony and wall.

They ambled past the jetty, then into a labyrinth of narrow alleyways away from the waterfront. Copies of the *Sun* and *Das Bild* were on sale everywhere, signs in English and German offered tours, fishing trips, money change.

Further on, they found themselves back at the waterfront at a small marina at the far end of the town. Fishing boats were moored to giant iron rings set in the wall. A blue-awninged ouzeri had refused to compromise to tourism. Its white metal tables were scratched, the chairs rickety. A waiter brought them ouzo and a plate of plump green olives. They sipped, hearing the lap of water against the stone wall and the chatter of Greek around them.

Ella sighed contentedly, taking a lungful of pine-scented air.

'Where next?' asked Luc. They'd relaxed today, but for how much longer? Earlier, when Liz and Tim had returned to the villa, she'd immediately become uneasy. Liz had frowned at the discarded Scrabble set and the sticky plates covered in pips and watermelon skin.

'What do you mean?'

'We can't stay at the villa all week.' Luc had been reassured by the dozens of signs saying Rooms to Rent. Ella and Liz rarely endured each other's company for more than a few hours before nerves were grated.

'Why not? Tim's offered.'

'It's an imposition.'

'Rubbish. I'm family. You're honorary family.'

'But . . .'

'But nothing.'

The old port had grown up round a semi-circular inlet. Compared with the main town a mile away, it was as tranquil as a monastery, the buildings far more delapidated, their paint blistered. A few yachts had dropped anchor in the middle of the bay. Swaying with the current, their lights danced on the water. Others were moored at the quayside, near a chandlers and a tiny café sheltered by a trellis. A crowded taverna, and a bar further on, had been built over the water.

'Didn't wait for us, did you?' Ella sat down, knocking the table. Wine sloshed in the glasses.

'Yes,' snapped Liz. 'You said eight-thirty.'

'You're usually late. Well, Tim is. Sorry.' Ella sounded anything but. 'That fish looks good.' Lighting a ciggie, she poured herself and Luc some wine.

'We're eating.' Liz fanned the air.

Tim gently ssshed her.

'Beautiful place,' said Luc, feeling unsteady after three ouzos.

'You look rrrested. Much better.' Marina smiled, her ringed fingers patting Luc's arm. A violet silk blouse was knotted under her bosom, showing off her tiny brown waist. She was as warm as the sun that had tanned her. 'Don't they, *cara*? Alex?'

He pushed his plate away, picked up a toothpick and studied Ella's tattoo. 'Next time, get D. U. M. B. engraved on your arm.'

'D. U. . . . Dumb?' Ella was indignant.

'Or has hitching suddenly become clever?'

'Alex,' protested Marina.

'I think Ella and Luc have learnt a lesson,' said Tim.

'We were unlucky,' said Luc.

Alex pulled a face. 'You make your own luck.'

'I hope you don't write in clichés as well,' said Ella. She turned to a waiter. 'Menu?'

'Please,' added Alex. 'No manners as well as no street sense?'

Ella smiled beatifically at the waiter. '*Kataloghos, parakalo. Ef karisto.*' She was rewarded by a huge grin. 'Depends which street.'

Alex raised an eyebrow. 'Forgot. Avenue, crescent and mews sense with you two. Snug inside the leafy environs of Knightsbridge, aren't you?'

'Chelsea. Let's guess who's been talking.' Ella glanced crossly at Liz.

The next day, Tuesday morning, Luc went into town with Tim. Liz had given him a shopping list and orders to wear a sunhat.

'We must need about Factor Three Million between us,' he said ruefully, peering at his freckly arms. Block-out cream was stuck to the gingery hair. 'How's the neck?'

'Much better.' She cleared her throat. 'Thanks for coming to our rescue, letting us stay. We were both feeling so miserable that we were thinking of going home.'

'Pleasure. You're staying on with us, aren't you?'

'I don't want to impose . . .' Luc had planned to check out Rooms to Rent.

'It would do Ella and Liz good to share some time together. Super bougainvillaea.' His myopic eyes were fixed on the splash of purple against a crumbling whitewashed wall. 'They need to put the past behind them. Do persuade Ella to stay on.'

'We were thinking of going to Hydra.'

'Well, I'd love you to stay. Interesting roof.' Being with Tim was like going out with an I-Spy book. 'Still draw?'

'A bit.' Luc wondered if she should try to sketch the villa as a present for him and Liz. He might appreciate it, but what about her? Liz was so finicky that the cleaning stuff under her kitchen sink was colour co-ordinated.

'You shouldn't waste a talent like that.' He drew to the side of the dusty road as some scooters hurtled by.

They passed the bakery. 'Alex's cheese pies,' said Luc.

'We'll get them on the way back.' Tim fanned himself with his sunhat. 'I'm afraid he can seem a bit abrasive. He's under a lot of pressure at the moment. His job, the book, Marina . . . She's super, of course, but it can't be easy. He never expected her to leave her husband.'

'Oh.' Luc hadn't wanted to pry. Too obviously. There hadn't been much opportunity. Alex was always tap-tapping away on his laptop while Marina lay on a lounger by the pool, shut off in her own world behind her dark glasses and Walkman.

'It's all very recent. She walked out of her marriage one morning and turned up at his flat. Not something he'd bargained for when their affair started. And he now feels responsible for her.'

Tim consulted his shopping list. 'Fish last. In this heat. Adultery is wrong, that sounds old-fashioned, but he's paying quite a price for his sins. I know he thinks the world of her, but I feel quite sorry for him.'

'You do?' Luc was amazed. She felt quite sorry for Marina, having to put up with Alex.

'He's got to finish the book, but Marina is a distraction. Don't mind him, will you?'

''Course not.' Luc smiled weakly. Being with Alex was like the walk back to the villa; hard, uphill work. He seemed to be carrying the weight of the world's injustices on his incomparable shoulders. At dinner the night before he'd banged on about the inadequacies of state education. The fault it seemed, to Luc's bafflement, lay with people like her and Ella who should pay more tax.

'Sorry, Luc. Just got to pop in here.' Tim halted outside a photo shop.

Ella had once said that if Tim got mown down by a hit-and-run driver, he'd probably apologise for being in their way.

'He called.' Liz sounded ecstatic.

'Von Retzen?' Tim took off his sunhat and wiped his forehead. 'That pool looks good, doesn't it, Luc?'

'He might come. Friday.'

Grimacing, Tim turned to Luc. 'Von Retzen is a rather difficult banker. Gnome from Zurich. Or rather Geneva. He's got this huge place on the lake that he's gutting. I've been commissioned to do the refurb. The client from hell.'

'He is perfectly charming,' said Liz.

From her lounger, Ella peered over her book and grinned. 'So charming you almost curtsied as you answered. He's only a count, they're two a penny in Europe.'

Liz ignored her. 'Now, Timmy, I've put the proposals out on the sitting-room table, just as well you listened to me and brought them, so we'll have a quick run-through.'

'We've got a few days in hand,' hedged Tim, gazing longingly at the pool, clearly unhappy at the thought of being cooped up indoors.

'It won't take long.' Liz was insistent.

'Poor Timmy's on holiday,' said Ella. 'Leave him alone.'

'Keep out of this, please,' snapped Liz. 'Some of us have a living to earn. And if you must smoke, vile habit, use the ashtray.'

Ella ground out her cigarette and stood up, wearing nothing but her bikini bottoms, her tattoo and a scowl. Tim averted his eyes. 'Beach?'

Luc nodded. The jasmine-scented air was getting heavy with the threat of tempers about to be lost.

Liz's mouth narrowed. 'And if our client turns up, and if, if, you're still here, could you try and remember your top?'

Ella grinned at Liz's almost flat chest. 'At least I've got something to put in it.'

*

Hours melted away, time evaporated. Luc and Ella squandered another day, just lying in the sunshine, swimming, snorkelling, reading. The guidebook told them about the church's architecture, a hermitage in the pine forest on the other side of the island, about a sea battle off the old port. They could've ridden horses, hired mopeds, gone on a cruise round the island, played tennis.

To Luc, just reading about all that activity was draining. She felt oddly tired all the time.

'Tomorrow.' Ella yawned, turning the page and checking her tan against the white skin under a ring. 'No rush.'

'But we're missing out on the real Greece,' sighed Luc. Perhaps she should have taken a package holiday; she was a tourist, not a traveller.

'Read Mary Renault.'

'What about Hydra?'

'What do you think?' Ella didn't lift her eyes from the book.

'I don't know.' Luc sighed. The thought of moving on again was unsettling. Why was she so tired?

'Decide later, shall we?' Ella yawned again and glanced round. 'I can't believe we've been away almost a week. Had the sun, had the sea. What about the rest?' She glanced round the tiny beach. 'Nothing here.'

'You've had Yannick.' Luc ignored the stab of resentment.

Ella threw herself on to her back, her hair getting encrusted with sand. 'Why did they have to leave? He was so gorgeous . . .'

'Can I help?' asked Luc.

Tim shook his head, puffing at the charcoal. 'Sit down and have a nice drink.' There was a jug of Pimms on the table, perfectly cut slices of oranges and lemons floating in the amber. Glasses waited, full of mint.

Alex arrived and peered at the glow. 'Hours to go yet. Wood shavings?'

'You're the expert.' Tim adjusted his apron.

'Being Australian,' said Luc. She smiled, wishing he wasn't so intimidating. 'How's the book going?'

'It's not. What's that you're reading?' Luc held it up. '*Hollywood Wives*? Bit grown-up for you, isn't it?'

'Ignore him, Luc,' said Tim.

Alex raised an eyebrow. 'You can manage without moving your lips?' Turning his back as if dismissing her, he peered at the barbecue. 'More charcoal.'

Luc left them to it. Where was his loincloth and woad? Why were men who never set foot in the kitchen always so proprietorial about barbecues?

She stared out at the sea, glowing gold in the evening sun. A mellow saxophone was coming from the stereo in the sitting room. What about Hydra? If the uneasy peace between Liz and Ella held, why not stay on?

'You've caught the sun, *cara*.' Marina patted her arm before languidly dropping into the chair beside her. 'Fabulous with your hair.' She glanced in Alex's direction. 'He's like a bear with a migraine this afternoon. His book. I'm sick of his book. No wonder my seester thinks I'm crrrazy.'

'She does?'

'Of course.' Marina glugged back some Pimms. 'Why do I leave my nice husband and my nice life in Wimbledon? She thinks I thrrrow away everything. Thrrrow away what? I'm Latin. Love is very important. Alex is a brilliant lover, verrry passionate.'

Luc shifted uncomfortably in her seat.

'You have a nice boy in London?'

'No.' Why should she have a nice boy, rather than a brilliant, verrry passionate lover? Was she that dull and colourless?

'You will.' Marina touched her arm again. 'Some sweet English boy, like you. Quiet, shy, restful to be with. Has Tim got a brother?'

Luc felt even more invisible.

'I told you. No smoking in the house.' Liz's squawk could be heard from the kitchen. 'And if you had to take every single ice-cube, why couldn't you refill the trays?'

'Sorry.' Ella's sigh was like a hurricane.

'Lizzy, Pimms,' called Tim anxiously.

Liz came out with a tray of cutlery. She was wearing a black linen shift, tight red lips and narrow eyes. 'How do you put up with living with Ella? She's the world's most selfish person.'

Luc felt she was the rope in a tug of war.

The table looked beautiful, flowers and vines curling round the candles. Ella always mocked Liz for arranging every meal as if for a photo shoot, but the truth was she took pleasure in simple things done well. She and Tim enjoyed cooking. They pored over new recipe books and went on pilgrimages to out-of-the-way shops. They made their own pasta and sour-dough bread. The mullet, marinated in herbs and lemon, was perfect.

'All this basil everywhere.' Liz glanced round the terrace. 'We should make some pesto.'

'Is there a pestle and mortar in the kitchen?' asked Tim.

'Should have brought ours.'

Ella rolled her eyes.

'Isn't that what delicatessens are for?' asked Marina, astonished.

'Marina's idea of a recipe book is the *Good Food Guide*,' said Alex, leaning over and kissing her brown shoulder.

'Town later?' Ella turned to Luc.

Liz was dismissive. 'It's like a zoo at night. Wall-to-wall discos, football matches, there's even a karaoke bar.' She sounded as if the plague were preferable. 'It's just ruined by tourists.'

'You're a tourist,' said Ella. 'You are. What are you then?'

'Stop being obtuse. You know what I mean.' Liz frowned. 'Timmy, you've forgotten the figs.' Apologising, he dashed to the kitchen. 'It's very short-sighted of the locals here to cater to the lowest common denominator.'

'They're catering, if they must be catering, to their wallets. They want to earn a buck. Who can blame them?'

'As if you know anything about earning a buck,' snapped Liz. 'Cheese, Alex?'

Ella glared at her. 'I know that if I were a local, tourists spending money on a good time would be preferable to tight-arsed tight-wads, sitting on their nice terrace carping about the rabble.'

Tim brought out a green marble board which showed off the purple figs. 'You must agree, Ella, that Ia is in danger of getting spoilt.'

'Spoilt for who?'

'For whom,' corrected Alex.

'For who,' repeated Ella, frowning as she dug into the pockets of her combats. 'People like you who come out for a fortnight wanting good olive oil and picturesque poverty?'

Alex reached down. 'Yours, I believe.' He handed over a small clear plastic wallet.

'My light . . . thanks.' She looked sheepish.

Liz stared. 'Is that what I think it is? It is, isn't it? Where did you get it?'

'What's wrong?' Marina was puzzled.

'Drugs. You brought drugs through Customs, didn't you?' screeched Liz. 'You stupid, stupid . . .'

'Oh, Ella.' Tim's face creased with disappointment, as if she were a prize pupil who had just flunked all her exams.

'And you, Luc?' Liz turned on her. 'I thought you were sensible.'

Luc wriggled.

'Liz, calm down,' pleaded Marina.

'Look at you.' Liz glared at Ella. 'Tattoo, that thing through your nose . . .'

'Don't forget the scarecrow clothes,' retorted Ella.

'You're a prime target to be searched. What if you had been?'

'We were. Well, Luc was,' said Ella blithely. 'Got away with it.'

'Don't smile,' hissed Liz. 'You think you're so clever, don't you? That rules don't apply to you because of all your bloody money. Well, while you're staying here they do. Get rid of that stuff. Now.'

'What's today? Tuesday?' Ella's clogs skidded on the gravelly pot-hole. The road was poorly lit. Liz had refused to let them borrow the moped. 'Let's go to Hydra tomorrow.'

'Wonder what time the *Flying Dolphin* leaves.' Luc hoped first thing. The fragile ceasefire between Liz and Ella seemed about to end, normal hostilities to resume.

'That'll give us three days before we go home.'

'Home.' Luc sighed.

'What's up?'

'Just realised I don't have much to go back to.'

'Ginger whinger. Not moaning about the lack of a man again, are you?'

'Lack of everything. Career, direction, money.' Luc stumbled on another pot-hole. Suddenly aware of the call of the cicadas in the undergrowth, she shivered.

'You've got loads of everything. Youth, health, brains, beauty. And a brilliant best friend.'

Luc smiled ruefully. 'Everyone else seems to be so sorted and settled.'

'Who? Me? Timid and Miz? Actually they're very well matched. Miz has found a slave for life who matches her decor. Poor guy.'

Luc rolled her eyes. 'Perhaps the *Dolphin* office is still open.'

The road along the waterfront was thronged with crowds. People were sitting on the sea wall eating ice creams. The thud of music from the rival clubs and bars could be heard from the tiny chapel a quarter of a mile away. After all the peace of the beach and the villa, it was refreshing to be amongst a throng. They felt more energised with every step. Life force seemed to be surging through them.

Outside a club, the stones under their feet seemed to be vibrating with the music. They had to push their way through a crowd lost in a dance trance. The heat made the walls sweat and the music was so loud the barmen had to lip-read. Luc ordered two beers. Within minutes, she was being chatted up by a sweet-looking boy from Athens with big brown eyes, a mobile phone and a polo player on his shirt.

'And?' demanded Ella, when Dimitri went back to join his gaggle of well-dressed friends.

'And I'm not old enough to want a toyboy.' Luc sighed. 'He's eighteen, Daddy owns a huge villa here. Worse, he wants to be a tax lawyer.'

'Not much poetry in his soul then. Next.'

As Ella got talking to a local with a goatee beard, Luc lost herself in the pounding frenetic beat of the music. The noise, the crowd, the steamy heat were a world away from the sedate dinner at the villa.

A grown-up version of Dimitri was hovering. Luc hastily looked in the opposite direction, her expression hardening to discourage him. She suddenly felt wary, on the alert. Her eyes automatically checked the exits. Had the attack on Praxos made her suspicious of strangers for ever?

'We're leaving.' Ella grabbed her arm.

'What's wrong?'

'Him.'

'Yous nuts,' shouted the goatee beard, screwing up his face and jabbing his finger at his temple. He reached out and grabbed Ella's arm. 'And yous stinks of garlic.'

'Good. It'll ward off creeps like you.' She pushed him away.

'Come on, Ella,' pleaded Luc, uneasy at his malevolence and Ella's fury. People around them were staring. 'Ella.' Luc grabbed her and pulled her through the throng towards the exit, the goatee beard still screaming abuse at them.

'What was all that about?' She was grateful for the cool calm of the waterfront.

'Fucking pickpocket. I thought he might have some E.' She delved in her pockets and pulled out her purse and the grass. 'Wrong guy. Wrong pocket. Shall we?' Ella halted outside the noisiest, most crowded, most touristy bar near the jetty.

Luc grinned. 'Why not?'

It was dark, packed full of Brits. Two men in Arsenal shirts clutched each other up on a tiny water-soaked stage, shouting along to 'My Way' on the karaoke machine. The crowd was booing. A Spurs shirt with a shaved head threw a chunk of pineapple from his cocktail at them.

Ella pushed her way to the bar and had to yell. 'Tim told me that Liz was so appalled that she might be lumped in with this lot, she insisted they spoke French. Snotty *vache*. Slammer?'

'Slammer.'

Ella asked for a salt cellar. She smiled at Luc. 'Three, two, one.' They licked their hands, poured on the salt, licked again and drank the tequila in one, slamming their glasses on the bar and sucking the lime. It hit Luc like a punch. She coughed. The barman grinned.

'Another?'

Luc nodded. To deafening booing, the pair of Arsenal supporters were staggering from the stage, giving two fingers to the Spurs shirt.

Eyes watering as she sucked the second slice of lime, Ella then ordered two Margaritas. To cheering from his mates who were sitting round a beer-soaked table, the Spurs shirt leaped on stage, his arms aloft. The Greek MC announced Tommy from Tottenham. 'I heard it through the Grapevine' came over the speakers.

Tommy from Tottenham was awful. If Marvin Gaye had

been around, he would have cut the power supply. Ella and Luc clutched each other and collapsed into giggles.

'Get off,' yelled Ella, throwing a slice of half-chewed lime high over the tables. Tommy headbutted it. 'Off, off, off,' cried Ella. Blowing ear-blasting whistles through her fingers she chucked three more. The Arsenal shirts cheered as two landed right in the centre of Tommy's Spurs shirt, the table of mates half stood up to get a better look at her through the throng.

' "Heard it through . . ." You're next, blondie,' called Tommy.

'No worries,' Ella yelled back, reaching into the ice bucket on the bar and chucking some cubes at the stage. The barman crossly snatched the bucket out of her reach. She ordered two more Margaritas.

The bar erupted into more booing as the song finished. Tommy from Tottenham took bow after bow, then peered through the gloom. 'Blondie the Gob. Still there?' There was a shriek of feedback.

'Here.' Ella raised her arm.

The feedback squawked again as his eye fell on Luc. 'And Blondie's mate.'

Luc went scarlet as the bar burst into applause and cheering. Every eye was on them. Where was the door?

'Cheers.' Grinning, Ella raised her glass to the table of mates and gulped down her Margarita in one. 'Come on, Luc.'

'No way.'

'Lukewarm . . .'

'No.' Despite Ella's tug, Luc stood her ground. She watched in disbelief as a smiling Ella shoved her way up on to the stage. 'Sorry?' One of the Arsenal shirts was beside her at the bar. In all the noise she couldn't hear what he was saying. He repeated it. Luc stared at him in horror, then at the wet stage floor, then at Ella up on stage, then buried her face in her hands. 'Oh God.'

Ella towered above the Greek MC. Tommy from Tottenham put his arm round her shoulders and kissed her cheek before he jumped off the stage, almost crashing into a table. Grinning, she took the microphone. Her call of 'Blondie the Gob from Chelsea' was greeted by whistles and footstamping. Luc cringed.

'Once I was afraid . . .' The music pounding, Ella squinted at the pingpong above the lyrics to 'I Will Survive' and belted out the words with gusto. Luc stood at the bar, too frightened to look at the stage, braced for the inevitable outrage. Ella was quite capable of decking half the men in the room.

'So now go . . .' Giving the finger, Ella ducked an orange segment then picked out a pineapple slice stuck in her hair and chucked it back into the crowd. 'You're not welcome any-more . . .'

As the MC tipped the jug of water down over Ella's front, the bar erupted into roaring cheers as if everyone's team had just scored the winning goal in the FA cup. Tommy's mates leaped to their feet, the barman clapped, the Arsenal shirt beside Luc whistled, flashbulbs flashed. Every man's eyes were glued to Ella's soaking wet T-shirt.

'Did I crumble, did I lay down and die? Oh no, not me . . .' As if nothing had happened, Ella carried on to the end. Praying that Liz wouldn't walk in, Luc gulped back her Margarita. The applause was deafening.

'Thank you.' Breathless, Ella bowed. She handed the micro-phone back to the MC.

'Lady and gentlemens. The clear winner tonight, you must agree, is Blondie from Chelsea.'

'Very clear,' shouted the Arsenal shirt, gawping at Ella's braless bosom.

'Your prize.'

Ella took the T-shirt and held it up to the cheering crowd. Luc saw two arrows and the logo 'Temperature Gauge'. She cringed. Then, as casually as if she were alone in her bedroom, Ella stripped off the wet one. Jaw-dropping disbelief turned to disappointment as she put on her prize.

*

'Nice time in town?' asked Tim the next morning.

'Great.' Behind her dark glasses, Ella's eyes were bloodshot. Her head pounded. 'Bloody creepy walking back. You could've loaned us the moped.'

'And you could've got your own,' retorted Liz, peering over her cup of jasmine tea. 'Though thinking of your unhappy history with anything motorised, perhaps not.'

'What?'

'Hungover, are you?'

'No,' fibbed Ella. When Tim set down a plate of scrambled eggs in front of her, she swallowed hard.

'Morning,' said Luc. Her bruises had faded almost to nothing, she could move her neck properly, her middle no longer hurt. She was hungover, still tired, but mentally geared up to move on. What time did the *Dolphin* leave?

'Sleep well?' asked Tim. 'Coffee?'

'Here.' Shuddering, Ella handed her the plate of eggs.

'Anyway,' continued Liz, 'I doubt if you could be insured for a moped because of that drink-drive business.'

Ella sighed. 'It's got nothing to do with anything. You're just being stingy as usual.'

'Stingy? I'm not . . .'

'Of course you are. You wouldn't part with your vomit.'

'Ella,' hissed Luc.

'Ella,' thundered Tim. 'That's a disgusting thing to say to your sister.'

'Half-sister,' snapped Ella and Liz simultaneously.

'It's a disgusting thing to say to anyone. You're staying with me and I'd be grateful if you were civil.' He picked up a fork. 'Now, Luc, how was town? Meet anyone nice?'

'So sorry, how nice, such lovely, lovely people.' Ella mimicked Tim. 'Stepford husband or what? Isn't the world ever shitty for you?' She leaped to her feet. Two minutes later the front door slammed.

'Typical.' Liz delicately mopped her lips with her napkin,

giving an I-rest-my-case look at Luc. 'Constant melodrama. Just like her mother. I don't know why you let her take such advantage.'

Luc was in limbo. Where was Ella? What about Hydra? Should she go riding or sightseeing? What if Ella came back? Her sense of being deserted was reinforced by the others who were planning to go off to a beach on the other side of the island.

'If Alex ever finishes his chapter.' Marina scowled. 'He was up at five again this morning. On that keyboard like Fozzy Bear the Muppet playing the piano.'

'He's very dedicated,' said Luc politely.

'To his work.' Marina plaited the fringe on her sarong. 'Gordon at least gets decent money.'

'Gordon?'

'My boring husband.'

'What about him?' demanded Alex.

Luc jumped. His arrival was so unexpected she wondered if he'd been spirited on to the terrace by a genie. Marina squirmed guiltily.

'Ready?'

Waving them off, Luc wondered what she should do. Pack? Go to town? Explore the island? Get down to the *Dolphin* jetty? Brain-scrambled from the tequila, it was even harder to decide.

She plodded back into the Presidential Suite and got some books and her sketchpad. Settling herself under an umbrella on the seaward side of the swimming pool, she studied the villa. It was hard to believe that they had left London exactly a week earlier. With two days of travelling and two further days virtually written off after they'd arrived on Ia, the holiday had been a change, not a rest.

It was Wednesday, there were only a few more days left. She felt dissatisfied, almost cheated in some indefinable way. Perhaps she should have taken a package, even gone away on her own. At least she'd have been settled in one place, instead of scurrying from one island to the next. She could have relaxed properly, recharged, got her thoughts together and planned the rest of her life.

Instead she had almost ended up in gaol, almost been raped, been in a car smash and been on edge ever since, expecting the fragile ceasefire between Ella and Liz to collapse at any moment. She felt more exhausted now than when she'd left London. Unlike Ella, she couldn't afford to go away again for months.

Were they going to Hydra or not? Part of her was glad that Ella had disappeared, taking her foul black mood with her, but it was irritating to be left hanging around. Was Liz right about Ella taking advantage of her?

Pencil in hand, she hesitated, like a diver poised on the top board. Could she draw? Did she really have talent, as Tim always suggested? Tim was always kind. Perhaps if she had gone to art college as she was meant to, she would have known. She would soon be closer to thirty than to twenty; she'd never find out now.

Her pencil tentatively made a few lines, then she stopped. Then a few more and then more. Without realising it, she lost her self-consciousness. Absorbed, she was oblivious to the sun beating down out of the cloudless sky and the warm, scented breeze. Occasionally she heard the cicadas, the tap of the swimming-pool filter and the distant murmur of the waves breaking on the beach far below.

'Sorry.' Ella sank down on the lounger beside Luc. It was almost four o'clock. 'Sorry for being ratty.'

'Don't worry.' Luc stretched indolently. She had enjoyed her day, delighting in having the pool and terrace to herself. She'd drawn, she'd read, she'd gone for lazy swims, then lay down on the baking stones, feeling their warmth on her wet skin.

'Hungover. And I needed some space, I guess.'

Luc had realised they both needed it. They'd been in each other's company for a week. Initially exasperated by Ella's disappearance, later she'd been glad she'd gone. And taken her horrible mood with her. 'Where did you go?'

'Sulking. Beach on the other side of town. Sulked. Had some lunch. Sulked. Bought a paper. Still raining at home. Slightly cheering. More beach. Thought about Yannick. Decided we were strangers in the night.'

'Busy? The beach?' asked Luc quickly.

'Packed. Zoo-like as Miz would say, though it was nice to people-watch. Most of the guys wanted to watch me. Blondie the Gob, the wet T-shirt queen. Tommy bought me an ice cream.' Smiling, she picked up Luc's sketches. 'They're brilliant.'

'A souvenir for Liz and Tim. To say thank you. I'll get them something else back in London. God knows what.' She quailed at the thought of choosing a present for Liz.

'No need.'

'They're so, well, particular.'

'Fussy,' corrected Ella. 'These will be perfect. Restrained, tasteful. Very them.' She reached into her bag. '*Flying Dolphin* timetable. One leaves for Hydra at eight o'clock tomorrow. We can have two full days there.'

'Oh.'

'Oh what?'

Luc pulled a face. 'It's just, just, we were meant to be going this morning.'

'Don't you want to go?'

'Yes, but . . . I wish you'd make up your mind.'

'Sorry.' Ella wrinkled up her snub nose. 'I couldn't think straight this morning. That hangover. And Miz giving me grief. God, she's such a cow.'

The thought of further tension between Ella and Liz decided Luc. 'So, eight tomorrow it is.'

Liz and Tim arrived back just before six, dusty and thirsty after their ride along the pot-holed roads.

'I'm filthy.' Liz brushed down her white shorts, giving a proprietorial glance around the terrace. Her deep tan showed up the jab scar on her stick-like arms.

'Pimms?' asked Ella.

'I'll have some tea.' She straightened a cushion on one of the loungers. 'Camomile. These roads.'

'Hello, you two. Good day?' asked Tim. 'We found a super little beach. Real *Desert Island Discs* place, wasn't it, Lizzy?' Luc and Ella exchanged glances, remembering Praxos. 'But the best are reached by boat. Alex has gone off to see about hiring one. Should've done it days ago.' He smiled. 'You two are very glamorous. Off to conquer Ia?'

'It's our last night,' announced Ella. 'We've decided to go to Hydra tomorrow.'

'Really?' Tim seemed disappointed.

'Really?' Liz sounded relieved. She sniffed. 'That's my perfume.' She glanced accusingly at Ella. 'You've been in our room.'

Luc wanted to melt into the wall.

'Only to borrow your hairdryer. Problem?' There was a pause. 'So, we'll be out of here first thing tomorrow. Luc's got you a thank-you present.' She turned to Luc who squirmed. 'Go and get them.'

'Don't be polite.' Luc bashfully handed Tim the sketches. They seemed so inadequate. 'I know they're not . . .'

'But they're wonderful,' exclaimed Tim, studying them. 'Aren't they, Lizzy? What a kind thought. Thank you.' He kissed her cheek.

'Very sweet.' Liz handled the paper gingerly, as if the sketches might bite her.

Luc guessed she was wondering where she could put them in her immaculate house.

An hour later Ella and Luc ambled down to the old port, passing the taverna and the bar built over the water. Yachts and cruisers were moored along the quayside, their crews enjoying a drink in the evening sunshine.

'They must be good friends,' said Ella, glancing at a thirty-footer which had six people on board, crammed knee to knee.

Luc tried to imagine everyone from the villa in such a confined space. After ten minutes Ella would be Fletcher Christian to Liz's Captain Bligh.

'Tacky.' Ella dismissed a neighbouring fifty-foot cruiser, then laughed at herself. 'It's just that when you look at these you realise *Les Voiles Blanches* was really something. Wasn't she?'

'Um.'

'Hard to enjoy pilchards after you've eaten caviar.'

The water shone like a golden mirror, reflecting the rainbow of flowers growing up on the crumbling walls. A man staggered past them weighed down by huge blocks of ice. Approaching a tiny chandler's, they were hit by a smell of diesel from the petrol pump.

Further along was a tiny bar, shaded by trellising. They sat on the plastic orange rope seats and ordered ouzo. Music came from a radio somewhere in the back. Few people were about. *Blind Date* nites might as well have been on the moon rather than a mile round the shore. At the far end of the quay was a circular jetty. Luc shaded her eyes and watched as a cat lay down smack in the middle of a large white cross painted on the stone.

'X marks its spot,' said Ella yawning. 'Early dinner, then bed?'

The sky was pink and indigo as they strolled back to the taverna. They were given a table on the waterfront. Luc threw a piece of bread into the glassy sea. Scores of black minnows darted towards it.

A toad-like man of about sixty was glad-handing all the waiters as he was ushered towards a table. Diners were trying to catch his eye and smiling sycophantically in case they did. In his wake trailed three much younger women, glamorous and over-dressed, pretending to be unaware that everyone was looking at them.

Ella shuddered. 'Probably what that English couple had in mind when they said a rich husband.'

The taverna was filling up. Voices rang out, waiters worked harder, dashing between the tables, the bar and the kitchen. Halfway through their octopus, Ella gave a muted groan behind a beaming smile. Tim and Alex were heading their way.

'Stop it,' hissed Luc, also smiling. 'We've got to be sociable. It's our last night.'

'Hello, gorgeouses,' said Tim. 'Let's move this table, shall we?' He fiddled about putting paper napkins under the legs to make it steady. Ella pulled faces.

'You're leaving tomorrow,' said Alex, sitting beside Luc.

She nodded. 'Going to Hydra.' He made her feel small; physically, intellectually, morally. Once again he induced a nervous shyness in her, although part of her wished she'd had the chance to get to know him better. 'How's the book?'

'Don't ask. Where's the waiter?' He turned round.

'Yoohoo. *Yassoo.*' Liz waved.

Ella's smile was forced.

The toad had turned round to stare as Marina sashayed past, looking like a corrupt Vestal Virgin in a tight white dress with a plunging neckline. She leaned across the table and smiled warmly at Luc. 'Your little drrrawings are beautiful. Charrrming. Liz says they'll go in her boxroom.'

Liz squirmed in her seat. 'I'm sure Luc understands that they don't really harmonise with our existing space. Menus, Timmy.'

'Don't . . .' began Luc.

'Space?' Ella snorted. 'Please. It's a house, not an exhibition hall.'

'A wonderful house, no?' Marina touched Liz's arm. 'Cool and peaceful. So clever, *cara.*' She turned to Ella. 'You have a place like it?'

'Not remotely.'

Tim smiled. 'Environmental health people condemned it yet? Ella's forte isn't really housework, is it?'

'Or any other kind of work, come to that,' said Liz.

Ella pushed away her plate. 'Even Howard Hughes would've found your house, sorry space, oppressively sterile.'

'Sterile?' Liz sighed. 'Just because some of us don't want to live in a penicillin lab.'

'Just because you want to put people in prison for bad taste,' retorted Ella.

'That's pathetic.'

'Thank God you don't have any kids.'

'And what's that supposed to mean?'

'All the dolls would have to be dressed in safe beige and soft neutrals. Let's face it, a style fascist like you isn't cut out for motherhood.'

Liz gasped. Tim's face crumpled with hurt. Sensing Ella had gone Too Far, Luc gave a silent prayer of thanks that they were leaving for Hydra.

'Marina, let's order.' Alex stared at Ella. 'You've got a smart mouth on you, but could you keep it shut for a bit?'

She was as stunned as if he'd proposed marriage.

'We'll have some fish, shall we?' said Liz. 'Tim?'

'Fine.'

Luc was puzzled, his voice sounded wobbly, his smile was forced.

'Wonder where we can get this boat from?' Liz pressed on. Tim shrugged, uninterested.

A wolf whistle echoed off the water. 'Hey. It's Blondie the Gob.' Standing at the entrance were Tommy and his friends. Half of their heads were shaved and their beefy tattooed forearms were shown off by their singlets.

Smiling, Ella stood up and waved. 'Hello again.'

Liz looked as if she'd seen an open tin of maggots.

'Give us another look.' 'Best sight on Ia.' 'Ever done page three?' They were interrupted by one of the waiters who shook his head regretfully and pointed at the tables. They were all full. 'Catch you later, eh?' they called, waving at Ella as they disappeared.

'Blondie the Gob? Page three?' said Liz icily. 'Friends of yours?'

'Met them last night,' said Ella, waving. 'At the karaoke bar.'

'Karaoke?' Liz's voice was Antarctic.

'Where I won the wet T-shirt competition.' Ella couldn't resist winding Liz up.

'What?' shrieked Liz. 'You are joking, of course.' She looked at Luc. 'Is she? She's not. You, you . . . In front of those, those . . .'

'Animals?' suggested Ella. 'Tommy and his friends are soldiers.'

'Squaddies,' said Liz witheringly.

'Don't be such a snob. They're nice.'

'Snob? I'm not . . .'

'You are. "Oh it's Tommy this an' Tommy that an' Tommy go away". But it's 'Thank you Mr Atkins', when the band begins to play." ' Ella smiled. 'Kipling could've written it for you.'

Luc wished they could leave for Hydra that night. She glanced at Tim, oddly silent, who was shredding his napkin.

Alex glared at Ella. 'When you've finished the poetry lesson, Blondie the Gob, we can order.'

Marina glanced longingly at the yachts and cruisers moored in the distance. 'Perhaps we can 'itch a rrride?'

'Ask an expert,' said Alex, pointing at Luc.

Marina wagged her finger. 'No more 'itching for Luc, eh, *cara*? Prrromise me.'

Alex was frowning. 'There must be millions of bucks' worth of boat out there. Rich boys' toys.'

'I'd like to play with them,' muttered Ella.

'Most of them are probably only used for a few weeks a year. The obscenity.' He shook his head. 'And acquired by the sweat of some other poor bastards.'

'Not necessarily.' Ella sounded sceptical. 'Oh, sorry, I forgot. You know the history of every owner of every boat, don't you?'

'Sorry. I forgot,' countered Alex. 'You could be an owner too, couldn't you, Ella? You're one of the privileged few, aren't you?'

She blushed scarlet in fury.

'Or did you think that your silly little tattoo would make us forget about the house in Knightsbridge and the trust fund and the share portfolio? Bet Tommy and his mates were impressed.'

Ella threw aside her napkin, got to her feet and stalked off as Marina protested to Alex that he was being unkind.

Luc was shocked. Ella's finances had always been a forbidden subject. Taboo. *Verboten. Interdit.*

'Unkind?' said Alex. 'Why? She knows her position is indefensible. That's why she's finally shut up.'

'That's not quite fair,' said Luc.

'Life isn't, sweetheart.' He poured out some more wine. 'That's exactly my point. But poor little rich girls like you have yet to realise it.'

Luc was about to protest that, if anything, she was just plain poor, but she was intimidated into silence by his unflinching stare.

'Ella has her problems too, you know,' said Tim quietly.

'Like what?' scoffed Alex. 'Trying to decide between Gucci and Prada?'

'Prada? Gucci?' Liz sounded incredulous. 'All she has to choose is between one layabout bit of rough and another.'

'For God's sake,' muttered Luc, standing up. She'd had enough of their carping. Pushing her way past the tables, she headed for the loo.

Ella stood in front of the mirror, scowling as she put on some lipstick. 'Obviously that cow Miz has told that prig Alex about my business. Fucking cheek.'

'Thank God we're leaving tomorrow.' Luc was suddenly weary, feeling like a UN negotiator whose peace mission was failing.

'I'm going to choke on that humble pie. Sorry.' Ella shook her head. 'It was a huge mistake coming here. Liz and I have never got on. Will never get on. Sorry about dragging you and everyone else into it.'

'Let's finish dinner and go somewhere else.'

'Sorry about spoiling your evening. Everyone's evening. Everyone's holiday.'

'You haven't.' Luc tugged a comb through her hair.

'I tried.' Ella sighed. 'Tried to be nice to Liz. But it's impossible. I'm surprised she hasn't got shoulders like Atlas, the amount of emotional baggage she's carting around.'

'Ella.' Luc was growing exasperated. 'Let's just eat and go.'

Back at the table their chicken was waiting. It was stone cold, probably frozen by Liz's expression. Ella forced a smile and poured out more wine. 'Thank you for letting us stay.' She raised her glass.

'Pleasure.' Tim patted her hand. 'Any time. Eh, Lizzy?'

'Any time,' she agreed briskly, flashing her teeth. The fish was set in front of Alex, who began filleting it. 'Now, sorry to bring this up.' Liz was brisk. 'We might not see you tomorrow. Money.'

'How much?' said Ella.

'Well, we haven't really thought about it.' Tim seemed uneasy. 'Whatever you think is fair.'

'We were paying about a tenner a night on Praxos.' Ella was swift. 'That OK?' Liz was hesitating. 'What's up? You honestly expect more than that for the Presidential Suite?'

'It's not just the room. It's the whole package. Location, pool, terrace . . .'

Ella noticed Luc's sudden anxiety. 'Let's sort it out later. Quietly. OK, sis? Don't worry, you'll get your money. Don't forget, I can afford it.' She glared at Liz. 'Actually, you never forget, do you? Always yakking about my business.' She turned to Alex. 'Next time you file a story, don't bother with a satellite phone. Use Liz.'

Luc buried her face in her hands as Liz began squawking that Ella was exaggerating as usual. Ella denied it, Tim tried to sssh them and Alex muttered could someone get a bucket of water to throw over the pair of them.

'Everyone. Please,' soothed Marina. 'No silly arguments. This is your last night.' She gave an ecstatic sigh. 'What a beautiful boat. Look, Alex.'

He glanced up from the fish. 'Ideal playpen for Luc and Ella.'

Luc followed his gaze. She squeaked.

'Oh, come on, Alex.' Marina laughed. 'Even you must be a little impressed.'

'OK, it's beautiful. I approve on aesthetic grounds.'

Ella's brown eyes lit up. She shrieked in delight, grinning a grin of delirious happiness. 'It is, isn't it?' she whispered to Luc.

Everyone in the taverna grew hushed. Some stood up to get a better view as *Les Voiles Blanches* glided across the inky water. She was lit up like a film star at a première.

'Now, that is stunning,' said Tim. 'Look at those lines.'

'French.' Liz squinted. 'What else? So elegant.'

'Could be Italian,' protested Marina.

The harbour master was waiting further along the water-front, minions at his elbow, walkie-talkie in hand.

'Deeper water?' asked Alex. 'Or poll position for an ostentatious swank?'

'Oh God,' muttered Ella, wriggling in excitement. She grinned at Luc. 'Got to be cool. Got to be cool. Shit, supposing he's met someone else?'

A grating sound echoed round the bay as the anchor chain was dropped.

'Have you got worms?' asked Alex, seeing Ella squirming in her seat.

She lit a cigarette with shaking fingers, causing Liz to fan the air. 'Not hungry?' asked Tim. The chicken was untouched.

'Comb,' hissed Ella to Luc, who discreetly fished it out of her bag and passed it under the table. 'Eyeliner?'

Alex caught them in mid-transaction and smirked. 'Think these two are hoping for an invite aboard.'

Liz snorted, amused. 'The karaoke bar and Tommy are more Ella's milieu.'

'Playing for high stakes, aren't you?' Alex picked his teeth.

'Us?' said Luc airily.

'Who can blame them?' said Tim. 'What a piece of design.'

'Think they've got designs on the owner.'

'Definitely not.' Ella got up to revisit the mirror. Luc could see Bertrand up on deck throwing a line to a fisherman.

Liz watched Ella disappear. 'She looks as if she should be selling the *Big Issue*. That dress. Those creases. Has she ever owned an iron, Luc?'

'It suits her,' said Marina. 'Very good-looking girl, your sister.'

'Half-sister. She's with us, not out in the woods with those road protestors. She could've made an effort.'

Luc took a deep breath, glad she only had to spend a few more hours in Liz's company. Inspired by *Les Voiles Blanches*, Tim again wondered where they could get a boat. Ella came back, growing more desperate as minutes, then a quarter of an hour ticked past.

'Madame must be on board,' she whispered to Luc. 'She's not going to let them out.'

Luc glanced up the quayside and nodded fractionally. Henri, Yannick and Bertrand were making their way down the gangplank. Rigid with anticipation, Ella didn't dare to look.

The waiters rushed forward to greet the three men. Like everyone else, the toad and his over-dressed harem had quietened, necks craning as they peered round to gawp. Ella blushed.

'Handsome guys,' whispered Marina to Liz. She flicked back her long curls and tried to catch Henri's eye as he swept past. Alex frowned.

'I'd like to talk to them about the yacht,' said Liz, giving Yannick the once-over. 'For research purposes, of course.'

'Of course.' Marina laughed.

'What else? I'm giving a conference paper on premium design, limited space next month, you know.'

None of the three noticed Luc and Ella amongst the jammed throng. Seeing Ella paralysed by uncharacteristic shyness, Luc got to her feet and made her way to their table. 'Henri,' she called, as he was about to sit. '*Bonsoir.*'

'Luc.' He roared with delight. 'Luc. *Ma petite. C'est vrai?*' Ignoring her outstretched hand, he wrapped her in a bear-hug, kissing her on both cheeks. 'More beautiful than ever.' He took a step back and looked her up and down. Bertrand and Yannick were grinning. 'Where's Ella?' demanded Henri.

'*Voilà.*' Luc beckoned her.

'Ella,' Yannick rushed over and threw his arms around her. 'Ella, Ella.'

Clinging to him, Ella looked as if she could faint from happiness.

'You've had dinner?' asked Henri. 'But you'll join us for a drink? If your friends allow.'

Luc glanced across at Liz and the rest, who seemed utterly pole-axed. As Henri took charge, instructing waiters to bring more chairs, she went and collected her bag.

'Old friends?' Alex looked at Henri, emphasising the old.

'Met them in Praxos.'

'You've been on the yacht?' asked Tim. 'How super. You must . . .'

'Your bill.' Liz held out a piece of paper. 'We did it separately.'

As Luc rummaged in her bag for some money, Henri snatched the bill from her hand. '*Non.* Mine.' He turned to Alex and Tim. 'I hope you don't mind us borrowing your beautiful friends.'

Chapter Five

─────◄०∞○►─────

'*Santé*.' Henri raised his glass. 'To fate.'

'To fate.' Ella radiated bliss, her eyes sparking like fairy lights.

'Fate.' Yannick smiled his sweet smile. More tanned, dreadlocks blonder, he was even more gorgeous than he'd been on Praxos.

The other four were leaving. Marina was pouting in Henri's direction, re-arranging her dress top so as to draw attention to her cleavage. Liz was staring with such undisguised curiosity that she tripped over a chair leg. Sitting between Bertrand and Henri, Luc waved back at Tim. ''Bye.'

'Greek wine.' Henri grimaced. It tasted far better than the house plonk that Luc and Ella had been drinking. 'So, when did you arrive?'

'Sunday,' said Luc.

'But you were enjoying Praxos. Why change your plans? Heartbroken that we left?'

'God no,' she blurted out, then squirmed. 'I mean . . . er . . . something happened.'

'What?' He looked alarmed. 'You weren't hurt?'

'More shocked.'

'Tell us,' ordered Henri. Luc glanced at Ella, who pulled a face. Neither of them wanted another lecture. 'Speak.'

Luc spoke. As she finished, Henri was shaking his head and tutting. 'You don't have to say it. We know we were stupid.'

'Those two are lucky we left.' His expression was as black as his eyes. 'I would've killed them.'

'With my help.' Yannick clutched Ella's hand. 'Thank God you're safe. If we're back in Praxos we'll hunt them down for you.'

Bertrand held his finger up to his throat and mimed a slice.

'You would?' Luc found the idea rather comforting.

'Who wants a caring new man?' murmured Ella. 'He's just a re-branded wimp.'

Henri deftly filleted the fish. 'Excellent. Here.' He offered Luc a forkful.

'Um. Delicious. How long are you staying?'

He shrugged. 'Until Friday, maybe Saturday. Madame keeps changing her mind. We waited in Athens, then she told us Ia. Who knows, tomorrow she might say somewhere else. You leave for London, when?'

'Saturday. But we're going to Hyd—' Luc shut up as she felt a kick under the table. Ella was obviously changing their plans.

'Ia's nice?' asked Bertrand.

Luc winced guiltily. 'This bit is far nicer than the main town.'

'Luc's done nothing but loaf by the pool and struggle a hundred yards down to the beach.' Ella grinned.

'You haven't done much more,' protested Luc.

'*Méchantes.* Lazy girls.' Henri lightly pinched Luc's cheek.

'It's not that,' she said, feeling pathetic. 'I've been so tired. It must be the sun or something.'

Henri shook his head. 'Luc, you've been in shock.'

'I have?'

'Of course. You too, Ella. It's obvious, no? Sunstroke, being attacked, a car crash. Then your room. It's shock. Simple. Why blame yourself for feeling, how you say, out of sorts? Shock.'

Luc looked at him as if he'd just solved a puzzle that had been eluding her for days. It explained everything; her weary lethargy, being jumpy, feeling unsettled, her broken sleep. Why hadn't she realised something so simple? Having been diagnosed, she felt almost better. She smiled at Henri in wonder.

'So tomorrow, after Madame calls, we explore together?'

Luc hesitated, playing for time. 'There don't seem to be many sites to see.'

'Who wants sites?' demanded Henri. 'Paris has the sites. We'll see the coast. Take a picnic.'

'On *Les Voiles Blanches*?' Ella gasped. Every stroller on the quayside was stopping to admire her.

Henri shook his head. 'The harbour master has offered us a speedboat. We'll use that.'

As soon as he finished his fish, Bertrand wished them goodnight and sped off towards *Les Voiles Blanches*.

'Now the skipper can relax,' said Yannick. 'Xavi left us in Athens.'

'He really jumped ship?' Ella sounded surprised. 'Why?'

'He had his reasons.' Henri was curt. 'So, would you like a job, Luc?'

'I, er . . .' Luc blushed.

'I would,' wheedled Ella. 'Please.'

'I'm not asking you,' reproved Henri, turning to call for the bill. He squinted at *Les Voiles Blanches*. 'A digestif? I can offer you excellent French brandy, not Greek petrol.'

A gang of local teenagers on mopeds had halted near the gangplank, revving their engines as if they were on Harley Davidsons. One of them dismounted and edged nearer to the yacht as if he were playing Grandmother's Footsteps. Henri cursed and leaped to his feet. Calling something to Yannick, he sprinted off.

Yannick paid the bill. 'Let's go.'

'Anything wrong?' hissed Ella, noticing Luc's apprehension. 'Oh. Oh.' She cottoned on. 'Henri isn't going to bite her, is he?' As Yannick laughed, Luc squirmed, mortified. 'Luke-warm . . . stop being silly and come on.'

The gang had retreated, intimidated by Henri's wrath.

Walking towards the yacht, Luc told herself to stop fretting. Why go back to the villa? For what? An early night in the cell-like Presidential Suite? She peered along the quay to the bar over the water. It looked so inviting. The light from the candles on the tables seemed to be floating on the water. And there were scores of people who would prevent Henri from pouncing.

But as she stepped barefoot on to the gently rocking deck, Luc again felt that she was being transported into a more enchanted world. The colours were more jewel-like, the air sweeter. 'This must be one of the most perfect . . .'

Yannick and Ella were disappearing below, stumbling as they kissed. Steadying Ella, he laughed, then gazed at her with longing. His topaz eyes were filled with wonder as if she were his three wishes come true.

'À demain. Sleep well,' called Henri, watching them indulgently. 'Ella, Ella, Ella. That's all he's talked about for days.'

Luc forced a smile, trying very hard to be glad for Ella, trying very hard to stamp out the kindling of resentment that was beginning to flicker inside her.

'A drink?' Henri's coal-black eyes were lingering. Her sense of claustrophobia returned.

How could Ella have left her stranded with him? The flicker was turning into a flame. She feigned a huge yawn. 'I should be getting back.' She would have to walk back to the villa on her own, along that dark lonely road where the leaves rustled as if someone was hiding in the undergrowth. The flame was becoming a bonfire.

'Stay here,' offered Henri.

'I'm sorry?'

'Stay.'

Luc's heart sank. Which was worse? A spooky, scary walk or a night-long tussle fending him off? It was as appealing as choosing between scabies and lice. 'I can't.'

'I'd walk you back, but after those boys, I don't want to leave. You're not going alone, it's not safe.'

'I'll be fine.' Remembering what happened on Praxos, she knew she'd be terrified every step of the way.

'You wanted to sleep on a boat. So sleep.' He held up his hand, silencing her hesitant objections. 'Luc. You can trust me, you know. You are beautiful, but not irresistible.'

'I'm not? Oh.' Luc giggled, finally meeting his eyes.

'That's better.'

'Perhaps I could get a taxi . . .'

'Luc, Luc, Luc. You think I'm like those men in the jeep on Praxos? I'm not. And it's offensive that you think I might be. Come. I'll show you your quarters.'

She followed him below. They passed through two saloons, went along a passageway and reached a teak door. The cabin was snug. Wood-panelled, softly lit, it had a thick blue carpet on the floor. Crisp white sheets and a hillock of snowy pillows covered a double mattress on a platform. Sea breeze blew in from the open portholes. Luc smiled in delight. 'Here?'

'*Moment.*'

As Henri disappeared, her nervousness returned. Was this his cabin? She looked round for signs. What was he doing? Getting condoms? What was she doing? No engine parts would be arriving from Mathi this time. Should she make a run for it or clamber out of the porthole?

'For you.'

She froze, praying whatever was for her wasn't some ghastly negligee. Turning round, she saw Henri holding out a toothbrush still in its wrapper, a towel and a *Voiles Blanches* T-shirt.

'Sleep well, Luc.'

Luc woke up as her face was warmed by the sun streaming in through the porthole. She lay still, being gently rocked, feeling as if she was floating. She could hear the water lapping against the side, the creak and distant rattle of the lines and anchor chain as they grew taut and slackened. Somewhere, coffee was being made.

The shower room was tiny but pristine. She opened a tablet of rose-scented soap and had a shower, fire-hose in pressure compared to the intermittent trickle at the villa. Finding some aftersun, she tried to wipe off last night's make-up.

A pale watery blue, the sky seemed freshly colour-washed. The sea sparkled, the breeze was a sigh. Beneath her bare feet, the deck was still damp with dew. She gazed up at the sturdy masts. The neatly stowed sailbags, the coils of rope were at odds with the satcom aerial and the electronics that could have been on Concorde's flight deck. For the first time it struck her that the yacht was more than just a pleasure palace, built to idle in ports looking beautiful. Suddenly she longed to understand how it all worked, to be aboard under full sail.

'You slept well?' Henri had a pair of half-moon spectacles on a chain around his neck.

'Amazingly well.' She smiled, her wariness of him had vanished. 'You?'

'Well enough. I was up at five. Breakfast?'

She followed him below towards a compact galley at the stern. While he boiled eggs and buttered bread, she sipped coffee, studying the coastal map on the chart table. It was covered with neat pencil markings. A compass and set of dividers were to hand. The books on the shelf above were all about navigation and the stars. How did he plot a course, taking account of the winds and tides and shifting sand bars? How could he get *Les Voiles Blanches* into a safe mooring, let alone across the Atlantic?

Luc was awestruck. 'I can't even steer a pedalo. It's all so daunting.'

He grinned, taking the eggs out of the boiling water. 'And unnecessary. The computer can do it.'

'Then why do you?'

'Computers can go down in a storm. I like to keep in practice.'

Just then Ella arrived. 'JFL?'

Luc studied her, feeling a pang of envy. She nodded. 'JFL.' Ella's 'Just Fucked Look' was written all over her contented face.

'He didn't?' said Ella, as they walked past the church up to the villa. 'Nothing?'

'Nothing.'

'Disappointed?'

'God, no. Grateful. I had the most brilliant sleep.' Luc glanced at Ella. 'More than you did by the look of it.'

'Too busy.' Ella giggled.

'So, we're not going to Hydra?'

Ella shook her head. 'Lost its charm, somehow, hasn't it?'

'Oh, hello.' Tim peered over *Hollywood Wives*. Like him, the rest were stretched out on loungers beside the pool. 'We were thinking of sending out a search party. Nice time?'

'Brilliant,' said Ella dreamily, giving a luxurious stretch. 'Wasn't it, Luc?'

'Tim. Ten o'clock.' Liz tapped her watch. 'Shade. So how was the yacht? One assumes that is where you spent the night?'

'Beautiful,' breathed Luc. She jumped as Alex dived into the pool, splashing her with cold water.

'Come on. Tell.' Smiling, Marina rolled over, showing off her teak-coloured back. 'You met them in Praxos, yes? How?'

'In a bar,' said Luc. 'We just got chatting.'

'Picked us up,' added Ella cheerfully.

Luc cringed.

'And they chased you across the sea. Rrromantic.'

'Coincidence,' said Luc. 'We didn't expect to see them again.'

'Didn't you?' Liz raised an eyebrow. 'Tim. Please. Shade.'

'They were very pleased to see you,' said Marina. 'They both seem smitten.'

'Hope so,' said Ella, as Luc began to protest. 'Henri? 'Course he's smitten.'

'He is.' Marina laughed. 'It was so obvious. And with a yacht like that, Luc, you want it to be more than a holiday romance.'

It dawned on Luc that they all assumed not only that Henri owned *Les Voiles Blanches*, but worse, that she had slept with him. Just as she was about to straighten the record, Liz asked if they shouldn't be packing. 'The next *Dolphin* leaves in an hour.'

'Um.' Ella cleared her throat. 'Would it be all right if we stayed on?'

'What?' Liz frowned at her. 'I've already told Elena to wash your sheets. By the way, your room was like a pigsty.'

'Sorry. I can untell her. You see, we've changed our plans. Haven't we, Luc?'

Ella meant that Ella had changed their plans, not that Luc minded much. Henri's unexpected gallantry had doused the previous night's bonfire of resentment. Somehow, sometime, during the best night's sleep she'd had all year, she had come to accept the situation between Ella and Yannick.

Luc heard Liz's exasperated sigh. 'We don't want to put you out. Ella, let's go to a hotel.'

'Why not a yacht?' asked Alex, floating like a starfish in the pool.

Luc was suddenly aware of her tousled hair, smudges of eye make-up and yesterday's knickers.

'Oh Liz, please. Tim?' pleaded Ella. 'It's not as if we'll be in your way.'

'A hotel?' said Tim. 'Don't be silly. Of course you can stay. Can't they, Lizzy?'

'Fine.' Liz sounded as if it was anything but. 'Timmy, shade. Please. We don't want you burning.'

'Thanks.' Ella whooped. 'Must go and get ready.' She dashed across the terrace. 'Come on, Luc, we'll be late.'

'For what?' asked Tim.

'We're going round the island,' said Luc.

'Do be careful on these roads.'

'We're going by boat,' called back Ella.

'How wonderful,' said Marina. 'Lucky girls, eh, Liz?'

'Um.' Liz snatched up her book.

From the pool, Alex stared at Luc. 'Nice to have a ninety-foot yacht. Get a thrill out of waving to the plebs?'

Henri expertly manoeuvred the speedboat out of the old port and into the open water. Rounding the headland, they saw the tiny chapel. Racing the length of the town, they passed the jetty where passengers were boarding a *Flying Dolphin*, then swept on past the marina. 'That's the ouzeri,' yelled Ella, pointing. 'Nicest place in town.'

'What about the karaoke bar?' Luc giggled.

Ella shot her a look.

It was hard to talk above the roar of the engines. The wind whipped their hair, salt spray dried on their lips. Henri occasionally glanced down at a chart, full of circles and crosses and markers. Sitting beside him, Luc tried to work out their position.

The town petered out, giving way to pine tree-covered hillsides, scored by dusty tracks. The boat cut on through the water, speeding past dozens of deserted coves and a few beaches, empty apart from a handful of people. On the horizon far in the distance towards Hydra, lay a tiny island shrouded in heat haze.

Walls of rock became gentler, the landscape more wooded. Rounding a headland, Henri slowed the boat, then cut the engines. They were in a cove. As they drifted towards the white sands of the shore, the stillness echoed around them.

'*Déjeuner*,' called Henri an hour later.

Luc peered into his bucket of salt water. Floating inside were prickly black conker shells.

'Sea urchins.'

After a swim, she'd sat in the shade drying off while he dived among the rocks. Ella and Yannick had disappeared, clambering up over the rocks and into the woods.

Henri opened the cool-boxes packed by Bertrand. Inside were two bottles of Meursault, water, grapes, figs, a Camembert and thick slices of buttered brown bread.

'It seems unfair Bertrand's missing out,' said Luc.

'The crew follows orders.' Henri frowned. '*Les citrons? Voilà.*'

Luc thought back to her last picnic. She and Ella had gone to Primrose Hill with a bottle of warm plonk, screwtop because they'd forgotten a corkscrew, and some bought sandwiches in a supermarket carrier. It had rained.

She winced as Henri plunged his knife into the thorny black ball. It reminded her of a baby hedgehog. 'Aren't they poisonous?'

He tutted. 'Delicious. Look.' The inside was coral-coloured. 'You've never eaten one? Then you must, and make a wish.' He squeezed on some lemon juice and spooned out the flesh. 'Close your eyes. Wish.'

She swallowed, her mind going blank. What could she wish for? Suddenly she realised there was so much missing in her life, she didn't know where to begin.

'Hello,' called Ella. She and Yannick were hand in hand. From the contented look on their faces, it was easy to guess they hadn't been shrimping. Luc realised how much they suited one another; tall, blond, honey-tanned children of nature.

As they all stretched out on the sand, drinking the wine and picking at the food, Henri asked Ella about the villa. 'This sister and you have the same mother?'

'Half-sister,' corrected Ella. 'Same father, he died about six years ago.'

'I'm sorry.'

'Thank you. But I never really knew him. Liz was devastated.'

'And your mother?'

'Janie? Cancer got her.' Ella screwed up her face. 'Eight years ago. I was devastated.'

'Poor Ella.' Henri clasped her hand.

Ella shrugged. 'Poor Luc. She's an orphan too.'

For the briefest moment it seemed as if the sun had gone in. 'Poor Luc.' Yannick squeezed her fingers. She smiled forlornly. 'Liz?' he asked. 'She was the pretty one in white?'

'No,' protested Ella. 'She was the skinny, chic one in black whose mouth was like a cat's bum.'

'Married to?'

'Timid. Tim. The washed-out skinny one with the glasses.'

'Ella,' sighed Luc. 'Be fair. They were there in our hour of need.'

'True. Tim's nice.'

'And the tough guy?' asked Yannick.

Luc and Ella grimaced at one another then giggled. 'Alex the Aussie,' said Luc. 'He doesn't approve of us. One bit. Thinks we need a crash-course in growing up. He's surprised I can read without moving my lips.'

'Sue him for slander,' shrieked Ella. She noticed the scar on Henri's back. 'What's that?'

'Someone didn't like me a long time ago.'

'Who?'

'Whoever.' He shrugged. 'It was dark.'

Ella frowned, intrigued. 'Where?'

'Chad. Africa.'

'When you were a mercenary?'

He smiled. 'Soldier of fortune.'

'That's just a more romantic description.' Ella pulled a face. 'I don't understand why anyone would want to join the military.'

'What about Tommy from Tottenham?' asked Luc. Ella frowned at her.

Henri shrugged. 'Easy. Adventure, excitement, brother-hood . . .'

'Money?' asked Luc.

Henri's face hardened. 'So, you'd be happier if I'd always fought for a noble cause. Which cause?'

She was taken aback. 'Defending your family . . .'

'Not my family,' muttered Ella.

'Freedom,' added Luc.

Henri scoffed. 'Freedom from what?'

'Tyranny. Oppression.' Suddenly she wished Alex was there to argue for her.

Yannick yawned. 'Aristotle said tyranny might be preferable to civil war.'

Ella whistled, impressed. 'Not just a very pretty face, are you? Ow.' She screeched as he bit into her shoulder. Rummaging in her bag, she brought out her pipe. '*Déjeuner sur l'herbe*, anyone?'

Drowsy from the wine, Luc lay on her stomach in the shade of a rock, hot sand between her toes. Her thoughts drifted like seaweed. Yannick and Ella had disappeared again. She realised he had become as familiar as Tim. If she owned a Monet or a Leonardo, how long would it be before she ceased to marvel and it became nothing more than priceless wallpaper?

'You look like a mermaid.' Water dripping from him, Henri sat down beside her. He was too muscly. He looked as if he'd been squashed in a press, inches taken off his height and squeezed down on to his shoulders and chest and arms. 'But mermaids don't wear T-shirts.' Gently he tugged at it.

'Mermaids don't get burnt.'

'You needn't.' He poured some sunblock into his palms. 'Let me.'

She tensed as he began to rub cream into her back, thumbs circling round each vertebra, his fingers digging between her ribs. He eased deeper into the flesh on her shoulder-blades.

'All this tension is bad for you. Relax.'

It was oddly pleasurable. Gradually she let go. Closing her eyes, listening to the soothing whisper of the waves, she felt her body becoming liquid, melting into the warm sand. 'Ummm. Where did, ummm . . .' His fingers were kneading into her neck. 'Where did you learn to do this?'

'Sweden.'

'When you were a merce . . . soldier of fortune?'

'After. When I was married.'

'Was married . . . not now? Ummm. Any children?'

'Two sons. Grown up now. Relax.'

The relentless pressure of his hands on her back made Luc want to purr like a cat. As he pulled off her T-shirt, her resistance seemed to have dissolved away. A distant voice was warning her about something, but she was too lazy to listen to it. 'Aren't you getting bored?'

He tutted. 'With you? Never.'

'Good.' She smiled contentedly. 'Why did you divorce? What happened after?'

'Why? Long story. After? I went around the world. Three times.' He started telling her. His voice was like chocolate, as seductive as his fingers.

'"Jolly boating weather, hail harvest home . . ."' Gazing out at the old port, Ella stood at the rail of *Les Voiles Blanches* clasping a lime daiquiri.

'Sssh,' hissed Yannick. 'Henri talks to Madame.'

'Where is she?' asked Luc.

'Paris. I think she's arriving in Athens tomorrow.' He sighed. 'So we leave tonight.'

'What?' Ella spun round, horrorstruck. 'Leave? You can't.'

'Madame whistles, we run.'

'Tonight?' gasped Ella. 'Can't she meet you here?'

He laughed incredulously. 'And how is Madame to get here? By ferry?'

'*Flying Dolphin.*'

'Madame? You're insane. Ella, remember this is her yacht.'

Ella glanced round, her face sullen. 'So it is.'

From below, Henri was summoning Yannick and Bertrand. *Tout de suite.*

Back at the villa, Ella sank dejectedly on to the bed. Galvanised by Madame's call, Henri had told them firmly that it would be better if they left, making them promise they'd meet for dinner later. 'Fairy-tale's over,' said Ella. 'I can't believe he's sailing off into the sunset.'

'It'll be dark by then.'

Ella gave her a baleful stare. 'Don't joke.'

'Sorry.' Since Luc had heard that Henri would be leaving, she'd been as relieved as a defendant on a murder charge hearing a Not Guilty verdict. Distaste and shame had filled her for the past few hours. On the beach, the wine, the heat and Henri's caressing fingers had lulled away reality.

Opening her eyes as he kissed her, his heavy, hairy body pressing her into the sand, she knew she was fooling them both. His open-pored face was lined as if a knife had carved into it, his skin lax and oily. Itchy as a Brillo pad, his moustache and chest hair were greying. When his fingers had edged inside her bikini bottoms, she had stiffened in alarm and yelped no.

'Tonight then. All night,' he'd promised his innocent English rose, while Luc had tried desperately to think of how to break it to him in the politest way possible that actually she found him repulsive.

Suddenly she had heard a tactful call of hello from Ella, who was picking her way back across the rocks. Luc had pushed Henri off her and scrambled to her feet, blushing scarlet when she'd met Yannick's topaz eyes and secretive smile.

As the speedboat had bounced across the water, she'd tried to keep her distance from Henri but he insisted on holding her hand. It lay inertly in his, while mentally she recoiled from his touch. Later, as they walked along the quayside of the old port, he'd put his arm round her shoulders. At the taverna, waiters were setting the tables for the evening. When Luc met their eyes, she'd wanted to scream, this isn't how it looks, I'm not really with him.

'He loves me, he loves me not.' Ella picked at her split ends. 'Oh God, I'm going to be a one-night and one-day stand.'

Luc sighed. 'Doubt it.'

'What's up?'

'Nothing.'

'Yannick says Henri's obsessed with you.' She grinned.

'Oh God.'

'Aren't you flattered?'

'No.'

'Why not? You seemed to be having a good time, writhing on the sand. *From Here to Eternity*, part two.'

Luc snatched up her towel. 'I'm going for a shower.'

Ella was bewildered. 'What's wrong?'

'Nothing.'

It was almost ten o'clock. The taverna was packed. For the third time the waiter asked them if they were ready.

'Perhaps they're staying on board after all.' Ella sighed. '*Kalimari, salata, psomi*.' She scanned the decks of *Les Voiles Blanches*. 'Perhaps Madame has changed her mind again. They can't leave without saying goodbye.'

'*Octopodia, salata*. Water, *nero*,' added Luc. 'They won't.'

The waiter scowled, unimpressed by their meagre order. Just as the plates were put in front of them, the three men arrived. The waiter sighed in exasperation as Ella and Luc changed tables.

'*Chérie*.' Henri kissed Luc's hand, which she immediately wanted to go and wash.

To discourage him, she'd deliberately made herself as unalluring as possible. Scraped-back hair, no make-up and a baggy T-shirt. But he seemed not to mind, and kept hold of her hand. 'We leave.'

'Oh.' Luc felt relieved.

He smiled but seemed distracted, barking out questions in French. Whispering in Ella's ear and clutching her hand, Yannick was ordered to concentrate.

Bertrand muttered to Luc that it was always the same before Madame arrived. 'Everything has to be checked, rechecked and checked again.' He scowled. 'It must be perfect.'

'But it is.'

'Then we redo it.' He sighed heavily. 'We need Xavi.'

Ella wanted to enjoy her last precious moments with Yannick, but had to put up with Henri's interruptions. 'Tyrant, aren't you?'

'I have to be.' He turned to Luc. 'When are you leaving?'

'Saturday.' She could hear Ella pleading with Yannick to write long romantic letters.

'So, we miss you.' He shook his head. 'Madame wants to come to Ia. She tried to get a helicopter from Athens, but it was impossible. We go and return Sunday. So I'll miss you.' He looked round for the waiter. '*L'addition*. Time runs out.' He squeezed Luc's hand more tightly, his black eyes imploring. 'Come with us. The job is still there.'

'I can't.' Luc felt claustrophobic. 'I must go back to London.'

'Sure? We need a fourth.'

'I'm sure.'

Across the table, Ella sat bolt upright, ssshing Yannick. 'What about me?'

Henri picked at his teeth. 'What about you?'

'For the job. Henri, I'm serious. Please. Please. I don't have to go back and you need a fourth. *Je parle un peu de français et j'apprends vite, parce que je suis très intelligente.*'

Henri dug deeper with his toothpick, frowning at Ella.

Bertrand stared. 'Why not? We need . . .'

'Listen, I'll keep my tattoo covered up.' She took out the stud in her nose. 'I can be very housetrained and I'm dead cheap, free even, and I won't mutiny.'

Henri was sceptical. 'When Madame and her guests are on board, it's different. Very hard work. You must keep out of her way.'

'No problem. Please. Please.'

'No drugs.'

Ella reached into her bag and handed her pipe and stash to Luc, who dropped it into her pocket as if it were scalding her. 'No drugs. Please.'

Yannick smiled. 'We need a fourth.'

'*Attends.*' Henri held up his hand and rattled something at him.

Ella guessed the gist of what he was saying. 'We'll take a vow of chastity. Promise. Please, Henri. You need a fourth. How about a trial? Until Sunday. If it doesn't work out, you can make me walk the plank.'

There was more chit-chat in French. Henri finally said, 'We leave at midnight. You'd better get your things.'

'You're doing what?' squawked Liz. 'Don't be so ridiculous. She can't, can she, Timmy?' They were hovering in the doorway of the Presidential Suite, watching a breathless Ella cram her stuff into her backpack.

'I can.'

'You can't.'

By the window, Luc prayed there wasn't going to be a row.

'Why not?' demanded Ella. 'You're always going on about how I should get a job. Well, now I've got one.'

'A proper job. Not messing about on a boat.'

'I won't be messing about. I'll be cooking and cleaning and stuff.'

'Cook? Clean? You?' Liz let out a mirthless laugh. 'Just as well you're not signing a contract, they'd sue you for breaking it.'

Ella muttered piss off. 'Can you take this stuff back home for me, Luc?'

'You can't swan off with a bunch of strangers,' insisted Liz. 'If my father were alive . . .'

'He's not.'

'And what sort of people are they?'

'Nice. Aren't they, Luc? Shit. Where's my passport? Your father, my father, wouldn't have cared, he never did. Not about me.'

'Ella, I don't think you've thought this through properly.' Tim polished his spectacles on his polo shirt. 'We're only worried about your welfare. You don't really know these Frenchmen. It's a bit of a risk.'

'Rubbish.' Ella began fastening her backpack straps.

'Remember what happened on Praxos.'

'Yachts can be highly suspect,' declared Liz. 'Fronts for money-laundering, gun-running, drugs. In the paper last week . . .'

'Do shut up,' ordered Ella. 'Where's my credit card?'

Liz's neck went as red as a turkey's bill. 'So, you intend to do nothing with your life apart from sleep your way round the Mediterranean?'

'No. I intend to shag my way across the Atlantic and round the Caribbean too.' Ella's eyes narrowed. 'Wouldn't you, given the chance? But you'd never get that chance because you've got no guts and no soul.'

Liz's lipsticked mouth narrowed. 'Who'll pick up the pieces when you get yourself into the inevitable mess?'

'I won't get into a mess. Where the fuck is my credit card?' She tipped her bag on to the bed.

'You won't get into a mess? And what happened last week?' demanded Liz. 'Your stupidity almost got the pair of you raped and killed. And who did you come running to?'

'You didn't have to bother,' said Ella.

'Of course we had to bother,' shrieked Liz. 'You bloody blackmailed us, with your pathetic hard-luck story. Which probably wasn't true. These Frenchmen turning up out of the blue when you're so conveniently in Ia. Did you think I wanted you here ruining my holiday? The sight of you makes me feel ill.'

By the window, Luc froze.

'Liz,' pleaded Tim. 'You didn't mean that.'

Ella smiled nastily. 'You're still so bloody jealous, aren't you? Get some help.'

'Jealous of you? Your imagination . . .'

'Why else did you try and get me put into care?'

'Ella,' warned Luc.

'Why? Because you were an uncontrollable monster and a wayward slut. Just like . . .'

'Go on. Say it,' taunted Ella. 'Just like Janie. Jealous of me, jealous of her. Just like your boring, plain, petit bourgeois *Dreadnought* of a mother, aren't you?'

'Ella, Liz, please.' Tim was getting desperate.

'And the father you fucking revered was only interested in getting his hands on my money, wasn't he? He tried so hard, and when he failed, he told me that bitch, your mother, put him up to it.'

'They had your best interests . . .'

'Bullshit. I should go down on my knees every morning and thank God my mother had the dominant genes.'

Over by the window, Luc needed air, the room was so full of vitriol.

'Leave. Now,' ordered Liz, her voice shaking with rage. 'Jealous of an insecure, spoilt, attention-seeker like you? You're very wrong. You've got a pathetic, shallow life, which you try to escape with drink and drugs.' She stared at Ella. 'Go off on that yacht. Let's face it, all you've got to go home to is Mummy's money.' Turning on her heel, she swept out.

Swallowing hard, Ella watched her go. 'Right.' She slung her backpack on her shoulders. 'I'm off.'

'I'll give you a lift on the moped,' offered Tim.

'Thanks.' She took a deep breath. 'Better hurry.' Close to tears, she hugged Luc. ''Bye. See you whenever.'

Chapter Six

'*Signome.*'

Luc opened her eyes and saw Elena backing out of the Presidential Suite, mop and bucket in hand. She looked at her alarm clock. It was already ten. She had found it difficult to sleep; acrimony had seemed to linger in the room for hours after Ella had gone.

After a shower, she pulled on a thin white dress. Like the rest of her clothes it was creased, slightly damp and greasy to the touch. Suddenly, she longed to be home. Why had they come to the villa? As she'd always suspected, they weren't welcome. And now, after blithely insisting they stay on, Ella had abandoned her.

Nervously, she crept on to the sun-filled terrace. Marina, lying out like a sacrifice on an altar, jiggling her toes in time to the tune on her Walkman, languidly raised an arm in greeting. Sitting at the table in the shade of the umbrella, Liz was making a list in her beautiful italics. Luc quailed.

'Morning.' Cheeringly, Tim's smile was as warm as the sunshine. 'Breakfast?'

'Elena's just finished cleaning the kitchen,' said Liz, without glancing up.

'I'll get something in town.' Luc cleared her throat. 'I've got to check on the ferry and *Dolphin* times. If I can't get a ferry, is it all right if I stay here tonight? I'll be out of your way first thing tomorrow.' They assured her that it was, Tim more convincingly than Liz.

'You seem sad this morning,' called Marina, lifting the speakers from her ears. 'Pining for your handsome Frenchman? You should've gone with Ella.'

Liz's face clouded.

'Page 276.' Alex strode up behind Luc, making her jump.

'Thanks.' She looked at the title. A poetry anthology. Poetry? Him? It was so unlikely she almost dropped it.

'Thought of you,' he called, taking a running dive into the pool.

She thumbed through the pages to *The Rime of the Ancient Mariner*.

The alleyways were cool and shady. Feeling as unwelcome at the villa as the Kiwi gatecrashers at Liz's party, Luc was spinning out her time in town. She ambled past restaurants, souvenir shops and the fish market, stopping outside a jeweller's window.

No gaudy beads threaded on bits of leather, no fake coins. Everything was way beyond Luc's budget. Her eye was caught by a pair of lapis lazuli cuff-links. Each of the stones was joined by a thin gold link. Luc was mesmerised. The blue was so rich, so deep that she wanted to dive into it.

Disheartened by the price tag, which was more than her whole holiday had cost, she walked on. A scruffy girl in a dress similar to hers was approaching. A split second later Luc realised the scruffy girl was herself reflected in a full-length mirror outside a clothes shop. She couldn't look that bad, could she? She could. From her hair tied back any old how, down to her battered espadrilles via her crumpled dress.

Even more dispirited, she found herself at the ouzeri overlooking the small marina. Apart from one table in the centre, it was full. She hesitated. She was thirsty, and besides, why go back to the villa? Self-consciously, she pressed her way through the throng and sat down. The table was cluttered with dirty crockery.

Around her, groups of people were laughing and talking. As the minutes ticked past, she felt as if a big neon sign had grown on top of her head and was flashing 'Sad Fuck. No Friends'. If only she'd brought a book to engross herself in. Not a travel book. When travel writers sat in cafés, they always got talking to fascinating, cultured locals who invited them to a cousin's wedding being held just around the corner in half an hour's time.

'*Kali mera.*' It was a spotty waiter rather than a fascinating, cultured local.

Luc jumped. '*Parakalo, kafe, cola. Karisto.*' Guilty at occupying a table all by herself, she felt obliged to order a coffee she didn't want. She stared out at the marina where a rusting cargo ship was being unloaded. Water taxis were speeding to and fro. All the bustle and purpose made her feel even more alone.

The walk back, carrying jumbo bottles of lemonade, oranges and pistachios, was more than usually like a trek across the Gobi. At the villa, Luc again felt like a trespasser. She went into the cool, stone-flagged kitchen, where Liz was arranging flowers, and told her she'd be taking the *Flying Dolphin* back to Athens the next morning.

'Oh. Not tonight's ferry?'

'No.' Much as she wanted to escape the villa, the thought of another overnight journey, this time alone, was too daunting. The ferry left at midnight, arrived in Piraeus at five-thirty, and there were no berths.

'You'll be able to entertain yourself, won't you?' asked Liz. 'My spirokopittas.' She dashed over to the oven. 'Count von Retzen is arriving. Tim's only booked a table for five.'

'I'll be fine. Have an early night.' Luc wondered if she was turning green and hairy, she felt so gooseberry-like. She wished she'd opted for the ferry, even if it meant freezing on deck all night.

Liz pulled out a batch of filo pastry parcels. 'Just a few eats. Where are those chives? Poor Luc, deserted like this. So typically selfish of Ella. Really, you shouldn't let her take such advantage of you.'

'She doesn't.'

'Doesn't she?' Liz put the parcels on a cooling rack. 'Well, you're more forgiving than me. I wouldn't like it if I went on holiday with a friend and got dumped because she found someone better to play with.'

'It wasn't like that. It's a brilliant opportunity.'

'Skivvying. If that's what she's doing.'

Luc thought back to the night before. Henri had been focused, in command, thoroughly professional. 'I think she'll have to work quite hard.'

'Work hard?' Liz snorted. 'Ella is to hard work what couture is to Camden Market. She needs to get a proper job, have some direction in her life. Messing about on yachts doesn't count. These Frenchmen. What are they like?'

'Charming.' Yannick and Bertrand were anyway.

Liz started tying chives around the parcels. 'Obviously.' She looked Luc up and down. 'Will you be seeing him again?'

'Doubt it.'

'Just as well. He's far too old for you. And that sort of world isn't all it's cracked up to be.'

'What world?'

'The super-rich.' Not giving Luc the chance to explain about Henri not owning *Les Voiles Blanches*, she added, 'I've worked for them, remember. Quite frankly, you'd be out of your depth.' Her eyes flickered over the creased dress and battered espadrilles. 'Better if you found a nice, normal boy of your own age.'

'Um.' The prospect was as uninspiring as flat tonic water.

'The bigger the bank balance, the more monstrous the ego. Look at Ella.'

'Ella's not super-rich,' protested Luc.

'Not in your Frenchman's league, no.' Liz got some lemons

out of the fridge. 'But far too much money, far too young. You know how much she's worth?'

'No,' said Luc. 'No, I don't. She never talks about it. She's not flash or showy. In fact, she's the most unmaterialistic person I've met.'

'She can afford to be,' said Liz sharply. 'Alex is right, she's just like Marie Antoinette. Ella plays at slumming. It's all a pose. Those bypass anarchists would've lynched her from that tree if they had known.'

'Ella would rather have Janie than the money.'

'I'm not saying she wouldn't.' Liz sighed. 'It's just that it would've been better if Janie had left the whole lot in trust until Ella was thirty.'

'Would it?'

'That's what my father thought. That's why he started the proceedings. Not to get his hands on the money. For Ella's good.'

'But it was Ella's . . .'

'Ella was seventeen. And wild. And grieving. By the time those wretched lawyers pulled their fingers out, it was too late. She was of age.'

'Despite everything, she's done all right. Brilliant A-levels, Cambridge, her degree . . .'

'And since then?'

'She's travelled . . .'

'She's drifted. The money hasn't allowed Ella to find her own way in the real world.' As a knife sliced through the lemons, the sinews in Liz's thin wrists stood out. 'Of course, exactly the same thing happened to Janie. Spoilt. Completely isolated from reality. Thought she was above the rules. She and Ella could've been twins. What she put my mother through . . .'

Luc grew uneasy. 'It must've been quite hard on her.'

'Quite hard? Imagine your mother telling you that you've got a little sister. I was nine, didn't understand why she was crying.' Liz's thin face hardened. 'You liked Janie, didn't you? Everyone did. Charming, fun, warm, pretty, rich. Father didn't stand a chance. Stupid fool.'

Ella's father, Liz's father, had been an Army doctor. His brief fling with Janie had been the most extraordinary episode in a dull, blameless life, according to Ella. Janie had told him that she was going to call Ella Fait, as in *fait accompli*.

Liz reached for a tiny tin and began rubbing her temples with tiger balm. 'Muggy, isn't it? I mustn't get a head today. Where's that jug?' She began searching through the cupboards. 'Homemade lemonade is so much nicer, I can't think why we didn't make it before.'

'Refreshing,' agreed Luc dutifully, glad of a change of subject.

Liz looked up at the clock. 'Two. Tim wants to go to the church on the other side of the town. If he doesn't get a move on, we'll run out of time.' She called out, telling him to put on a long-sleeved shirt. And proper trousers. And a hat.

Luc wandered out on to the terrace, dazzled by the glare. The light bounced off the water in the pool, the white walls, the stones, bleaching their colour. The breezeless air was stifling. She flopped down listlessly in a chair under the shade of the umbrella and picked up the poetry anthology.

It was too hot to concentrate, too hot to swim, too hot to breathe properly. When Liz and Tim called their goodbyes, it was almost too much effort to reply.

'Scorching, isn't it?' Alex sat opposite her, sweat trickling down his chest. Head back, he gazed up at the blue, blue sky, his long legs stretched out in front of him. Luc drew away, thinking how he always assumed more territory than necessary. 'Another day in paradise. When are you leaving?'

'Tomorrow.'

'Surprised you didn't hoof it with Ella. How's the Ancient

Mariner?' Grinning, he turned to look at her. 'Gives me the creeps.'

Luc blushed. 'The boat sank, didn't it? After they shot an albatross or something.'

'Seemed very afloat yesterday afternoon when you two walked hand in hand up the gangplank.'

Luc's blush deepened. 'It wasn't how it looked.'

'Good.' Alex shrugged. 'Because it looked pretty sick.' Luc gasped. 'Oh, come off it, Luc. What's with the hurt? It's true, it was sick. The guy's what? Fifty? Do you always go for old men?'

'No. I didn't . . .'

'Or does it depend on the size of their yachts?'

'I'm going to pack.'

Luc spun out her packing for as long as possible, telling herself that Alex was not, not, not going to upset her. It was only two-thirty. A whole afternoon and evening and night of nothing stretched out before her. Why hadn't she booked herself on to the ferry?

She decided to go for a swim, but seeing Alex and Marina stretched out on the loungers, she scurried through the garden towards the beach path. The sight of them holding hands, him soft-faced as he smiled at her indulgently, made Luc feel even more fed up.

The beach was deserted. Her feet were scalded as she headed for the shade of a scrubby tree. She tried to swipe the sand off herself, but it stuck itchily to her skin. A swim was suddenly unappealing, because of all the palaver with sunscreen after-wards. She picked up her book. Her eyes followed the lines but she took in nothing.

She gazed out at the blue horizon. Had they navigated by the stars, followed the moonlight as they cut across the velvet black sea, the sails full? Why hadn't it been *her* steps moving to the rhythm of the pitch and the roll, why wasn't *she* learning how to plot a course, why wouldn't *she* be exploring sundrenched ports and idyllic coves?

Luc picked up a handful of sand and threw it. She wondered what the time was. Perhaps she should get the midnight ferry? Why stay on at the villa to be sniped at by Alex? Why stay on, knowing she was only there on sufferance as far as Liz was concerned? To be exiled from the company of a boring banker?

She and Ella should've gone to a hotel days ago. Last night's horrible row had been brewing ever since they arrived. It was folly to think that the brilliant sunshine would melt away decades of jealousy and bitterness. Why hadn't she insisted they leave? Why hadn't she told Ella to chuck away the grass? They might be in gaol now. Why hadn't she objected to hitching a lift? As Liz pointed out, they could've been raped or killed.

Luc realised that ever since the start of the holiday, she'd been in the supporting role. Her part in the script had been to trail along behind the leading lady and let herself be half seduced on a beach. She felt soiled and grubby as if the imprint of Henri's fingers was still on her skin. And now the leading lady had sailed off over the horizon to live happily ever after with the handsome hero.

Would she have abandoned Ella, like Ella had abandoned her, to live the fairy-tale?

The sun beat down relentlessly, seeming to suck the energy from the waves, which only managed an exhausted sigh. Just as Luc was beginning to lose herself in her book, two Greek couples arrived, together with what seemed like a village of children. Shrieking and laughing, some raced into the water, two boys began to play football, a radio was switched on and a baby started to wail.

Luc tried to ignore the commotion. Ten minutes later, when the football bounced off a rock and on to her book, she surrendered. Getting her stuff together, she dragged herself up the path back to the villa. Should she get the ferry?

The terrace was deserted. She paced round the pool, but couldn't be bothered to swim. Out at sea, a yacht was heading east. She looked away. From an open window on the first floor, she heard a cry: 'Si.' Then another, slightly louder. And then another, louder still. Luc deduced that Alex was proving his skills as an amazing lover. Unable to bear it, she stomped indoors.

At least the Presidential Suite was cool. It was almost four. Only six hours to get through and then she could go to bed.

Why hadn't she thought of going to Athens? At least it would be somewhere new to explore. Or would most of her day have been swallowed up looking for a room, lugging her bag around? Unlike Ella, she hadn't travelled round India and south-east Asia. Unlike Ella she had a bag, not a backpack. A bag now made even heavier because of Ella's stuff.

Luc stared at Ella's empty bed. 'Thanks.'

Her espadrilles filled with dust and grit as she plodded down the hill, her sketchbook under her arm. She had no idea where she was heading. The stone walls seemed to be crumbling in the heat, the flowers wilting. Apart from the cicadas, the world was asleep.

Lost in misery, she jumped when the horn from a taxi hooted behind her. The shock caused her heart to race and more sweat to trickle down her back. She stood at the crossroads near the church. Town or old port? Right or left? Did it matter? She just needed somewhere different to kill some of the five and a half hours left before she could say farewell to a horrible day.

She went right, along the parched road down to the old port, passing the spot where *Les Voiles Blanches* had been moored. She hurried on past, blinking hard and swallowing back the sudden tightness in her throat. The taverna was deserted, its tables shabby without their paper cloths. The bar on the water was locked. She'd never got round to visiting it, never would now. Liz had made it very clear she wasn't welcome to join them that evening. She'd make an omelette, then try and lose herself in one of the pile of books she was taking home for Ella.

Luc ambled on, keeping her eyes on the ground, shutting herself off from the crews on the boats moored just feet away from her. Passing the chandler's, she came to the trellised bar where she and Ella had drunk ouzo that night *Les Voiles Blanches* had arrived. The taxi which had startled her earlier was parked outside, blocking the quayside, the driver talking to the bar owner. Luc sank down on an orange rope seat, grateful for the shade.

When the mineral water finally arrived, she downed half of it at once. The chill hit her throat, making her realise how hot the rest of her was. Her dress was sticking to her, her hair under her hat was plastered to her scalp, sweat oozed from her pores as if they were open sluices. Opening the sketchpad, she marked the paper with grubby fingerprints.

Fewer boats than usual were moored along the quayside. Others would soon be arriving. They were far out in the open sea and seemed motionless in the flat calm. 'As idle as a painted ship upon a painted ocean.' Remembering the lines from *The Ancient Mariner*, she scowled and picked up her pencil.

Halfway through her second bottle of water, Luc was distracted by a woman strolling across the deck of a large white cruiser moored close to the bar. Late thirties? She was hard-faced, hard-bodied and leanly attractive. Her tiny black bikini showed off a long waist and pancake-flat stomach. Her short blonde hair was slicked back, her nails varnished and her wrap-around glasses were, unlike Luc's, unsmeared, their lenses very black. She was so arctic cool, she'd never even glow.

Luc hated her on sight. She immediately wanted to hide in a large sack. Back home, she'd thought a long frock and shady hat would make her ethereal and romantic. Now she felt ridiculous and looked worse. Her sunglasses kept on falling down her sweating nose. She snatched them off and dabbed at her face with a napkin.

Trying to focus on the taverna in the distance, she heard a muffled roar. Assuming it was a speedboat, she scanned the harbour, then her eyes were drawn up and up. A helicopter was approaching, the sun glinting off its bubble window. The roar became louder. Around the quayside, people were coming out on to the balconies, intrigued. Crews gazed up. Even the chic woman on the cruiser was staring.

The roar became deafening. The helicopter was preparing to touch down on the circular jetty at the far end of the quay, where the cat had sat on the giant white cross. Some men were waiting nearby, Luc recognised the harbour master.

The water rippled as the helicopter hovered, its whirring blades like giant fans before it touched down. Crouching low the harbour master ran forward and opened the door. A passenger jumped out. He reached inside to shake hands with the pilot, moved away and watched until the helicopter was airborne once again and heading over the sea.

The taxi driver said something to the bar owner, then sprinted off along the quayside. The passenger began walking towards them, the harbour master and his lackeys at his heels like courtiers.

Luc squinted, making out slick-backed blond hair and sunglasses. Elegantly lean, he was unaffected by the heat despite his dark suit. His pale blue shirt would've suited the lapis lazuli cuff-links. Not Greek, decided Luc. Too tall, too fair. Scandinavian?

The blonde on the boat must be waiting for him; they were made for one another. They could be in a feature on the lifestyles of the blessed and the beautiful.

Unhurried and unsmiling, he was glancing round him with cool detachment, getting his bearings, as the trotting harbour master escorted him round the quayside. The taxi driver scurried up, almost tugging his bag and briefcase from him, pointing at the Mercedes.

He drew nearer. Luc froze, knowing that her eyes had met his, despite the camouflage of his dark, dark glasses. She knew that he was looking at her.

Blushing, she forced herself to look down at her sketchpad, but knew he'd stopped just feet from her. The taxi driver was yelling '*Nero*'. Even when he took the glass of water, she knew his eyes were still on her. She looked up again, staring into the black, feeling giddy. The world around her had seemed to stop. Dazed, she tried to focus on the paper, her pulse racing, her blush deepening.

'*Ef karisto.*' He left the water almost untouched on the next table. Unable to stop herself, she looked up and watched him reach in his jacket pocket and pull out some cigarettes.

'*Kyrie.*' The taxi driver was holding the door open.

He nodded, still looking down at her, but he neither smiled nor spoke as she was expecting. As he walked away, she wanted to scream 'Wait'. But, as in a nightmare, no words would come out.

Liz was sitting under the huge umbrella, wearing more make-up than usual. Her scent overpowered the jasmine and basil in the pots. She raised an eyebrow at Luc's dusty dishevelment. 'You do look hot and bothered.'

'Do I?' A teapot, glasses and a jug of Pimms stood on the table, along with the filo parcels and some olives.

'Some Pimms?'

'Thank . . .' Luc followed Liz's gaze across the swimming pool and realised the offer was directed elsewhere. Gasping, she almost dropped her sketchbook.

'Lucasta, Count von Retzen. Count, Lucasta James. Lucasta's been sketching,' added Liz hastily, as if this might excuse Luc's tattiness. 'Anywhere nice?'

Luc heard nothing. The world might have been exploding into a million pieces around her and she wouldn't have noticed.

No longer hidden behind dark glasses, the eyes were lapis lazuli blue.

'How long was the flight?' Liz handed him a glass, then poured herself some more camomile. 'Count von Retzen arrived by helicopter.'

'I know,' whispered Luc.

'Fifty minutes. Please, Lorenzo,' he corrected, his eyes not leaving Luc's.

'Luc, Pimms?' asked Liz for the second time.

Still feeling giddy, Luc forced herself back to reality. 'Thanks.'

Alex arrived with Tim, who looked far smarter than usual in a pale linen suit. Swigging beer from a bottle, Alex was in tatty jeans and barefoot. However, he was sitting up straight as if he were being put on his best behaviour.

'Cooler, thankfully,' announced Marina, slinking across the terrace. 'Please, Lorrrenzo.' He'd half got to his feet, but she touched him on the shoulder. 'We're verrry inforrrmal here.' In a short black evening dress that showed off most of her bosom, high heels, a cream silk wrap, hair up, she was wearing half of Tiffany's.

'We are?' said Alex drily.

Focusing on the horizon, Luc gulped back her Pimms. The glass cooled her sticky hands as the chit-chat picked up. She was too nervous to look at him properly, anxious that she'd betray herself. His feline calm emphasised her jitters. From Marina's questions, she learnt that he was Italian-German and lived in Geneva. They broke into musical Italian. He'd studied at Harvard, was a banker, did business in Eastern Europe. When Liz clucked that so much travelling must be hard on his wife, Luc drained her Pimms and got to her feet.

'I'm not married.'

Luc paused.

'Off to pack?' asked Marina.

'You're leaving?' A flash of lapis lazuli blue.

'Tomorrow morning.'

'But you're having dinner with us?'

Luc hesitated.

'Luc's got a very early start tomorrow,' cut in Liz.

'You'll be wanting an early night, won't you, *cara*?' added Marina. She touched the blue-shirted arm. 'Luc's been having such an exciting time, little wonder she looks so exhausted. Chased across the sea by a handsome Frenchman with a beautiful yacht.'

Lorenzo raised an eyebrow.

Marina's fingers seemed to have taken root on his sleeve. Luc noticed his cuff-links. Lapis lazuli. 'Alex called him the Ancient Mariner, but that's unfair, isn't it, Luc? He was scarcely fifty.'

The eyebrow went higher.

Luc wanted to garotte Marina with her cream scarf.

Alex poured out some more Pimms and smiled at Luc. 'I think you should come with us. As it's your last night.'

'Of course you must,' agreed Tim.

Luc had almost finished drying her hair. The clothes that she'd so carefully packed had been pulled out of her bag and lay strewn across the bed.

'Ready?' Liz bustled in and examined her reflection in the mirror. 'Isn't he charming?' She sighed. 'I do wish Marina would be a bit more piano and stop thrusting her chest at him.'

'Thanks.' Luc handed Liz the hairdryer. Black dress, or was that trying too hard? Besides, Marina was wearing one, an expensive one. Last night's skirt and what? Her only clean top was Baci da Roma, Kisses From Rome. Too childish.

'These painkillers are taking their time. Surprised he isn't married,' said Liz. 'Still, I'm sure there's no shortage swooning at his feet.'

Kisses From Rome would do.

*

Lorenzo announced he'd prefer to walk down to the old port. He had showered and changed out of his suit, but was still formal in a white shirt and blue jacket.

'So we go together,' declared Marina. 'Cancel the taxi.'

Flanked by her and Liz, he strolled ahead. The two women were laughing and chattering like the unseen cicadas. Luc could scarcely get a word out of Tim and Alex, whose eyes were fixed on the group ahead. They were unsettled, wildebeest who scent the approach of a leopard.

Dusk had fallen by the time they arrived at the taverna. '*Yassoo.*' The mâitre d' beamed at Liz and Marina. 'The two most beautiful ladies on Ia.'

'Creep,' muttered Luc, wishing she'd worn her black dress instead of the T-shirt.

Liz took charge of the placement, putting Lorenzo at one end of the table, between her and Marina. Luc was at the other.

'You remember how to walk?' muttered Alex to Marina, as they arrived at the crowded taverna. 'Thought your idea of a hike was Harrods' food hall.'

Unruffled, Marina beamed at him and sank gracefully into her chair.

At the other end of the table, Luc wondered how he could be half Italian with his colouring, his cool, feline reserve. How old? Late thirties? Forty? She guessed his contemporaries must envy his full head of thick blond hair and his lean, gut-free frame.

He pointed across the bay. 'That's where we came in.'

'Heard you land.' Alex poured olive oil on to his bread. 'Thought helicopters were only for medical emergencies.'

'I pleaded sea-sickness.' Liz and Marina laughed, a fraction too loudly. 'A contact in Athens arranged it.'

'Friends in high places,' said Alex. 'Useful, that.'

'Shall we have some snapper?' cut in Tim.

'Very useful.' Lorenzo shrugged. 'It saves time, of which I

have too little.' He pulled out a packet of Lucky Strike and a flat gold lighter. 'May I?'

'Please,' urged Liz. There was none of the pointed air-fanning that Ella induced. 'A change from our usual?' she suggested brightly to Tim, who was studying the wine list. 'Alas, a rather limited choice,' she confided to Lorenzo. 'Few whites compare to the German and Alsace, do they?'

Listening to them compare vineyards and vintages, Luc suddenly realised Gewürztraminer wasn't a horrible disease.

Marina swallowed a yawn. 'Liz, *cara*, so knowledgeable.'

'Oh, wine's so fascinating, isn't it?' Liz smiled at him. 'One can never know enough.'

'One drinks, one enjoys.' Marina held up her glass to his. '*Prost.*' Her wrap slipping down her shoulders, she said something in Italian.

'Please enlighten us. If it's not too much trouble,' said Alex.

'A toast to wine, women and song, *caro*.' Marina began talking opera.

'Do you share this enthusiasm, Alex?' asked Lorenzo minutes later, after Marina had finished her tour of works, houses and singers, with frequent lapses into Italian and much touching of the blue sleeve.

'Alex?' trilled Marina. 'He doesn't know Wotan from Mimi.'

Alex's expression darkened. Fortunately, the waiter arrived with the snapper.

Wotan? Mimi? Luc was adrift on a sea of inadequacy. Mute, gauche, dressed like a bumpkin compared to Liz and Marina, she felt like a child allowed to stay up and have dinner with the grown-ups.

'Have you seen her?' Marina was asking.

'Once,' said Lorenzo. 'At Verona.'

'La Divina,' Marina turned to Alex. 'A mezzo . . .'

'Mezzo soprano,' Alex cut in. 'Thank you, Marina. Even I've heard of Yasmina Bois.'

Even Luc had heard of her.

'Not hungry?' asked Tim, seeing her toy with her fish.

'Perhaps Luc's pining for her sailor like Madame Butterfly,' said Marina. 'So rrromantic, don't you think, Lorrrenzo?'

'Very.' For the first time since she'd been sitting on the terrace, he seemed to notice her existence. The blue eyes met hers. He didn't smile. Luc's insides withered. Why hadn't she explained about Henri when she'd had the chance?

'Madame Butterfly?' said Alex. 'Wasn't she a hooker?'

Luc wished he would get on a surfboard, aim for Sydney and start paddling.

Marina was certainly drinking and enjoying. Her dark eyes shone, her laugh became louder, her touch on the sleeve more lingering. Like a pupil trying to get a teacher's attention, she kept butting in on Tim, who was talking architecture.

Liz cleared her throat. 'Tim's mentioned you're a collector, Lorenzo. The Constructivists . . .'

Luc was not only adrift, but drowning in her sea of inadequacy.

'Done her homework, hasn't she?' muttered Alex to Luc. 'This contract means a lot.'

Detached from the villa for the past few days, Luc had almost forgotten that Lorenzo was Tim's client. She noticed Liz forcing a smile as Marina went off on some tangent about astrology.

As they finished dinner, Liz suddenly winced and rubbed her temples. Alex and Lorenzo started talking about the political situation east of the River Oder. Listening, silent, Luc had drowned. She needed a lifeguard and mouth-to-mouth resuscitation. Alex was predicting the resurgence of communism.

A frown crossed Lorenzo's face. 'I hope that you're wrong. As for the future . . .'

'I can tell you your future,' cut in Marina. Her dark eyes were slightly glazed from the wine. Her animation was in sharp contrast to Liz, who'd become oddly subdued. 'I read palms. Show me.'

Lorenzo shook his head. 'I don't believe in fortune-telling.'

'Just in having one,' muttered Alex.

'Show me,' insisted Marina. He held out his hand. 'Long fingers,' she cooed. She began tracing his palm with a crimson fingernail. 'I have gypsy blood, you know,' she confided in a velvety voice. 'My grandmother was pure Rrromany.'

'As well as being Queen Victoria.' A black frown crossed Alex's face.

Marina blushed. 'It's the truth.'

'Bullshit.'

Marina screeched something in Italian.

'Lie to your husband, not to me.'

The screeching became louder.

'What the fuck are you on? Showing yourself up like this?'

Marina leaped to her feet and snatched up her glass. The wine missed Alex. Luc cried out as it hit her eyes. The sting was like an acid burn. For a moment she panicked thinking she was going to be blinded permanently. She heard Marina's dismayed apologies and Alex's curt 'Goodnight, everyone.' Her eyes watered, clearing her vision. 'Excuse me.'

'Where's . . .?' Returning from the loo, where she'd washed her eyes, Luc was bewildered.

'Our hostess fears a migraine. I insisted Tim take her back to the villa.' Lorenzo held back the chair next to him. 'Still stinging?'

'I'm fine. Thank you.'

'You'll join me for a drink, I hope?'

He sounded so indifferent. 'Perhaps I . . .' stammered Luc.

'Does the signora always star in her own melodrama?'

'She's very sweet . . .'

'She's too old for drunken histrionics.' Luc quailed at his disdain. 'A drink? Shall we go?'

They walked in silence round the quayside towards the bar over the water. The flickering candlelight on the tables danced on the water to a slow, jazzy piano tune. Walking in, Luc wished she'd worn anything but her stupid T-shirt. The bar was packed with expensively labelled women. As it was Friday night, it was crowded to standing room only with weekenders from Athens. Crushed in all senses, Luc felt like a mongrel beside the Best of Breed at Crufts.

She peered out wistfully at the tables on the breeze-cooled jetty. 'Pity . . .'

As she wondered where else they could possibly go, Lorenzo intercepted the black-tied maître d', whose expression changed from chill to interest, to beaming sycophancy. Luc followed them outside to the waterfront. The maître d' whisked a reserved sign off the table, made sure they were comfortably seated and begged them to enjoy their evening. As two whiskies were ordered, a tip was handed over so dextrously and pocketed so quickly, that Luc thought she'd imagined it.

'Baci da Roma.' He lit a cigarette. 'You know Italy?'

'No. It's a present. From Ella. My best friend. Liz's half-sister.'

'And where's Ella tonight?'

'Athens, perhaps. She left yesterday. Got a job on a yacht.'

'The same yacht that pursued you across the seas?' He almost smiled.

Luc took a deep breath. 'That yacht. Yes. But it wasn't in pursuit. Ella and I were in Praxos last week and we met up with the crew. Frenchmen. We left and came to Ia. And they turned up the other night. Purely by chance. A coincidence.'

'How fortuitous. Baisers de Paris from a handsome Frenchman with a beautiful yacht.'

'No.' Luc choked on her whisky. 'I wasn't interested. Everyone at the villa just assumed. Like they assumed he owned the yacht.

He skippered it. Ella fell for another crewman and I just tagged along. It all got so awkward . . . I'm glad he left.'

'And if he'd owned the yacht?'

'What if he had?' Luc was puzzled. 'It wouldn't have made any difference.' She stared at her drink. 'This is a long way to come for the weekend.'

He shrugged. 'I wanted a swim.'

'People don't just fly hundreds of miles to swim.'

'I wanted to look at sea the colour of lapis lazuli.'

'Like your cuff-links.'

'Like my cuff-links.'

'I saw some this morning.' Luc sighed, remembering the price tag. She glanced round. The motor-cruiser blonde, now in a simple linen dress, was sitting at the next table. The squat man beside her was as bald and fat as a Buddha. Ignoring him, she was gazing hungrily at Lorenzo.

'Where are you taking me next?' he asked abruptly.

Luc was dismayed. 'Don't you like it here?'

'A charming spot. But full of too many well-dressed people bored with life.'

Rounding the headland, they followed the road running beside the sea and came to the tiny chapel on the outskirts of town. The door was ajar, two black-clad crones sitting guard at the entrance. Uncertainly, Luc followed him inside, breathing incense and sudden tranquillity. Dark, Byzantine-style portraits of saints glowed in the candlelight. For several minutes he stood in silence, studying them.

A hunched old man shuffled in and genuflected.

'Come,' whispered Lorenzo.

Tiptoeing, Luc followed him outside. The town lights seemed even brighter and gaudier.

'A pity you can't visit Mount Athos.'

'Mount Athos?'

'In the north. The holy mountain, with hundreds of monasteries. Some seem to hang in the air.'

'You can stay at them? With the monks?'

He nodded. 'You stay, you walk to another.'

Luc was puzzled. 'Like a religious retreat?'

'Exactly. A retreat with exquisite art and learned minds.'

What had he needed to retreat from? Luc longed to ask, but her courage failed her. 'Why couldn't I go?'

'You don't know?' he asked. 'No women. Nothing female is permitted. Not even hens.'

'Perhaps I could smuggle myself in, in disguise.'

'You? A man? For a start, I wouldn't let you cut off all that beautiful hair.'

They stopped in front of one of the nightclubs near the *Flying Dolphin* jetty. Music pounded out. More her age than his, punters were spilling from the door. Still dancing frenetically, swigging from bottles of water, they were dressed to sweat.

'Here?' asked Luc doubtfully.

'Why not?'

Inside, it was baking-oven hot. Even the walls were sweating. Coloured lights flashed, giant speakers vibrated with the bass, hundreds of bodies were abandoned to the beat. But if Lorenzo felt out of place in his blazer and Gucci loafers, he didn't show it.

At the bar, as he ordered two more whiskies, the barman lip-reading, Luc sneaked a glance at his profile. The straight nose, the lean jawbone, a face almost forbiddingly cold in its classicism. Watching the dancers, they let the noise wash over them. She was grateful for the music, grateful not to have to talk. Talk about what? Banking? Orthodox liturgy? Her chit-chat was more soap opera than opera. Did it matter? Tomorrow, she'd be gone. The day after that, he'd be back in Geneva.

A blond, hair matted into long dreads, touched the sleeve of the blue blazer and smiled beatifically. He whispered something, shrugged, then drifted away. Luc was astounded to hear a laugh. 'It's been years since anyone promised me ecstasy.'

Outside was cool after the fetid air in the club. The waterfront pulsated with music, the squares and alleyways were thronged with people as if it were midday, not midnight. Luc fretted about where to take him next.

He peered into the karaoke bar with disdain. 'Definitely not.'

Luc shuddered, imagining him catching her knocking back slammers and Ella winning the wet T-shirt competition.

They stood outside another bar, where a soccer match was being shown on a giant screen. Scores of people were heckling. 'Orgasmatron.' He read the chalkboard. 'What's that?'

'Some sort of cocktail, I guess,' said Luc.

'Let's try it.'

They pushed their way past the hecklers, all staring at the screen.

He raised an eyebrow. 'Your national game?'

'What's the Swiss national game? Making money?' Luc was getting a hangover just by watching the barman pouring the different spirits into the blender. 'I don't know much about Switzerland.' Apart from the Chalet School books. She was obviously as well read as she was well informed.

'I'm not Swiss, only resident there. My passport's German.' A huge cheer went up as someone scored. He winced. 'Outside?'

Ushering her to the only free table, he asked the waiter to clear the debris and bring a clean ashtray. Two glam English girls with long blonde perms were staring at him. Luc wished she'd at least ironed the T-shirt and had strappy sandals like theirs rather than her espadrilles.

Sipping the drink he frowned. 'What do you think?'

Luc tried to be polite, then gave up. 'It's disgusting.'

'Good. Let's go.'

Where next? As they walked, Luc fretted, blaming herself for the gaudy neon, the souvenir shops full of tourist tat. A paralytic girl was puking in a doorway. Lorenzo's expression was Antarctic. Luc was suddenly fed up. The evening was turning into a disaster. All he wanted was a companion to go sight-seeing with, except the sights he was seeing were obviously not to his liking. Nothing was good enough for him.

At the ouzeri by the marina, she felt as self-conscious as she had that morning, stranded on her island of solitude. It was like trying to amuse a cool, beautiful cat that never once broke into a purr. Why bother to try?

'Nice place.' He glanced round. 'So you live in London, you sketch, you wear large hats. What else? Any secrets?'

Luc wished she could confess to interesting vices, wished she could be a woman of mystery and intrigue. 'None. Have you?'

'Maybe.' He swallowed the ouzo and shuddered. 'So, where are you taking me next?'

'You've seen the town. Back to the villa, I guess.' She felt like Cinderella with midnight approaching. Ella would've chatted and charmed with her usual assurance. Ella wouldn't have felt intimidated and tongue-tied. Ella wouldn't have been boring.

'Why? Of course, you've got an early start, haven't you?'

Luc hesitated.

'A final drink?'

She nodded. 'Where?'

'The place on the quayside. Where I first saw you. Where we should've spoken.'

There was a long line waiting near the waterfront for one of the island's few cabs.

'Oi, mate. Learn to queue,' yelled someone, as Luc slid guiltily across the seat, trying to ignore the disgruntlement. It was the same cab as that afternoon; the driver having recognised Lorenzo and a good tip.

Ten minutes later, she watched the bar owner swipe the

orange rope seats with a tea-towel, before ushering them to sit. She wondered if everyone put themselves out for Lorenzo: Liz with her lists, the taxi driver, the mâitre d', the waiter at the Orgasmatron bar clearing the table.

The moon shimmered on the water like mercury, the yachts and the cruisers tugged on their mooring ropes as if yearning to be out on the calm sea. His flat gold lighter drew attention to the chipped white paint on the rickety tables. Their whisky glasses were scratched.

A small yacht had moored next to the cruiser. Two couples, fattish, fiftyish and tipsy, were settling themselves for a final drink. The *Dance of the Sugar Plum Fairy* poured from their stereo.

'You'd prefer the other place?' He pointed up the quayside to the jetty bar with its candle-lit tables.

'With the well-dressed people bored with life? Is that you?'

He lit a cigarette. 'Why should I be bored?'

'You shouldn't be. No one who can fly thousands of miles for a swim should be. You're not having a mid-life crisis, are you?'

'A very ugly phrase.' He frowned. 'Perhaps you should stop talking in clichés and start using your mind.'

Luc's insides withered. She wondered what she could possibly say next. If only she could talk opera or art or politics or banking. What was the point? She was nothing more than a convenient companion to idle away a few hours with. On the yacht Tchaikovsky had given way to *Carmina Burana*. She felt even more gauche, knowing the fact that she immediately associated the music with adverts would earn her minus cultural Brownie points.

Suddenly she longed for home. Home, home. Not the villa. The evening was proving as much of a disaster as the rest of the holiday. Here she was in the middle of an audition for a part she'd waited for all her life and she was fluffing her lines, before drying up completely. If only someone would call out thank you and put her out of her misery.

'Don't frown. It doesn't suit you.' He'd been watching her. 'Would you like to dance?'

'Sorry?' The *Blue Danube* was filling the air, the quartet on the yacht humming and swaying in time. 'Seriously?'

'Please.' Laughing, he stood up and took her hand, leading her to the quayside. She felt his arm round her waist and mentally counted off one two three, one two three as she tentatively followed his steps. She found her rhythm, lost her self-consciousness and suddenly she was waltzing. The music was becoming louder, the boats and the bar spinning in front of her eyes as he whirled her round the quayside as if it were a ballroom.

Breathless and giddy, she began laughing with utter delight as she turned and turned and turned.

A round of applause broke out when they finally stopped. Luc blushed, realising that people had slowed to watch them. Lorenzo bowed to the four on the boat and thanked them in German.

'What were they saying?' asked Luc.

'That we looked very romantic.'

The bar owner was sweeping up, lights were going off on the yachts. It was two o'clock. Up near the cat's jetty where his helicopter had landed, battered rowing boats seemed almost becalmed in bath-deep water and oozy mud.

'Can we borrow one?' asked Lorenzo.

'No oars. You'd have to paddle.'

Luc went out on to the jetty, standing on the white cross. She gazed up at the sky and gasped in wonder. Thousands of stars punctured the blackness. 'It's so beautiful.' Transfixed, head back, she slowly walked round gazing and gazing and gazing. 'That can't be a satell—'

'Luc.'

His warning came too late. For a split second she was

freefalling, then she was under water, then she surfaced again, coughing and spluttering. Her clothes billowed out around her as she kicked towards the jetty. The water was freezing. 'It's not funny,' she coughed.

'It is.'

Able to touch the bottom, she stood up and waded towards the jetty's stone steps, wiping the water from her eyes.

'Venus from the waves.' He held out his hand to steady her.

'I've lost my shoes.' Water was streaming from her clothes, mortification was running through her. 'I'm not even drunk. Promise.' Her teeth began to chatter.

He pulled a strand of seaweed from her hair. 'I'd better get you back.'

Grit from the stones dug into her bare feet. 'I don't usually do things like this.'

'Like letting enchantment get the better of you? Why not?'

One of the Germans on the yacht was still on deck. Lorenzo called something. Glancing at Luc in disbelief, laughing, he went below and came back with a towel.

'*Danke schön*.' Lorenzo took off his blazer and handed Luc the towel. 'Wear this. It's presumptuous, but I suggest you get out of your clothes.'

'What? Here?'

'Otherwise you'll get a chill.' He turned his back to her, saying something to the German who also turned away.

Luc hesitated, then, covering herself with a towel, pulled off her sopping T-shirt. 'It's like doing the Dance of the Seven Veils.'

'Intriguing.'

'Jacket, please.' When the jacket was safely on, she stepped out of her skirt. Puddles of water were at her feet. Luckily the jacket came well past mid-thigh. She wrung out her knickers and put them back on. 'Done. Thank you.'

He turned round and looked her up and down. 'It suits you. We'd better find a taxi. *Gute nacht*.' He handed the German back the towel. '*Vielen Dank*.'

'*Bitte schön.*' The man called out something.

'What was that?' asked Luc, hobbling rather than walking.

'That I should take better care of you. He's right. Shall I carry you?'

'No. I'm far too heavy.' Why hadn't she gone on a diet before coming away? 'Ow.' She winced as her little toe caught the edge of a stone.

He stopped and crouched down. 'Come on.'

'Where?'

'On me. A piggy-back.'

'You can't.'

'Why not?'

'Because. Because. Because it's silly. It wouldn't suit you. You're too much of a grown-up.'

'Don't be ridiculous. Jump.'

She leaped on his back and grabbed his shoulders. His thick blond hair smelt of citrus. She could feel the muscles in his long, lean back, his hands round her bare legs. His watch strap was cutting into her thigh. 'Please put me down. You don't . . .'

'Sssh.'

Just as she was protesting, he turned right into the jetty bar. 'We can't.' Luc was horrified.

'Why not?'

'I'm not dressed. Stop.' Suddenly they were under the lights, surrounded by people who looked at them in astonishment. 'Put me down,' hissed Luc, tugging down the back of his jacket.

'Good evening again.' He wheeled round, addressing the maître d'. 'Two whiskies and a taxi. We'll sit here. The lady will get cold outside.'

The maître d' of coursed, sir. He showed no reaction to Luc's bundled skirt and T-shirt dripping water on to his floor. The motor-cruiser blonde strolled past, staring at Luc as if she was something that the cat had sicked up. Luc hastily slithered back on to her feet and dashed to the loo. Her hair was a sopping tangle. Her mascara was streaked down her face like black tears.

She cringed with embarrassment. How could she have been so dumb? She should be auditioning for a farce.

She rubbed at the mascara remains with loo paper, practised an expression of lofty nonchalance, then gave up. It was hopeless; even Bette Davis couldn't pull off looking poised after falling off a jetty in front of someone like Lorenzo. At least it had amused him, perhaps she should apply for the job of jester. The thought was profoundly depressing.

She slunk back to the bar, trying to ignore the sniggers. 'I hope your jacket isn't ruined.' The shoulders and lapels were soaking.

He got to his feet and pulled back a chair for her. 'Goats get rained on.'

'Goats?' Cashmere. She should've guessed.

'So, you live in London, you sketch, you wear big hats, you fall into harbours, you can waltz. And you're leaving in a few hours.'

The taxi was disappearing down the hill. Luc felt a pang. Was it turning back into a pumpkin? 'So, you live in Geneva, you fly in helicopters, you wear cashmere. You'd never fall into a harbour in a million years. And you're leaving on Sunday.' The villa gates were like bars to a prison.

'I can't persuade you to stay?'

'What?'

'Change your flight. Leave on Sunday.'

'What?' she gasped, gazing up at him in the darkness. 'Why?'

'So you can look at sea the colour of lapis lazuli. Why else?'

'I can't.' Whatever he meant, she couldn't change her flight ticket.

'Pity.' He sounded indifferent. 'You'll watch the sun rise with me, won't you?'

Luc had a shower, trying not to think of the murk in the

harbour water and panicking about what she could wear next and whether she should bother with make-up. Why had she given Liz back the hairdryer? Why worry? He wasn't remotely interested, he just wanted some company.

Dressed, hair tied back, she found him in the kitchen. He was sitting at the table, smoking. He'd made some coffee. Luc was surprised that he had done something as mundane as use a stove, as well as being practical enough to find some blankets and a torch.

'Are you sure you don't want to go to sleep?' She noticed bruise-like shadows under his eyes.

'I've got all day to sleep. After my swim. Come.'

Down at the beach, he spread out one of the blankets. They sat side by side in silence. Far out in the distance shone lights from fishing boats. The waves sighed contentedly, as if marvelling at the moon and the stars. Staring up, he seemed disinclined to talk. Luc kept quiet, fearing she'd say something silly. If only she weren't the sort of gauche dullard who mistakes shopping channel satellites for shooting stars.

'Are you always so restful to be with?' He lay on his back.

'Are you?'

'No. Ask Madame Royer.'

'Who's she?'

'My assistant.'

'What's she like?'

'Madame Royer? Fierce. Fifty. Efficient. Keeps out intruders.'

Luc imagined a guard dog chained to his office door. 'Intruders?'

'On my time.'

'And she's always Madame Royer?'

'Of course.' He sounded puzzled. 'What else?'

'Not a first name? How formal.'

'I don't *duessen*.'

'*Duessen?*'

'You don't speak German?' He tutted. '*Du* is the familiar. *Duessen*. Like *tu*. You learnt some French, I hope? Good. *Du* is being used too frequently.'

'But not by you?'

'Rarely.'

'So, Count von Retzen, you like people to keep their distance.'

'Yes.'

'Oh.' Luc felt crushed. If she weren't suddenly so tired, she'd start swimming and not stop until she got to Egypt. She needed to break the silence. 'Tim's a brilliant architect, isn't he?'

'He is.'

'I thought you came here to check the plans. Isn't Tim redesigning your house?'

'I came for a swim. I don't need to check the plans.'

'Why? Aren't you going ahead?'

He looked at her. 'The house is almost done.'

'But . . .' Luc frowned, puzzled.

'Tim is a wonderful architect. And a wonderful time-waster. I don't have the time to waste for him to decide whether he wants to supervise the project or not. I've given it to another architect.'

'You can't,' protested Luc. She sensed there was something wrong, almost unethical. 'It's Tim's project. His plans.'

'If he were serious, he would've been more professional. I told him from the start, I was his priority. Over the months it's become clear I wasn't.'

'The client from hell,' said Luc. She was troubled.

'Just a client.' He shrugged. 'I'll sort everything out with him on completion, otherwise there'll be more complications. More time-wasting.' He glanced at her. 'I'd rather you didn't mention any of this to Tim. Or to Liz.'

'I won't,' said Luc, not wanting to get involved.

She wrapped the second blanket round her shoulders. Over in the east the blackness was fading to charcoal.

'May I?' He sat up. Pulling the other half of the blanket round himself, he edged closer, so they were sitting shoulder to shoulder, thigh to thigh. Despite their closeness, Luc felt as if he'd built an impregnable wall around himself, patrolled by a snarling Madame Royer.

The silence grew louder, the minutes ticked away. Although her eyes were fixed on the eastern sky, she was conscious of nothing but him. Almost aching with desire, she reminded herself that she was nothing but a convenient companion to idle away some time with.

He lit another cigarette. 'Where shall we meet?'

It took a few seconds for his words to register, he sounded so off-hand. 'Meet?'

'Geneva? London? I need to see my tailor. Halfway? Brussels has good food, but little else. Amsterdam? Dull food.'

Luc was pole-axed. 'You are joking, aren't you?'

'No.' He smiled. 'I must see someone who could've drowned because of the stars.'

He couldn't mean it. 'Another whim?' She was suddenly very fed up.

'Maybe. Madrid? Oslo?'

'Paris?' snapped Luc.

'Not Paris.' He shook his head. 'Definitely not Paris.'

'Why not?' She noticed him scowl. 'Oh, that's trespassing. Fine.' She sighed. 'Listen, if you've finished your fantasy tour, I want to go back to the villa.' She began lumbering to her feet with all the grace of an arthritic camel.

'Stay. Please.' He finally looked at her. 'I want to see you again.'

'You do? Truly?'

'Truly.'

'When?' Luc sank down.

'As soon as I can. I warn you I'm busy. Can you wait? Or will you forget me?'

His touch on her cheek was so light she wondered if she were imagining it. The elation surging through her made her breathless. 'No, I won't forget.'

'Good.' He wound a lock of her hair round his fingers and pulled her to him.

The sun had appeared above the horizon, the sea was pale gold. Luc lay back on the blanket studying him. She felt the peace of utter contentment. He stretched out, holding her snug to him. 'Madame Royer is going to be busy sorting out appointments with my tailor in London.'

'Is she?' Luc smiled. She picked up his gold lighter and turned it one way and then the other so it caught the rays of the sun.

'Very busy.'

'Arranging helicopters for Count von Retzen?'

He laughed. 'No. Ordinary plane tickets. Anyway, Lucasta, to you I'm Lorenzo.'

'*Il Magnifico.*' Luc snuggled closer to him. Even the waves seemed to be murmuring 'Lorenzo, Lorenzo, Lorenzo . . .'

'Kiss of life,' he whispered, bringing her back to consciousness. How had she drifted off to sleep? She gazed into the blue depths of his eyes. 'You can't be real.'

'It's almost seven. Time to go back, if you must go back today.'

'I must.'

They folded up the blankets and walked across the sand to the path which led back to the villa. He stopped near the garden wall door and brought his mobile out of his jacket pocket. Luc was about to protest that he shouldn't be so crass as to bring a phone to the beach, when he asked for her number. He stored it in the memory. 'I'll call you.'

'Promise?'

Nodding, he gazed down at her as if storing her face in his memory. 'Promise. Have a good trip back.'

'Aren't you . . .?' It took time for her to realise that he was saying goodbye, that he wanted her to go back to the villa alone. 'I get it. No intruders, no gossip?'

'I'd prefer discretion.' He kissed her hand. 'I hope to see you again very soon.'

'Have a good swim.' Allowing herself one final look at him, she stood on tiptoe and kissed his cheek, rough with blond stubble.

Halfway across the terrace, Luc realised that Alex was sitting at the table. He was reading the poetry anthology, a mug of coffee at his elbow. As she was wondering if there was any way to avoid him, he squinted up at her. 'Morning. You're up early. Saying a final goodbye to the beach?'

'Um.' She prayed she hadn't said a final goodbye to Lorenzo.

'Listen, Luc. About last night. Marina was off her face . . .'

'When? Oh, that. Doesn't matter.' It seemed so long ago, so trivial. She'd better scarper before Lorenzo arrived, before Alex made the connection.

'She'd be very contrite, if she were awake.' He sighed. 'Which won't be until about midday. She spent most of the night throwing up.'

'Oh dear.' Luc scanned the peach-tree wall.

'Anything wrong?'

'No, of course not.'

'Tim set me right about you last night when we got back. I didn't realise . . .' He broke off. 'Another early riser.' Alex raised an eyebrow. 'What's he doing with those blankets? He can't have slept on the beach. There's no room service. Oh.' He stared at her. 'Oh. I get it. Tut tut, Lucasta. Doing your bit for European integration, aren't you? Frenchman one day. German-Italian the next.' Luc squirmed. 'You're so predictable. A very handsome, very rich guy. Very right up your leafy avenue.'

Chapter Seven

'Luke? That's a fella's name. Can I have my chair back?'

'Sorry.' Luc told herself to stop apologising, she was getting as bad as Tim. Mandy made her feel nervous. She'd already said sorry for drinking out of Mandy's mug and sorry for using Mandy's coat hanger.

Mandy had swept into the office at ten to ten, complaining about her train being delayed.

'Wrong sort of snow?' asked Shirl. Outside it was blazing sunshine. 'Leaves on the line?'

'Cheeky.' Mandy sniffed. 'So, come on, ask me. Ask how was your holiday, Mandy? How was your week of sun, sangria and shagging while I was stuck in this dump?'

Shirl bit into her iced bun. 'How many waiters?'

'One. And he wasn't no waiter. Not really. Training to be a bull-fighter.'

'Bull something else more like.' Shirl sniffed and waved the bun in Luc's direction. 'Luc's been away. Greece.'

Mandy gave Luc a sharp once-over. 'Weather wasn't up to much then.' Luc's skin had returned to its usual paper white. 'You should of seen the hotel. Beautiful pool. Satellite telly in every room.'

While Mandy showed Shirl some photos of Pablo the bull-fighter, Luc tried to concentrate on her computer screen. If she lost herself in the work, the time would go faster. Unable to resist, she glanced at her watch. Three minutes to ten.

Hornbeam and Harold was a shipping company, with offices in a back street near Warren Street Tube. Luc had started temping there a week before and had wanted to bolt as soon as she'd walked through the door. The work was scream-makingly dull. Filing, copy-typing, more filing, photocopying, unjamming the photocopier and making coffee for Mr Harold. Shirl called him Mr Haytch. Mr Haytch called Luc the temp. 'Shirl, give this to the temp.' 'What'syourname, the temp, any chance of a cup of wet?'

Carole, the temp controller at the Agency, had said Luc might be offered the chance of being a courier. The last girl had taken some documents to New York. Luc suspected this was a fib. The closest she'd ever get to a plane was keying in the flight number on an invoice.

Luc stuck it out. The Agency said there wasn't much work about. After Greece, her bank balance was in a worse state than usual. She wished she could find a nice permanent job with paid holidays.

She'd rubbed along with Shirl well enough the previous week. Shirl was three stone overweight and devoured Lincoln Creams and Barbara Cartlands. Despite her kindness to the potted plants on the filing cabinets, her husband had run off with her best friend.

Mandy's arrival had changed the atmosphere in the office. By wasting no time in reclaiming her territory, she'd put Luc in her place. She was an attractive, vibrant twenty-two-year-old, so trendy she looked as if she were going clubbing rather than to work. Luc wondered why Mandy was stuck in a dull office like this. Luc then wondered why Luc was stuck in a dull office like this.

A telephone rang. 'He never,' guffawed Shirl. 'Hang on.'

'The temp can get it,' hissed Mandy. 'Answer that, can you?'

'Hornbeam and Harold. Can I help you?' Disconcerted by Mandy's mutter of 'Dead posh, ain't she?', Luc missed what the caller was saying and asked him to repeat it. She turned to Mandy. 'What's your extension?'

'Who is it?'

Luc winced. 'Sorry.'

Mandy tssked. Luc looked at her watch. Seven minutes past ten.

The morning dragged on. Mr Harold appeared. 'Hello, Mandy. Nice break?'

'Lovely, Mr Haytch.'

'Ready, willing and able to take down my,' he paused, 'dictation?'

'Sauce.' Mandy giggled. 'I'll do you for sexual harassment.'

'Anytime, darlin'. What'syourname?' He clicked his fingers. 'Lynn, Louise . . .'

'Luc.'

'Luc. Cup of wet, please. Three sugars. Want one, Mandy?'

'Ta. Two sugars.' Mandy held out her mug. 'Come on, Mr Haytch. You're supposed to say I'm sweet enough.'

As the kettle boiled, Luc stared out of the grimy window on to the litter-strewn courtyard where Mr H parked his Daimler. Because of the ox-blood brick buildings towering round it, the area was in permanent shade. The window-sill was limed with pigeon droppings. She peered up. Far, far above, the tiny patch of sky was brilliant blue. Almost the blue of lapis lazuli. Three minutes past eleven.

The clock hands edged so slowly towards her lunchbreak, Luc wondered if time had stopped. Asphyxiated by exhaust fumes, she mooched along Tottenham Court Road. It suddenly seemed the most uninspiring place in the universe. The bright sunlight illuminated the grumpiness of the office workers' faces. How much had she earned that morning?

There was a long queue in the sandwich bar. As Luc pulled out her purse, a dry-cleaning ticket dropped out. She picked it off the grimy floor. The cheese was curling up to die in the display counter. She watched a sniffing assistant make up an egg mayonnaise sandwich. His hairy hands took a greasy £5 note, then counted out the change.

'Next.' He sniffed at Luc. 'You wantta?'

'Nothing.'

Outside, the temperature had hit 88 degrees. Inside the office, the afternoon was crawling. Every minute lasted an hour, as if the heat had drained time itself of energy. Shirl crunched on Lincoln Creams while arranging a shipment to Auckland, and a giggling Mandy got chatted up by someone on the line at the Southampton office.

Updating the data-base, keying in address after address, Luc tried to work out how much she was earning each second.

The sunshine and blue skies begged for cooling swims in white-sanded coves and long, lazy lunches *al fresco*. Not this. Not this incarceration in an airless, dark gaol where the only visible blue was the letters on the screen.

Was *Les Voiles Blanches* scudding across an azure sea under full sail? Or being admired in some pretty harbour, where the stonework resembled lace? Why hadn't she just accepted Henri's offer? Said yes, I'll do it, I'll spend the summer sailing round the Mediterranean.

Ella had said yes. Ella had seized the opportunity. Ella would never have told herself better safe than sorry, that mantra of the spineless and the pathetic. The blue letters on Luc's screen began to blur.

If she'd sailed into the moonlight that night, she'd never have met Lorenzo and wasted the past ten days obsessing about a man with eyes the colour of lapis lazuli who lived hundreds of miles away. A very good-looking, very rich, very successful man, who was so far out of her league he breathed different air.

He'd never call. She'd just been someone to idle away a few

empty hours with. How many times had she relived their time together, from that moment she'd seen him getting out of the helicopter to those last seconds out on the terrace in the early morning light? Going to the chapel, waltzing on the quayside, on the beach . . .

He'd been with her as she went to sleep and when she'd woken up. Like the waves, a voice inside her had been constantly whispering 'Lorenzo, Lorenzo, Lorenzo'. Even as her euphoria had gradually seeped away.

That Saturday morning she'd been floating on joy. The taxi ride down to the jetty, the hours on the *Flying Dolphin*, the journey across Athens had been a blur. She'd seen nothing but him, heard nothing but what he'd said to her, smelt his aftershave. In her daze of ecstasy, she had forgotten that Ella's grass was still in her skirt pocket until she was through Customs at Heathrow.

Throughout the last week she'd jumped every time the phone rang. Each time before she answered it, she prayed it would be him. When it wasn't, she'd sounded so disappointed that everyone calling had asked her what was wrong. Since Wednesday she panicked countless times that he'd keyed the wrong number into his mobile's memory. On Thursday, she'd called home from Hornbeam and Harold to check the answering-machine was working. On Friday night, having got no calls all day, she'd phoned the engineer to test her line.

She'd asked herself a million times why she hadn't had the presence of mind to get his number.

Her yearning had grown worse over the weekend, matched by her deepening despair. At home, at a loose end, with too much time to brood, she dragged herself round, picking up books and magazines only to throw them aside unread. She'd planned to bake a birthday cake for Quentin the Zit, had got the ingredients out of the cupboard, only to abandon the whole thing after weighing out the flour. It was still on the scales in the kitchen. She'd thought Quentin's party would be a distraction, but she'd left early.

For most of Sunday she'd slumped on the sofa, staring at the phone, willing it to ring. Outside it was a beautiful day, but she'd chosen to stay indoors with the blinds half shut and only her apathy for company. If Ella had been there, Ella would have got her organised, got her out of the house with a picnic or a trip to the coast or a jokey game of tennis with their old racquets and bald balls. She'd even forgotten that the Wimbledon men's final was on until it was over. She had actually imagined she was fond of the routine at Hornbeam and Harold, which at least provided her with a few hours of relief from pining.

'Louise, Lou.' Mr H popped his head around the door.

'Luc.' Her voice sounded thick, muffled.

'Cup of wet? Ta.'

Sniffing, Luc got up. She had played it safe. And she was so sorry.

Luc sat at her desk until five thirty-two. The extra two minutes were a penance for the sudden guilt she felt about clock watch-ing. 'See you in the morning.'

' 'Bye, love,' called Shirl, the Lincoln Creams packet almost empty.

'Far to go?' asked Mandy.

'Chelsea.'

'Chelsea. That's nice, intit, Shirl? Posh.' Mandy gave Luc a cold, satisfied smile. 'Tube's on the blink. Was earlier, leastways.'

Mandy was right. There were notices at Warren Street station warning of severe delays on all lines due to a generator failure. Eyes searching for a guard amongst the throng of sweltering, furious commuters, Luc got whacked by a backpacker's rucksack. Turning round to apologise, he trod on her foot.

'Normal service will resume in approximately one hour,' said a voice over the tannoy. 'We apologise . . .' The voice, which sounded smug rather than contrite, was drowned by collective commuter groans.

Sticky, thirsty and fed up, Luc stomped towards Gower Street, hoping to catch a bus. The three lanes of fume-belching traffic were at a standstill. When a packed bus eventually arrived, she was queue-barged. The conductor refused to allow her on.

More than an hour later, Luc got back to the Mews. The twenty houses were all different shades of pastel. Flowers tumbled from window-boxes, vines covered walls, bay trees stood sentry on the cobblestones outside the front doors. The residents got used to captivated tourists lingering by the entrance. It was so pretty, so tranquil and so close to Harrods.

Ella called number seven the Doll's House because it was such a great place to play with. Going inside, Luc slung down her bag and went up to the first-floor kitchen, where she downed two glasses of water straight off. The rays of sunlight through the windows showed up all the grime, almost ordering her to do some cleaning. The horrible stench from the bin told her she was an idle slut too lazy to take the rubbish out. She humped the sack down the stairs.

Outside, seventy-something Dolly Tilling who lived opposite was watering her window-boxes. Wearing a floral patterned silk frock, chiffon sleeves covering up her aged arms, she was dressed for a night out.

'Ella back yet?'

Shielding her eyes from the sun, Luc peered across. 'Not yet.'

'Good for her. What an opportunity.'

'Isn't it?' agreed Luc, a shade too heartily.

'You should've joined her. You don't want to be stuck in a stuffy office at your age. Get out and see the world.'

Luc's smile was forced. 'Are you going away?'

'September. Walking.' She lifted up her skirt and pointed to a pair of sturdy walking boots. 'New today. Got to break them in. Patagonia isn't the park.'

Feeling even more fed up, Luc abandoned her plans to clean the kitchen and poured herself a whisky. She went up three flights of stairs and opened the door on to the roof terrace.

Closing her eyes, she sipped slowly, feeling a softer sun's warmth on her face. She heard the two American bankers call good evening to Dolly Tilling. Everyone living in the Mews was politely friendly to their neighbours rather than popping-in-and-out matey.

Luc took another sip, soothed by the splash of water in the tiny fountain. Bees droned lazily round the honeysuckle that Janie had planted on the terrace years before. Neglectful of most things, Ella tended it fanatically. The whisky was peaty. Luc had never really drunk it until that last night in Greece and had spent her remaining few drachma on a bottle of duty-free at Athens airport.

She told herself that Dolly Tilling hadn't meant to rub her nose in it, but Luc didn't need another galling reminder that Ella had seized that chance to see the world while she herself was stuck in a stuffy office. Where was *Les Voiles Blanches* now? Another idyllic Greek island? Portofino? St Tropez? Madame probably hadn't turned up, so the regime would be relaxed, leaving Ella plenty of time to learn to sail, to navigate, to be blissfully happy with Yannick as they explored new places together.

Luc slumped back in her chair. It was just her luck that Henri had fallen for her, just as she had fallen for a man who lived hundreds of miles away, who she'd never see again.

For the past week she'd been making excuses for Lorenzo; pressure of work, his hectic schedule. Even, with straw-clutching desperation, the time difference. As if he were in the Galapagos rather than Geneva.

What if he'd called? What on earth would she have to say to him? She was bound to let slip how she'd been checking his horoscope and the temperature in Geneva – Mars had entered his sign and it was a constant 21 degrees. And how she'd been reading the foreign news in the paper looking out for stories about Switzerland. And, worst of all, how she'd bought the *Financial Times* for the first time in her life because it carried a special report on Swiss banking.

How would someone as cool and polished as marble react to such confessions of juvenile idiocy? With his impeccable manners, he'd even hang up politely.

She had to accept it. She would never see Lorenzo again.

Pouring the whisky into the rain gulley, Luc jumped to her feet and went downstairs to her room. She yanked the sheets off her bed, gathered up her dirty washing and threw out the tickets for the plane and the *Flying Dolphin* that had been cluttering up her bedside table.

Somehow, Luc got through the week. On Friday, she was pleased to see thunder in Geneva and money matters needing urgent attention. She hoped Lorenzo's house would be struck by lightning and he would go bankrupt and end up in a debtors' prison.

The office was deserted, Mandy and Shirl were at the pub. Shirl was comforting Mandy about not hearing from Pablo the Bull-fighter the Bull-shitter. Mandy had been far from pleased when Luc pointed out that holiday romances were usually as long-lasting as a suntan.

'Don't our Luc sound bitter, Shirl? Voice of experience?'

Luc got out her cheque-book. After 'Pay' she wrote 'Ella Parr'. She filled in the cheque, then scribbled a note to an obscure, very smart bank in the City asking for it to be paid into Ella's account – a copper-bottomed account which matched the copperplate print on the bank's letterheads.

Where was *Les Voiles Blanches*? Speeding across a sea the colour of lapis lazuli, or being admired in a picturesque harbour where the stonework was like lace?

Luc reflected bitterly that she could be learning to navigate, reading tide tables and charts rather than the Tube map and the *A to Z*. She could be going ashore to get provisions from a market or a tiny bakery, rather than trailing round a supermarket pushing a trolley. It could have been her scrubbing the wooden deck in the sunshine, rather than mopping the lino in the kitchen.

She stared at the pile of paper on her desk. Another afternoon updating the data-base. How many hours did she have to work before she stopped putting money into Ella's bank account and started earning for herself?

Suddenly Luc remembered Ella handing over her credit card at Mathi airport. That tiny bit of plastic emphasised the gulf between them. When was the last time Ella had been forced to get up in the morning to do a job she hated? She'd never had to, would never have to. With that fake platinum in her fist, she could stick two fingers up to anyone.

'Nothing?' squawked Liz down the phone the following Monday morning. 'Not a word?'

'No,' said Luc, glancing anxiously at the clock. Ten past eight.

'Timmy, Luc hasn't heard from her. Luc, sorry. This is all I need. I've told Tim not to worry. Should we call the police? How do you get hold of Interpol?'

Luc heard Tim asking 'Camomile, Lizzy?' She was already behind and still had to have a shower. 'I'm sure there's nothing to worry about. Ella's disappeared before now.'

'That's just what I've been saying to Tim. She vanished for months in India. Though quite honestly I don't know why she bothered. All she did was hang around with other backpackers, so much for travel broadening . . .'

Luc was almost dancing a jig in her impatience to hang up. 'I'm sorry, I've really got to go, I'll call you this evening.'

'I knew those Frenchmen were dubious. Yachts are often fronts for some very shady operators. God knows what Ella's got herself mixed up in. The Mafia, money-laundering, gun-running, drugs. Though that would hardly be a surprise . . .'

'Liz, I'll call you later. I must go. 'Bye.' Cursing herself for going out the night before, instead of having her usual getting-ready-for-the-working-week quiet Sunday evening, Luc shoved on the iron and dived into the shower.

Three minutes later as she was frantically ironing, towel falling off her, the phone rang again. Expecting it to be Liz, she ignored it, letting the machine pick up. Instead it was the Agency.

'Carole?'

'Luc. I've caught you. Good. Listen, I've just had Hornbeam and Harold on. They've cancelled the booking.'

'Oh. Why?' As much as she'd loathed her fortnight in the cramped office, she still had an irrational sense of being rejected.

'You've finished the job, that's why. Next time, don't be so efficient. You're squeezing my margins . . . Cheeky, enough of that you . . . Still there, Luc?'

'You've got something else?' Luc was anxious. She couldn't afford a day's idleness.

'Yep. Got a pen? You can do shorthand, can't you?'

Luc quailed. 'It's a bit rusty . . .'

'They said just in case. Right. It's the usual. Perm's got a sickie. Julian Group. Property. Report to Juliet Beak. New client, so do your best.'

Luc read back the address, then turned the already chaotic sitting room upside down looking for her *A to Z*, before remembering it was amongst the pile of cookbooks in the kitchen. Green Park seemed the closest Tube. Carole had warned her to get a move on. She still had her shirt to iron and her make-up to put on and why hadn't she polished her shoes?

'Shit.' A button fell off as she fumbled to do up her shirt. Her left eye was smarting after she stabbed it with her mascara wand. Vowing to keep her jacket done up, she fastened her shirt with a safety pin. Where were her keys?

'Shit.' After ten minutes' frantic searching, she found them in her bag hidden under the battered *A to Z*. It was five to nine when she left the house and three minutes past when she let herself back in, panicking she'd left the iron on.

*

'The Agency said you'd be here at nine.' Juliet Beak smiled glacially. In her late forties, she was immaculately groomed. 'I did explain we had a meeting at ten.'

'The Tube . . .' hedged Luc, trying not to pant. Mrs Beak's coolness made her feel hotter. The offices were closer to Hyde than Green Park and she'd had to sprint along the streets.

'Well, this is your desk. You're familiar with the switchboard? And the computer?'

'Which package?' Luc tried to sound efficient. Having caught a whiff of Mrs Beak's Diorella, she realised she'd forgotten to put on any anti-perspirant. Sweat seemed to be gushing from her armpits.

'Package?' Mrs Beak raised a plucked eyebrow so it was almost level with her huge helmet of salt-and-pepper hair.

'Computer package.'

'You people know about that sort of thing, don't you? There's bound to be a manual somewhere.' Mrs Beak waved in the direction of the desk, then spun round on crocodile heels. 'I'm on extension 555.'

Luc watched the retreating Valentino suit, then tried to take stock. On the first floor of a converted Georgian house, the Julian Group's offices would get the Liz-approved stamp for order and restraint. Cream carpet ran throughout. Luc's desk in the reception area was pale blond wood opposite a low cream sofa. It was bare apart from the computer and a vase of tulips.

The phone rang, unnaturally loud in the cloistered hush. She stared at it before realising it was her job to answer. 'Hornbeam . . . The Julian Group. Good mor . . .'

Juliet Beak tutted. 'Internal call, Miss James. Let's not waste any more time. When Casey arrives, tell him to come through.' She hung up.

Casey? Luc sat at the desk and opened the drawers, searching for clues to get her bearings. Temping was like constantly being the new girl at school; if you were lucky, you met a kindly fellow pupil who offered you some coffee, showed you where the loo was and explained procedure. Just as you found your way round, got to put faces to names and learned that only prefects are allowed to use the front stairs, it was time to move on.

The drawers were the tidiest Luc had ever seen, with sharpened pencils lined up in rows. Whoever she was replacing obviously fitted into the immaculate surroundings.

'Having a snoop?'

Startled, Luc almost fell off her chair. 'Mr Casey?'

'Just Casey.' He was so short and fat that he was almost spherical. His skin was the colour and texture of lard, his brown eyes like currants in an uncooked bun. 'You are?'

'Luc James. The temp.' The trousers of his pin-striped suit almost came up to his chest. He couldn't have been much older than her, but weight added years to him.

'Mrs Beak in yet?'

'Yes. She wants to see you.'

He threw a pile of mail on to Luc's desk. 'Do the usual.' He smiled and began to waddle away.

'The usual?'

'Open and sort. The usual.'

As Luc was opening the mail, Juliet Beak buzzed her, asking if a fax had come through. 'Fax?'

'Facsimile.' Mrs Beak lengthened every Home Counties vowel as if they were on a rack.

Luc peered around. 'Is there a machine?'

'Behind you.' Luc swivelled round and saw a long, low unit. 'Behind you,' repeated Mrs Beak.

Imagining her in a pantomime audience, Luc suppressed a giggle. There were no handles. 'I can't open it.'

'Bottom, Miss James.' A heavy sigh. 'From the bottom.'

Luc tugged and yanked. Nothing. It finally yielded to a gentle press, and the sound of Mrs Beak's manicured nails beating a tom-tom. 'Open Sesame.'

'I beg your pardon?'

'No fax, I'm afraid,' said Luc. On the shelves was the fax

machine, a printer, stationery and files, all so organised they seemed to be on an inspection parade.

Shortly afterwards Mrs Beak swept out, a waddling Casey in her wake. He was mopping his forehead with a red silk handkerchief and carrying her Louis Vuitton briefcase.

Luc switched on the computer. Casey had given her the drafts of some letters to type. 'Oh no.' The cursor was flashing at 'Password'. She tried Julian, JulianG, Juliet, Casey, Hello and Fuckit, which she quickly deleted.

'Typical.' She got up. What was she supposed to do now? The Odd Couple weren't due back until lunchtime. She felt completely cut off from the world. There were no windows in the reception area, no sound from the street outside or from the rest of the building.

She took out a file, hoping her predecessor had left some clue. It was full of bumf about a development in Bracknell. Luc read through it, gleaning nothing, then through a second, yawning loudly. After a third, something about Basingstoke, she paced up and down the office, which was beginning to resemble a padded cell for affluent lunatics.

Luc was trying out the sofa, lying down, stretching out, re-arranging the cushions and wishing she had her book, when the telephone rang for the first time. Despite sprinting across to it, she picked it up too late and had to make herself heard over the answering-machine's recorded message, bleeps and feedback.

'Miss James? For goodness sake . . .' Mrs Beak's whispered voice sounded a mite pained.

'Sorry.' Luc managed to switch off the machine. No, the fax hadn't arrived. No other messages. Would Mrs Beak know the computer password? Another pained sigh was followed by a mutter of 'Deal with this, Casey, I don't know what the girl is talking about.'

'Mario,' announced Casey.

'As in Supermario?' asked Luc.

'Who's Supermario?'

'The Gameboy plumber.'

'You what? No. Mario as in Mario Lanza.'

'Who's Mario Lanza?'

'The singer.'

'Oh.' Luc winced as she caught another 'For goodness sake' in the background. Whoever Mario was, it worked. The screen came to life and Luc got on with trying to decipher Casey's doctor's prescription handwriting.

'Lunch? Lunch?' Lines appeared between Mrs Beak's brows as if she were suffering a headache to be bravely borne. 'So be it.'

'I'll be back at two?' Luc wondered why Mrs Beak was so taken aback. She was planning to have a sandwich, not indulge in some light cannibalism.

'Very well.'

Out in the street, Luc felt as if she'd escaped from a Trappist convent, if such places existed. After the air-conditioned, cell-like seclusion of the office, Mayfair suddenly had all the colour and vibrancy of Rio during the carnival. She found herself in Shepherd's Market where crowds were gathered outside pubs, basking in the sunshine. On the spur of the moment, she dived into one, ordered half a lager and stood at the bar enjoying the blare from the juke-box.

Two o'clock came round too fast. Luc sensed that her presence in the office was an irritant to Mrs Beak, as if she personified an upset to her normally smooth routine.

'Would you like me to do anything?'

'Do?' Mrs Beak peered over her half-moon spectacles. She was sitting at another pale wood desk studying a report, a bottle of Evian and a tumbler at her elbow. There was an ugly modern painting on the wall behind her, all khaki and orange splotches.

'I've finished Mr Casey's letters . . .'

'Miss James, I'll let you know. I'll thank you to close the door on your way out.'

Luc went back to her desk and counted the petals on the tulips. 'He loves me, he loves me not.' Becoming even more fed up when it turned out he loved her not, she began recounting.

At the end of the afternoon, which had been enlivened by a rebuke that all typing was to be done in bold, Luc was horrified to be told that she was expected at eight-thirty the following morning. 'Is there a problem, Miss James?'

'No,' said Luc faintly. 'Eight-thirty.'

She decided to walk home, cutting across Hyde Park. Revelling in the early evening sunshine and green open space, she felt like a convalescent allowed out after being cooped up in a nursing home. The path along the Serpentine was thronged with joggers and bladers and Arab families.

A toy yacht was being floated into the water. It reminded Luc that she'd promised to call Liz. She sighed, anticipating what Liz would say and hating it. She didn't need another lecture about Ella being irresponsible and feckless. She didn't need another reminder that Ella was sailing round the Mediterranean, while her own treat for the day was a sight of the murky Serpentine. Above all, she didn't need to be told that Ella had more money than sense, when she was heartily sick of being skint and sensible.

It would soon be three weeks since Ella had slung her stuff into her backpack, leaving half her clothes for Luc to bring back. Luc had brought them back, washed them and dried them, folding them up neatly and leaving them in Ella's room. She'd stared at the pile of laundry, wondering if Ella would have done the same for her. Knowing the answer, Luc had felt a hideous black resentment. For more than a fortnight, she had looked after Ella's house, tended Ella's honeysuckle and paid Ella's rent.

Luc was untroubled that Ella hadn't been in touch. She knew

Ella was fine. She didn't want or need to know that Ella was having the most brilliant time on *Les Voiles Blanches* with Yannick, while she herself was having one of the most miserable times of her life, crying over someone who'd deleted her from his memory.

If Ella were in trouble, Luc would hear from her. Ella would call when she wanted something, like she'd called Tim and Liz from Athens. 'I'm family,' Ella had announced on Zia Marina. But Ella's ideas about family seemed to be based on *The Godfather* rather than the *Brady Bunch*.

Why had Ella bothered with her? They'd only got talking at school one morning because Ella wanted to borrow Luc's prep. Ella had quickly scribbled a copy of a Latin exercise that Luc had spent a painstaking hour on. Sister Barnabas had been suspicious about the similarity, hinting that Luc should do her own work. Grade A Ella, of course, would never cheat.

Lorenzo had needed a companion to idle away a few hours with; had Ella just needed a partner in crime? Someone for all those trips to the pub, those cigarettes behind the pavilion, those joints up in one of the music rooms. Not finding anyone else as acquiescent, she'd settled on Lukewarm. Looking back, it hadn't been Ella who kept their friendship going after they'd left school. Ella had rarely called, never suggested a meeting. While Luc was at secretarial college for a year, had Ella put herself out to come to Oxford even once? She'd always expected Luc to come to Cambridge and to fit in with all the new people she was meeting at university.

Ella had let her student friends be so patronising and dismissive about seccy coll as they called it. Had Ella ever stuck up for her, put them right and explained that Luc could also be doing a degree but because of family circumstances and mix-ups over money, she was learning shorthand? No.

Lukewarm. Is that why Ella had been drawn to her? Had Ella recognised someone who'd never steal her limelight, but was acceptable enough to be invited on to yachts? The same acquiescent, lukewarm Luc who'd let Ella smuggle grass, hitch and almost get them killed.

Why had Ella suggested she move in? Because it was useful to have a house and honeysuckle sitter from whom she could borrow Tampax and tights? Ella didn't need the rent. For company? Next time, Ella could get a Border terrier.

'I missed her. I was back later than usual.'

'But where is she?' demanded Liz.

'Corfu, I think. The line was bad.'

'And what did she say?'

'Nothing much. Wish you were here.'

'Wished I was there?' Liz sounded puzzled.

'No. Me.' Luc was apologetic. 'Wished *I* was there.'

'Yes, well she'd hardly want me around, would she?' said Liz tartly. 'So she's alive. Not in prison, not kidnapped by white slavers, not down with some horrible disease?'

'Doesn't sound like it.'

Liz sighed. 'I'll tell Tim. It's so typically selfish of Ella to cause all this worry and fuss . . . Tim, Ella's called Luc. She's in Corfu. She's fine. The asparagus kettle? Where it always is . . . Luc, can you come to supper on Friday?'

'Friday? Yes. I'd love to. Thanks.'

'Very casual. Fling some pasta in a pan. Luc?' There was a pause. 'No, it can wait. Eightish?'

Luc hung up. Liz's very casual meant wild flowers and the heavy white Tuscan plates. The pasta would probably be Tim's home-made pappardelle.

Corfu. The line had been crackly and Ella sounded as if she were under water. The message was short. 'Hi, Luc. Sorry I've not touched base before. Living in interesting times. Wish you were here. Call you later.'

Hearing the message echoing around the sitting room had shocked Luc. Over the past fortnight, her mind had acted like a distorting mirror at a funfair, distorting Ella so her selfishness and egotism had grown to monstrous proportions, while her good qualities had shrunk. Until she heard Ella's voice, Luc hadn't realised how much she'd demonised her, how strongly she'd resented her, almost to the point of loathing.

Going into the Julian Group office the following morning, Luc armed herself with a book, a paper and her address book. She could while away a few hours reading and writing some letters.

Mrs Beak was already at her desk, the horrible painting contrasting vilely with her lilac suit. 'Casey and I will be in conference from eight forty-five. No calls, please.'

The tulips matched Luc's spirits. Wilting. As soon as she'd walked into the office, she'd felt herself becoming deadened by the hush and order. Hornbeam and Harold at least had some vitality about it. The phones ringing, couriers coming and going, Mandy's incessant chat. The immaculate Mrs Beak wouldn't be caught dunking Lincoln Creams into a Garfield mug of instant.

Despite reading through the files, all Luc had been able to grasp in the haziest possible way was that the Odd Couple bought up plots of land, got planning permission for development and sold them on. She told herself to pay more attention. Perhaps they needed an architect, Tim for example. There might be a juicy corruption scandal hidden among the pages.

She resisted the temptation to get out her novel. Carole at the Agency said that she should make temping work for her. Be (shudder) proactive. Network. Once, at a party, a jowly stockbroker had given her his card, saying she must pick up all sorts of intriguing gen. Like what? Whispers of mergers, takeovers, new products. Sort of stuff to affect the share price.

Luc had said she was usually too preoccupied with finding the photocopier, unjamming the photocopier and replacing the fax paper to worry about the stock-market. And even if she heard a whisper, so what? Ella was the one with the share portfolio. Ella played the markets.

'Morning.' Casey waddled in, sweat glistening on his forehead.

'Morning. Anything you'd like me to do?' She'd be delighted to make a cup of wet.

He smiled vaguely, making his eyes disappear into his fat cheeks. 'Not at the moment. Conference. No calls.'

Luc blew on the tulips, scattering a few petals, then turned to her paper. Her horoscope said it would be a good day for communications. True. The gas bill was lower than expected. She refused to read Aquarius. Or the temperature in Geneva. In Corfu, it had been 31 degrees of sunshine.

'Shit.' In her haste to hide her novel, Luc overturned the vase. It landed on the cream carpet with a thud and rolled towards the crocodile heels. Water cascaded over her desk and on to the floor.

'Sorry.' Cringing, she hastily wiped the sopping file cover with her sleeve.

Mrs Beak raised an eyebrow, but made no attempt to pick up the vase or the scattered tulips lying at her feet like a tribute to a Roman emperor. 'I believe you'll find cloths in the ground-floor cupboard.'

'I don't think the carpet will mark,' pleaded Luc.

Yet again Mrs Beak had her headache-bravely-borne look. 'When you've dealt with this, kindly come through. You do shorthand?'

After mopping up, Luc went through. It was almost midday and she'd done nothing all morning except answer a few calls, book a table for lunch and read three chapters.

Allowed to go at four-thirty, after a victory over Mrs Beak about the spelling of legitimate, but defeat on the use of a comma rather than a semi-colon, Luc arrived home. She immediately called the Agency to demand how long the assignment would last.

'At least a week,' said Carole.

'What?' Luc was horrified.

'Problem?' Anticipating hassle, Carole sounded guarded.

'It's so boring. I'm going mad. Isn't there anything else?'

'In a word, no.'

'There must be. It's summer. Thousands of people are away . . .'

'Luc, can I remind you that you're getting bored at top rates.' Carole was sharp. 'They're a new client, so don't let me down.'

'The Julian Group consists of two people doing very little at a smart address. You won't be getting much business out of them.'

'That's my concern. OK?' Carole sounded sharper. 'So, will you be in tomorrow or not? Tell me now and I'll get someone else.'

Luc sighed heavily. 'Have I got a choice?'

'If you want the money, no.' Carole suddenly became conciliatory. 'This isn't like you, Luc. What's up? Man trouble?'

'Haven't got a man to give me any trouble.' Not for eighteen days.

'Great. Young, free and single. Enjoy it.' Carole picked up her other line, asking them to hold. 'Stick with the Julian mob and I'll look out for something really plum for you. OK, love? Come in and have a chat on Friday. 'Bye now.'

Luc made herself some tea and settled down on the sofa. Sunlight filled the first-floor sitting room, showing up how the carpet needed a vacuum and the windows ought to be cleaned. She reached for the remote and put on *Neighbours*.

Twenty minutes later, just as the episode was reaching a cliff-hanging climax, the phone rang. Cursing, Luc got up, her eyes fixed to the screen. 'Hello.'

'Lucasta James?'

The voice was low, vaguely familiar, but she couldn't place it. '. . . Lorenzo?'

'How are you?'

Excitement surged through Luc like electricity. Delirious joy filled her. Sinking to the floor, automatically tidying her hair, she told herself to sound cool. 'I'm well. Very well. How are you?'

'What's that?'

It was the *Neighbours* theme tune. 'Television.' Mortified, Luc stabbed at the remote's off button. Why hadn't she been caught listening to something highbrow on Radio 3? 'I was just waiting for the news. How are you? Where are you?'

'Better today. I'm on a small airfield outside Geneva.'

'You're going away?' How could she sound cool with her pulse racing so hard she could feel it in her throat?

'No. I've been flying this afternoon.'

'Flying? You're a pilot? Like Biggles?'

'Who's Biggles?'

Luc wasn't exactly sure, never having read the books. 'He was a heroic pilot who said chocks away, Ginger, and shot down lots of Germans. I think.' She cringed. 'Shit, you're German. Perhaps you're more like *Top Gun.*'

Lorenzo laughed. 'No. I certainly don't shoot down Germans and I only fly small planes. How was your trip back from Ia?'

'Fine. Did you swim?'

'Yes. Then I spent the afternoon sleeping, which I fear spoilt our hostess's plans. We had dinner, then Alex and I played chess. What have you been doing?'

'Working. Meeting friends. The usual.' Luc wished she could boast about curing leprosy or winning the Nobel Peace Prize.

He tutted. 'Work? You should be on a *chaise longue* reading poetry. Have you fallen into any more harbours?'

Luc winced. 'No. How's your jacket?' She remembered how it had felt wrapped round her, how his aftershave seemed to be woven into it.

'I need another.'

'I didn't ruin it?' Her sopping hair had soaked the lapels and shoulders.

'No. I have to see my tailor.'

'As one does,' teased Luc. 'Where is he?'

'You don't remember? London.'

'London?' Luc caught her breath.

'I have some meetings towards the end of next week.'

Next week. Next week. He was going to be in London next week. Would he . . .? 'I suppose you'll be very busy.'

'Some of the time. What about you?'

'What about me?' Why wasn't her brain working? She was either gibbering about Biggles or barking questions like a Gestapo interrogator.

'Have you any plans for next Thursday evening?'

She had, but she cancelled them. 'No.'

'Then you can meet me in the bar of the Chester Hotel at seven o'clock. Chester Street, Belgravia.'

Luc hugged herself, her face lit up with joy. 'I can.'

'Until then. What are you doing tonight?'

'Friend's birthday party.'

'Enjoy it. See you Thursday week.'

And he was gone, before she had a chance to ask for his number.

Petrol had been chucked on the barbecue. Acrid smoke was filling the tiny garden, making eyes water. Made in the washing-up bowl, the punch should've been labelled radioactive. Someone was bringing round a plate of pitta bread and a sludgy dip that looked as though it had already been eaten and thrown up.

'Luc?' Maggie the hostess was taken aback. 'Have you been on a diet or something? You look so well, it's sickening.'

'Do I?' She was floating, wrapped in bliss.

'Thanks for the postcard. Good time?'

'Wonderful.'

'Holiday romance? Thought so. Some hunky local like Tom Conti in *Shirley Valentine*?'

Luc laughed. 'Nothing like him.'

Fuelled by the punch, the noise levels rose. The sausages tasted of firelighters, remains of banoffee pie got trodden under-foot. All evening, Luc was somewhere else. Watching a helicop-ter land, seeing eyes the colour of lapis lazuli, a beach as the sun rose. People were talking to her, but she could only really hear what Lorenzo had said, his words going round and round like a loop tape.

'Luc. Wonderful.' Tim pecked her on the cheek. 'Come in.'

From the outside, the Edwardian terrace house was no dif-ferent from any other in the tree-lined street in Kew. Inside it was as strange as entering Dr Who's *Tardis*. Luc gingerly edged past a floor-to-ceiling sheet of greenish opaque glass that used to be the hall wall.

In the sitting room, Liz was straightening magenta and violet suede cushions on the two sofas, the colour of orange creams. It all somehow went with her red lipstick. 'Hello, Luc. You've brought the weather, we'll have to eat indoors.'

Drizzle had started falling on Luc's walk from the Tube. 'For you.' She shyly held out a small box of ultra-expensive choco-lates, having agonised for hours over what to bring. Flowers would provoke endless fussing and probably wouldn't match any-thing. Wine, after all that expertise shown on Ia, was out.

'Lovely, thank you.' Liz squinted at the box to check the per-centage of cocoa solids. 'Drink for Luc, Timmy?'

'Fizz OK?'

'Thanks.' The fizz came in a thin-stemmed flute, so fragile Luc wondered if it would smash when she touched it.

The white room was empty apart from the two sofas and a perspex table between them, so perfectly unmarked it gave the illusion that the glasses were floating in the air. Ella was right, the place was a showcase rather than a home. It had been featured in countless style magazines. The camera loved the empty space, the stainless-steel kitchen, the glass walls, the sandstone staircase. Perched on the edge of the pale sofa, afraid she'd mark the pristine upholstery, Luc knew she'd be more comfortable if the place was how it used to be; an ordinary, cluttered terrace.

'What's your news?' asked Tim. Like Luc, he'd lost his tan. 'Where are you working?'

'For a property company. The Julian Group.'

Liz looked up. 'What sort of property? Do they need architects?'

'Lizzy,' protested Tim.

'Doubt it,' said Luc. 'They're middlemen. I think. Not involved in any actual building.'

'Bosses from hell?'

'Strange. There's Mrs Beak, the unmerry widow, and Casey, the Pilsbury Dough Boy.'

'Isn't it about time you got yourself something permanent?' asked Liz. 'All this temping can't be good for your CV.'

'Always the bridesmaid.' Luc sighed, downcast. 'I've been for loads of interviews but never landed the job.'

'You will,' said Tim, squeezing her arm. 'Look on the positive side, Lizzy. Luc copes with being thrown into new places every couple of weeks. It shows she's adaptable. Resourceful.'

Luc smiled, Tim always managed to say something nice.

'At least you're working.' Liz smoothed the cushions. 'Heard from Ella again?'

'No. Nothing since Monday.'

'She's very lucky that you're around to keep an eye on her place. You can't just abandon a house in London for months. Anything could happen. Flood, fire . . .'

'Pestilence? Plagues of locusts?' Tim winked at Luc.

'Burglars and squatters,' added Liz coldly. 'If Ella had actually had to go out and work for that house of hers, she might take better care of it.'

'Music?' said Tim, getting up.

'Schubert?' Liz frowned at the interruption. 'If Ella deigns to call again, tell her that the Trustees need her. There's some papers she has to sign. I don't know why they're bothering me.'

'I'll tell her,' said Luc.

'She might not have a job, but she does have responsibilities. One of them is to protect her inheritance. Which she can't do if she's swanning around on some yacht all summer.'

Luc mmmed neutrally.

'And if I were you, in exchange for all this house-sitting, I'd make sure Ella waives your rent,' continued Liz. 'She's just taking advantage.'

The doorbell rang and Alex walked in, clutching a bottle of wine.

'No Marina?' asked Liz.

'Sorry, tried to call but my mobile died. The charger's been eaten by the car. She's stuck in Salisbury. Her sister had a scan today. Expecting twins.'

'Twins?' Tim's face lit up. 'How wonderful.'

'Apparently not for Gina and Bill. They'd find it difficult moneywise with one. Hello, Lucasta.'

'Hello.' Yet again she was intimidated by him.

'Not run away to sea yet? Gather Ella's still enjoying life on the ocean wave.'

Re-arranging the dining table, partly hidden by another sheet of greenish glass, Liz ummed sceptically. 'Are we warming the bread, Tim?'

Alex grinned as Tim scuttled towards the stainless-steel kitchen. He looked round. 'Very stylish, but cosy it isn't. So, Lucasta, how's life?'

'Fine, thanks.' She glugged her drink. 'You?'

'Off to Soviet Central Asia tomorrow. Covering the elections.' He swiped some brick dust off the sleeve of his crumpled black suit. His tie was askew and his shirt collar frayed. 'Usual panic over visas.'

Luc envied him his passport, guessing it would be battered and extra large, with pages stamped at hundreds of strange frontier posts. 'How's Marina?'

'Fine. Thinking of giving Italian lessons.'

'Good idea,' called Tim from the kitchen.

'Thinking.' Alex scowled. 'She should've been a cat. All she wants to do is lie around in the warm, look graceful and get fed.'

Liz's casual meant a clothless dining table, decided Luc, admiring the white flowers among the candles on the scrubbed wooden surface. Did she possess a tin-opener? The tuna and anchovies in the salad niçoise were fresh.

'Twins?' said Tim. 'Boys? Girls?'

'Didn't ask,' replied Alex.

'Nice to get it over with in one hit.'

'Two lots of noise.' Liz shuddered. 'Two lots of mess. Two lots of hard work.'

'Two lots of joy?' suggested Tim, polishing his glasses with his napkin. Without them as a shield his eyes seemed vulnerable.

'Let's not start, shall we, Tim?' Liz forced her lipsticked lips into a smile. 'More bread, Luc?'

'Liz is a bit anti-children at the moment,' said Tim. 'My cousin's pack came round last weekend and got crayon on the sofa.'

'And wrecked the garden. And marked the walls. And spat out my lemonade.' Liz was indignant. 'Quite honestly, seeing that lot, Herod had the right idea.'

'Lizzy, you don't mean that,' protested Tim. 'Little Barnaby is so sweet.'

'Little Barnaby is a spoilt monster.'

Alex looked round the pristine emptiness. 'This isn't quite the environment for kids.'

'You're not about to do an Ella, are you?' Liz groaned. She began gathering up the plates. 'Style fascist, taste policeman . . .'

'Me? I'd rather do rat poison than do an Ella,' cried Alex. 'Need a hand?' Liz shook her head. 'I just can't imagine this place being littered with plastic toys and sticky handprints.'

'Come round when Barnaby's here.'

'It was great,' murmured Tim forlornly.

The pasta was Tim's home-made linguine with crab. It was followed by three different sorbets, which looked more like a work of art than a pudding.

'Don't you two ever slob out in front of the box with a Pot Noodle?' asked Alex.

'Drugs? Us?' Liz was aghast. 'Of course not.'

Alex laughed. 'You explain, Luc. Have you got a television?'

'In there.' Tim pointed at a sitting-room wall. 'That's all cupboard, believe it or not. Amazing piece of joinery, isn't it? Liz found the carpenter.'

'Very stylish,' said Luc cautiously. All the cool space demanded best clothes and best behaviour.

'It's minimalist, but it's a house just like anywhere else,' said Tim. 'We often chill on the sofa with some grub and watch the box.'

Liz nodded. 'Like last night. Pizza and *Goldfinger*.'

'I missed it?' Luc was dismayed. 'That's the best Bond movie. The Aston . . .'

Tim smiled. 'The documentary. On Erno Goldfinger. The architect.'

Luc felt a philistine twit.

'Don't worry,' said Alex. 'I haven't heard of him either. And I bet it was home-made pizza, thin crust, with organic tomatoes and lots of basil leaves.' He winked at Luc. 'So, Tim, how's work? That von Retzen guy still giving you grief?'

Luc's passionfruit sorbet went down the wrong way.

'Don't ask,' pleaded Tim. 'I doubt if that project is ever going to get off the ground.'

'Of course it is, after all your hard work. It's stunning. And you've been paid for the plans,' said Liz.

'Thanks to you.' He smiled. 'You should've heard Liz haggling in French the other day. It's wonderful, but for me to establish myself, buildings must be built. Not just stay on the drawing-board. Bloody clients.'

'Don't be so defeatist, Timmy,' chided Liz. 'There's lots in the pipeline. Don't forget Glasgow.'

'Another possible project,' explained Tim. 'At the moment I'm in a beauty contest with other firms. Another chance to be runner-up. That's why Geneva is so important. It's the best work I've ever done. Perhaps award-winning. I need to complete it.'

Luc felt a cold dread inside her.

Liz sighed. 'I must admit Lorenzo has proved a mite disappointing. We're completely stuck until he gives the green light.'

'How is the lovely Count?' said Alex. 'He just invites typographical errors.'

Luc blushed.

'Somewhere in the wilds of the Baltic states,' said Liz. 'We haven't spoken directly since Greece. It's all been via some froideur-ridden hag of a PA. Madame Royer. I forgot, you met, Luc, didn't you?'

'Lorenzo?' Her voice was squeaky. 'Yes. That last night.'

'Gave him a tour of Ia's hot spots, didn't you?' said Tim.

'And the beach,' said Alex.

'We just had a few drinks.' Her cheeks were burning like a furnace.

'He and Alex had a marathon game of chess,' said Tim. 'Hour after hour, only to end in a draw.'

'Great game.' Alex yawned. 'Didn't like him any better for it.'

'He's perfectly charming,' said Liz.

'You were charmed. Marina was charmed. I bet Luc was charmed.' Alex glanced at her. 'To me he's as smug as fuck and as cold as charity. He was born on a golden escalator and his life has been one steady, smooth ride upwards ever since.'

*

After dinner, Liz asked Luc to come up to her study. The sketches of the villa had been photocopied and laid out on the desk. Liz explained that she'd sent the originals to the villa's owner as a thank-you present. 'I thought she'd appreciate them more.'

'That's fine,' said Luc, expecting them to have been chucked in the bin. Liz was ruthless at purging clutter. 'They're not really for here, are they?'

'Can you do some more? She's selling the villa and wants them as a keepsake. I've got extra prints of our photos, so you can work from them. Of course, you'll be paid.' Liz mentioned a sum.

'What?' Luc was dumbfounded.

'I thought that was quite generous.' Liz was tart. 'I had to work quite hard to get it up that high.'

'No, I didn't mean . . .'

'You'll do it? They're for her gazebo.'

'Gazebo?'

'A summerhouse by water. Didn't those nuns teach you and Ella anything? I'm redoing it. Why, I don't know. She's a nightmare client . . .'

Luc couldn't help glancing round for any evidence of Lorenzo's number.

'. . . I've talked her out of some ghastly Art Nouveau riche wallpaper, but she still wants curtains that should be worn by the chorus of the Folies Bergères.'

Towards midnight, Luc got up to leave. 'Hitching?' asked Alex.

'Cab.' She was frosty.

'I'll give you a lift. It's on my way.'

Luc had to move a pile of old newspapers, notebooks and tiny cassette tapes from the seat of his ancient rusting BMW. The phone charger was buried beneath them. He told her to chuck it all in the back.

'How's the Ancient Mariner?' he asked as they sped eastwards from Kew. Even with the seat fully back, he seemed to have to hunch over the wheel.

'Who?' She was puzzled. 'You mean Henri? Don't know. Don't expect to hear from him again.'

'Really? Thought he'd have swathed you in diamonds and furs by now. Or have whisked you off on his yacht. So, it was just the holiday hots?'

'Firstly . . .'

'You mean first.' He grinned. 'Continue. I'll sub you as you go along.'

'First,' said Luc, through clenched teeth. 'First, there were no hots and second . . .'

'Secondly.'

'And second, the yacht wasn't his. He was the skipper.'

'Were these two issues related?'

Luc saw red. 'Stop the car.' They were on Chiswick flyover. 'Let me out.'

'Don't be such a drama queen.' Alex laughed, adding to her irritation. 'Sorry. Oh God, you're not sulking, are you? I can't bear pouty women.'

Still infuriated, Luc tried to re-arrange her face. 'What's the wetsuit for? In the back. Scuba diving?'

'Surfing. Not that there's much here.'

'Cornwall?' suggested Luc.

'You are joking.'

'There is.'

'Sure. Cross a dog turd-covered strip of grey sand and paddle out among the sewage. Great. You English don't know how to live.'

'You're living here.'

'Not for ever. I'll head home as soon as I've found fame and fortune. Won't be too long now.' He smiled. 'Just given my manuscript to my agent.'

'You have? That's brilliant. Good luck with it.'

'Thanks.'

'How long have you been here?'

'Four years. Four years too many to spend on an overcrowded little island with a bad climate. Didn't think I'd last a month.'

'Why not?' asked Luc.

'Because I wasn't used to wearing a tie, let alone an old school one. Because I wasn't used to saying sir and being stonewalled. Because I wasn't used to nervous men.'

'Englishmen aren't nervous.'

'The Poms? Dead scared. They think all the Aussies are over here to steal their jobs and fuck their women.'

Luc was startled. 'But you're not.'

'But we are. I am.' He grinned. They began speeding up the Cromwell Road. 'Never been to Australia, have you? It would do you good.'

'You make it sound like a health farm.' If the whole country were full of Alexes, Luc suspected she'd rather go to a leper colony.

'Might temper your restraint and your frightfully good manners, my dear. If you ever visit, look us up.'

'Us? You and Marina?' She hadn't realised it was quite so serious between them.

'She'll be filing for divorce any minute. I'm thinking of applying for a job in Sydney. We might be there in time for summer.'

'It is summer.' Luc was bewildered.

'The Australian summer. Call this a summer?'

'Next left and left again,' said Luc, longing to get out of the car. He made her feel as if she were to blame for her country's ills.

'Nice neighbourhood.' He peered down the Mews. 'Have to be. Can't see our Lucasta doing the badlands of 0181 country.'

Luc told herself to let it pass. 'Say hello to Marina for me. If either of you are passing, look in. Number seven.' She said it, not meaning it, out of routine politeness.

'Marina said she'd like to see you. I'll get her to give you a call, shall I?'

'Sure.'

'What about your landlady?'

'Ella? What about her?'

'She'd put out the not welcome mat for me. Still, the dislike is mutual.' He glanced at Luc. 'Must be good for the pair of you to be split up for a while, mustn't it? Gives you the chance to stop slip-streaming.'

'What?'

'Your best mate casts a huge shadow over you. Get out of it and you'll start growing.'

Luc tossed and turned in bed, thumped the pillows, turned on the light, turned it off five minutes later then turned it on again. She gazed at the lilac walls and purple dado rail and cerise window frames. There was a patch of damp in a corner by the window. The ground-floor bedroom had been Ella's. It hadn't changed in a decade when Luc used to sleep across the hall in the spare room in the school holidays. She'd never thought much about the colour scheme before, much less disliked it. What would Lorenzo think of it?

Would he really come to London? As the week had passed, her hopes had dwindled. Over the past few days, she'd played superstitious tricks on herself. Tempted fate, made bets. 'He'll come if the next bus is a 14.' It hadn't been. 'He'll cancel if the dry-cleaner's is still open.' It had been shut.

She picked up a library book on opera plots. She still didn't know Wotan from Mimi. It was almost as boring as the books on Swiss history and aeronautics, which lay on top of a massive volume on modern European banking.

What she really needed was *How to Be Cultured, Interesting and Sophisticated Made Simple*.

*

The following morning a postcard arrived from Corfu, showing a golden-sanded beach and sea the colour of lapis lazuli.

'*Don't you wish you were here? Send books and clean knickers. All love Ella.*'

Luc picked it up off the mat as she let herself in, laden down with paint-pots, rollers and brushes. Where was Ella now? Drifting up the Ionian, the Adriatic or across the Mediterranean? Was Madame with them, making Henri nervous? Or had she returned to France, leaving the crew with little to do but sunbathe on the deck of *Les Voiles Blanches*?

She cleared out the bedroom, dusted and opened the windows. Across the Mews, Dolly Tilling was peering at her bay tree. 'Morning, Luc. Ella back yet?'

'Not yet.'

'Excellent. Good for her, isn't it?'

'Very,' agreed Luc with as much heartiness as she could muster. 'How are the boots?'

'Given me the most God-awful blisters.' She peered down. 'Just starting to get the better of the buggers.'

Luc turned on the radio. Since Lorenzo's call, it had been tuned to either Radio 3, 4 or the World Service. She was trying to enjoy them as much as her usual pop stations. After pouring paint into a tray, she hesitated. This was Ella's room, had been since she was born. Perhaps she ought to wait and ask Ella first?

Outside, Dolly Tilling was demanding to know what someone was doing. Luc went over to the window. Two slouching youths mumbled something back. 'Well, you can stop it and go and do something useful. Kick a football. Now, be off with you.'

Luc watched them skulk off. Dolly Tilling turned to her. 'Toads. Probably thieves. Just as well you're a homebody and can look after things for Ella.'

Homebody? Homebody? As Luc was gnashing her teeth, the shipping forecast started on the radio. 'Viking, Forties,

Cromarty . . .' By the time it had reached Biscay, most of the
paint in the tray had been rolled on to the lilac wall.

'Over here.' A horn tooted. Marina was sitting behind the wheel
of a red open-topped Alfa Spyder. With a scarf wrapped round
her ringlets and in her dark glasses, she looked like something
out of *La Dolce Vita*. The car was parked blocking the pavement
outside the Julian Group offices.

'Lovely to see you, *cara*. You look even more beautiful than
you did on Ia.'

It was Tuesday evening. The day before Luc had been surprised when Marina called and even more surprised when she
asked her to come to the cinema.

'Alex has just gone. Not that it matters. Like all men, he hates
subtitles.' She had offered to pick Luc up from work; they'd have
a drink and then go on to the film.

'Nice car,' said Luc, as Marina accelerated, tyres screeching.

'Which costs a fortune in taxis,' called Marina. 'I have to leave
it in the car-park at Cadogan Square.' Barely slowing down at a
junction, she hurtled into a stream of rush-hour traffic racing
along Park Lane.

'Why?' yelled Luc, convinced they were going to slam into a
cab.

'Someone slashed the roof outside Alex's. Barrrstarrrd.'

Was the bastard the roof slasher or the van driver who was
hooting furiously at being cut up? At Hyde Park Corner, the
traffic lights turned to red. Luc put her foot on an imaginary
brake, Marina put her foot down on the accelerator pedal. A
coach missed them by inches. Luc squeezed her eyes tight shut.

'So, where shall we go?' called Marina, about to turn off
towards Knightsbridge. 'I know.' She wrenched at the wheel and
they continued back round and exited towards Piccadilly. Pulling
her seat-belt more tightly round her, Luc wondered if Marina
had actually passed her driving test. Turning left with more tyre-

screeching, they sped along a narrow street, almost on the back wheel of a pushbike courier.

'Nice legs.' Marina leaned out of the side window to get a better look and nearly swerved into a pedestrian. 'Here we are, *cara*.' She braked to a violent stop outside an imposing Georgian town house. Again the wheels were on the pavement.

Marina loosened her scarf and strode up to a glossy black front door. A uniformed doorman touched his cap. 'Good evening, Mrs Jones.'

'Clive, *caro*. Is your mother better? Wonderful.' Marina gave him the car keys. 'This is my friend Luc.'

She greeted the receptionist, signed them in and led the way to an oak-panelled bar, where she ordered a bottle of champagne. 'Now, *cara*, tell me your news.'

'Not much to tell. Work, home, work . . .' said Luc, gazing about her and feeling scruffy. She was disoriented, trying to adjust to the change in Marina. Was this woman-about-town with her red suit, red sports car, Hermes bag and membership of a club reeking of exclusivity the same bikinied, flip-flopped flower-carrying Marina on Ia? 'And you?'

' 'Ectic. Drrramas with my seester, drrramas with my 'usband, drrramas with Alex. 'Opefully his temper will improve in whichever boring khan or stan 'e's gone to.'

'I saw him on Fri—'

'We 'ad such a fight on the way to the airport. Just because I told 'im the trrruth.' She held up her glass. '*Salut*. I told 'im, Alex, your flat is sort of OK, sort of, but the arrrea's a dump. A dump. Trrrust me, Luc.' She leaned forward and held Luc's arm. 'It's like a shanty town in centrrral Amerrrica. My car's been attacked, next I'll be attacked. And you know what 'e said? Stop exagerrrrating. 'Ow you like that, Luc? I said, it's OK for you, you're almost two metres, you don't 'ave a 'andbag, you don't 'ave diamond rrrings, no one will attack you. But me, I'm scared to walk down the strrreet.'

Her heavily made-up eyes alight with indignation, Marina

chattered on, pausing only to spit olive stones into her fist. Luc contributed the occasional yes, no and really.

'. . . And of course, what Alex cares about is not my safety, but me going back to my 'usband. I tell 'im until I am purrrple in the face, that I am not going back to Gordon. I am not wasting my life peeling the carrots while 'e is on the golf-course.'

After half a bottle of champagne, Marina's driving was even more erratic. Somehow they made it to the cinema. The film was Italian, beautiful, and made them both cry a little.

'That was wonderful. Thank you,' said Luc, as Marina stopped at the entrance to the Mews. 'Are you sure you don't want some coffee or something?'

'Thank you, *cara*, but it's getting late.' Marina glanced at her Rolex. She was distracted, edgy.

'Like to borrow a baseball bat?'

'I'd prefer to borrow your neighbourhood. Call you soon. Big kiss. *Ciao*.'

Luc waved her off. It was only nine-thirty. She wondered why Marina was in such a hurry to get back to an empty flat.

Chapter Eight

'Is there something troubling you, Miss James?'

'No, nothing,' said Luc airily.

'Your concentration seems a little awry.' Mrs Beak studied the report on an infill site outside Slough. She wore her headache-bravely-borne look. 'I recall asking you for double spacing and bold.'

Luc winced. 'So you did. Sorry.'

'This sentence. "The area comprises seven litres . . ." Litres?'

'Hectares, I think.' Luc squirmed. 'Don't you?'

'Indeed I do. Now, "according to the surveyor, Mr Lorenzo Wilkins . . ." Are we sure that is correct?' An eyebrow shot up to the helmet of salt-and-pepper hair.

Luc checked her notebook. 'Leonard. Mr Leonard Wilkins.'

'Quite so. This final sentence. You've omitted an "a".'

'Does it need an "a"?' hedged Luc.

'It does.' Mrs Beak handed back the report. 'It's perhaps fortunate you're not a journalist. We might find you omitting the not in not guilty.' Luc blushed. 'Kindly do the amendments. I'll thank you to close the door.'

Feeling wormlike, Luc scurried back to her desk. She looked at her watch and wiped her palms on her skirt. Three o'clock. Zero minus four hours.

How long would she have to sit around in a hotel bar before

she admitted to herself that she'd been stood up? Would she be able to linger? Suppose, horror, the staff mistook her for a call girl? He was bound to have changed his mind. Why hadn't he confirmed? Why hadn't she got his number?

She dialled directory inquiries. Heart pounding, she then called the hotel. The voice sounded efficiently charming. She took a deep breath. 'Good afternoon. Is Loren . . . Mr . . . Count von Retzen staying with you?'

'Just one moment, madam. I'll check.'

'Miss James, is my report ready yet?' Mrs Beak was approaching the desk.

'Almost.' Luc hung up as if the receiver were scalding her. 'Almost.'

As the taxi rounded the cream stucco of Belgrave Square, Luc wanted to order the driver to turn round and take her back home. Suddenly, she yearned for an ordinary dull night in; vegging out in her trackpants, *EastEnders* on the box and a plate of pasta on her lap. For the past ten days, she'd imagined zero hour arriving. Now that it had, she'd prefer to go to the dentist and have her wisdom teeth yanked out.

The taxi pulled up. She wondered why it was stopping, until she caught sight of the unobtrusive brass nameplate. The Chester Hotel. It was small, discreet, but looked so forbiddingly smart. Even if she had the courage to walk up to the door, would someone intercept her halfway and order her to use the tradesmen's entrance?

Lorenzo wasn't going to be there. She knew for absolute certain. Should she tell the driver to wait? When he told her the fare, she decided she'd get the bus home. Hands trembling, she handed over a tenner. Exhaling slowly, she walked towards the black door.

There was no sign of him.

'Can I help you, madam?'

Luc spun round, bewildered. Inside was minimalist modern,

as if it had been designed by Tim. It wasn't at all what the exterior had led her to expect. Footsteps sounding too loud on the charcoal granite floor, she went over to a sandstone slab, presumably the reception desk.

'Thankyouyes.' Her voice sounded as if she were being strangled. 'I'm supposed to be meeting someone.' She blushed. Please God she wasn't mistaken for a hooker and ordered off the premises.

The clerk behind the slab nodded. 'May I ask who, madam?'

'Lorenzo von Retzen.'

'Ah yes. Miss James?'

Luc nodded. He'd called from Geneva and cancelled.

'Count von Retzen sends his apologies and regrets . . .' Luc was filled with a horrible bleakness '. . . that he's been slightly delayed. If you'd care to wait in the bar? This way, please.'

She amazed herself by automatically ordering a glass of champagne. Somehow the surroundings demanded nothing less. It would be so easy to get used to the very good life. Sitting in such quiet luxury reminded her of being on *Les Voiles Blanches*. The world suddenly seemed a more magical place.

Ten minutes passed, then a quarter of an hour. Having cooled, her angst began to simmer again. He wouldn't turn up. Were her black dress and velvet jacket too funereal for a July evening? The skirt was too long, but at least it sort of covered her ankles, swollen by the heat. Sort of. Should she go to the ladies and try to cool them down under a washbasin tap? No, she'd only fall over and end up in a graceless heap on the floor . . .

'Hello, Lucasta.'

Luc's heart stopped. He was more of everything than she remembered. Taller, leaner, blonder, those eyes holding hers bluer than lapis lazuli. He was more mesmerising than when she had first seen him walking along the quayside and more heartbreaking than in those last seconds on the terrace.

'Hello.' Dissolving with happiness, she could only whisper.

He sat down. 'No Baci da Roma?'

'Sor . . . my T-shirt? No.'

'No hat?'

'No blazer.' He was wearing a black suit, white shirt and dark tie.

'No harbours for you to fall into.'

'Not in Belgravia.'

'Pity.' Smiling, he ordered some drinks. 'You're not too hungry, are you? We're eating at nine.'

'We are?' She could've cartwheeled around the bar with joy. Deep down, she'd dreaded they'd have a drink and he'd get a taxi called for her. 'Where? Here?'

'No. Wait and see.' He got out a packet of Lucky Strike and his flat gold lighter. She remembered how she'd lain beside him on the beach that morning, held it up and watched it glint in the rays of the newly risen sun. 'Dawn light.'

So, he remembered too. For the first time in weeks, she felt the peace of utter contentment that had filled her then. It was worth every second of those endless hours of bleak misery and black despair she'd suffered since.

'For you.' He reached into his pocket. 'To make up for your leaving that morning.'

Frowning, she opened the tissue paper and then a box, and stared at him. She gently touched each cuff-link, identical to those she'd seen on display in the jewellers in Ia. 'Lapis lazuli.'

'Cuff-links.' He finished his whisky. 'Would you prefer something more usual? Earrings, perhaps?'

She shook her head. 'These are perfect. Thank you. Thank you so much.' She was overwhelmed. On the beach she'd fiddled with his cuff-links, sleepily telling him how she'd seen some that were similar, that lapis lazuli held a mysterious magic for her, conjuring up images of Xanadu and stately pleasure domes.

'My pleasure.'

A silence fell. Once again, he reminded her of a cat. Cool,

sleek and self-contained. He watched her playing with the cuff-links, her fingers growing more agitated. Finally, she met his gaze. 'Something wrong?'

'Everything is suddenly very right.'

'Sure?' She wished she could stop blushing. Not only was it pathetically juvenile, but it clashed horribly with her hair.

'I'm certain.' He continued studying her. 'Would you mind postponing dinner for a while?'

'Why?' She was bewildered. 'Have you another meeting?'

Half an hour later, Luc opened her eyes, smiled slowly and stretched.

The arm around her tightened and Lorenzo pulled her closer. 'Stay here.' He grinned. She was wriggling, trying to dis-entangle herself from the sheet that had wound itself round her like a mummy's bandages.

'I'm staying.' She curled up even closer to him. 'Such a nice, soft carpet.'

He raised an eyebrow. 'That's the only reason?'

'Why else?'

'Perhaps there was another reason.' Luc laughed in delight. He gently ran a finger the length of her profile. 'Do I pass?'

'Faultless.' He nodded. 'Very classic.'

'Nonsense.'

'Perfectly straight.'

'My nose?' She wrinkled it up. 'Small and silly. Ella once said it would preclude me from ever being taken seriously. That I ought to have blonde hair and big tits and no brains to match it.'

'How horrible.' He shuddered. 'Thank God you're nothing like that.'

'It was ages ago. When we were at school. There wasn't much to do except skive off hockey and fret about how we looked.'

'No boys?'

'None. Like, what was that place? Mount Athos. Mount Athos in reverse.' Idly, she played with his fingers. 'Why did you go there?'

'Long story. I'll tell you one day.' Hugging her tightly, he kissed her again. 'Hungry?'

'The truth?' Luc giggled. 'Starving.' She looked at his flat gold watch. 'It's already quarter to nine.'

He reached across her to the telephone on the bedside table. 'Von Retzen.' From underneath, Luc studied his jawline. 'I've been unexpectedly delayed.' He frowned as she giggled. 'You'll call . . . nine forty-five . . . Thank you.'

Wrapped inside a huge robe, Luc came out of the shower and found him watching a report on the New York stock-market. Kissing her cheek, he gave her a glass of champagne, his eyes immediately returning to the screen. Holding his hand, she watched him watching, so happy she could burst.

'Good day?' she asked when the bulletin had finished.

'Excellent.'

'Are you even richer?'

'Yes.' He laughed. 'Where are we? A battlefield?' Immaculate when they had first walked through the door, the room was chaotic. Clothes and pillows were strewn across the carpet, a picture was aslant, knocked when he'd pinned her against the wall, a pile of documents was scattered across the desk.

'Looks like home,' said Luc.

'Not for the same reason, I hope.' He gently bit into her arm. 'No? Good.'

While he was in the shower, Luc switched to MTV. For the first time, she tuned into the words of a love song that had been in the charts for months. Suddenly they made sense.

'Where did you get your looks?' he asked, after they were seated.

'Hair from my paternal grandmother, eyes from my mother. The rest? Who knows?'

'Your parents live in London?'

Luc shook her head. 'They died when I was two. In a mud slide in Honduras. They were aid workers.'

'I'm so sorry.' Lorenzo held her hand. 'An orphan. That's unusual these days.'

'Isn't it? The little match girl, Oliver Twist. But I had my aunt, Sophie. Who was brilliant.'

'Was? She's not . . .'

'No. She's in Canada. With her husband.' Luc pulled a face. 'He and I never really got on. From the start. I guess we were competing for her attention. He's mean. Stingy.' Bryn had been the one who insisted that once she left school, Luc went to sec-retarial college rather than art school. Because of complications over loans, missed application deadlines and the general wran-gling and muddle, she'd complied. 'He belongs to one of those weird fundamentalist sects. So does Sophie now. It's like she's been brainwashed. We can't really communicate.'

'I'm sorry.' Lorenzo squeezed her hand. 'You seem very well adjusted.'

'Bryn wasn't around until I was about fifteen. And when he was, I spent the holidays with Ella and her mother, Janie.'

'Ella? Liz's sister? The one who left on the beautiful yacht with the Frenchman who pursued you across the seas?'

Luc laughed. 'He didn't.'

'Why not? I would. I have.'

Each course looked jewel-like and tasted sublime. With eyes only for Lorenzo, Luc could've been at a McDonalds. It was only later that she realised that although the food and service were impeccable, the restaurant was devoid of atmosphere, like a tomb. With Michelin stars in their eyes, the people around them behaved as if they were in church.

'What shall we do tomorrow?' asked Lorenzo as coffee was brought.

'You're free? No meetings?' He shook his head. 'When are you going back to Geneva?' Not wishing to confront his leaving, it was something she'd been too chicken to ask earlier.

'Saturday morning. First thing.'

Luc felt despair sweep through her.

'I'm being presumptuous. You're probably working tomorrow.'

'No.' Luc grinned. 'I think I'm ill. Food poisoning.' Hearing her, the waiter who was pouring more coffee looked horrified. 'What would you like to do? Sightsee? Day at the races? Night at the opera? An outing to the Zoo or the Imperial War Museum?'

'An outing?' He locked his fingers round hers. 'Can't we stay in?'

Entwined around Lorenzo, Luc woke as usual at six forty-five. Gazing and gazing at him, she stayed absolutely still for minutes.

After they'd got back to the room, she'd realised she would need some clean clothes. He'd arranged for a car to take her home first thing. 'I want to make sure you come back.'

'I'll come back. Promise. For breakfast.'

'Only for breakfast?' he'd asked.

'What else?'

Kissing his shoulder, Luc got up. She dived into the shower, brushed her teeth with his toothbrush and tried to clean off her make-up with a soapy flannel. Deciding it would be too tacky to wear her evening clothes, she grabbed one of his shirts and put it on instead of her velvet jacket.

'A car was booked. Room five.' As the receptionist's eyes flickered over her, Luc was glad she'd tied back her hair and put on Lorenzo's sunglasses. She could almost pass for going to work.

'Von Retzen? It's waiting outside, madam.'

It was the same black Daimler that had taken them to the restaurant the night before. The driver touched his cap and held open the rear door for her. Getting into the back, Luc wished she'd had deportment lessons.

'Newspaper, miss?'

Alfred assured her she should take her time. Longing to get back to Lorenzo, Luc tore up the Mews and into the Doll's House. Seeing her unmade bed, the scrambled egg pan in the sink and the Lorenzo homework books piled up on the sofa, she thanked God she'd not suggested he come with her.

A magazine was open at a 'Who's in control of your relationship?' quiz. She'd done it, then written Lorenzo, Lorenzo, Lorenzo at the bottom and, shudderingly, a row of hearts. Hastily closing it, she dashed upstairs to change.

'Day off?' asked Dolly Tilling, examining her window-boxes as Luc frantically double-locked the front door. 'Don't blame you. Beautiful morning. Far too nice to be stuck . . .'

'Shit.' Luc had forgotten to call the Agency. Unlocking the door, she hurtled up to the sitting room. Misdialling twice, she noticed the answering-machine was flashing that she had two messages. They could wait.

'Carole?' Luc tried to sound pathetic and unwell. 'It's Luc James. Sorry, can't make it today, something I've eaten . . . Haven't slept . . . Up all night . . . Oh God, better go, think it's happening again . . . 'Bye.'

As she hung up, Luc felt rotten about telling such dreadful fibs, especially as Carole had been so sympathetic. Had her small nose grown, like Pinocchio's? Would Lorenzo suggest coming round? Panicking, she shoved the homework books and the magazine under the sofa cushion, then dashed to the kitchen and hid the sopping scrambled egg pan in the fridge.

'Ella not back?' called Dolly Tilling as Luc was finally leaving.

'Not yet.'

Miss Tilling peered up at the Daimler. 'Found a fairy godfather, Lucasta?'

As she approached the car, parked at the bus stop on the main road, Alfred leaped out to open the door. Luc caught a glare from a waiting *Militant* reader.

Sitting at the desk, towel pharaoh-like round his waist, Lorenzo was in the middle of a call. Smiling, he put his fingers to his lips as Luc arrived. Beside him were a pile of faxes, the *Wall Street Journal* and a laptop. Another business programme was on the box, share prices flashing across the bottom of the screen.

He'd ordered breakfast. Luc crept across the room, poured herself some coffee and buttered a croissant. He was speaking what? Portuguese? Polish? Watching him, she longed to touch him, to bury her hands in his hair, to feel his long, lean muscles. He was the colour of honey.

Tanned from where? Tanned with whom?

Just as Luc suddenly felt pangs of unease, he smiled at her and beckoned her over. His hand tightened around hers. His lips on her face and his breath on her ear were like a balm, healing her insecurity. Still listening to his caller, he pulled her on to his lap and played with her hair as she clung to him like a koala.

'Lucasta,' he said, hanging up. 'That was supposed to be a very important call.'

'It was?' she murmured. His cheek was stubbled, slightly rough against hers, but his shoulders felt velvet warm.

'It. Was. How. Can.' Every word was punctuated by a kiss. 'I. Concentrate. With. You. Beside. Me?'

'Sorry.' Luc wasn't in the least. 'Where. Were. You. Calling?'

'The Czech Republic.'

She pulled back from him. 'You were speaking Czech?'

'What else? Swahili?' Her surprise amused him. 'I do a lot of work there.'

'English, French, German, Italian, Czech . . .' She counted off. 'Anything else?'

He shrugged. 'Russian. Latin.'

'Latin? No one speaks . . .'

'To read, not to speak.'

'Oh.' Luc felt inadequate. 'I've forgotten it. *Amo, amas.* How does it go? I love, you love.' Her voice trailed off. Her thoughts suddenly became confused. '*Amo, amas, amat.*'

'And the rest?' Fingers in her hair, he lifted his eyes to hers.

Luc's face was scarlet. 'Forgotten.'

'*Amamus.* We. Love.' Once again, he kissed her between each word. '*Amamus, Amatus. Amant.*'

'*Amamus*,' she murmured, kissing him back, tightening her arms around him.

'Time for our outing.' Lorenzo smiled.

Outside was a perfect summer's day. The sun shone, the air was freshened by a warm, soft breeze. 'Can't we stay in and risk Seasonal Affective Disorder?' Luc snuggled closer to him.

'What?'

'The depression you get in winter because of a lack of light.'

He laughed. 'No. Eleven o'clock. Time to get up.'

'Eleven?' Disbelieving, Luc looked at his watch. 'You mean we've spent . . .'

'A very enjoyable morning. But now we're going to look at some paintings and have lunch.'

While he was in the shower, Luc gathered up her stuff which was littering the floor.

Her pinafore dress lay in a crumpled heap where he'd dropped it. Where were her knickers? She ferreted around in the bedclothes, stained with cherry and watermelon juice. Where was Lorenzo? She was missing him already.

'I can't wear them,' she wailed, emerging from the bathroom in her dress, white shirt and ballet pumps. The cuff buttons didn't undo.

'Very Gigi,' he said, looking her up and down. 'All you need is a straw hat with ribbons.'

*

'This one,' he announced half an hour later.

They'd walked across Green Park, where skiving office workers were sprawled on deck-chairs soaking up the sunshine. The world was suddenly a playground, designed to amuse her and Lorenzo. The Julian Group offices, only a few minutes' walk away, could have been on Mars.

Lorenzo had whisked her up Bond Street and into the hat shop. Each one she tried on got a no, despite her protests that each was beautiful. The assistant insisted that a creamy confection was made for Luc.

'This is the one. Try it.' Luc obediently put it on. The hat was fine pale straw with black edging and trailed long black ribbons. 'Perfect.' He smiled in satisfaction.

'I'll box it up,' said the assistant.

'No, she'll wear it.'

'Lorenzo,' gasped Luc. 'You can't.'

'Why not?'

'Because . . .' she spluttered. Because she'd just caught sight of the price tag and realised that the hat probably cost more than her entire wardrobe of clothes put together.

'Because you don't like it?'

About to put his credit card through the machine, the assistant froze.

'I love it.'

'So do I.' He adjusted it. 'There's one problem. It makes it harder to kiss you.'

Luc had assumed that seeing paintings meant going to the Tate or the Royal Academy. Instead she found herself breathlessly following Lorenzo in and out of the scores of galleries and auction houses around Mayfair and St James's. She felt like a tourist in her own city. After an hour, Victorian water-colours, eighteenth-century oils and contemporary bronzes were merging into a dizzying kaleidoscope.

'Are you always so decisive?' she panted, after they had walked in and out of a show of abstract seascapes in two minutes flat.

He shrugged. 'I've a good eye.'

'And no sense of false modesty,' she teased.

He paused in front of a window, staring at a muted oil of a distended grotesque face. Luc found it creepy. 'Francis Bacon?' she asked.

He nodded, not taking his eyes from it. Her attention wandered to the display in the clothes shop opposite.

'Good morning, sir. Madam.' A pin-striped, stripy-shirted Henry unlocked the door to the gallery and let them in. His manners were as polished as his brogues.

'The Bacon. Is it for sale?'

'Indeed, sir.' The Henry glanced at Lorenzo and then launched into a longwinded ramble about technique and provenance. It was so disguised that it couldn't possibly have been a sales pitch.

'And the asking price?' said Lorenzo finally.

'Rather a lot, as one might expect.' The Henry smiled regretfully. 'Six hundred thousand, sir.'

Luc flinched, but Lorenzo remained poker-faced. 'Dollars or sterling?'

She could have guessed, blindfold. By the air-conditioning. The lower the temperature, the higher the chic and the prices. She tried to read the menu but kept on glancing round for Lorenzo, somewhere in reception. The hotel had called with an urgent message. She peered again, already missing him. A puppy entrusted to a new owner, she needed him constantly close.

The Henry had got the Bacon from the window, so Lorenzo could have a closer look. She'd held back, fearful that her breath might damage more than she'd earn in a lifetime's work.

Then Lorenzo had whisked her across Piccadilly and into Jermyn Street, where he'd insisted on getting her some shirts.

No, she couldn't try them all on, there was no time, they were already late. Clutching her armful of white shirts, cotton, silk, linen, she'd felt like Jay Gatsby.

'Is there a problem?' she asked when he sat down. He seemed preoccupied. Her mouth went dry. 'You have to go back to Geneva?'

'No.' He ordered a bottle of Meursault. 'Another outing. We have to leave by three.'

'Another outing?'

'A night at the opera.'

'Sorry. Too fast.'

Luc smiled, gloriously content. 'Flattering.'

'Even if you missed out on your pudding?' Less than fifteen minutes before, she'd been a spoonful into her chocolate mousse when he'd grabbed her arm, rushed her outside and into a cab. He stroked her face. 'You look different.'

'J F L. As Ella says.'

'The German machine tool company?'

Luc let out a peal of laughter. 'Just Fucked Look.'

'Strange to be wearing black tie in the middle of a perfect summer's afternoon.'

'You could be a bouncer about to start work.' She giggled at his look of distaste. 'That first night in Greece. We were on a horrible overnight ferry and an American was amazed that I'd never been to Glyndebourne. And now . . .'

'Now you are.'

'Strange . . . fate.'

'It's just chance,' said Lorenzo. 'Not fate. Not the stars. You don't read horoscopes, I hope?'

'Not seriously.' She cringed inside, thinking how she'd scoured hers and his most days since they'd met. 'But, but surely, sometimes . . . sometimes, some things are so right, so perfect, that they were almost ordained to happen?'

'A determinist?'

She wanted to ask him what on earth he meant, but he was punching out a number on his mobile. He began speaking French, motioning her to pass him his briefcase.

An unease seeped through her. The man she'd thought she'd got to know was vanishing. The Lorenzo who'd tenderly fed her cherries, played with her hair and indulged her with beautiful hats was replaced by a cold, focused businessman, who'd never waltz on quaysides.

His expression reminded her of that last morning on Ia, when he'd said goodbye. He could build a wall around himself, shutting her out. He'd retreated behind it when she'd asked about Mount Athos, or mentioned Tim, or asked about his childhood.

In February Ella had dragged Luc to an experimental production of *The Magic Flute* in a smelly, stifling theatre above a pub. It had been so dire they would've fled after five minutes if they hadn't been hemmed in the middle of a row. The pages of the score had been turned with such tortuous slowness that they seemed stuck. She thought she'd be trapped on the concrete-hard bench for ever.

Watching *Don Giovanni* from the comfort of the stalls at Glyndebourne, Luc sat enraptured from the opening bars of the overture.

'You like picnics?' asked Lorenzo during the Long Interval, seeing her astonishment at the sight of the tables around the lawns.

'Picnics?' They were more like exceptionally grand dinner parties. Linen, crystal, silver and candelabra were set out. Long frocks and black ties were busy unpacking food from cool-boxes and opening bottles of champagne.

Having lugged a hamper from the car-park, Alfred hoped that everything was to their liking and disappeared. Luc knelt on a tartan rug and peered at a gourmet's Aladdin's cave inside the wicker.

'Poor Donna Elvira, going to a convent,' mused Luc on the journey back to London. 'Shut up with all those nuns.'

'Preferable to the fate of Don Giovanni, surely?' suggested Lorenzo.

'Not if you were at my school.' Clasping his hand, she pecked him on the cheek. 'Thank you for a wonderful evening. A wonderful day.' Did it really have to end? He played with her hair. The darkness in the car seemed to intensify the faint citrus smell of his aftershave. Soon, the smell, the touch would be gone. She knew the answer, but asked anyway. 'Must you go back?'

'Yes. There'll be other wonderful days, I hope?' He pulled her closer to him. 'Soon?'

'Ummm.' Her pain receded as she curled up closer to him. 'Very soon?'

'Very soon.' He kissed her cheek. 'I promise.'

That night, they made slow, tender love. Afterwards, he picked up his fountain pen. 'Staking my claim.' He wrote MINE across the inside of her wrist.

As the Daimler moved off the next morning, Luc crossed the road to the newsagent's opposite the Mews. She was carrying her enormous pink hat box and the shirt bags. It was only seven-thirty, the streets were almost deserted. Another beautiful day was promised. She dithered about buying the *Financial Times*, then opted for the *Mail*.

'Shit,' she muttered, walking into the Mews. In the distance, a tramp was huddled outside the front door of the Doll's House. She'd have to wake him up, move him aside and send him on his way. Where was Dolly Tilling? And there was a bottle beside him. She prayed he wasn't going to be drunk and abusive.

'Hello . . . Ella?' Luc gasped.

Ella slowly unpeeled her eyes, red and piggy with tiredness. Under her beanie, her blonde hair was filthy, tangled almost into dreadlocks. Her brown face, like her hands, was streaked with dirt. 'Hello, Luc. Time to kill the fatted calf. The prodigal returns.'

Chapter Nine

—⋙◆⋘—

Stumbling with weariness, Ella dragged herself up the stairs to the sitting room. 'God, it's good to be home.' She tugged off her hat and dropped it on the floor, then kicked off her clogs. Her feet were dirty and calloused, one toenail black. 'Any food? I'm starving.' She wandered into the kitchen. 'Why's this eggy pan in the fridge?'

'Sit down,' said Luc hastily. 'Breakfast? Tea? I'll run a bath, shall I?'

'Thanks.' Ella yawned. She pressed the answering-machine. ' "Hello, Luc. It's me. I'll be back Friday night, Saturday morning. Please leave the key out if you're out." That was Thursday. Where have you been?'

'Here and there,' hedged Luc from halfway up the stairs. 'Boiled eggs? Your mail's on the table.'

Ella threw herself down on the sofa and started tearing open envelopes. 'Bill, bill, telly licence . . .' She sniffed. 'Do I look as rough as I smell?'

'Worse. What's happened to you?'

'Long story. I should burn these clothes.' They were tatty and torn. 'Car tax renewal. Oh God, better call Liz. Ben's having a party. Had a party. Last night. Did you go?'

'No,' called back Luc.

'What's in the box?'

'A hat.'

'Let's see. Been to a wedding?' Ella had to repeat herself as Luc turned on the bathtaps. 'God, Luc, this is beautiful.' Coming back down the stairs, Luc tried not to mind as Ella put the hat on her greasy, matted hair and posed in front of the mirror above the fireplace. 'Must've cost you a fortune.'

Luc stared at her. 'You've got so thin.'

'Haven't eaten properly for ages. So. Who is he?'

'Who's who?'

'Whoever you spent last night with. And Thursday night. The one who bought you the hat and the shirts. And who took you to Glyndebourne.' She waved the programme, which Luc had tried to hide under the *Mail*.

Luc hesitated. Could Ella be relied upon not to blurt something out to Tim and Liz? She didn't want to end up the piggy in the middle of a wrangle between them and Lorenzo.

'Good-looking?' asked Ella. Luc nodded. 'Rich? Stylish, if that hat's anything to go by. Cultured. Most straight men would rather have dysentery than go to the opera. Bright? Old?'

'Forty,' said Luc. 'Boiled eggs?'

'When can I meet him? You've already asked me about the eggs. Why are you going all furtive on me?'

'I'm not.' Luc blushed.

Ella followed her into the kitchen. 'Come on. You've met this handsome, rich, older man. Sounds perfect. Sounds too good to be true.'

'He is.'

'Things that sound too good to be true are usually exactly that. Where does he live? What does he do? How did you meet him?'

'Geneva.'

Ella frowned. 'Geneva? And you'd walk a million miles for one of his smiles?'

Luc turned on the grill. 'You bet.'

Having shooed Ella upstairs and into the bath, Luc finished

making breakfast. She was curious to hear about *Les Voiles Blanches*. Had sea-sickness caused Ella to lose so much weight? She sensed that something was very wrong, that something weird had happened. 'Where's your backpack?' she asked, setting down the tray on Ella's bedroom floor. 'Ella?'

The bathroom door was ajar. Surrounded by bubbles, Ella lay in the steaming water, fast asleep.

'My backpack?' said Ella. It was six o'clock. She and Luc were sitting on the roof terrace overlooking the Mews. Her collar-bones were sticking out like knives. Her hair, bleached by the sun, was still wet from the second bath she'd taken half an hour earlier. The water had turned black from all the dirt still encrusted in her skin. 'Stolen.'

'Not from *Les Voiles Blanches*?' Luc thought back to what a security fanatic Henri had been.

'On Corfu.'

Luc imagined long, lazy days on the yacht, island hopping around the Aegean and sailing up the Ionian Sea. 'Nice sail?'

'I flew.' Ella was terse. 'From Athens.'

'Why? Engine trouble again?'

'I was kicked off *Les Voiles Blanches* after two days. Sacked. Fired.'

'What?' Luc choked on her wine. 'What happened?'

Ella pulled a face. 'Madame and I loathed one another on sight. Actually, as soon as Tim dropped me off that Thursday night I knew Henri regretted offering me the job.'

'But . . .'

'I was given this platform in a stifling cubby-hole to sleep in, right next to the engine, and warned in no uncertain terms that Yannick wasn't allowed within a *mille* miles of me.' She scowled. 'Then Henri barked out all these orders in French as if he was still in the Foreign Legion. Coffee. Sandwiches. More coffee. If I were one of his soldiers, I'd have shot him. Then I had to spend hours cleaning the showers and the kitchen. Sorry, galley. So much for night sailing and seeing the stars, I had my eyes fixed on the lavs.'

Luc poured them more wine. 'And?'

'And at about three o'clock, I got sea-sick. It's not funny.' Ella's brown eyes narrowed. 'I lay in the cubby-hole thinking I'd died and gone to hell. God, all that rolling and pitching and tossing and the smell of the engine oil.' She shuddered. 'Then Henri appeared and started screaming at me about why hadn't I hoovered the saloon and I knew that I had gone to hell. He was furious. Idiot and imbecile are the same words in French, aren't they? He said there was no point in having a crewman who gets *mal de mer*.'

'Had a point, hadn't he?' said Luc.

'Anyway, somehow I managed to drift off to sleep. When I woke up we were in some port near Athens. Henri's first words were do the washing-up, then he gave me a whole list of other stuff. Iron the T-shirts, make up Madame's bed, it was endless. Yannick was up on deck. Again. Avoiding me. Anyway, no chance to doss around in the sun, I didn't even see daylight. Especially after the ego had landed.'

'What?' Luc was puzzled.

'Madame.' Grimacing, Ella wrinkled up her snub nose. 'She arrived that afternoon. It was about a thousand degrees and the stupid cow was carrying a sable coat. And a crocodile jewellery case. Makes you want to sign up to the Animal Liberation Front.'

'What was she like?'

'Looks twenty-five from the back. Tall, skinny, short skirt, long blonde hair. Then when she turns round . . . she's almost sixty and prune-like. It's weird, like seeing a beautiful girl then realising she's a transvestite. Anyway, she was practically piped aboard. Bertrand, Yannick and me were lined up to greet her, all in our ironed T-shirts and itchy blue trousers. Henri bowing and scraping. I was introduced, almost curtsied, but she looked straight through me.'

Luc was riveted. 'And?'

'And black mark, bottom of the class, immediately. She inspected every inch of the yacht and, of course, I hadn't made my bed. Or berth? Bunk? Whatever it was, I was summoned. She let off a tirade of French before she asked if I'd heard of "ship-shape and Bristol fashion". God, she and Henri would love Liz. Then they had lunch. Then we sailed to Aegina. So much for life on the ocean wave. I was below, washing up lunch, then hand-washing Madame's lingerie while she was sunbathing up on deck.'

'What about Yannick?'

'Yummy Yannick?' Ella smiled a lifeless smile. 'Blanked me.'

Luc frowned. 'But . . .'

'At first I thought it was because Henri had told him to keep well away. Then I was told to make some tea. Fortunately, Bertrand was there to tell me about the tray and the cloth and the china and the silver teapot. What a fucking palaver.' She took a deep breath. 'I went up on deck with the tray, like an animal emerging from hibernation. And there was Yannick, busy rubbing suntan oil into Madame's rhino-hide back.'

'You don't think . . .?'

'Luc, I didn't have to think. I knew.' Ella pulled a face. 'He's beautiful. Perfect toyboy material.'

'Are you sure?'

'And she's not bad-looking, gagging for it and incredibly rich. He's smart, lazy and has an eye to the main chance.'

Luc was pole-axed. 'But why did he want you there?'

'Dunno.' Ella shrugged. 'Probably took a punt that Madame wouldn't turn up. Or if she did, she'd be with husband *numéro cinq*.'

'You didn't just over-react?'

'That afternoon I sensed something. He looked so shifty. And she guessed there was something up between him and me. Took one sip of the tea from this poncy little cup then chucked it over the side, ranting on about who was this *Anglaise* who couldn't even make tea. I skulked below, stayed there until we arrived in Athenia where Madame took them all off for dinner. She insisted I stay behind, for security supposedly.'

'Not unreasonable,' suggested Luc.

'Oh, sure,' spat Ella. 'The old bitch was clutching Yannick's arm as she tottered down the gangplank, leaving me to guard an African mine of gold and diamonds, plus the little Matisse she takes with her everywhere. So there I was, on a beautiful yacht, on my own for hour after hour after hour. It should've been flying that special plague flag, I felt as if I had an infectious disease.'

Luc had rarely heard Ella sound so bitter.

'As soon as they came back, I crept into the cubby-hole. No Yannick. Waited and waited for him. Eventually slept, woke up early. And I caught him.' Ella bit her lip. 'Coming out of her stateroom. Great, eh?'

Luc squeezed Ella's hand. 'I'm sorry.'

'Anyway, we had this massive row. She stormed out and sacked me on the spot for disturbing her sleep. I told the old cow where she could stuff her yacht and Yannick and left.' Ella held out her glass for more wine.

'That was when? Saturday morning? Why didn't you come home?'

'Don't know. Athenia was nice, a bit like Ia. Found a room overlooking the port and just chilled.'

'And Yannick?'

'God knows.' Ella yawned. 'Sailed off into the sunlight never to be seen again.'

'Don't you mind?'

'I did. Heaps.' She drained her glass. 'Anyway, who is he?'

'Who's who?'

'This perfect man.'

Luc felt as if she were on the edge of the top diving board. 'Lorenzo. Lorenzo von Retzen.' Ella frowned. 'Yes, Tim and Liz's client. He arrived the day after you left.'

'The one Liz was panicking about?'

'The one. We all went out to dinner, then the others left and we went for a drink. And pow.' She studied the cuff-links. 'Then he was in London on Thursday.'

'Don't tell me you've finally fallen in love.'

'Completely.'

'The sonnets and the symphonies and the waves crashing on the beach?'

'All of the above. And more.'

Pent up for almost a month, the whole saga poured out of Luc like lava from a volcano. She told Ella the lot, from the first moment she'd seen him on the quayside until the last glimpse of him in the airport-bound Daimler that morning.

Luc made supper. Having been kept tidyish for the past month, the sitting room had quickly become littered with discarded papers, CDs, Ella's hairdryer, books and dirty crockery. She was reminded it was Ella's house.

'So why Corfu?' she asked, forking up some spaghetti.

'I was about to come back, but this travel agent in Athens had an ad for a dirt-cheap flight. So why not take it? Lick my wounds.' Ella grated some Parmesan, scattering it over the table. 'It was OK at first. Managed to avoid the Blackpool bits and found a room in a fishing village. Read Lawrence Durrell, prefer Gerald.'

'Then what happened?'

Ella sighed. 'One night I got talking to this couple. They seemed nice. Invited me to have a drink. And another. And another. Stupidly, I told them where I was staying and he must have got hold of my key. She kept me talking and he went to my room. Swiped the lot. Backpack, clothes, books, credit card.'

'What did you do?'

'Cried. And cried. Talked to the police. Luckily I had my passport and about eighty quid on me.' She sighed despairingly.

'It was the end. Getting attacked on Praxos, chucked off *Les Voiles Blanches* and then that.'

'Why didn't you call?'

'I tried. Collect. But you were never in. Also . . .' Ella's voice faded out. 'Also, I was knocked sideways for days. I kept on wondering about my judgement, about being so naive and dumb. Too trusting. I felt enough of a cretin without everyone rubbing it in.'

'Ella,' protested Luc.

'Not you. Miz and Timid and know-it-alls like that bloody Alex.' She scowled. 'So, I thought, I'll just try and get by on my own. No nice credit card to bail me out. See how I got on. Get a job, get by and save towards coming home.'

'And?'

'And.' Ella stared out of the window. 'And I was useless. Couldn't get a job. My snooty bank said it would take weeks to send me another credit card. And they quibbled about sending me money. Probably thought I was a scammer. Suddenly every last drachma counted. I thought I could sleep on the beach, but it was too cold and I was too scared. Didn't trust anyone.'

Thinking about all the hours she'd wasted away eaten up with jealousy imagining Ella having a wonderful time, Luc felt guilty.

'Anyway, I got a bus to Corfu town, ready to throw in the towel and throw myself on the mercy of the British consul. I'm full.' She pushed away her plate. 'Thanks. Delicious.'

'You've hardly eaten a thing.'

'It was so hot getting off that bus. Everywhere stank of fumes. It made me feel sick. The thought of trekking round was overwhelming. In fact, everything became too much. I just collapsed on this bench and cried my eyes out. That was when the knight in shining Armani was meant to appear. Well, he didn't.'

Luc took the plates to the kitchen and made some coffee.

'This French girl, Claudette, sat down. I didn't realise, but she was also in floods. Between us, Noah should've built another ark. It turned out she'd gone to Corfu with her fiancé, but had decided to dump him. She wanted to stay on and avoid the family flak. The upshot was that she had half of a return ticket to Lille that she wasn't using.'

Luc frowned. 'Those plane tickets aren't transferable.'

'We knew. Anyway I gave her fifty quid and my jewellery in exchange for the ticket and her coming to the airport and checking in. All she had to do was give me her boarding pass and pray that they didn't check it against my passport at the gate.'

'Ella, the risk.' Luc was horrified. 'They might have thought you were a terrorist or something.'

'Worth it. I just had to get out of Greece. It was one of those dodgy little airlines and I figured things might be a bit more relaxed. I was right. The hardest thing was making sure we avoided the fiancé.'

'So, you got to Lille. Then what?'

'I walked.'

'Walked?'

'What else could I do? I had virtually no money, so couldn't take the bus or the Eurostar. Couldn't face trying to bunk the train. Certainly couldn't hitch. I figured it wasn't that far to Calais. Patrick Leigh Fermor walked to the Balkans.'

'Who's he? Someone you met?'

'No.' Ella rolled her eyes. 'A travel writer.'

'You walked? You're barmy,' exclaimed Luc.

'I didn't have to walk that far. Only to a service station, where some Young Christians offered me a lift in their minibus. It was Kumbaya all the way to Balham.'

'Why put yourself through all that? You could've called your bank, got money wired, anything.'

'I couldn't think straight,' snapped Ella. 'I hadn't slept properly for days. Hadn't eaten. And . . .' She paused. 'And I thought I might be pregnant.'

'What?'

'Pregnant. Expecting. Up the duff. Knocked up. With child.'

'And you weren't.'

'And am I? Probably.'

Luc reached over. 'How late?'

'Almost two weeks.' She clung to Luc's hand and began sobbing her heart out.

The following morning, Ella looked more tired than when she had gone to bed. Her brown eyes were swollen, her face ugly with strain and lifelessness. She came downstairs and threw herself on the sofa. 'I've just been sick.' Crossly, she reached under the cushions. 'What are these?' She examined Luc's library books. 'Banking? Switzerland? Opera?' She chucked them on to the floor. 'A little light bedtime reading?'

'Coffee?' Luc ignored the dig. She had spent the hour after she'd woken up reliving every moment of her time with Lorenzo.

'Tea, please. Very weak. With lemon.' Ella picked up a paper, only to stare into space. The telephone rang. Luc's heart leaped.

'Hello, Miz.' Ella sounded fed up. 'Liz. Yes, I'm back, otherwise I wouldn't be answering, would I? Fantastic, thank you. The Trustees? That's hardly my fault, is it? What for?' She was suspicious. 'Luc, it's Miz. Liz.'

Luc gingerly took the receiver, feeling awkward as if she'd been caught out doing something she shouldn't. 'Hello. The sketches? Well, I've made a start. When's the deadline? That soon? No, no problem.' Luc winced. Preoccupied with and by Lorenzo, she'd completely forgotten about them. 'How's Tim? Very nice evening. I must call her, she'll be missing Alex. Yes. 'Bye.'

'What was all that about?' demanded Ella.

'Remember I did some sketches of the villa? Liz showed them to the owner, who wants some more. As a memento. She's selling it.'

'Oh.'

'I'm even being paid. Liz negotiated it.'

'Taking her cut, I bet.'

It was something Luc hadn't thought of. She shrugged. 'Well, even if she were, so what? By the way, I saw Marina earlier in the week.'

'Really?' Ella scowled and held her stomach. 'Is she still with that creep?'

'Um, except he's out in the wilds of Soviet Central Asia. Don't think she's happy about being abandoned.'

'What did she expect? The guy thinks he's starring in International Rescue.'

'I'll call her later.'

'Before or after you call Lorenzo?'

'I can't call him.' Luc sighed. 'I left a message yesterday.'

She finally had his number. It was engraved on her memory, but she'd written it down in three separate places in case she forgot it. The MINE on the inside of her wrist was fading, she wondered if she could get it tattooed.

Luc cleared the dining table, then fetched a sketchpad and the photographs. Ella flicked through the *Observer* only to throw it aside. She began fiddling with the radio. '*The Archers*? Now I know I'm back.' Abruptly, she turned it off. Wanting to settle down and concentrate, Luc tried to ignore her. After staring into space for a few minutes, Ella picked up the remote. 'Look. *Top Cat*.'

'Um?' Luc frowned, stifling her growing irritation. Her eyes remained on the photographs.

Stony-faced, Ella watched the box, then began pacing up and down. She went to the table and peered over Luc's shoulder. 'That's good. Can I have some paper?' Taking a deep breath, Luc tore a few sheets out of the back of the pad. 'Got a pen?'

'Here.' Luc tried not to sound churlish. She wondered if she shouldn't take herself up to the roof terrace.

A little later, she heard a choked-back sob. Rushing over to the sofa, she put her arm round Ella's heaving shoulders.

'What the fuck am I going to do?'

After 'Not so dear Yannick', Ella had scribbled half a page of vitriol. Her tears were making the black ink run. 'He said, he claimed, that he'd fallen in love with me . . . that he'd move to London . . . that we should live together . . .'

'What?' Luc was bewildered. 'But you'd only just met.'

'Why did he bother to say it?' She sniffed hard. 'It wasn't as if he had to spin a line to get me into bed, was it? Why did he bother? Why did the bastard promise me the earth only to snatch it away?'

'Calm down,' pleaded Luc.

Swiping away her tears, Ella tried. 'That first night on *Les Voiles Blanches*, I thought he was avoiding me because of Henri. Now I know he just didn't want me. The humiliation of it. The shame. Me following him around like some pathetic runt of a puppy that he just wants to dump in the nearest dogs' home. Why do you think I stayed at Athenia? Because I thought he might come looking for me, that's why.'

'Really?'

Ella nodded, her face desolate. 'I took a room so that I could see every boat, ferry and *Flying Dolphin* arrive. I sat on the balcony and watched and watched and watched for days. That's why I went to Corfu.' She shuddered. 'Because Henri mentioned that Madame wanted to visit this particular place. So who went there? Me. Alex was right. I should have "dumb" tattooed across my forehead.'

Luc glanced at the library books. 'Perhaps being lovesick is contagious.'

'Lovesick? I'd prefer smallpox. At least that only leaves scars.' Luc was puzzled. 'Wake up. The evidence of my stupid fling with that scumbag might be arriving next spring.'

For hours the night before Luc had tried to reassure Ella that it was probably a false alarm. Yet another scare. That her body clock was muddled because of the stress and lack of sleep, lack of food . . . Lack of bloody common sense, Ella had howled, before bursting into tears again.

'I'm sure you're not.' Luc tried to sound authoritative. 'Given up smoking? That's good.' Her voice faltered, she stared at Ella with growing alarm.

'I haven't given up. I can't smoke. God knows, I've tried. It makes me retch.' She began howling. 'I am. I know I am.'

This time, Luc was unable to contradict her. She got up to fetch some kitchen roll and handed a wad to Ella. 'What are you going to do?'

'I don't know.' Ella wiped her eyes. 'Have it? Me look after a baby? What a joke. I can't even look after myself.'

'You'd manage if you had to.' Luc looked out of the window at the other pastel-coloured houses in the Mews. 'At least you don't have to worry about money.'

'And you could always babysit. Joke,' added Ella hastily, seeing Luc's alarm. She began tearing the letter into tiny pieces. 'So, I don't fit the stereotype of a single mum jumping the queue for a council flat. But it would still be bloody hard.'

'Your mother managed,' pointed out Luc.

'Well, Janie found it tough. For all her Bohemian ways, she did want a man to share the load with. Especially when I was just a bawling, puking machine. And Pa would visit, until he was dragged off to Cornwall.' Ella smiled sadly. 'Janie really wanted me to meet a nice husband, settle down in the country and have a pack of children and dogs.'

'She did?'

'She said it during one of our last talks. Before things got really bad. Sorry, Mummy.' Ella took a deep breath. 'Sorry for messing up.'

'A baby isn't the end of the world.'

'End of one world.' Ella wiped her eyes and began shredding the soggy kitchen roll. 'You cross a Rubicon when you have kids. I'm not ready to make that leap.' In her frustration, she picked up a cushion and hurled it across the room. 'I can't. I won't.'

Feeling helpless, Luc tried to think rationally. 'You don't necessarily have to.'

'Oh no? Don't I?' Chewing her lip, Ella examined her rose

tattoo. 'I've got a big dilemma. The problem, the dilemma,' she paused, 'is that I can't bear the thought of having an abortion.'

'Oh.' Luc was guarded.

'What do you mean "oh"?'

'Oh. Oh, I'm surprised, I guess.'

'Why?' cried Ella. 'I couldn't do it. Not with my history. Don't you understand? Janie could easily have decided that I was a piffling inconvenience to be hoovered out of her and chucked into an incinerator.'

'Ella,' pleaded Luc, 'that's very . . .'

'That's the truth.' Ella began to weep again.

'I thought you were pro-choice,' said Luc finally.

'I was.' She sounded despairing. 'In the abstract. Before I had to make that choice.'

The following morning, Luc called the Agency. Carole was caustic, asking if she was better.

'Better?' replied Luc, then winced as she remembered that she was meant to have had food poisoning.

'Pity you were so ill,' snapped Carole. 'It was such a lovely day for a stroll with an incredibly dishy man. And a hat box, if my sources aren't mistaken.'

Luc quailed.

'Don't even think of doing that to me again, Lucasta James. If you weren't so bloody good and usually so bloody reliable, I'd tell you where you could put your next assignment. Say sorry, Auntie Carole.'

'Sorry, Auntie Carole,' mumbled Luc.

'You're forgiven. Just. Come in soon and tell me all about him. No more Julian Group, you'll be pleased to hear.'

'You've got something else?' Luc was anxious. Skiving off Friday had put another dent in her battered bank balance.

'Yep. Not exactly groovy, but should be interesting. Outfit

called Platform. A think-tank. Non-party political. Report to Nigel Mann, head of research.'

Luc's heart sank. 'Politics? I know nothing about politics.' Apart from the fact that she wasn't remotely interested in politics.

'Then you'll learn.' Carole sounded impatient. 'You didn't know anything about shipping or property. Now get off the phone and get down there. Got a pen?'

The offices were off Smith Square, near the Houses of Parliament. As Luc made a circle in the *A to Z*, Ella came downstairs. She was hugging her kimono to her like a comforter. 'Morning.' She switched on the kettle.

'Manage to sleep?'

'Eventually.' Her suntan was starting to fade, making her skin look sallow, almost dirty. 'Another present from Lord Snooty?' She stared at the lapis lazuli cuff-links accusingly. 'Are you sure that scumbag didn't try and call me?'

'Yannick? If he did, he didn't leave a message.' They had been through all that the day before. Suddenly Luc longed to escape to work, unable to face listening to Ella talk herself round in circles of confusion and unhappiness. 'Whatever you decide, you ought to go to the doctor.'

'S'pose so.'

'Shall I make an appointment?'

'For fuck's sake. I'm pregnant, not senile.'

The kitchen suddenly seemed too small for both of them. 'I'd better go or I'll be late,' fibbed Luc. 'Are you in tonight?'

'Dunno.'

'Perhaps we can go to a film or something. See how you feel.'

'Sick.' Ella's scowl deepened.

As she walked to the Tube, Luc felt helpless to prevent Ella tearing herself apart. The day before she'd been unable to offer any comfort as Ella had alternately cried her eyes out or cursed Yannick. Luc's suggestions of a picnic in the park, a visit to a gallery, getting a video, even a game of Scrabble had all been turned down flat. By evening she'd felt worn down and worn out.

'What the fuck am I going to do?' Ella had wailed for the umpteenth time.

However, Luc had switched off. Leafing through the Glyndebourne programme, her head had been full of Lorenzo. She'd resented the intrusion. 'I don't know. It's for you to decide.'

'I don't want to decide. I can't decide. Oh God, why has this happened to me?'

Because you were typically careless, because once again you were playing Russian roulette with your body, Luc had wanted to reply.

'Don't just sit there looking as smug as fuck,' Ella had yelled, as Luc turned the page. 'What would you do?'

Luc had put aside the programme. 'What would I do? I'd have no choice. I couldn't afford to have a child on my own and that is that. You've got money, so you've got the luxury of choice. I'm going to bed, I've got to be up for work.'

'Luxury of choice?' Ella had stared at Luc. 'Are you having a dig? You sound just like Miz or Alex.'

It was one of the rare times that Luc had openly referred to Ella's wealth. Waiting for a Tube at South Kensington station, Luc wondered what had goaded her into it. Wanting to shock Ella into shutting up? Irritation that her daydreams about Lorenzo had been interrupted? Or the prickles of jealousy that Ella's privilege and bank balance could buy her a conscience as well as everything else?

A few hours later Luc was thumbing through *Who's Who*.

Her terminal was dicky, invitations had to be sent out, and it would be smashing if she could possibly do the envelopes by hand, with a quick shufti to check on any gongs or baubles. 'Some of these chaps and chapesses get into a tizz if the CBE or whatnot is left off,' said Nigel.

Very tall and very thin with a beaky nose, he reminded Luc of a stork in a pin-striped suit. He wasn't that much older than she was but because of his arcane speech and general air of elaborate courtesy, he seemed to come from another generation. With much throat-clearing and pinking of cheeks, he'd confided that the, er, ladies' facilities could be found in the basement.

'You're in here. With my four wise men.' He'd thrown open a door. 'This is Miss James. Luc.' She'd blushed as four pairs of eyes glanced up from screens and documents. Nigel had introduced them all, but in her self-consciousness, she'd failed to take in their names.

Very soon the four were wrapped up in their work. None of them paid her any more attention, which gave her the chance to get her bearings. The office was in an eighteenth-century terrace of houses in a street whose hush was broken by the chime of Big Ben. She was sitting in what once had been a first-floor drawing room. Huge windows were at either end. The ugly metal shelving, crammed floor to ceiling with books, reports and Parliamentary papers, the dilapidated desks, the computers, were all unable to detract from its perfect proportions or cornicing.

The atmosphere reminded her of a boys' school, and she was stuck with the swots. Robert, Marcus, Hugh, Rupert. Who was who? Hunched over their desks, they were identically earnest. Their suits seemed too big, as if they were waiting to grow into them, their whiskerless faces were pallid, as if they'd spent too long on their studies and not enough time in the fresh air. While one dissected a Treasury forecast, another was writing a report on local government funding. Groovy they weren't; intimidatingly superbright they undoubtedly were.

The envelopes were to enclose an invitation to a lecture by the American Ambassador. As she wrote out the name of a member of the Cabinet, Luc half tuned in to a chat about the Test match. She looked up to find one of the Wise Men staring at her as if she were an alien species. Blushing, he hastily looked away. She realised that the four were probably all as shy of her as she was of them. Suddenly she felt comforted, like Snow White among the seven dwarfs.

The Test chat was interrupted by the telephone. 'Rupe,' said one of the other Wise Men – Marcus? – 'Your journo mate from Londoners' Diary. Trawling for some goss.'

Apparently things were quiet because it was near the end of term. 'Is that a fact?' drawled Rupert. He whistled. Putting down the phone, he announced, 'Whisper that Crummock's going to the Home Office.'

The news was greeted with the sort of excitement that was usually reserved for England winning the World Cup.

'How are we doing?' asked a voice after lunch. The Wise Men had disappeared, leaving the television on in the corner of the room. The cricket had started.

'Eighty for five,' said Luc idly, playing with her cuff-links. Eyes on the screen, she'd been daydreaming about Lorenzo. Turning round, she almost fell off her chair.

'Splendid,' boomed a former Prime Minister. 'Hear that, Nigel? Have them all out by tea.'

'Smashing,' said Nigel. 'Can I introduce you to Miss James?'

Nigel had called her into his office and asked if she could type his dictation directly into the computer. 'You don't mind being my amanuensis? Now, if you'd sit here.'

Realising they'd be sitting side by side in front of the screen, just inches apart, Luc felt a nano-second's unease.

'It's the conclusion to a report on the Education Green Paper. I hope you won't find it too dull.'

Her respect turned to awe as he delivered almost two thousand words in logically ordered, grammatically perfect sentences, only interrupting himself to ask if she'd like a break or care for some tea. 'Shall we continue then? Smashing.'

*

'Nerdy but nice,' said Luc, opening some wine. Buoyed up, she felt like celebrating. It had been one of the best days' work in ages. Nigel and the Wise Men were more likely to moon at Madam Speaker than click their fingers and call out, 'Oi, you, the temp.' The work had been a thousand times more interesting than the Julian Group. 'How was your day?'

Ella shrugged, frowning at her split ends. 'Fine.'

'Did you go?'

'Where?'

'To the doctor.'

'No.'

'Why not?'

'Why should I?' demanded Ella belligerently. 'Listen, Luc, just because you've finally got yourself sorted with a man and found a halfway decent job, don't start a lecture.'

'I'm not,' protested Luc. 'I just thought . . .' She shrugged. 'By the way, what's an amanuensis?'

'Someone who writes from dictation. For example, Milton's daughters after he went blind,' snapped Ella. 'And you might have asked me before painting the downstairs bedroom.' Luc gave a start, as if she'd been slapped. 'This is my house.'

'As if I could ever forget.'

There was a long silence.

Luc snatched up her sketchpad from the dining table. A half-completed sketch of the villa had a brown ring on it. Gasping with fury, she tore it out. 'Thanks.' Staring at Ella, she ripped the paper into eight and dropped the pieces on the floor.

The Doll's House was horribly silent. No music, no giggling as they sat in facepacks watching soaps, no clatter as they cooked, no muttering from Ella as she wrestled with the *Guardian* cross-word. Both lay on their beds two floors apart, thinking about a decade of friendship. And blaming the other for screwing it up.

Ella went out on to the terrace and fingered the honeysuckle. She'd expected to count on Luc's total support after all the hell she'd suffered: Yannick, *Les Voiles Blanches*, the nightmare journey home. The hell she was still suffering. Instead of support, there'd been indifference. Luc had either been a zombie – playing with her cuff-links and daydreaming about Lord Snooty – or snide, with her little 'luxury of choice' speech. Either way, she'd given the impression that she didn't care. The sudden mateyness with Liz. Changing the bedroom. The thought of home had been a beacon in the darkness. Now, more than ever before, Ella needed constants. Familiarity.

Downstairs, Luc tried to focus on her drawing. Why did Ella have to use her as a scapegoat for Yannick? For being dumb enough to get pregnant? Just as life seemed to be getting sweeter, Ella had to sour it with her nastiness. What more did Ella expect her to do? She'd been there for her, listened to her, offered practical advice which had been ignored. 'The downstairs bedroom': it had been her room for the past three years. The Doll's House had been her home. Who'd housekept, who'd been the homebody when Ella was away backpacking round Asia or on those road protests or swanning around the Greek islands?

To ease the ache in her lower back, Ella decided to have a bath. Her body felt bloated, her breasts tender, like the run-up to the curse. For the hundredth time that day, she was momentarily convinced she was all right, then a split second later knew she was fooling herself. The doctor would confirm it, a home testing kit from any chemist would confirm it; she'd avoided both because it meant the end of any hope. Something that brought joy to millions only filled her with terror and panic.

With child.

She slammed her fist on the side of the bath. She was knocked up, not with child. Why did that Victorian phrase keep echoing around her head? Why were these fleeting moments of satisfaction in her own fertility becoming more frequent? Why had she allowed herself dangerous daydreams about an adorable toddler with its father's topaz eyes?

'You wouldn't mind? Smashing,' said Nigel. 'I'm off to the House. Back at midday. Can I divert my phone to yours? Ta.'

Luc spent an agreeable time going through that day's papers and compiling any relevant cuttings. It gave her a chance for a clandestine browse through the fashion pages and gossip columns.

The four Wise Men were busy studying reports or tap-tapping away on their keyboards. They were getting used to her. Robert?, Marcus?, who had stared at her the day before, managed to smile without blushing. She was getting used to them, their cleverness, their earnestness, the ease with which they talked to the Great and the Good on the phone.

Flicking past a report on the Soviet elections, she wondered if Marina had found another flat. She must call her. Thinking of the situation at the Doll's House, Luc turned the page so violently she almost ripped it. Too angry and hurt to face Ella, she'd spent the whole of the previous evening incarcerated in her bedroom. Correction, the room she rented, which was now a million times nicer with its creamy walls than it had ever been in lilac and cerise.

Playing with her cuff-links, she read Lorenzo's horoscope. A good day for communications. He'd call her later, she knew. Sometimes she could almost feel the imprint of MINE on her wrist. The memories of their time together constantly waltzed around her head. One moment they were in the hat shop, the next lying on the beach in the dawn light. He was with her like her shadow. Had he written MINE on her soul?

Sometimes, her longing to be with him was so intense she couldn't breathe. Her craving was worse than a junkie's need for a fix. That morning, walking past a builder's van, she'd heard the same song that had been playing on MTV that evening in the hotel suite. She'd stopped and listened to it. Strap-hanging in the crowded rush-hour Tube, her head full of Lorenzo, she'd missed Westminster and found herself at Temple.

Everything she did, she mentally referred back to him. Working with Nigel and the Wise Men was far better than her usual run of jobs. And even Lorenzo would be slightly impressed she'd been given the run-down on the cricket by a former Prime Minister.

Could she kindly have a sort-through of the bookshelves? Smashing. Biogs, history, reference, just restore some basic order. Keep a look-out for a pile of EDMs that had gone walkies. Oh, sorry. Early Day Motions. And that had nothing to do with syrup of figs. Ha ha.

Used to the Wise Men politely ignoring her – they weren't hostile, just completely focused on their work – Luc was surprised when Marcus? Hugh? Robert? asked her if she'd like some coffee, then which was the better band.

'The Lemon Cakes,' said Luc.

'Hear hear,' called Marcus? Hugh? Robert?, as if he were already sitting on those green benches in the Commons' chamber. 'Did you see them at Glastonbury?'

'Did you go?' Luc was taken aback. Surely he was more Garsington than Glastonbury and only listened to Elgar?

It was as if Marcus? Hugh? Robert? had been sent ahead to scout a route which the others could safely follow. Luc idled away half an hour in chit-chat, then, curious to see whether von Retzen was listed, she flicked through an ancient, dog-eared copy of the *Almanach de Gotha*.

'Checking up on your boyfriends?' joked Rupert. 'Finding a suitable husband?'

'No,' squeaked Luc, slamming the book shut so hard dust flew up.

*

Ella spent the afternoon in the City with her Trustees and stock-broker, going through her share portfolio. Their chit-chats about yields and dividends, capital, liquidity, price-earnings ratios usually washed over her. This time, however, she sat up straight and listened, making notes. What was the difference between gilts and bonds? Puts and calls?

Her shaming ignorance tied her tongue. Who trusts the Trustees? She left, thoughtful.

'Perhaps she's finally growing up,' her stuffy broker remarked to his assistant afterwards. 'If only she'd take that dreadful thing out of her nose and put on some decent kit.'

At seven o'clock, Luc was back at the Doll's House.

From being home only a day earlier, it now felt like enemy territory. If she and Ella didn't make up, then what? Mentally she began removing her own books and CDs from the shelves where they were all jumbled up with the evidence of Ella's past, if fleeting, enthusiasms: yoga, Buddhism, alternative healing, antique textiles, bridge.

Hearing a key in the latch and Ella's footsteps on the stairs, Luc stiffened. If she'd turned round, she would've known that her paralysing awkwardness was mutual. They both realised that they'd been dreading this moment all day. Luc half acknowledged a cool, curt 'Hi'.

Ella flung open a window as if to dilute all the tension in the air. 'Nice day?' She sounded indifferent.

'Fine, thanks.' Luc was equally guarded. 'You?'

Neither could meet the other's eyes.

'Fine.' Ella's cheeks grew as pink as Luc's. She eyed a small bag on the table. 'New CD? *Don Giovanni* by any chance?'

'So?'

'OK. I'm just trying to make small, sorry, tiny talk, that's all.'

'Why bother?' Luc sighed.

'Oh, for fuck's sake. Pathetic.' Ella stomped towards the stairs.

'Me, pathetic?' called Luc. 'You're the one who started all this.'

Ella turned round, her face screwed up with misery. 'I didn't mean it,' she protested. She was close to tears. 'I'm sorry. Really sorry. I wish I could claim I don't know what's got into me. But I do. Yannick, unfortunately.'

'Don't cry,' pleaded Luc.

'All last night I expected you to say sorry. You usually do, even when things aren't your fault.'

'That's because I'm so wet.'

Rueful smiles began to relax their faces. 'Sorry about your drawing. I wasn't concentrating.'

'Sorry about the bedroom. Should've asked.'

'It's brilliant. We must get someone round to look at that damp. Anyway, I've decided the whole place needs brightening up. What colour should we have in here? Something grown-up and neutral, I guess. Apricot?'

'Perhaps.' Luc was cautious. The Doll's House had remained almost as Janie had left it. When Liz had once suggested some changes, Ella had gone ballistic.

Ella began pacing. 'Rip up the carpet. Get the sofas re-covered . . .' She sniffed.

'What's that?'

'What's what?'

'Your scent. New. Nice.'

Luc squirmed. 'Aftershave,' she admitted. 'Lorenzo's aftershave. Don't laugh. I know it's silly, but it brings him closer.' As she breathed in the citrus, images of him waltzed through her head.

Ella's eyes widened. 'God, Luc. You're obsessed.'

'I know.'

'You've never, ever been like this.'

'I know.'

'Next you'll be practising writing Lucasta von Retzen.' She grew alarmed. 'You haven't? Blimey.' She stared, troubled. 'What's his form?'

'What do you mean?'

'His past. Exes. Girlfriends. Why isn't this perfect man married?'

'Hasn't found the right person, I guess.' Luc smiled to herself.

'And you're thinking you might be her,' suggested Ella gently. 'Why couldn't either of us just have a normal holiday romance? Shit. Listen, Luc, be careful. You've fallen in love with a stranger who lives hundreds of miles away . . .'

'So?'

'So, there could be a lot of hurt in those hundreds of miles.'

Luc fiddled with her cuff-links, gazing into the blue depths. 'He's so perfect.'

'A perfect stranger,' said Ella. 'Drop the daydreams, forget the fantasies. Especially the one about being Countess von Retzen. You've only spent a few hours with the guy and you're already up the aisle. Still, better than being up the duff.'

Luc winced. She didn't dare ask outright if Ella had seen the doctor. 'What have you been doing?'

'Meeting with the Trustees. Had to sign some papers and stuff.' As usual Ella kept things vague. 'And then I went to the doctor.'

'And?'

'And? And either I should be painting the spare bedroom pink or blue. Or getting out the gin and running a hot bath. Confirmation via a thin blue line. I'm pregnant.'

As Ella worried at the *Guardian* crossword, the telephone rang. 'Luc.' She held out the receiver, mouthing, 'Think it's Lord Snooty. Nice voice.'

Luc swallowed hard. She had a rush of adrenaline, her pulse went nuclear. 'Hello.'

' "Tell me not, sweet, I am unkind . . ." Shall I go on?' Lorenzo laughed.

'You've been reading Lovelace,' exclaimed Luc, happiness coursing through her.

'You must be bored with men quoting him to you.'

'It's rarely happened. Where are you?'

'Car. At the airfield.'

Luc tried to imagine him all those miles away, parked near a tiny control tower, a windsock full of breeze, little planes like toys.

'Have you got a Russian visa?' he asked.

'No. Why?'

'Because I wanted you to come to St Petersburg. There's space on the flight from London tomorrow morning.'

'Tomorrow? I can't . . .' Luc was desolate.

'Next time I'll give you more warning.'

Hearing him light a cigarette, she remembered their time together on the beach in the dawn light. 'How long will you be away?'

'Until Friday.'

'And after that?' She prayed that he'd say he'd be in London.

'Vienna, Budapest, the Czech Republic.'

'Oh.'

'I need to see my tailor.'

'As one does,' said Luc, her heart thumping.

'Urgently. But I can't come to London in the next few weeks, so perhaps my tailor could come to me.'

'Perhaps.' A huge grin broke across Luc's face. 'So what have you been doing apart from reading Lovelace and going flying?'

'Listening to *Don Giovanni* . . .'

'Crikey,' exclaimed Ella, who'd tactfully tried to keep out of the way. 'An hour and ten minutes.'

Luc gave a dreamy sigh. 'I miss him so much it hurts.'

Ella rolled her eyes. 'Noodles or rice?'
'I just ache and ache and ache.'
'My back aches. Noodles or rice?'
'He's so perfect.'

'Dear Yannick'.

After Luc had gone to work the following morning, Ella began another letter in her bold italics. She crossed out the dear. 'Yannick, Remember me, Ella? The one who . . .'

The one who fell for a pretty face and all that laid-back charm, which belied a surprisingly sharp mind. The one who picnicked with you in a cove beside glass-clear water, allowed herself to get hazy on white wine and grass. The one who trusted to luck rather than to Durex. The one who'd like to delete you from her memory, but who can't, because her luck ran out.

She threw down her pen and examined the rose tattoo on her arm. Yet another drunken mistake, branding her for a lifetime. This other error needn't. A certain amount of discomfort, the doctor explained, but it was routine, safe.

Yannick, remember me, Ella? One of your romances that happened as you pursued your endless summers around the world on *Les Voiles Blanches*. You might have denied me as you massaged oil into Madame and went to her cabin, but I've got proof. I'd like to destroy the evidence and forget I ever met you, but it's not that easy.

'Just a few tiny minutes. Turn a blind eye, *caro. Por favore,*' wheedled Marina, who'd been pouting into a side mirror as she put on some lipstick. The Alfa was vaguely on a double yellow line, less parked than abandoned.

'A few minutes,' warned the policeman who was rewarded by a purr of '*Grrrazie mille*'.

Luc had hardly closed the door when the car roared off. The over-revving of the engine almost masked the crunching of gears.

Turning to look at her, Marina clutched her arm. 'You look marrrvellous. The new job, perhaps? Or a new boyfrrriend? The one who was calling for hours last night when I was trying to get through? *Cara*, you must tell me all your news.'

Luc wished Marina would keep her eyes on the road and her hands on the wheel as they hurtled round Parliament Square.

'And Ella's back, Liz told me. I can't believe those two are seeesters. So different. We go to my leetle drinking den for some nice refreshing champagne and then our movie. Such fun.' Marina gave her another squeeze and a huge smile.

'How's Alex?' yelled Luc, wondering how Marina could steer and change gear one handed, while the other held back her long dark ringlets.

'Still in his boring khan or stan.' Her melted-chocolate eyes grew still softer. 'We're meeting in Berlin soon. Oh, I'm looking forrrrward to it. We'll spend the whole time in bed.' She giggled wickedly.

'Any luck finding another flat?' asked Luc, when they were settled with their champagne and olives.

'What drrramas. What I'm going through, *cara*.' She leaned forward, ringed hand holding Luc's. 'Alex refuses to move. Refuses. Says it's too much hassle. I'll work on him in Berlin. Then my husband Gordon. The sheet. The bastard has stopped our joint credit card. And he's threatening to take my car back. My birthday present. I told him, tough sheet.'

'So you're in contact then?' said Luc. 'I suppose you must be, with the divorce and everything.'

'What divorce?' Marina spat an olive stone into her fist. 'Gordon just laughs. Refuses to consider it. Suddenly he's discovered he's a good Catholic. I have to go to my lawyers again. It's costing forrrtunes.'

'Perhaps he doesn't want you to leave him,' suggested Luc.

'He's just being a peeg. Yesterday I went round to find he's changed the locks on the house. My house.' Marina's voice grew shrill, people stared.

Embarrassed, Luc could only come up with a tame 'Oh dear'.

'And it gets worse.' Marina chomped on an olive, looking like an indignant rodent. 'He has found another woman. Some beetch is in my house, cooking for my husband, in my kitchen. He claims she's just a frrriend, helping him out. Pah. I know her. She's the ladies' captain at the golf club and a scheming *putana*.'

Luc thought her champagne glass would shatter.

'And that beetch, that bastard, are inviting my friends over for lunch on Sunday. How you like that?'

'But you're with Alex . . .'

'Alex,' cried Marina. 'Alex is in his khan or stan. What use is he? I cannot believe my bastard husband can replace me so easily. So queeeckly. The insult.'

Luc was bemused. 'But you've replaced him. With Alex.'

'Gordon knows nothing about Alex.'

'What?'

'Luc, Gordon doesn't know Alex exists. And no one who knows Gordon knows. They all think I'm staying with Gina, my seester. Not in some dump of a flat in a horrible place in fear of my life.' Seeing Luc's bafflement, Marina added, '*Cara*, with a mobile phone you can be anywhere in the world. Gina's, Liz's, England, Greece.'

'Why not tell your husband? About Alex.'

'One day soon. Not yet.' Marina shrugged. 'I want a settlement, Luc. Adultery means no alimony.'

Luc was speechless.

'I was a good wife to Gordon. I supported him by teaching when he had nothing. I put every penny of mine into the business, I helped him build the company. I put up with his obsession with golf. You know how we spent our honeymoon? At the British Open. I would never have met Alex if Gordon hadn't stood me up for two hours while he was on the driving range.'

Luc tried not to wince as Marina gripped her hand. 'And now he barricades me from my own house, refuses to take my calls, is leaving me penniless, while he spends money on someone else. When I think of someone sleeping in my bed, and she is, despite what he claims, it makes me sick to the stomach.'

'What does Alex say?' said Luc finally.

'He tells me I'm the one who's scheming.' Marina wiped her fingers on a napkin. 'Says I have no right to a settlement. That I should walk away. That I should be honest with Gordon. Tell him the truth about us. I will. One day soon. Not yet.'

During the film, Marina seemed possessed. Her body was clenched, she gnawed her lip, her eyes stared at the screen but she seemed to take in nothing. In the half-light Luc saw a bitter fury suddenly warp all of Marina's sweet prettiness. The distortion reminded her of the grotesque Francis Bacon portrait that Lorenzo had studied in the gallery.

As the days passed, Ella withdrew further into herself. Along with her suntan, all her vitality and zest for life were fading away. Apart from Luc, she cut herself off from her friends. The sitting room was chaotic; Ella had begun redecorating but had given up. The furniture was covered in dust-sheets, half the walls were newly painted in apricot, the rest yet to be done. Luc would return home from work and try and coax Ella out of her torment. Among the piles of books were pamphlets from the local church; one afternoon Ella had gone to see the priest.

'Why?' asked Luc.

'Because I needed help.'

'Did you get it?'

'Well, it's counselling on the cheap. Why waste money on psychotherapists?'

'Don't be flippant,' said Luc. 'Was it helpful?'

'Yes.' Ella fiddled with her bangles. 'I'd be killing an unborn child and that is that.'

Luc winced. 'Are things really that black and white?'

'They are to him. No weasel words like pro-choice. No comforting cosiness or excuses. He called it a death on demand.' Ella took a deep breath. 'It was refreshing, I guess. To talk to someone who's so ethically sure of himself.'

'I don't get it,' exclaimed Luc. 'You've never had any truck with all that. What about school? Telling Sister Joseph that the Bible was out of the Bronze Age.'

'I was being the little smart-arse show-off.'

Luc sighed in despair. Going to the kitchen to get some wine, she noticed the Yellow Pages was open under Pregnancy. Ella had ringed an ad for a clinic and noted down a time. 'What does TOP stand for?'

'Termination of Pregnancy.' Ella swallowed hard. 'I thought I ought to talk to them too. I'm going tomorrow.'

Ella went to the clinic the following day. Alone. She'd refused to let Luc go with her. She returned from the appointment grim-faced and wouldn't discuss it. Instead she began furiously to paint the wall around the fireplace.

Disturbed by Ella's visit to the priest, Luc was even more alarmed to find that she had got hold of some pro-life pamphlets and was sickened at the masochistic pleasure she took in reading out the gruesome details of the procedure.

'Stop it. There's no point in torturing yourself like this.' Luc leaped to her feet and snatched the papers from Ella's hand. She tore downstairs and dumped them in the outside dustbin. 'That's better.' She stared at Ella who was once again dissolving into tears. 'Ella. Sssh. Sssh.' Luc put her arms round her.

Ella clung to Luc. 'I'm going mad . . .'

'Sssh.' Luc's shirt was getting wet.

'I just don't know what to do . . . I'm so confused . . .'

'Wish there was more I could do.' Luc was also close to tears.

'I haven't got long to decide. You see,' she gulped, 'every day I'm getting more attached . . .'

'Perhaps you should go away for a few days,' suggested Luc, when Ella had calmed down. 'Help you see things differently.'

'Where?'

'Cornwall? Sea air, country walks.'

'I hate the country, it brings me out in hives. I always think there's a gibbet round the next corner.' Ella scowled. 'Cornwall? Oh great, perhaps I should touch base with the *Dreadnought*. No fucking way.'

'Just an idea,' said Luc apologetically.

'By the way, Liz called earlier. Something about those sketches.'

'I'll talk to her later. Listen, whatever you decide, I'm here for you. You know that.'

Clutching Luc's hand, Ella nodded.

While Luc felt sorry for Ella and tried to be supportive, nothing could dent her well-being and sudden zest for life. A parcel, FedExed from St Petersburg, arrived at the Doll's House. Inside was a huge tin of caviar.

Wrapped in joy, Luc almost skipped to the office.

Working with Nigel and the Wise Men was so congenial it seemed almost like a holiday. The hours flashed past, she learned a lot. At the end of her first week, she almost felt guilty about asking Nigel to sign her timesheet.

Lorenzo was with her constantly. St Petersburg, Vienna, Prague, he was as well travelled as he was well read. Luc was terrified that one day he'd write her off as a dull little homebody. The need to impress him whenever he telephoned her, to keep him interested, panicked her. Where was *How to be Cultured, Sophisticated and Interesting Made Simple*?

Suddenly she was buying new books, CDs. She gathered up

a rain-forest of theatre and concert schedules, prospectuses for evening classes.

She came home one night to find Ella going through a battered photo album. She was crying. Luc assumed it was because of all the hundreds of pictures of Janie, looking so much like Ella they could've been twins. It was only when she was close up she realised that Ella was looking at a black and white image, strange enough to be of the lunar surface. 'That's me, Luc. In embryo. When Janie had a scan. Now tell me life only begins at birth.'

Liz and Tim had paid their usual Saturday morning visit to the gym, when Luc arrived with the completed sketches. They were making brunch. Tim was poaching eggs in their operating theatre-clean kitchen. His skinny, freckled legs peeked out from under his apron.

'Gosh, Luc. Sight for sore eyes. You do look well. Glowing.'

'Been on a diet?' asked Liz, surveying her. She frowned at her own size eight reflection in the glass panel of the oven. 'I must. Put on almost a kilo according to the scales in the changing room.'

'Lizzy,' protested Tim. 'Don't be silly. There is such a thing as being too thin.'

'No woman can be too thin or too rich,' retorted Liz, smoothing back her shiny bob. 'Speaking of that, what's got into Ella? She was even more off with me than usual when I called the other day. Positively rude.'

'Perhaps you caught her at the wrong moment,' suggested Luc diplomatically.

'She had a cold, but that's no excuse. She should stop drinking and smoking so much. Destroys Vitamin C,' said Liz, who'd caught Ella during a bout of weeping.

'These summer colds are wretched,' said Tim.

'I gather she's redecorating the house,' continued Liz. 'About time. Very morbid, all this shrine-to-Janie business. She should've come to me. Trade. Still, if she's got the money to waste paying retail . . .'

'Let's eat,' cut in Tim hastily, spooning the perfectly poached eggs on to warm plates. 'Go through, Luc.'

Luc went through, gingerly edging past the etched glass wall into the dining room. The spare perfection of the decor reminded her of Lorenzo. 'How's work, Tim?'

'So-so. Still waiting to hear about the Glasgow project.' He passed her a basket of warm rolls.

'And there's Ladbroke Street,' prompted Liz.

'More clients from hell.' He pulled a face. 'She wants this, he wants that. It's more like being a marriage guidance counsellor than an architect. This is my very last domestic project, I swear.'

'And what about the other house? In Geneva?' Luc went pink.

'That?' growled Liz, about to butter her roll but changing her mind. 'Still no decision. We've more or less written it off. Apparently Lorenzo's in St Petersburg.'

'Really?' said Luc, trying not to think about the massive tin of caviar in the fridge at home.

'And, according to that hag Madame Royer, he was in London last week. Didn't even have the courtesy to call.' Liz was shrill with indignation.

'I admit I was surprised,' said Tim.

Luc squirmed in her seat. 'Perhaps he was busy.'

'Perhaps.' He reached out for another roll and got a warning 'Timmy' from Liz. 'I consoled myself with the thought that I wouldn't have to deal with him.'

'Oh?' Luc was puzzled.

'He's perfectly pleasant, of course. But Alex was right, he needs a lake of anti-freeze in his bloodstream.'

She wanted to protest that she'd seen Lorenzo's warmth, his tenderness.

'I hear you've seen Marina,' said Liz. 'She called last night.'

'In a bit of a state, wasn't she?' clucked Tim. 'Poor girl. Missing Alex.'

'Um. So she claimed.' Liz sounded sceptical. 'Thought I'd never get her off the phone.' She got up. 'Now, let's have a look at these sketches. Coffee? Latte? Decaff skimmed, all right for you, Luc?'

'Otherwise known as a "why bother".' Tim pulled a face. 'Lizzy's on the warpath about caffeine.'

'You're far too important to me to get a heart attack,' Liz briskly patted his arm. 'When you're seventy, you'll thank me.'

Tim smiled. 'How are the lobbyists, Luc?'

'Not lobbyists. Think-tank. Policy researchers. Great.'

'You're finally working somewhere convivial? Good for you. Any chance that something permanent will come out of it?'

Luc nodded. 'Possibly.' When she had gone in to get Nigel to sign her timesheet the day before, he'd hinted there might be a job for her. Smashing if she could let him have a quick shufti at a CV along with a brief line expressing her interest if something were to come up.

'You didn't mention anything about you know what?' Ella's expression was sour. She was still in her dressing-gown, sitting on the roof terrace. An unopened paperback and another half-completed letter to Yannick lay on the table at her elbow.

'Of course not.' Luc guessed that Tim was desperate for Liz to have some children. Ella's news would upset both of them.

'How's Miz and Timid?'

'Liz and Tim,' corrected Luc.

'Miz and Timid,' repeated Ella.

'He seems to be waiting for all these clients to commit. I was thinking, perhaps we could get them over for dinner.' Luc thought of the generous cheque in her bag that Liz had given her for the sketches.

'You can.'

'Oh, come on, Ella.' Luc sighed. 'Isn't it time you and Liz became a bit more, well,' she paused, 'sisterly?'

'Just because there's some vague, accidental blood tie . . .'

'Half-sisters is hardly vague.'

Ella's teeth were clenched. 'Liz and I don't like each other. Never have. Never will. You invite them over, I'll be in Outer Mongolia that night.'

Luc glanced at her watch, then at Ella. 'Come on. Get ready or we'll be late.'

'You go. I don't feel like it.'

'It'll do you good to get out . . .' She'd booked tickets for the matinee in Holland Park.

'It won't. Look, Luc, I know what's good for me and it's not going with you to *Il Trovatore* as part of your self-improvement programme to suck up to Lord Snooty. OK? Honestly, what's got into you? You're so priggish suddenly with all this pseudo highbrow bullshit. No soaps, no mags, no *Top of the Pops*, no *Daily Mail*. Actually, no fun. He's hundreds of miles away, you think he really cares if you listen to Radio 3? Which, incidentally, you don't enjoy.'

'You've got paint on your bangles.' Luc just about swallowed her fury. 'See you later.'

When Luc came back, Ella apologised, ruefully saying that she wished she could blame her foul mood on PMT. She had made dinner as a peace offering. Luc, whose afternoon had been almost spoilt by the outburst, forgave her and put it down to the strain Ella was under.

On the dust-sheeted sofa, they finished off the caviar watching a repeat of *Inspector Morse*.

'Another Saturday night in,' remarked Luc during an ad-break. The pre-Greece Ella who'd spent her nights partying and clubbing seemed to belong to a different age. 'Are we getting old or something?'

'Not old.' Ella adjusted a cushion to ease her back. 'Sad. Actually, not sad. Tragic.'

On Tuesday morning, having been urged by the Wise Men to go for it, Luc tentatively left an envelope on Nigel's desk. In it was a copy of her CV and a covering letter. She suddenly realised how sick she'd become of temping. She wanted the security of a proper job, the feeling of belonging, of being part of a team.

Despite her initial misgivings, she enjoyed being at Platform. Each day as she walked from Westminster Tube and across Parliament Square into the hushed, timeless streets behind the Abbey, she felt more at home. The work was interesting, her colleagues were kindly and good-hearted, even the offices suited her. Their cosy chaos was far more lovable than the Julian Group's soulless slick. Threadbare cashmere compared to immaculate polyester.

She was gradually getting to know people in the building. The tweedy young men, old before their time; the frighteningly clever women who had low voices, low heels, and lunched with Cabinet members. They followed the cricket as keenly as the men.

Why Platform? Considering that she hadn't actually voted at the last election, something she kept ultra quiet about, Luc wondered. She still couldn't name half the members of the Cabinet, let alone the Opposition Front Bench. She didn't understand how one of the Wise Men could describe politics as the best game in town. 'Cross between Snakes and Ladders and Cluedo, Luc.'

Ella had sneered: 'The place hardly sounds the cutting edge of cool.'

'It's not.' Luc had shrugged. Coming home every evening she felt that her brain had enjoyed a workout. Been stretched. She was getting blasé about bumping into faces she saw on *Newsnight*, which she'd started watching. A new world was opening up for her, one where she felt strangely at ease. One which would be approved of by Lorenzo, she was certain.

Having made up her mind to apply for a permanent job, she wondered how she had temped for so long, working for companies like the Julian Group or Hornbeam and Harold.

'Smashing,' said Nigel later, distracted. 'We'll talk properly at the end of the week. For the next few days, I'm afraid it's flap city. Shoulders, wheels, hands, deck et cetera. Wish we could have three months' hols like those blighters over the road.'

'Who?' She realised too late he was talking about the MPs.

Nigel looked exhausted. His eyes were red with tiredness. He was putting the finishing touches to a transport paper that was due at the printers on Friday afternoon. He'd been working over the weekend and until two that morning. 'Would you mind staying late tonight?'

Luc worked flat out, with no time for a proper lunchbreak, just sandwiches at her desk. Nigel had her typing, digging out files and cuttings, phoning information departments at ministries, oil companies, hauliers and scores of other places, whom she had to bully into faxing her statistics.

At ten o'clock, headachy and almost cross-eyed, she dragged herself wearily home. Ella was already in bed. The sitting room was finished, the dust-sheets put away. There was a message that Lorenzo had called. Could she call back, urgently. It jolted Luc. She'd hardly thought about him all day. Smiling to herself, she frantically began to dial, but there was no reply.

She called him the following lunchtime from a phone box outside St John's Church in Smith Square. Her palms sweated, excitement seemed to have unleashed a hundred wriggly eels into her insides. She knew the number off by heart, but still checked it against Ella's note.

'Von Retzen.' The voice sounded cool and crisp.

'Lorenzo? It's Luc. Is this a bad time?' Alarmed, she watched her money disappearing. With twenty pence left, she fumbled and fed another pound coin into the slot.

'No. Perfect time.' He laughed. 'Where are you?'

'A stinky phone box. Oh God, my money's running out again. Shit.'

'I'll call you back. What's your number?'

As she waited, Luc wondered if she'd need to earn the annual GDP of small African nation to afford to call Lorenzo. She pounced on the receiver after half a ring.

'A stinky phone box?' he continued. 'Why haven't you got a mobile so I can pester you night and day? How are you?'

'Well.' She was suddenly gloriously, joyously, laughingly well. 'How was St Petersburg? Thank you for the caviar. How are you? Where are you?' Her words came out in a rush. Just hearing his voice was making her melt.

'Beautiful. A pleasure. Could be better. Geneva.' He laughed again. 'I have a big problem.'

'What problem?'

'I have to see my tailor. Very soon. In the Czech Republic. Can I?'

Luc felt giddy. 'Does your tailor need a visa? How soon?'

'No visa. This weekend. Friday. Can I arrange a ticket?'

She didn't hesitate. 'Yes.'

Nigel let her go at six o'clock, puzzled as to why the highly conscientious, helpful, meticulous Luc had completely gone off the boil since lunchtime. In fact, she'd been more hindrance than help. She must realise how vital it was to get this stuff together. His wife, a radio producer, collected him from the office at ten-thirty.

'This arrived for you. Horny-looking courier,' said Ella, holding out an envelope. Luc tore it open and whooped. Inside was an open return ticket to Prague. Ella peered at it and whistled. 'Slumming it in business class, are we? Lord Snooty's work?' Luc nodded ecstatically. 'When are you going?'

'Friday night, I guess.'

'The day after tomorrow? You'll be away this weekend?'

Luc failed to register Ella's troubled expression. 'Shit, I've got so much to do. What am I going to wear? Better put on some washing. Must call the airline.'

Ella raised an eyebrow. ' "I would walk a million miles for one of your smiles". You would too, wouldn't you, Luc? He must really be something.'

'He is. I can't believe I'm going to see him so soon.' Luc squirmed and hugged herself in delight. 'Perfect, perfect Lorenzo.'

Chapter Ten

'Go away.' Sensing he was trying to pick her pocket, Luc wrenched her arm free of the whining beggar boy. 'Fuck off.' Startled by her malevolence, he scampered off into the crowd.

Her eyes scanned the cathedral-like railway station. There were statues, there was gilding, but where was the ticket office? Who could she ask? The words on all the signs were utterly alien, looking like a very bad Scrabble hand. She'd miss her train. A whistle blew, engines were rumbling. While she was stranded on her island of helplessness, people pushed past her, hurrying towards departing trains or for taxis. A deafening voice came over the tannoy. She couldn't understand a word; it sounded as if the announcer was brushing his teeth.

Time was running out, her panic mounting by the millisecond. She must buy her ticket and find the train. She only had a few minutes. 'Ticket office?' she cried at anyone walking past. Mute, they just stared back in reply. 'Ticket office. Please. Ticket office.' Her voice was becoming more hysterical. A middle-aged man jerked his thumb over his shoulder. Luc picked up her bag and her huge sugar-mouse pink hat box and started to run.

She found it. There were queues at all the windows. She had no time to be polite and stand in line. Shoving her way to the front and elbowing aside an elderly woman, Luc gasped, 'Sorry. Do you speak English? Karlovy Vary.'

The fat old clerk looked blank.

'Shit. Karlovy Vary. Ticket?' At this rate, she was going to miss the train. She swallowed a sob. 'Karlovy Vary.'

At last, comprehension lit up his doughy face. He nodded.

'Ticket.' Heart pounding, Luc pointed. The clerk said something. What? Behind her, the woman muttered crossly. 'One way. Prague to Karlovy Vary.' Thank God, he seemed to understand. She handed over a fistful of krona. 'Which platform?' Repeating herself like a language tape, Luc pointed towards the trains. The clerk smiled, making Luc want to slap him, before he held up four fingers. 'Four? Yes?'

She hurtled across the station concourse, dodging around people as if she was a rugby fly half powering through the opposition. As she arrived on the platform, a whistle was being blown. Yanking open a door, she threw herself into the train as though she was over the touchline and scoring a try. 'Jesus.'

Heart-rate going into meltdown, she fought to get her breath back as the train lurched its way along the platform and out towards the Prague suburbs.

She'd had no time to think, let alone to take in much of her surroundings. The plane had been late, she'd had a nerve-jangling wait to change money and then for a cab. All she knew was that she had to be on the 12.58 train to God-Knows-Where. She'd made it. Just.

Heart-rate almost back to normal, Luc wondered if she'd caught the right train. She was going to end up in Moscow. Or Budapest. Or Sofia in . . . Bulgaria? Romania? She imagined herself being shunted here and there across central Europe, unable to make herself understood. Her pulse went back to sprint.

There was no one to ask. The deserted carriage was dusty and old-fashioned, divided into separate compartments off a corridor. A faded poster of a lake surrounded by forest was on the wall. The train was gathering speed, the uninspiring concrete tower blocks and smokestakes of the suburbs giving way to flat, open countryside. Luc gazed out of the grimy window at what she thought was an oil refinery, but guessed from the sudden horrible smell must be a brewery. It was a beautiful day, blue-skied, cool-breezed. All she felt was stressed and thirsty. And insane.

A ticket collector came round a little later and obviously thought she *was* insane, as she repeated Karlovy Vary umpteen times. She hoped she was on the right train. In two hours she'd be God-Knows-Where. Apparently it was a spa town. As famous in its time as Bath.

Why hadn't she got a guidebook and *Czech for the Simple*?

Luc wandered up the almost deserted train in search of a buffet car. There wasn't one. People eyed her curiously. Fretting that her bag might be stolen, she hurried back to her dusty carriage. She tried to read, wishing that she'd brought a *Cosmopolitan* instead of *War and Peace*. It was more heavy-going than it was to carry and she was only on paragraph four.

What was she doing? What was she doing trundling across a dun-coloured plain in the backarse of the Czech Republic on a Friday lunchtime? With a sugar-mouse pink hat box the size of a small village? She didn't understand a word of the language, she'd been mercilessly ripped off by a cab driver, some child had tried to pick her pocket and she didn't know a soul.

Why was she putting herself through all this?

'I'd walk a million miles for one of your smiles.' Luc kicked her hat box. She'd crossed Europe for one of Lorenzo's. She was mad.

The countryside was one vast, monotonous hop-field. So much for her dreams of a joyous reunion with Lorenzo. She'd pictured hours of passion and strolling hand in hand with him through the medieval streets of Prague, which would be even more magical in the evening light. Instead she was on a scummy, almost deserted train, heading to God-Knows-Where in western Bohemia.

She had called him again on Wednesday, after she'd telephoned the airline. There was no evening flight on Friday. Laughing away her panic, he had told her to take the morning plane. His plans had changed. Some unexpected meetings meant that he'd have to stay longer in Karlovy Vary. Why not meet him there? They'd drive to Prague the following day. All she had to do was get on the train. The 12.58, he'd checked.

'Perfect,' she'd agreed. Bliss, relief and excitement had stilled her twinges of conscience about skiving off work and letting down Nigel and the Wise Men on that crucial Friday morning.

Nigel had been very put out when she'd blithely announced that, sorry, something had come up, she had to go away, and so she wouldn't be able to come to work tomorrow after all.

'I see.' He'd looked at her as if he'd like to turn her to stone. 'It must be important. So be it. Could you check whether the fax has arrived?'

When she'd asked at five o'clock if there was anything else he'd like her to do, he'd said she could go home as her mind clearly wasn't on her work and hadn't been all day. The rebuke, like everything else, had washed over her. All she could think about was getting on the plane and seeing Lorenzo. Zero minus twenty-one hours and counting.

Zero minus two hours and counting.

Luc picked up *War and Peace* and read half a sentence. In the distance the land was getting hilly, pine-forested. Supposing Lorenzo wasn't there when she arrived in God-Knows-Where? She knew for certain that she was going to be abandoned by him and would have to sleep on the station platform because there wouldn't be another train back to Prague. It would serve her right for being too wimpy to confront Carole directly. Instead,

Luc had left a rushed, unapologetic message on the Agency's answering machine just before leaving the Doll's House.

The train lurched to a sudden stop. Apart from some distant hissing there was lonely silence. She jumped up and leaned out of the window. It dawned on her that no one in the whole world knew where she was. If something terrible happened out here in the middle of the Czech countryside, who would know? Who'd care? A wave of homesickness hit her, a yearning for familiarity and routine.

She was all alone, in a strange country, on her way to meet a man about whom she really knew nothing. Why hadn't Lorenzo met her in Prague? Suddenly, the train jolted back into life, almost throwing her off her feet. Why weren't they meeting in London? It was home turf. Safer.

Needing distraction, she picked up her book again. She scanned the lines, trying to ignore the cold, harsh light of reason that was flickering inside her, illuminating her blind trust, blind faith, blind love.

The train chuntered on, deeper into the countryside. At each stop, Luc peered out of the window, wondering if she'd arrived in God-Knows-Where. Her unease grew with each mile. To distract herself she put on her hat and then tried to check the angle in the window reflection.

Tinker, tailor, soldier, sailor. Banker, pilot . . . It was insane to chase across Europe at the behest of a stranger, no matter how perfect. She didn't know Lorenzo. His enigmatic, feline cool could be hiding a dark, horrible secret. He could be anyone, anything, and she could end up drowned in an acid bath, her body dissolving into nothing . . . Luc wanted to pull the communication cord, jump out of the train and walk back to the Doll's House.

'On Karlovy Vary station she sat down and wept. I'm so sorry to be late. Hello, Lucasta.'

Luc stopped plaiting her hat ribbons and gazed up. 'Hello, Lorenzo.'

He had kept her waiting for a fraught-making twenty minutes on a platform bench in the wilds of the Czech Republic with a sugar-mouse pink hat box at her feet. Her heart had been heavier than *War and Peace* which she'd been tempted to leave on the train. Frantically chewing gum, she'd almost got lockjaw.

Her resentment dissolved on seeing him smile, smelling the citrus tang of his aftershave and feeling his lips against her cheek.

Smiling, he sat down beside her on the platform bench, winding her hair round his hands and scrutinising her face. She felt awkward, wondering if he had gone off her, if she were failing to measure up. 'Do I pass?'

'Flying colours. Five stars. Top of the class. Come.' He picked up her bag, laughing when he saw the hat box.

'I didn't want it crushed,' said Luc defensively.

'Flying colours. Why I was late. Sorry.'

'You've been flying?' She'd assumed a business meeting had delayed him.

As they walked side by side through the station, Luc stole covert glances at him, unable to believe he was hers. His leather jacket made look him blonder, younger, his faded black jeans more relaxed.

Catching her eye, he grinned. 'My tailor doesn't approve of such informality?'

'No, it's not that. It's just, just . . .' She laughed, once again feeling a blanket of joy and contentment wrapped around her. 'So, where am I?'

'Karlovy Vary. Also known as Karlsbad. Once the spa of emperors and princes, now full of rich Russians and coachloads of ugly, fat Ossi tourists.'

'Australians? They've come a long . . .'

'Ossi. East Germans. Would you like to go sightseeing?' He raised an eyebrow. 'An outing, perhaps?'

Luc thought of what she'd prefer to do and blushed, knowing that he was reading her mind. 'Whatever.' They were approaching a rank of drab-looking Skoda taxis. She hesitated, hating to admit something so prosaic. 'I'm starving.'

'No lunch? Poor Lucasta. We'll go back to the hotel.'

They passed the taxis. Across the street a tram hissed to a halt. Just as Luc was thinking she'd never imagined him catching public transport, her eye was caught by a length of gleaming black Aston Martin. 'It's like the one in *Goldfing*—.' Then she saw the Swiss number plate and gasped. 'Yours?'

'Mine. Like something else.' He examined the inside of her wrist. 'Or not.'

'It washed away.' Despite her best efforts.

Lorenzo unlocked the passenger door and held it open for her. As she eased herself into the seat, Luc wished she'd been to finishing school and had deportment lessons.

As the car roared off, she tried to concentrate on the view. They were in a valley, protected by steep hills of inky-green forest. It seemed as if she'd stepped back in time, into a toytown kingdom set along the banks of a meandering river of sparkling silver.

The sky was a freshly painted blue, the light crystalline. The air was as pure as on Creation Day. Each corner they turned was yet another perfect scene for a postcard. The wide, tranquil streets were spotlessly clean, the stately columned and stepped buildings resembled elaborately iced wedding cakes.

'A Disney castle,' exclaimed Luc, peering at a roof in the distance through some trees. It was studded with scores of spires and turrets.

'The hotel.' Lorenzo was amused. 'At your age you should know Disney was inspired by places like that, not the other way round.' They were climbing higher, away from the town towards the hills. 'How was the journey?'

'Fine.' She looked at him. 'Why here? Why not Prague?'

'Because I wouldn't have been in Prague until six at the earliest and I didn't want to miss out on three hours of seeing you.' He changed down a gear. 'Why else?'

'Why are three hours so important?' wondered Luc.

'You'll find out soon.'

As Luc was wondering if there was any chance she could be a squatter in five-star hotel suites for the rest of her life – clean sheets every day, huge towels, huger beds, room service – Lorenzo was on the telephone ordering some coffee in Czech, one eye on the Cable News business report.

'I have to make some calls. Sorry.' He began to pace, switching between French and German, frowning when she switched channels to MTV, blaring the latest Euro hit. Hastily, she switched back.

Luc went out on to the balcony and gazed down at the silver river threading its way through the green. 'Lorenzo, why do you need television? Look, it's so beautiful.'

'So, hopefully, are the markets.' He raised an eyebrow. 'You disagree?'

'The stock-market? I don't know my bulls from my bears from my dead cat bounce,' admitted Luc with a sigh. Yet another of her shaming chasms of ignorance.

'I'll teach you.' He twisted a lock of her hair round his finger. 'You must be hungry.' She nodded. 'Good. I've got you something.'

The coffee arrived along with some sandwiches – it took all of Luc's self-control not to stuff them into her mouth like a ravenous dingo. She sat on the sofa, trying to be decorous, as if she were having tea at a bishop's palace. From the armchair opposite, Lorenzo handed her a box, wrapped in gold and white paper.

'What is it?' she asked, curious. Too big for a ring. More tiara-sized. 'More caviar? Another hat?'

'The best of its type in the world.'

Inside the wrapping was a wooden box. 'From Vienna. How do you pronounce it? Sack . . .?'

'Za,' he corrected, 'Sachertorte.'

'Chocolate cake,' cried Luc, opening the box. The chocolate gleamed so dark it was almost black. 'Yum. Where's a knife? Quick.' She wanted to grab fistfuls.

He laughed. 'You're easy to please.'

'And easy to fatten up. Am I being uncool?'

'Yes.' He squeezed her hand. 'Don't worry, it's wonderful to watch. You're not one of the well-dressed people bored with life. Thank God.' He cut a sliver. 'It's very rich. You don't need much.' Luc wanted to say he was very rich and she needed heaps of him, but was shut up as he reached forward.

'Thank you. Delic . . .' Suddenly her mouth was full of cake and his fingertips. Heart hammering, she held his blue gaze.

They were strolling through a pastel-coloured promenade towards one of the baths. Like an elderly, deposed archduchess, the town was steeped in faded grandeur. The Belle Epoque villas and wrought-iron colonnades demanded frock-coats and crino-lines rather than coach parties and camcorders. Everywhere was so clean and pure and ordered that it would've passed Liz's housekeeping tests with gold stars.

'So you now know why three hours mattered.'

'So you could check the markets,' said Luc. 'I never thought I'd take second place to the Indonesian kong.' They'd somehow rolled on to the remote, turning on the TV, and she'd been taken aback to realise his attention had strayed to the Asian reports.

'The Indonesian dong,' corrected Lorenzo, causing giggles. 'Anyway you don't. Not to that. The greenback? Maybe.'

'Greenback? As in bacon?'

'The dollar. US. Not Australian.' He put his arm round her shoulders. 'Seen anything of Alex and his soap-operatic girl-friend? Maria? Mary?'

'Marina,' said Luc. 'He's away. She feels abandoned.'

'Perhaps she should go back to her husband.' He shrugged at Luc's puzzlement. 'I was told the story the morning you left Ia. Alex was in his room working. The whole story and the signora's warmest encouragement to call her. I think she was still drunk.'

'What?'

'She's abandoned her marriage. That morning she was wondering if Alex were the right replacement for it. And if he weren't, who else might be.'

'Marina?'

'I had the feeling I was a small insurance policy.'

'Marina hit on you?' demanded Luc. She was outraged. 'Hit on you. Came on to you. Chatted you up. She gave you her number?'

'Calm down.' Lorenzo was laughing.

'Why didn't you tell me before?'

'It was so trivial. Luc, what's wrong? Luc?' He was bewildered. 'If anyone should worry, it's Alex.'

She stared up at him. 'I suppose it happens all the time. To you. Getting hit on. Hundreds of Marinas.' She was blind to the mannerly streets of an old spa town, seeing only hundreds of vivacious, glamorous women with shiny little sports cars.

He stopped abruptly. 'And hundreds of Frenchmen pursuing you across the seas?'

'Of course there aren't.'

'There aren't? Perhaps I can leap to conclusions. Perhaps I can be as childish and irrational as you.'

Luc took a deep breath, trying to calm the molten jealousy burning inside her. 'It's just . . .'

He pulled her closer. 'If the signora could mind-read, she'd have known she was wasting her energies.' He stroked her hair. 'Enough. We're meant to be sight-seeing. You must drink the water. It's supposed to be therapeutic.'

Luc wondered if it would cure her sick-making insecurity. She tried to smile. 'Taking the waters. It's like something out of

Jane Austen.' She should be wearing an Empire-line dress and a bonnet.

'Last chance. Tomorrow we'll drive back to Prague.'

'We will?'

'You'd rather stay?'

'I really don't mind.' She didn't care. She could be in a shanty-town shack and really not mind. Well, almost. A shack with a decent bathroom and a hairdryer.

The spring was housed in a modern concrete building, smelling of rotten eggs. Hundreds of gallons of water gushed in a stream set behind glass. The aged, the frail and the infirm were gulping back water from the fountains set into the wall. At Lorenzo's insistence, Luc tried some, although the smell made her want to retch. It tasted foul, like scummy, salty bathwater.

'Therapeutic?' laughed Lorenzo.

'Um.' Her insecurity was miraculously cured, giving way to a distinct queasiness. All she could think about was not throwing up in front of the most perfect man in the world. 'Oh God.' She clapped her hand over her mouth.

'Luc? Luc?' Seeing her go green and white in stripes, he rushed her outside into the fresh air and into a café, where he ordered two glasses of slivovitz. 'Plum brandy. Cure for the cure.'

They were back at the hotel, curled up on the sofa together. While he distractedly played with her hair, Luc was watching him doing the crossword in the copy of *The Times* that she'd been given on the plane that morning. Revelling in such unexpected cosiness, almost domesticity, Luc's mind strayed to daydreaming about spending every evening like this with him.

'Smart, aren't you?' she teased, secretly mortified that she was unable to work out the answers even after he had inked them in.

'Not always.'

'When not?'

He shrugged. 'Whenever.'

'How not?'

'However.' Filling in three more clues, Lorenzo peered at her. 'You're not bored?' Smiling, she shook her head. 'Are you about to paint me? No? It feels like you're making a study. Perhaps I should get you a basket. So you could sit under my desk like a puppy.'

Luc's contentment vanished. She gulped back the fizz and poured herself another glass. He obviously thought she was boring, as dull as flat soda water. A dreary, meek, acquiescent little homebody. A puppy, happy to sit at his feet and chew his shoelaces, until he'd finished whatever he was doing. Scowling, she hacked at the Sachertorte and crammed some into her mouth.

'You're hungry.' He kissed her hand. 'We must get some dinner.'

'I never expected to see you in a leather jacket,' said Luc later when they were having dinner. The restaurant was dark and dismal, smelling slightly of damp, the food indifferent.

'A very old friend. I've had this jacket since I went round the States on a motorbike one summer.' He paused. 'When I was young.'

'Lorenzo, stop sounding as if you're ancient.'

'My soul feels ancient. Jaded. As if I've seen everything and done everything and there's nothing left. Except to take up golf.' He lit a cigarette. 'A deadening game. Never play it. The clothes are so horrible for a start. Worse than this food.' He pushed away his second steak, half eaten. The first had been sent back, to Luc's embarrassment. 'We'll go somewhere better in Prague.'

'Do we really have to leave on Sunday?'

'I have to go back to Vienna.' Luc caught her breath, hoping he'd say come with me. He added, 'You stay on. Explore. It's beautiful.'

Luc forced a smile. 'Maybe.' A waiter took away their plates.

She gazed at Lorenzo, so feline, so self-contained. Why couldn't she confront things? Afraid of destroying the dream? No news being good news? She began to trace the tablecloth with her pudding fork. 'What's your form?'

'My what?'

'Your past. Girlfriends. Wives. Mistresses.'

'No wives.'

'Why not?'

He became very still. Statue-still. As if he were carved from cold, lifeless marble. 'Why no husband, Lucasta?'

'You're not answering.'

'And neither are you.'

'I asked first.'

'You must be tired.' He looked round for the waiter. 'Let's get the check. Sorry, bill. You're English.' She wriggled, itching to speak. 'Hush.' He put his fingers to her lips. 'Mine.'

'Me? Or your past?'

'Both.'

She woke up the next morning to find him lying next to her talking softly into his mobile, one hand playing with her hair. She nuzzled closer and smiled. Closing her eyes, she imagined drifting in the ocean with Lorenzo, the bed a raft, a gentle breeze whispering through some palm trees on a beach in the distance.

Suddenly he pushed her off him. 'Ow.' Her yelp of protest would've been loud, but was stifled by his hand over her mouth. He said something in Italian to his caller.

'Do you think they guessed?' gasped Luc afterwards.

'Maybe.' Shrugging, he reached over for his cigarettes, then picked up the phone and ordered some coffee. 'We'll have some breakfast then go.' He pushed back the covers and got up. 'Another ersatz shower.'

'What?'

'The water pressure is non-existent.'

Luc frowned. 'Anything wrong? Apart from the shower?' The bathroom door was almost slammed shut in reply. She sat up, spirits crushed. He seemed so remote, as if they were separated by the ice-capped Himalayas. As if he'd like to leave her some money on the bedside table and go.

An hour later they were in the car, speeding on the road towards Prague. 'Perhaps I should've got up on your side of the bed,' apologised Lorenzo.

'Or stayed in there.' Luc tried to sound light. She'd wanted him close, afterwards, especially after someone had practically listened in. He'd obviously enjoyed it, she had at the time, but now the memory was disturbing, one she'd rather delete.

'Is that a reproach?' He glanced at her.

'Who was it? A business colleague? Shit.'

They were coming out of a bend, an ancient snub-nosed lorry was parked on the nearside facing them, a car approaching from the opposite direction. Lorenzo put his foot down, swerved out and sped past the lorry, avoiding the oncoming car by millimetres.

'Jesus,' gasped Luc.

'You buy this much power to get yourself out of trouble.'

'Sounds like a motto.'

'Possibly. Music? Choose.'

The CDs were stacked somewhere in the boot. She pressed the stereo and went from one disc to another, all classical. 'Not exactly road music.'

'We're not exactly on Route 66.'

An aria from *Norma* filled the car, sung by Yasmina Bois. It had been the theme tune to a tyre ad on the box. She'd heard it so often recently, it was beginning to sound flattened, its magic lost. Luc pressed again, recognising the opening bars of *Don Giovanni*.

Apart from a few lorries belching black exhaust fumes, they

passed little traffic. The countryside glowed gentle gold, but the villages looked lonely and down-at-heel. The roads were pot-holed, the few signs rusty. There was an air of scrimping and saving, making do and mending, as if everything had been on ration for years.

She caught him glancing at her. 'Don't stare.'

'Why not? I enjoy it. I spent most of the night doing it.'

Luc sat up in alarm. 'God, I didn't snore, did I?' Or, horror, dribble?

'No. Mouse quiet. You followed me round the bed. Making sure you were close.'

'I did?' Obviously her subconscious had given her away. 'Why didn't you sleep?'

'Thinking.'

'About?'

'This. That. You.' Luc wanted to ask him what about her, but suddenly he pulled over into the side of the road and stopped. The engine died. The music was suddenly far too loud. 'Like to drive?'

'I can't,' spluttered Luc. 'It's the wrong side of the road.'

He laughed. 'You've never driven on the right?'

'The wrong. No.'

'Another first then. I want to give you lots of firsts.'

'Like Sachertorte? And Glyndebourne and lapis lazuli and . . .'

'Out.'

Luc got out, staring at the bonnet with apprehension. All that horsepower. She'd never been able to control a pony prop-erly. And the only cars she'd ever driven had been biscuit tins on wheels. 'Are you sure? Supposing I crash? Am I insured?'

'No. If we live, the car gets fixed.'

She sat in the driver's seat and adjusted the mirrors. Turning the key, she fired up the engine. And crashed the gears. She winced. She tried again, only to stall. At her fourth attempt the car kangeroo hopped a few yards, before she slammed her foot on the brake in panic. Stalling, the car lurched to a halt.

'It's a long clutch.' Lorenzo was amused.

Luc rested her sweating forehead on the steering wheel. 'I can't believe you're letting me do this.'

'It's just a car. Anyway, it gives me a chance to admire your profile.'

A few more false starts later she was driving. Very slowly. So slowly they got overtaken by a fume-belching Lada. Lorenzo laughed. Luc imagined Aston Martin sueing her for defamation. Five miles later she relaxed, forgot that she was in charge of something more valuable than the average house, and put her foot down. The Czech countryside flashed past, she flashed past the Lada. It was the most glorious drive of her life.

'So. Where am I?'

'Prague. On Charles Bridge. Overlooking the Vltava.'

Luc peered down into the murky water. 'Not the Danube? It's not very blue.'

'Shall we waltz? Don't fall in.'

'There aren't any stars.'

It was almost seven. Luc felt exhausted. No sooner had they arrived in the hotel, than Lorenzo had dragged her out, insisting that she must see one of Europe's most beautiful cities. They had been walking for almost six hours round the red-roofed lanes of the old town, up a hill to a castle. Gothic, Baroque, tiny passageways, boulevards, frescoes, squares, vaulted ceilings, statues, concert halls, opera houses, Art Nouveau, Neo-classical; each corner she'd rounded, she'd thought a place couldn't get any more perfect. Until the next one.

The city deserved a lifetime's exploration, not a few hours. Luc yawned. Lorenzo's arm was round her shoulder, she leaned closer into him. 'You should work for the Prague tourist board.'

'We're tourists?' He looked horrified. 'Not travellers?'

'Ask a local. Ask any local, anywhere. All so-called travellers are tourists to them.'

'Dream wrecker.'

'Am I?' said Luc.

He held her gaze and shook his head. Wrapping his arms round her, he pulled her to him. Oblivious of the crowds walking past, they slowly kissed and kissed and kissed. Luc heard every sonnet, every symphony and the waves crashing on the beach.

'Let's go back,' whispered Lorenzo, stroking her face. 'Bedtime.'

'Cab?' smiled Luc.

They turned round to see a woman hovering a few feet from them. 'Excuse me. Do you speak English?' The accent was American, she was an over made-up blonde, face almost glowing orange with foundation. Her shiny bob was as immaculate as her scarlet gilt-buttoned jacket, at odds with her scruffy combats and sneakers. 'Cindy Lopez, US Cable News.' She flashed a smile. 'Here on honeymoon?'

Arm round Luc, Lorenzo glanced over the woman's shoulder. His eyes narrowed at the sight of an idle film crew who were hanging around about thirty feet away. 'You've been filming us?'

'Enjoying Prague?' She turned to Luc. 'Been here long? Isn't it just so romantic?'

'You've been filming us without permission?' cut in Lorenzo. 'Press pass.' He held out his hand.

As she delved into her pockets, her smile seemed painted on. You're not Czech, are you, Mrs . . .?' Lorenzo gave a warning glance at Luc. 'We're doing a story on the local tourism explosion post-Velvet Revolution. From Dubcek to travellers' cheques. Get the drift?'

'Press pass,' repeated Lorenzo.

'Great footage. Lovers on the bridge, setting sun reflected in the water, backdrop of statues and spires. Can we interview?

Short piece. Won't take a moment.' She handed Lorenzo a laminated card. 'What's your names?'

He studied it with distaste, then handed it back. 'Ms Lopez. Lose the film of us. Or you and your colleagues will lose your jobs.'

'Hey, now, wait a minute . . .' She bristled with indignation.

Luc held her breath as Lorenzo reeled off a list of names. 'Familiar to you, Ms Lopez? They should be. On your company's board. What's the American phrase? Higher up the food chain than you.'

'Are you threatening me?'

'We do business together. I'll be calling them.'

'Listen, aren't you over-reacting a little here?'

'I don't like my privacy being invaded.'

'Well, mister, you and your lady friend are very much in public. Or hadn't you noticed?'

'Our mistake. But not one to be compounded by you people.' Lorenzo stared down at her. 'August. Slack news time. Usually. Or haven't you noticed there are a few civil wars going on not so very far from here? Any good reporter would be covering those.'

Under the orange, the face turned red with fury. Luc shivered at Lorenzo's iciness. He looked across the bridge where a couple were smooching, smiling into one another's eyes. 'Love's young dream. There's your interview, Ms Lopez. They even look American to me.'

'Don't tell me my job.'

'I'm not. Just advising you. If you want to keep it.' He grabbed Luc's hand.

'Was it such a big issue?' pleaded Luc back at the hotel. Lorenzo's Arctic cold anger hadn't abated. He was pacing the room, as frustrated as a big cat in a zoo cage.

'I'm not being used as mindless entertainment for every mindless fifth-rate executive in every fifth-rate hotel.'

'Don't they all watch the porn channels?' She sighed.

'That's hardly the point.'

Luc unlocked the minibar. 'Whisky?' She didn't dare admit that she'd be delighted to have had that moment recorded on film and beamed around the world by one of those satellites she'd mistaken for a shooting star. 'Will you really be calling those board members?'

'I was calling her bluff.'

'You were?'

'There was a report about them in one of the papers last month.' He shrugged. 'I've got a good memory.'

'You should play poker,' exclaimed Luc. 'You sounded so convincing.'

'Good. Let's hope Ms Lopez thought so too.'

'You fooled me.' She handed him a glass. 'It's not the end of the world.'

'I don't like the Press, I don't like gossip and I don't like being taken advantage of.'

'It wasn't deliberate. Forget it.' Smiling up at him, Luc reached out for his hand. 'Anyway, it's not very flattering that you're so embarrassed about being seen with me. Anyone would think you've got something to hide.' Her smile vanished. 'You haven't, have you?'

He sipped his whisky. 'Such as?'

'Wives. Children. Time in prison. Photos of you in flares and platforms. Being an axe murderer.' She tried to sound light-hearted.

Lorenzo grinned, relaxing for the first time in more than an hour. 'None of the above.' He pulled her towards him. 'Where were we? Before we were interrupted?'

Later that evening they went to a tiny bar in a cellar. It was dim, smoke-filled, the gravelly growl of Tom Waits could be heard singing 'Tom Trabant's Blues'. They sat at one of the long benches and drank beer. At the next bench a couple were playing chess. Opposite Lorenzo, an unkempt man was writing in an exercise book. He had greying bristles and his scruffy, dandruff-shouldered jacket smelt of damp dog. He wore his shabbiness smugly, like a CBE, as if his mind were on higher things than shaving or having a bath.

Luc sat in silence as he and Lorenzo began talking in Czech. She tried to revel in the atmosphere, tried to pretend to like the beer. Tried to force herself not to be bored.

Lorenzo interrupted her reverie. 'He's asking who's your favourite Czech writer.'

She was blank. 'I don't know any.'

'But you must have read Kafka. Even in translation.'

'No.' Ella had, Ella had read everything.

'You haven't?' He was astounded.

'No,' snapped Luc irritably. Lorenzo translated for the benefit of the stubble, who was smirking. 'Sorry. Not even in translation.'

'I'll call you very soon,' said Lorenzo the following morning. Kissing her on the cheek, he got into the car.

Luc stood outside the hotel and watched the Aston roar off until it had disappeared. She felt plodding, lead-heavy, over-whelmed by the same sense of aimless emptiness she'd felt that Friday on Ia before she met him.

The hotel would look after her bag, the porter had assured her. She could come in and collect it on her way to the airport. She looked at her watch. Six hours to kill.

She told herself to be positive and use the time productively. It was a glorious summer's day and a whole city was at her feet to be explored. It was just pathetic to wish she could crawl back into bed and pull the covers over her head. Patrick Leigh Thingy had walked to the Balkans, surely she could manage to walk round Prague? Marcie and Sherry would have planned their schedule and been up at dawn.

Taking a deep breath, she went back into the hotel and asked the concierge for a map and the must-see sites. The list was endless.

She felt herself deaden the same way she had on a visit to the British Museum, when confronted by bits of Etruscan pottery that were meant to be so fascinating. But weren't.

Chapter Eleven

———◆◆◆———

Ella was lying on the sofa watching the end of *Casablanca*. It was almost eleven o'clock. 'Luc? Why are you back?'

'Because.' Exhausted, Luc threw down her bag.

'Get yourself a glass of wine or something.' Eyes back on the screen, clutching a cushion, she lip-synched Bogart's 'One day and for the rest of your life' parting speech. As 'The End' appeared, she let out a huge sigh. 'It gets better every time.' She turned to Luc. 'They'll always have Paris. So, how was Prague?'

'Beautiful.' Luc sounded as flat as she felt.

'And Lord Snooty?'

'Great.'

Ella peered at her. 'What's up? Have you just spent a dirty weekend with a great man in a beautiful city or had your wisdom teeth yanked out without anaesthetic?'

'Anti-climax, I guess.' Luc shrugged. 'Anyway, how are you?'

'Better.' Seeing Luc frown, she added, 'Drama over.'

'You didn't . . .?'

'I was going to. Saturday morning.'

'What?' Luc was horrified.

'Had myself booked into some clinic. The forms were filled in, the legal niceties complied with. Told to eat and drink nothing after Friday evening.' Ella fiddled with the ends of her hair. 'On the runway, ready to go.'

'And?'

'And I was in the taxi. And it was eight-eighteen. And we were alongside Chelsea football ground. And I told the cabbie to turn round, take me home. Actually, I made him stop off so I could get two jumbo bags of Maltesers.'

'You were going to . . .?' Luc's voice trailed off. 'When did you decide? Why didn't you tell me?'

'Wednesday afternoon. Why didn't I tell you?' Ella squinted at a split end. 'Because you were so preoccupied with seeing Lorenzo, you had no mental space for anything else.'

Luc jumped as if she'd touched an electric fence. The pair stared at one another. 'That's not true,' she said finally.

'Come on, Luc. If I'd told you, what would you've done? Told him, sorry I've got to cancel, something's come up? Forget it.' Ella's smile was far too bright to be natural. 'Anyway, it was probably for the best. With you around, I might never have had that epiphany.'

'The what?'

'The sudden blinding revelation. Outside the Stamford Bridge stadium, of all places.' She laughed suddenly, joyfully. 'I'm going to have a baby. Perhaps I'll call it Chelsea.'

Luc's eyes widened. 'Are you sure?'

'About the name? No. About it?' She nodded, hugging herself. 'Sure I'm sure. I've never been so certain about anything. Ever. We should be opening the fizz to celebrate.'

'Well, let's.' Luc tried to sound happy, to keep the caution out of her voice.

'Except I can't drink for a while.'

'Oh. Of course not.' Luc looked at Ella, glowing with contentment. 'A baby. You. A mother.' She was shocked to the core. 'Are you sure you'll be able to cope?'

'Yes.'

'What about Yannick? The father?'

'I wrote to him yesterday morning. To tell him. If he gets in contact, it's up to him.'

'You don't sound very bothered.'

'I'm not. What do we need him for?' She patted her tummy.

'Support?' suggested Luc.

'What sort of support?'

'The normal sort of support that fathers are supposed to give.'

'Sure. And how many do? All those marriages that end in divorce,' Ella scoffed. 'Quite honestly, most women should cut out the disappointing reality and just go straight to a sperm bank.'

'Yuck.' Luc shuddered at the thought. 'Ella.' She hesitated, trying to find the words. 'Your views are a bit clouded by how you were brought up. Janie going it alone. But you're not Janie, are you? Are you absolutely certain about this?'

'Yes.'

'As you said, half the time you can't look after yourself . . .'

'But I have, haven't I? Realistically.'

Luc thought of Ella smuggling grass, Ella on her cocaine binges, Ella losing her licence, Ella's brains being fried by Ecstasy, Ella insisting they hitch. Ella being too restless to settle down to a proper job. Ella with a succession of men like Tas. Little about Ella suggested she was ready for responsible parenthood. 'Have you?'

'Yes.' Ella eyed Luc. 'I've done a lot of thinking recently. And I've realised I've looked after myself since I was seventeen. Contrary to expectations, the house hasn't been burnt to the ground, I haven't ended up a junkie or in prison. Or been kidnapped for the white slave trade.'

'Get real, Ella, neither do most people.' Luc laughed mirthlessly.

Ella's look was sharp. 'And I haven't frittered away my inheritance. A lot do. Easy come, easy go.'

'Not many. Not everyone has an inheritance,' snapped Luc.

'True. I'm lucky. But I haven't blown my luck. Have I? Not according to my stockbroker, anyway.' Ella stood up. 'Cocoa?'

'What?'

'I need more calcium and I can't have cheese. Well, not soft cheese. Listeria risk. So I've got to drink more milk, according to the doctor. Do you want some cocoa?'

From lines of coke to cocoa. In less than two months. Luc couldn't believe it. 'Wine,' she said faintly, holding out her glass. From the kitchen she heard Ella saying something about folic acid. The Doll's House was going to turn into an ante-natal clinic. Her heart sank.

Looking at her watch, she yawned. She'd better get to bed. Work tomorrow. She froze, mouth half open. Where was she working tomorrow? Platform? 'Did the Agency call?'

'No. Marina did. Quentin the Zit did. Who else? Patrick. He's having a party. Your post's on the table. I've started swimming. Every morning. The doctor said it was the best exercise, less strain on the joints.'

'Really?' Yawning, Luc picked up the three envelopes. 'Bill, bill, what's this?' The postcode on the thick white envelope was SW1. She ripped it open. Written on Platform's headed paper, it was dated Friday and all of three lines. She read them and re-read them, swallowing hard.

'Bad news?' asked Ella, returning with a glass of wine.

'Yep.' She held out the letter.

Ella raised an eyebrow. 'He should've saved his time and computer memory and just written Fuck Off.'

'Um.' Luc couldn't speak. Of all the rejection letters she'd ever received, this one hurt the most. Nigel Mann hadn't even bothered with the face-saving, pride-salving courtesies. In-this-instance-regretfully-your-application-has-not-been-successful. Of-course-we'll-keep-your-name-on-file-for-the-future. He'd been direct, brutal. Platform needed reliable staff who demonstrated commitment. In view of this, she'd probably be happier working elsewhere. Yours sincerely.

'I thought a permanent job was in the bag,' said Ella.

So had Luc. She was choked. She'd felt cosily at home in the grand-shabby offices, which seemed to have been marinated in decades of courtesy and charm. She'd enjoyed being gently teased by the Wise Men who seemed to accept her as part of the team.

Ella sipped her cocoa, re-reading the letter. 'Rude shit.'

'My fault.' Luc's voice was cracking.

'Come on. There'll be plenty of other jobs. With nicer people. Perhaps it just wasn't meant to be. I wouldn't want to work for him.'

Luc glared at her. 'You don't have to. You don't have to work for anyone, do you? When was the last time you had to do something whether you liked it or not?'

'I . . . I . . .'

'Don't start patronising me, because you've got no idea what you're talking about.'

Open-mouthed, Ella could only stare at Luc. 'I'm just trying . . .'

Luc cut her off. 'Know something, Ella? You should get out more. Find out what the real world is like. For those who aren't lucky enough to be trustafarians. Remember them? They're the ones who don't have stockbrokers to look after their odd few million quid.'

Ella took a deep breath. 'I can't handle this. Not now.'

'Why not now? Because you've decided to have a baby? Which, incidentally, is a very bad idea.'

'What? Why?'

'You're not ready to settle. You said it, Ella. You can't look after yourself.'

'Oh, thanks for all your support. Look, Luc, not now. Stress is bad . . .'

'Stress?' Luc scoffed. 'You don't know what stress is.'

'What's that supposed to mean?'

'There are millions of women out there who don't have your choices. They're not only single mothers, but they have to go out and work to put food in their kids' mouths. Your biggest problem will be which nanny.'

'Tell me something, Luc.' Ella's brown eyes narrowed. 'Why's it all right for Lorenzo to have money and not me? Some fucking feminist you are.'

'Lorenzo works . . .'

'How do you know? He's an aristo. I'd put this house on the fact that he was born loaded. Your sudden scruples about family money don't extend to possible husbands, do they?'

'Lorenzo's diff—'

Ella shouted her down. 'But I wouldn't hold your breath waiting for him to propose. Face it, you're probably Lorenzo's Tas.'

'Meaning?'

'Meaning you play with them, you don't marry them.'

Luc recoiled as if she'd been punched.

'Sorry to be brutal, Luc. No one wants to trade down.'

The following morning, Ella went to the pool. Luc called the Agency.

'Is that the Lucasta James who used to be my most reliable temp?' Carole's voice dripped with sarcasm. Luc was relieved to be told there was nothing right at that moment, but something might crop up later that morning, so act the Boy Scout. 'Be prepared. Stay by the phone. That is, if you want to work. I've got a brontosaurus-sized bone to pick with you.' Luc shuddered. Fortunately Carole's other line rang. 'I'll be picking it later.'

Luc made herself a mug of tea and crawled back to bed. She'd had an awful night, tossing and turning and finally dozing.

Suddenly so full of promise after meeting Lorenzo, life seemed to have taken her into a cul-de-sac. A dead end where she could see no Exit signs. Everything pointed to No Career or No Money or No Home of her Own. And the biggest sign of all said No Future with Lorenzo.

She was finally facing what she couldn't confront the day before in Prague. What her zombie-like sightseeing had enabled her put to put on hold. She was in love with Lorenzo. She could give him aching out-of-control obsessive love. What was she getting in return?

Luc gulped the tea, hardly noticing it was scalding her mouth. Even as he'd driven away, leaving her standing on a Prague pavement, part of her had refused to accept that he was going. She'd expected him to turn round and say, come with me. Come to Vienna, then we'll go to Geneva, come and spend the rest of the summer with me, come and spend the rest of your life with me.

You play with them, you don't marry them. No one wants to trade down.

She hadn't expected to be back at the Doll's House, hadn't expected that she'd have to be calling the Agency, had never considered that the weekend would end and she'd be in a worse position than when it started. She'd blown her chance with Platform, she'd taken her foul mood out on Ella, and Carole was clearly very pissed off.

Hearing a key turn in the front door, she sat up. 'Hello, Ella?'

Ella's wet hair was tied back in a pony-tail. She stood at the bedroom door and gave Luc a cool glance. 'Not working?'

'There isn't anything.'

Ella threw her bunch of keys up to the ceiling and caught them, before squinting down at the carpet. 'Could do with a proper clean.' Pulling a face, she said, 'I think it would be for the best if you found somewhere else to live.'

'What?' Luc was dumbfounded.

'No rush. Let's say, in a month, shall we?' She shrugged, finally meeting Luc's eyes. 'I can't cope with any emotional stress. Not now. And quite frankly, Luc, you're upsetting me. Big time.'

Luc swallowed hard. 'I see.'

'Do you?' Ella's voice was shrapnel-hard.

'No.' Luc frowned. 'No, thinking about it, no. No, I don't see at all.'

'You should see how you've changed. You're so snide and

bitchy all the time. As bad as Liz, as bad as that fucking oaf Alex. Who, incidentally, will be calling you.'

'What?'

'He's back. As large as life and twice as disagreeable. He was at the pool. Went berserk that I was in the wrong lane. Apparently I was trespassing in the one for goggle-wearing guided missiles. Shouted loud enough to cause a tidal wave.' She felt her hair. 'I'd better not get a cold.' Outside it was a sunny 25 degrees.

'So, you're kicking me out,' said Luc, feeling as if she was being mugged. 'You can't.'

'Listen, Luc, I'm sorry, but I can. What I can't do is deal with you.'

'With me?'

'With you. All your hostility. Your jealousy. I don't want to live dreading your coming through the front door.'

'Jealousy? Of what?'

Ella went over to the window and peered out at the Mews. 'The material stuff. Correction, the immaterial stuff. This place. The Trust. You've suddenly become some Maoist and I'm the capitalist swine who should be shot.'

'Don't be so stupid,' protested Luc. 'Perhaps your hormones are . . .'

'Don't blame it on hormones,' hissed Ella. 'That's just female-as-victim bullshit. It's simple. You resent me. Yes, you do. And your resentment re-opens the wounds. The Janie wounds. Which still hurt. A lot.' She straightened her shoulders. 'So, it would be easier on both of us if you were to move out.'

Half an hour later, Luc heard the front door close. She hadn't moved in that time, just stared up at the ceiling, paralysed by shock. She knew that Ella had made up her mind and wouldn't be changing it.

What was she going to do? The Doll's House had been her home for the past three years. It had been her refuge for more than a decade, ever since she'd first come to stay that Easter holiday. She had looked after it as much as Ella had looked after the honeysuckle.

No money, no career and soon, no home. What a brilliant start to the week.

The thought of needing money for a deposit on another place panicked her into scurrying out of bed and under the shower. She hoped that getting herself dressed and vaguely together would make her feel better, but with Ella's words echoing in her head, her hand shook so much she could hardly put on her mascara.

Going up to the sitting room, she rang Lorenzo's mobile. 'Bastard,' she cried, hearing the recorded message. She needed comfort, not voice mail. She called the Agency, determined to try to make amends, but Carole was in a meeting.

No money, no career, no home. She sank on the sofa, utterly defeated. What was she going to do? Just a week earlier, everything had been on the brink of being settled. Now all she saw was rubble and wreckage.

'Hello.' Picking up the phone, she tried to sound normal.

'Luc? Alex. Alex Ireland. Got a cold?'

'No.'

'Just a call to say thanks for seeing Marina when I was away. She really appreciated it.'

'Fine.'

'Anything up?'

'Nothing.' Luc swallowed. The room began to swim.

'Sure? Did your landlady tell you I had the pleasure of seeing her this morning?' Luc's um was more of a squeak. Alex sounded concerned. 'Luc, something's wrong, isn't it?'

'Nothing.' She gasped. 'Everything.' And suddenly she was sobbing so hard she couldn't hear him.

'I said what number are you?' repeated Alex. 'Seven? I'll be there in ten minutes.'

'Don't,' pleaded Luc, but he'd hung up.

He stood barefoot and Raybanned at the front door, towering above her, blocking out the light from the Mews. He'd just had a number one cut, so his hair was almost non-existent. 'You look like shit. Day off? Right, get your sunnies. Let's have lunch.'

'I don't feel like going out,' said Luc in a pathetic voice.

'Tough. We'll be in Brighton by two.'

'Brighton?'

'The seaside.' He rolled his eyes. 'You don't have an ocean here, do you?'

'Brighton? It's miles away.'

'Sixty miles. We drive that to get a packet of fags back home.' He looked at his watch. 'Come on. Or we'll miss the last overs before lunch.'

A few minutes later, Luc found herself on the threadbare seat of the rusty BMW. As he belted out of the Mews in reverse, she began to protest that perhaps she ought to stay at home. Alex ssshed her. The radio commentators were analysing how a wicket had just been taken.

They shot down the King's Road and over the Thames, heading towards the South Circular. Luc felt as if she was pickled in misery, her tongue seemed set in concrete. No career, no home, no money. Occasionally random thoughts intruded, such as why had she agreed to go to Brighton with someone she found so overbearing.

'Why are we doing this?' asked Alex, turning off the radio somewhere south of Clapham. 'I'm sure I don't even like you.'

'The lack of feeling's mutual,' replied Luc drily. 'Shall we turn back?'

'Nope. Nice day.' He glanced through the open sun roof. 'Pity to waste it. And we could both do with some sea air.'

'Why do you need it?'

'Later. Over a nice bottle or three. Can you drive?' Luc thought back to driving the Aston Martin. 'You can bring us home.'

'All right.'

'Your lovely landlady said you've been in Prague. Filthy weekend?' Luc stiffened. 'Someone nice?'

'Very nice.' Luc took a deep breath.

'So why the glums? Come on. Shoot.'

'I've blown my chance for a decent job. And Ella's chucking me out. Month's notice as of this morning.'

Seeing desolation break over her, Alex turned the radio back on to listen to the news. With his cropped hair, combats and black T-shirt he ought to have been driving a tank into battle. 'There's a food guide in the back somewhere. Book a table, can you?'

He chucked her his mobile. Luc reached into the back seat, piled high with old papers, magazines and notebooks. And probably a colony of mice. She found the guide under his wetsuit. 'Been surfing recently?'

'Hardly. No waves that side of the Urals.'

'How was it?'

'Difficult. Desolate. Beautiful. My interpreter got the heebies. Frightened of the Mafia. I got the runs. We got car-jacked by some kids. And then my stuff gets canned. People are more interested in some minor royal's wedding.'

'I know I am,' admitted Luc, cringing.

'Next time I'll run a story past you instead of a news editor.'

'How's Marina?'

'At her sister's.' He braked as they came up to yet another set of traffic lights. 'The joys of the open road.'

Brighton was on holiday. The pebbly beaches were crowded with sunbathers, office workers were stretched out on every available patch of grass.

'We need an MP.' Alex frowned as they drove past the Taj Mahal domes of the Pavilion. 'Keep your eyes open.'

'For an MP?' She winced, remembering Platform.

'Miracle Park. Parking space.' He suddenly spun the car 180 degrees, spotting some people getting into a tiny Fiat. There was probably a millimetre of space either end, but he managed to get the car in first go. He reached for his shoes and a crumpled linen jacket. 'Hungry?'

Luc nodded, realising she hadn't eaten properly since Saturday night's dinner with Lorenzo.

Alex led her through some side streets, slowing down to squint at piles of secondhand books outside the bric-à-brac shops. 'Don't look so sad,' he pleaded. 'Everyone will blame me for making you unhappy.'

He'd wanted to go to a fish restaurant. Sitting at an outside table in the shade of a huge umbrella, surrounded by girls in summer dresses, Luc felt she could've been on holiday somewhere in Europe. The air smelt different from London's. She sipped some white wine, then suddenly put it aside.

'Corked?' asked Alex.

'No. It's just . . . I . . . I shouldn't be here.'

'Don't like the company?' He raised an eyebrow. 'I'm not that bad, am I?'

'No. No, it's not that.' She fiddled with her bread. 'I should be working. Or rather finding work. And somewhere to live.'

'And you can't do that eating *fruits de mer* in the sunshine. Luc, you weren't going to do anything today in London except panic.' He refilled their glasses. 'Instead I'm offering you the chance to be productive.'

'How?'

'By letting me tell you my troubles.'

'Marina?' Luc stared at him. 'Alex, I really don't want to get involved. Anyway, how was Berlin?'

'Marina cancelled at the last minute. Something about her sister.'

'Oh.'

'I reckon she wants to be back with Gordon the Golfer, God

bless his sweet suburban soul.' He gulped back some more wine. 'Perhaps I should let her.'

'If you love something, set it free,' suggested Luc.

'And if it doesn't come back, hunt it down and kill it. Just a saying.' A waiter set a huge platter in front of them.

'All your plans together. Going to Australia . . .'

Alex shrugged. '*Que sera, sera*. As the song says. Or as a mate said, married woman? Root by all means, just don't fall in love with her.'

Luc winced. 'And have you?'

'Dunno, Luc. I just don't know. When I first saw her, I knew I had to have her. Beautiful, isn't she? But breaking up a marriage? Hard one, that.'

'Then don't do it.'

'She won't be honest with me. One minute she's saying let's go to Sydney tomorrow, the next shrieking about some girlfriend of her husband's commandeering her kitchen.'

'Perhaps she's confused.'

'Perhaps she really wants Gordon the Golfer. Perhaps she only wants him because another woman does. Perhaps she's an emotional terrorist, the Red Army Faction of relationships. Perhaps, perhaps, perhaps. Shit, I've been hearing too much of that Doris Day CD of hers.' He peered at the various skewers and pincers on the plate before them. 'If you don't fancy eating, we can always perform open heart surgery.'

Luc peeled a prawn. 'How's the book?'

His expression darkened. 'My agent's on holiday. Umbria, where else? Being comfortable in her clichés. I'm going to have to write postscripts to the postscripts to the postscripts at this rate.' He attacked a crab claw with a nutcracker. 'My absence hasn't made Ella's heart grow any fonder. Why the parting of the ways? Had a dust-up? Surely not over a bloke?'

'No. Money.'

'Not paid your share of the milk bill? Why should that worry her? She's loaded.'

'That's the problem. Apparently. She thinks I hate her for it.'

Alex peered at her over his sunglasses. 'Do you?'

'No.' Luc sighed. 'But somehow after I came back from Greece it became an issue. For the first time. I've been fed up with playing Cinderella.'

'To Ella's privileged little princess. Tough shit, Lucasta.'

'Thanks.'

'Lesson number one in growing up, life isn't fair. Didn't I tell you that in Greece? You should've listened instead of running off with the Ancient Mariner.' Alex curled his lip. 'He's not your man in Prague, is he?'

'No,' yelped Luc.

'Thank God. Have some more bread, you look peaky.'

Picking at the food, Luc only half listened to Alex's stories about his trip. She tried to focus on him and not on her troubles, which seemed to be crowding her head so much she thought it would explode. Suddenly she got up, asking him if the restaurant had a phone. Her heart sank when he offered her his mobile. 'Call Timbuktu if you like. One of my perks.'

She hesitated, then dialled. She should have called the Agency, she could have called friends to find out if they knew of anyone needing a lodger. There was only one person in the world who could make her feel better. But once again she only got his voice mail.

It was almost four-thirty when they left the restaurant. Alex suggested they walk along the beach. They began ambling down a lane crammed with antique shops. 'Well, I feel better. Even if you don't.'

'I do,' protested Luc. 'Thanks for lunch.'

'You're still haunted. Despite my best efforts to distract you.'

'Sorry.' Luc hung her head. 'Lots on my mind. Homeless. Jobless.'

'Maybe you should start thinking it's all for the best. A chance to change your life completely.'

Startled, Luc glanced up at him. He ordered her to stay where she was and dived into a dark Aladdin's cave of a clothes shop crammed with sarongs, batik print dresses and henna kits. Incense and zitar music wafted out of the front door. It was the sort of place that Ella would have rummaged in for hours.

'Beach,' said Alex, re-appearing.

The sun was way past Cornwall, the beach bathed in mellow warmth. Turning their backs on the gaudy pier, they walked at the water's edge. Luc caught Alex casting appraising glances at the bikinied bodies. 'Babewatch?' she teased.

'A few. Too few.' He winced, seeing a lobster-red beer gut hanging over a pair of multi-coloured trunks. 'Don't fancy yours.' Luc giggled. 'Fie fi foe fum, who's afraid of Englishmen?'

'All right, Alex,' sighed Luc. 'We all know you've got the best body on the beach.'

'How do you know?'

'I saw it, remember? In Greece.'

'Thought you had eyes for nothing but fuck-off yachts.' Luc pulled a face. 'Joke. So, back to changing your life. Go anywhere, do anything, become a junkie, a shepherdess, but never set foot in Switzerland.'

'Switz . . .?'

'Where you called, wasn't it?' He picked up a pebble and sent it skimming across the sea. 'I'm a journo. Curiosity comes with the turf. Noticed the dialling code.' He picked up another. 'Why there?' Luc blushed. 'Our man in Prague's on a business trip?'

'He lives there.'

'No one lives in Switzerland. They count their money.' He froze, staring down at her. 'It's not, is it? You haven't? You haven't been seeing Lorenzo von Retzen?'

Hesitating, Luc turned beetroot. Alex was bound to tell Tim and Liz.

'You have.' Alex groaned. 'No wonder you're unhappy. Very nice? The guy's a cold, soulless shit.'

'He's not.'

Alex shook his head in disbelief. 'Jesus, you've got bad taste in men. I suppose you've fallen madly in love with him.'

'Yes.'

'Poppet, you're nuts. And a masochist. He'll break your heart. You won't break his, he hasn't got one.'

'He has,' protested Luc. 'You don't know him.'

'And you do?' Alex sent another stone across the mirror-like sea. 'How can you? There's a small matter of about seven hundred miles separating you.'

'We manage. He comes to London.' Luc tried not to think that he'd only come once. 'And I went to Prague.' She refused to listen to a voice reminding her that she'd had to trek out to God-Knows-Where because Lorenzo had wanted to go flying. 'And I was supposed to meet him in St Petersburg. And there's the telephone,' she added feebly. Which she'd been kept waiting by for more than two weeks after she'd returned from Greece.

'Ever thought this is a holiday romance that should've ended after one night on the beach in Greece?'

Luc threw a pebble. 'No.' Instead of bouncing, it sank with a dismal plop.

'He can't help you up and brush off your knees, give you a hug and set you on your way via satellite,' said Alex. 'Isn't that what you hoped for when you called just now? A bit of moral support?'

'Yes.'

'Well, he won't give it to you. The only person's comfort Count von Retzen cares about is his own.'

Luc was becoming mulish. 'I think I know him better than you do.'

Infuriatingly, Alex's next pebble almost went to France. 'Then you know he's the most self-centred, conceited man on the planet.'

'He's not. You don't know him.'

'I saw enough of him. In Greece. Remember? He's psycho-pathically selfish. Look at the way he's been giving Tim the run-around.'

'That's . . .'

'You're broke, homeless and jobless. Your priority should be you, not being a bit of far-flung R and R for the unlovely Lorenzo. He's not for you.'

'They don't trade down. You play with them, you don't marry them.' Luc was close to tears. 'So who is he for?' She hurled a handful of stones into the water. 'Marina? She didn't take long to make a pass at him, did she?'

Alex flinched. 'What?'

'Couldn't wait to give him her number,' spat Luc, almost boiling with rage. 'Is that why you're so horrible about him? Feeling threatened?'

She was appalled as what she said sank in. He frowned as if he might have been trying to solve a riddle, then enormous hurt seemed to engulf him. 'Sorry,' whispered Luc. It was like watching a lion being felled by a tranquillising dart. 'Sorry. Forget I said that.'

The thousands of lights on the pier were shining brighter, the helter-skelter tower was in silhouette as the sun went further west. Alex shook his head, gazing out at the horizon. 'Can't take that one back, Luc.' His voice was unnaturally quiet. 'Wish you could.' He didn't look at her. 'Listen, leave, will you? Quick smart. Even someone as dumb as you can find the station.'

It was almost nine o'clock when Luc arrived back at the Doll's House. Just missing an express, she'd had to wait ages at Brighton for another train which then seemed to stop at every tree. She longed for bed and the oblivion of sleep. If the day were a dog, she'd have had it put down.

Dressed in leggings and a T-shirt, Ella was in the kitchen

making a huge salad. 'Just in time. Hungry? I'll lay the table.'

Luc was wrong-footed; she'd expected cold hostility, not baked potatoes. 'Thanks,' she croaked. 'Any calls?'

'None. But I was at a yoga class.'

'No messages?' Luc went over and checked the machine. No Lorenzo.

'Been working?' Ella lit some candles, then began arranging place mats and cutlery.

'I went to Brighton. With Alex.'

'Really? Why?' Some of Ella's serenity seemed to vanish.

'Because he's in fact a very nice guy. And could've been a very good friend to have.'

'My enemy's enemy is my friend.'

Luc felt too defeated to argue. 'So, you and I are suddenly enemies. Fine. Great. I'll be moving out as soon as I can. Don't make it any harder on us until then. Please.'

'Shit. I'm sorry. Come back. Luc, we've got to talk . . .'

But Luc was already halfway down the stairs to her room.

The following morning Luc got up early. She was on the Agency's doorstep in the dreary hinterland behind Victoria Station just after eight.

'Dr Foster, I presume.' Carole peered over her huge spectacles. None of her partners had yet arrived in the office. 'No, he went to Gloucester. Luc James buggered off to Prague.'

'Your bone,' said Luc dully, sitting down and bracing herself for a telling off. She fiddled with her lapis cuff-links. 'Pick it.'

Carole took a sip of her take-away cappuccino. In her mid-thirties, she was born to wear shoulder pads, be efficient and close a deal. 'You went after a permanent job on the sly, according to that pompous prat, Nigel Mann. That's doing me out of commission, that's breaking the rules.'

Luc stared at the wall behind Carole's ear. 'I didn't get it. The job.'

'That's not the point. And I don't like getting a bollocking and having to grovel to twits like Nige because one of my temps decides the weekend starts on Thursday.'

'Sorry. Something came up.'

'I bet it did. I don't want the gory details of your dirty weekend, Luc James, thank you very much.' She stared at Luc. 'I'm well pissed off with you.'

'Fair enough. Understandable.' Luc stared back. 'Now what?'

Carole bit into a huge apple Danish. 'You tell me. Forget shorthand, I need reliability. And I can't rely on you if you're going to drop everything to go gold-digging in Prague.'

'Sorry?'

'Your dishy bloke. Loaded, isn't he?' Carole ran her tongue over her teeth. 'Come on, Luc, I can tell a man's net worth at five hundred paces. While your mind's on the job with him, I can't see how you can concentrate on any other job.'

'Please, Carole, I need to work.' Luc sounded desperate.

'Well, you've got a funny way of showing it.'

'Are you telling me to go to another agency? There are lots of others, you know.'

'I do know.' Carole sat back. 'But they won't give you our rates. Or our consistency. You've worked every day you've wanted to since you joined.'

'But . . .'

'But nothing. There are lots of other temps, you know. You're not that special, Luc.'

The pair of them glared at one another. In the silence, Luc realised she couldn't afford to fall out with Carole. Why was she screwing everything up all the time? Ella, Alex, Nigel, now Carole. Feeling utterly crushed, she screwed up her eyes and sniffed. 'Sorry,' she said in a small voice.

Suddenly Carole broke the Danish in half and offered it to Luc. 'Eat. It's high time you thought about getting a permanent job, isn't it? Something you can build a career on. A girl needs a career these days. Unless we can land millionaires who can keep us in Dom Perignon and chocolate-coated peanuts.'

'I hate chocolate-coated peanuts.' Luc grimaced.

'But you wouldn't mind the millionaire? I wouldn't mind your millionaire. He's gorgeous, you lucky cow.'

'Isn't he?'

'When do I buy a hat? For the wedding.' Carole saw Luc's eyes widen. 'I'm jumping the gun?'

'I only met him two months ago.' Luc was sullen. *You play with them, you don't marry them. No one wants to trade down.* Remembering what Ella had said, she realised that marrying Lorenzo was as likely as winning the Nobel Prize for Physics.

Carole's partners arrived, the phones began to ring. 'Let's have a drink one night and you can tell all.' Carole finished off her coffee. 'Froth moustache? No? Sure? Luc, I don't want to lose you, but I don't want to lose business either. Drop your knickers but nothing else for Mr Loaded. And from now on, follow the rules. Understood?'

'Understood.' Luc nodded. 'Sorry.'

'When Steve gets in, I'll bung him your CV and he can check the perms for you. Permanent jobs. In the meantime, you really want to work? Yes? Good girl.' She peered at her computer screen. 'Our old friends. The Julian Group.'

Luc tried to hide her dismay. 'How long?'

'Till the end of the month.'

'Usual rates?'

'Top rates,' chided Carole. 'Yes.'

Mrs Beak, the cloistered calm, the scream-inducing boredom. But, Luc reasoned, she'd be earning and she'd have plenty of opportunities to ring round about flats. 'Fine.'

It was as if the weeks hadn't passed. Luc could've sworn the same tulips were in the vase. Mrs Beak's soul was still in the deep-freeze. She showed no surprise at Luc's sudden re-appearance, just handed her a ream of paper to fax.

At lunchtime, Luc dashed out to the newsagent's and bought an *Evening Standard*. She scrutinised the rentals columns, almost fainting when she saw the prices being asked. No, extorted. Even a tiny studio within a five-mile radius of the Doll's House would gobble up her salary. She had a choice; paying rent or having a life which included eating.

The afternoon had passed with Luc either blinded by panic that she'd end up sleeping rough, or depressed at the thought of life permanently on the brown cards of the Monopoly board.

Walking home, she realised how cushy it had been living with Ella. Fabulous address, nice neighbours, nice house, token rent which, she was suddenly aware, was way below market rates. For three years she'd been insulated from reality. The Doll's House was nothing like her previous flatshares, with their inevitable squabbles over cleaning and bills. The thought of tensions arising over whose turn it was to take out the rubbish was grim. Flatshares could start off like *Friends*, but end up more like *Single White Female*.

Plodding down Knightsbridge, eyes dazzled by the west-bound sun, she could almost feel her lungs being blackened by the car fumes. Perhaps she should move to the country? Which country? Switzerland? Would there be a message that he'd called? She stopped, then retraced her steps and stood blocking the pavement as she gazed into a shop window.

Half an hour and hundreds of pounds on her credit card later, she was the owner of a mobile phone. Five minutes after-wards, she wondered if she ought to see a financial advisor. Or a psychiatrist.

Ella was in a bikini, sweeping the roof terrace, almost skipping with excitement. Her brown eyes gleamed. 'He called. He's coming to London.'

Luc gasped. 'Lorenzo?'

'Yannick.'

'Yannick? Oh.'

'Isn't it brilliant?'

Luc sank into one of the chairs. 'He got your letter so quickly?'

'No. He called completely out of the blue. He was supposed to be racing at Cowes or something, but it's fallen through. This time tomorrow, he'll be here.'

Luc's gaze fell on Ella's tummy. 'Does he know?'

'No, not yet. Best to tell him face to face.'

'What about . . .?' Luc groped for a way to be tactful.

'What about that business with Madame?' Ella shrugged. 'He swears I leaped to conclusions. Nothing happened between them. He claims he was delivering her early morning tea.'

'And you believe that?'

'Don't know.' She started throwing the dead leaves into a rubbish sack. 'Have to work that one out when he gets here. Thank God he gave me some warning, gave me a chance to clean up. I found an orchard of mouldy apple cores under my bed.'

Luc stopped tapping Lorenzo's number into the mobile's memory and looked up. 'He's staying? For how long?'

'Depends. Anywhere between one night and for ever.'

'Oh.'

'He's the father of my child.'

Luc was filled with disquiet, suddenly realising the enormity of what Ella was doing. Motherhood would put her in a different world, one from which Luc was excluded until she had children of her own. Having a child meant putting away those childish things. Luc wondered why no one had ever told her that when a friend has a baby, it's more of a seismic separation than having a boyfriend or even getting married. That she'd feel so alone and left behind? And so very single?

'How's Lorenzo?'

'Don't know.' Luc took a deep breath. 'He hasn't called?'

Ella shook her head. 'Call him.'

'I did, yesterday. Twice.'

'Call again.'

'No, no way. He'll think I'm going to tell him to play "Misty" for me as I boil his bunny.'

Down in the Mews, Dolly Tilling was calling her cats. Far in the distance over the huddle of roofs and spires a plane was heading for Heathrow. The gentle splash of water in the fountain masked the hum of traffic.

'I should find somewhere else soon.' Luc tried to sound casual.

'Fine.' Ella concentrated on the leaves.

'And I'll make myself scarce when Yannick's around.'

'Thanks. Time for my yoga class.'

Luc stared out over the roofs and spires. Ever since Ella had turned up at school in the middle of term quoting Lovelace and being ordered to tie her hair back and lengthen her skirt, she had been Luc's rock. A fixed anchorage in the rocky seas of adolescence and growing up. With her parents dead and Aunt Sophie in Canada, Ella and Janie and the Doll's House were the closest to home and family Luc had. Now, Ella was having a family of her own and Luc would be relegated to occasional visits as a guest.

'What was so urgent? You've lost your hat?'

It was past midnight. Yawning, Luc forced her mind into gear. 'Worse.'

'Nothing can be,' said Lorenzo. 'Apart from getting your hair cut off.'

'Where are you?' She curled up on the sofa, closing her sleepy eyes against the dazzling lamplight.

'Geneva. In my beautiful house.' He sounded smug.

'The work's all finished?'

'Yes.'

'It's that beautiful?'

'Of course. What was so urgent?'

'I didn't get the job. And I have to move out of here.' She scowled as a blast of opera came down the line.

Lorenzo apologised. 'Sorry, my new toy. What were you saying?'

'That I'm going to be homeless and jobless,' snapped back Luc. A horrible crackling followed. 'Is there something wrong with your phone? Lorenzo? Lorenzo?'

'Still there?' he asked as she was about to hang up. 'I was down in the cellar. Where were we?'

'I'm still where I was, homeless and jobless,' seethed Luc. Was he opening drawers and cupboards? 'Where are you?'

'Kitchen. Shall I give you a tour? The lighting is incredible. I'm almost tempted to learn to cook.'

'Jolly good,' scoffed Luc, now wide awake and furious.

'This fridge . . .' marvelled Lorenzo.

Luc couldn't believe her ears. The man who quoted Lovelace's poetry down the phone was now going on about chill compartments. 'Lorenzo,' she interrupted a eulogy to his new dishwasher. 'I'd better go.' She added, 'It's late. And I'm tired.'

'You should never be too tired to talk to me.'

'Listen to you, you mean.' Luc slammed down the receiver.

Mrs Beak was put out that her favourite restaurant was fully booked. She seemed to blame Luc, who was trying not to yawn.

'The Ritz it'll have to be, then.' She sighed, martyr-like, as though it were McDonalds, and peered at the list of messages, holding them at arm's length. That morning the phones had been unusually busy. Through her haze of tiredness, Luc wondered what was going on.

'Lucasta, double spacing and bold please, I've forgotten my reading spectacles.'

'Don't worry. Men don't make passes at girls who wear glasses,' quoted Luc, then froze.

'I'll bear that in mind,' said Mrs Beak drily, a hint of a smile between the helmet of hair and the fuchsia suit. 'You'd better answer that call.'

Luc scuttled out, wondering what sort of man would dare make a pass at Mrs Beak. It would be as impertinent as pinching the Queen's backside or chatting up Lady Thatcher.

At lunchtime, she bought an *Evening Standard* on her way to the sandwich bar. Ignoring the horoscopes, she turned straight to the rentals columns. It was all so daunting. Looking up places that sounded promising, she had to turn to pages in the *A to Z* that she'd never looked at before. Surely Theydon Bois was in France?

Back at her desk, she pulled out a Yellow Pages and looked up the number for the lettings agency Marina had recommended.

A Super-Sloane answered. 'Per week?' asked Joanna, hearing Luc's budget. 'A month? Oh.' She sniggered. 'Oh. Last time you could rent a flat for that I was a sprog. Vair, vair sorry.' Luc was about to speak but the line was dead.

She stared at the receiver in disbelief. Three more agencies were equally dismissive, getting rid of her so fast that she had the impression they only dealt with Donald Trump and her modest budget might put him off.

Crushed, she fiddled with the tulips. It looked like she'd have to share. She got her address book out of her bag and began a round of calls. Ben, Maggie, Quentin the Zit, Jamie . . . She worked her way methodically through, getting answering-machines. Did anyone know anyone who had a room to rent?

Liz's neighbours in the street of Edwardian terraces were enjoying a summer evening in the suburbs. Smoke wafted from barbecues, footballs were kicked, lawns and borders were being watered.

In contrast, Liz's garden consisted of decking and a few sculpted bushes and eucalypts surrounded by white-grey gravel that was raked into swirly lines. It felt Japanesy. If a weed dared grow it would be made to build the Bridge on the River Kwai.

Not wanting to intrude on Ella's reunion with Yannick, Luc had been delighted that afternoon to be asked round to supper. It was a spur of the moment invitation. Tim was away overnight, for another meeting in Glasgow.

'Have you and Ella fallen out?' Liz poured some wine.

Luc hesitated. 'Not exactly. But perhaps we're starting to get on each other's nerves. Ella wants some space.'

'Space? She's just greedy. A house that size to herself. It's almost immoral.'

'She won't have it to herself for long. Yannick's arriving today.' Luc didn't dare mention that Ella was pregnant.

'Yannick?' Liz frowned. 'The Frenchman? From the yacht?' Luc nodded. 'And you don't want to stick around playing gooseberry.'

'Not really. That's why I'm trying to find somewhere else. But God knows where I'll end up.' She told Liz about the letting agencies.

Liz offered her an olive. 'What about buying somewhere?'

'Me?' gasped Luc.

'Why not?'

'Because . . .' Because house-buying, like having milk and the papers delivered, was for grown-ups. 'No one would give me a mortgage. Anyway, I could never afford one.'

'You couldn't afford a mortgage on a place like Ella's, you mean,' said Liz. 'Who can? Think about getting your foot on the property ladder, talk to your bank manager. We'll eat out here, shall we? Let's hope next door's boy is parked in front of a video and keeps quiet.'

While Liz bustled about in the operating-theatre kitchen, Luc was pensive. It had never occurred to her to buy somewhere. Was it possible? Interest rates were low, but supposing they spiralled up? She'd be falling off that ladder and hurtling down into a black hole of negative equity. But did she want to rent all her life, going from shared flat to shared flat? It was an unappealing prospect at twenty-something, what about at forty? Or sixty?

'Sorry it's so scratch.' Liz put down a huge round plate. Prosciutto, new potatoes, fish, salad were arranged like a photograph of a recipe in a lifestyle feature. It was almost a shame to eat, it looked so beautiful.

'Could I really get a mortgage?'

'I don't know. Find out.' Liz glanced at Luc. 'I'll be on your back until you do. And I wouldn't want me on your back.'

'You wouldn't?'

Grinning, Liz shook her head. 'I'm the organiser from hell. Ask any builder, plumber, curtain-maker in London. Ask Tim.' She passed Luc the bread basket, full of warm sour-dough rolls, home-made. 'Moving out might be the best thing that's happened to you.'

'Can't see how,' said Luc despondently. 'Funny, Alex said something similar.'

'Perhaps he also thinks that Ella's a spoilt monster.' She hushed Luc. 'I know she's your best friend, but she is. While you're so strongly attached to Ella, you can't do much for yourself. And it's time you started.'

'Is it?'

'You're what, mid-twenties? You should be laying the foundations for the rest of your life. Ella's already got the security that most people never have. Including you.' Liz refilled their glasses. 'Stop drifting and get anchored to a career and a place of your own.'

Luc sighed. 'You're right, but . . .'

'And don't for one moment think that some knight in shining armour is going to come along and sweep you off your feet.'

'A knight in shining Armani,' mused Luc, thinking of Lorenzo. Suddenly, she yearned to talk to him. 'He might.'

'For goodness sake.' Liz rolled her eyes. 'He won't. Just

because you look like something out of a fairy-tale doesn't mean you have to believe in them.'

'I don't,' protested Luc.

'Sure? I did, at your age.' Liz smiled wryly. 'I honestly thought that one day my handsome, clever, brave prince would come.'

'Really?' Luc couldn't imagine it.

'Of course. Most of my girlfriends did too.' There was a thud as a football hit the party wall followed by a woman yelling 'Theo' and then an unrepentant 'Sorry, Mum.' 'Doesn't that child have a bedtime?' Liz frowned. 'Where were we?'

'The brave prince and your girlfriends.'

'Him. It took one evening, five of us, probably ten bottles of wine and the horrible thought that we had more than half a century of dating between us to realise the obvious.'

'What obvious?'

'The prince doesn't exist.' She added, 'Neither do knights in shining armour. Neither do real-life Mr Darcys. We had more chance of meeting Father Christmas.'

Luc sipped her wine, feeling rather smug. Lorenzo was handsome, clever, brave. She must, must, must call him. 'Perhaps you just didn't come across the right men.'

'But we did,' retorted Liz. 'We just didn't know it. We were so blinded by the search for the non-existent Prince Right that men like Tim were always second-best.'

'But Tim's perfect for you,' said Luc. She couldn't imagine Liz being with anyone else.

'He is.' The football thudded against the wall again. Liz winced. 'Sometimes I'd rather have rats living next door. That's the only cloud, you know. Between Tim and me. He's desperate to have some children. I'm not ready yet. As I told him, there's plenty of time.'

'There is?' Luc tried to be tactful. Liz was, what, thirty-four?

'A good few years. I'm not ready yet, we're not ready yet. I don't want to be bullied or pressured. And Tim must be properly established first.'

Luc wondered how Tim would react when he heard Ella's news.

Although the evening was still warm, the sun was going down. While Liz cleared the plates, Luc studied the garden, so odd in suburban Kew. Apparently the neighbours had scoffed at first, but as their lawns turned to dustbowls because of the hosepipe ban, they'd become more appreciative.

'What's the project in Glasgow?' she asked, as Liz returned with summer pudding.

'Probably another false lead.' Liz sighed. 'Between ourselves, things have been so hard Tim's thinking of giving up and going back to his old firm.'

'Would that be so bad?'

'Not the end of the world, no. But it's not what he wants. Or deserves. He's got too much talent to be one member of a huge team where the boss takes all the credit and gets the knighthood.'

Luc felt a sudden pang of disquiet.

'He needs the work to get the name, but without the name it's impossible to get the work.' Liz pulled a face. 'Lorenzo von Retzen was almost the last straw. Tim put so much into that. It would've been such a showcase, then the bastard changes his mind.'

Luc squirmed in her seat, concentrating hard on her pudding. She was relieved when Liz went inside to answer the telephone.

'Marina,' announced Liz, coming back. She sighed. 'On her way round. Apparently she's been trying to reach you. She's sounding the hysterical end of stressed. What's wrong?'

'Nothing,' muttered Luc. She felt distinctly uneasy. Alex had obviously reported back. Marina would be furious about Luc's tales of her chatting up Lorenzo. Luc imagined herself back in the Middle Ages, being ducked in the village pond for gossiping.

The bell rang urgently. Horror-struck, Luc suddenly realised that the saga of her and Lorenzo would come out in front of Liz. Anticipating Liz and Marina's joint verbal

Desert Storm, she was tempted to climb over the wall and leg it.

'Come in,' Liz was saying. 'Drink? No champagne, I'm afraid, but some rather good chardonnay. Unoaked.'

Luc was thrown by how dreadful Marina looked. Her white summer dress was grubby and creased, the flat plimsolls made her dumpy and her long curls were greasy and lank.

'Water.' Marina seemed breathless from the short walk from the car. She stared round the garden. 'Elegant, yes. But Liz, *cara*, too much control. You boss, boss, boss even the nature.'

Liz forced her lipsticked mouth into a smile. 'Do sit down, Marina.'

Marina waited until Liz was settled, then pounced. 'You saw Alex on Monday?'

Luc froze. Surely Marina didn't suspect her of trespassing? 'Yes. We went for lunch. In Brighton.' Having visions of all those hotel rooms rented by the hour, Luc pressed on hurriedly. 'He was being kind. I think he felt sorry for me.'

'Sorry for you,' repeated Marina distractedly. 'You had lunch, then what?'

'We went for a walk. Then I caught the train back.' Luc blushed. 'He's really nice.'

There was a long silence. While she was trying to work out if Alex had landed her in it, or whether Marina suspected her of having a fling with him, Luc swirled around the wine in her glass so hard that half of it ended up in her lap. 'You're very lucky,' she added lamely.

'I was.' Marina shrugged. 'Alex finished with me this morning. On his way to Belfast to do another boring story.' She glanced at Luc. 'Don't gawp, *cara*, it doesn't suit you.'

'Finished?' Liz was incredulous.

'*Finito.* All because of some silly fib.' Marina folded the hem of her dress, her nail polish was chipped. 'You really spent Monday with Alex?'

'I was upset and . . .'

Marina interrupted. 'I told Alex I spent the day with you.'

'Oh.' Luc frowned. 'Oh. Why?'

'I panicked. Said the first thing that came into my head. He's a bastard. Question after question. How's Luc? Where did you go? What did you eat? Where did you park? He should've worked for the Gestapo.'

'It's over? But all your plans,' cried Luc. 'He can't mean it.'

'He does. Said if I want to see my husband so much, I should go back to him.'

'Is that where you were?' demanded Liz. 'With Gordon?'

Marina nodded. 'Walking round the bloody golf-course with him.' She frowned down at her legs. 'Even my knees are starting to look middle-aged. Almost forty and I'm on the shelf.'

'You've put yourself on it.' Liz was brisk. 'Quite frankly, Marina, the best thing you can do is forget about Alex and go back to your husband.'

'That's just what Alex said.'

'He did? Well, better late than never.'

'He says he doesn't want to be responsible for ending a marriage. But there is no going back.'

'Of course there is. You just drive across Richmond Park.'

'No, Liz. It's not controllable, like your leetle garden. The irony is I finally told Gordon about Alex.' She smiled forlornly. 'So, they've both finished with me.'

The Doll's House was deserted. A dusty backpack was propped up against the sitting-room wall and the ashtray was full of Gitanes stubs. Going into the kitchen to get some water, Luc saw an enormous bunch of white flowers in the sink. Lucky Ella . . .

Gasping, Luc ripped open the tiny envelope. ' "If to be absent were to be, Away from thee . . ." Distance is no excuse. Forgive me. Lorenzo.'

All her resentment and doubts vanished. Less than thirty seconds later she was through to Geneva. 'You're forgiven.'

'So easily? You should be my priest.' He laughed. 'Hello, Lucasta.'

'How's your house?'

'Still beautiful. Some magazine people are coming round to photograph it tomorrow.' Luc knew she should mention Tim, but didn't. 'How are you?' asked Lorenzo. 'Still beautiful?'

'Well. I'm very well.'

'But you're homeless and jobless.'

'Details,' giggled Luc. 'Are you going to give me another tour?'

'No. I'm in bed. Wish you were here.'

'Do you?' Luc melted. 'Really?'

'Of course. My book's a classic. Therefore worthy but dull.'

'I don't think I want to sit on the subs' bench to a book.'

'Subs' bench?'

'Where footballers wait until they're swapped with a player on the pitch.' Luc began to feel like a dictionary. 'Don't you have soccer in Switzerland?'

'Of course. It's not all cuckoo clocks and Heidi.'

'Isn't it?'

'You've never been to Switzerland?'

'No,' admitted Luc. 'Never had a reason to go.'

Until he said goodnight, promising he'd call her soon, he gave her plenty of reasons to go, including skiing which she loathed and climbing Mont Blanc which was insane as she got vertigo going up a step-ladder.

Putting down the phone, Luc wished they'd stop going off on nonsensical tangents. Why hadn't she'd just come out and said that the only reason she'd set foot in Switzerland was to see him and where was the invitation?

Why, why, why couldn't she close a deal?

Chapter Twelve

Gorgeous, thought Luc the next evening, as Yannick leaped to his feet. One of Ella's sarongs was wrapped round his waist. Exclaiming delightedly, he kissed her on both cheeks. As gorgeous as ever. Apollo on the drachma note, Apollo bringing life-giving sunshine. Seeing him, the world was suddenly a better place.

Ella watched him, her smile self-satisfied and indulgent as if she had created a wonderful work of art. The pair of them had idled away the afternoon lying about on cushions drinking Pimms on the roof terrace. Yannick had used some of Lorenzo's flowers to make a garland and woven it into Ella's hair.

'Join us, Luc. I'll get you a glass,' he said, darting downstairs.

'Going well?' asked Luc in a low voice.

Ella nodded. 'Great.' She touched the flowers. 'You don't mind, do you?'

' 'Course not. There were too many for all the vases.'

'Santé.' Yannick handed Luc a Pimms and settled himself beside Ella on a cushion. 'To Greece. Ella tells me you fell in love there. With a man who sends you beautiful flowers and meets you in Prague. Henri will be heart-broken.'

Luc jumped. 'How is he?'

'Happy, I guess.' Yannick grinned. 'New crew to bully up and down the Côte d'Azur. Madame to be bullied by. The yacht to worry about. He's pig in sheet.'

'Shit,' corrected Ella. 'Apparently he's still pining for you.'

'It's true.' Yannick nodded. 'His little English rose.'

Luc groaned. 'I've got sharp thorns.'

'You?' He laughed. 'I'll tell him. He owes me some wages. Love suits you, Luc. You're looking well. When do I meet this Lorenzo?'

'I don't know,' sighed Luc. 'When do *I* meet him again? He lives in Geneva . . .'

'Ella told me.' Yannick kissed Ella's cheek and reached over for his cigarettes. 'And he's a busy and important man. What did you have to forgive him for? I read the card.'

Luc was startled by his candour. 'Not much. I was fed up and he wasn't very sympathetic. He had a lot on his mind.' Like chill compartments.

'When did you meet him? After we sailed?'

Luc answered question after question, blossoming under his gaze like a flower given water. Reliving the saga, she forgot her angst about intruding, all the recent awkwardness between her and Ella. Yannick seemed so genuinely interested that she felt enormous warmth towards him. Smiling contentedly, Ella played with his fingers and gazed out over the chimney-pots silhouetted against the sky.

'Love's expensive,' said Yannick, when Luc told him about the mobile.

'She's obsessed.' Ella yawned, tugging at his hand. 'We ought to get ready. The table's booked for eight.'

'And you're obsessed by food.' He pinched her tummy. 'Ella's fatter, isn't she?'

'Well, that's hardly surp—' Luc was silenced by a warning frown from Ella, who had stiffened in alarm. As their eyes met, she realised Ella hadn't told him. Luc stammered, 'She's given up smoking.'

'Thanks,' mouthed Ella, a few minutes later as Yannick gathered up the cushions.

'Why haven't you told him?' mouthed back Luc.
She was answered by a shrug.

The Doll's House to herself, Luc had a do-the-chores evening, interrupted by phone calls. No rooms, but how nice to hear from her. Why had she gone to ground? Maggie was particularly blunt. 'New man, Luc? Neglect your old mates until you want something?'

'Morning,' said Yannick. Wearing the sarong again, he was standing in the kitchen waiting for the coffee to drip, drip, drip through the machine. His dreadlocks were in silhouette like a halo. 'Sleep well?'

Luc yawned in reply. She hadn't. Maggie's words had cut her and she'd spent half the night awarding herself nil points for effort and focus. She'd neglected her friends, hadn't bothered to make an appointment with the bank or even to update her CV.

She filled the kettle, squinting against the light that was pouring in. 'How was your dinner?'

'Awe-full. Ella should let me cook instead of wasting her money.' He peered out of the window. 'Nice area. Nice house.'

'Um.' Luc didn't need reminding. She shook some cornflakes into a bowl.

'And you're leaving soon. Happy about that?'

As he eyed her, Luc was reminded that she was only wearing a long T-shirt. She felt a sliver of weird unease. 'Hope we've got some milk.'

'I can persuade Ella to change her mind.'

'Where's the sell-by date?' Peering into the fridge, Luc pointedly examined the carton. 'Don't bother. About changing Ella's mind.'

'Why not?'

'She won't. You'd be wasting your time.' For some reason, she couldn't meet his gaze. 'Your coffee's done. The cups are behind you.'

'I know.' He smiled, but made no attempt to move.

'In the cupboard.'

'The kettle's boiled. English tea . . .'

'Better hurry, I'll be late for work . . .' Taking the few paces towards him, Luc kept her eyes on the clock, then on the kettle. She could smell Ella's shampoo that he'd washed his hair in. His skin smelt of the sun.

'For an English rose.'

'With sharp thorns,' said Luc, staring at the kettle as if it held the Holy Grail. The touch of his fingers on her neck was so light she asked herself if she weren't imagining it.

'Ella will do anything for me,' he whispered. 'We could have such a good time together. The three of us. Think about it.'

Frozen under his touch, Luc thought. Horrified, she fled downstairs.

Unease went to work with Luc. The vague stabs of disquiet unsettled her, making it impossible to concentrate.

She relived the scene, trying to dismiss it, trying even harder to laugh it off. A proposition from Yannick? A proposition from Yannick in the kitchen before breakfast? She'd imagined it. Over-reacted. He couldn't be that much of a bastard to Ella.

The cloistered hush in the office did nothing to soothe her turmoil. Casey waddled in, chucking a pile of post on Luc's desk. 'Morning.'

'Morning,' said Luc. 'Coffee?'

'Heartburn.' Shaking his head, he sucked harder on a Rennie. 'I need a plumber.'

Luc grimaced, thinking he was referring to his guts. She didn't want to imagine the state of lard-tub Casey's insides. 'A plumber?'

'My boiler's on the blink. The usual bloke's on holiday. Ring round and get some quotes, will you?'

She stared at him, resentment welling up. Surely sorting out Casey's domestic problems wasn't part of her job?

'My details.' He handed her a card.

'NW3?' She added bitchily, 'Gospel Oak?'

'Hampstead,' he corrected huffily. 'Try Yellow Pages. P for plumbers. Where's Juliet?'

'Dentist.'

'So she is. Oh, run down to the dry cleaners for me, will you?' He got two tickets out of his wallet. 'And while you're about it, drop into the chemist and get me some Milk of Magnesia.'

'Anything else?'

'That's it. Hang on, how are we off for teabags?'

'I'll check.' Luc's teeth were gritted, hard.

His currant eyes blinked in his Pilsbury Dough Boy face. 'Know something, Miss James? Your expression is saying "What did your last slave die of?" '

'Is it?' Luc raised an eyebrow. 'Well, Casey, what did your last slave die of?'

'Answering back.'

Juliet Beak swept into the office on her crocodile heels just as a phone rang. Luc picked up the receiver but the ringing continued. It took an age to realise it was her mobile in her bag. Snatching it up, she was gasping hello just as the phone on her desk rang.

'Hang on.' Luc dropped the mobile as if were white-hot and pounced on the receiver. 'Hornbeam and, Plat . . ., sorry, Julian Group. Good afternoon, I mean, good morning. No, it's after twelve . . . Sorry.' She glanced up and saw Mrs Beak had her headache-bravely-borne look. 'She was in a meeting. I'll check.' Luc pressed hold. 'Are you in?'

'For whom?' Mrs Beak was glacial.

'Er, I'm not sure.'

'You'd better put it through to my office.'

Flustered, Luc pressed some buttons on the switchboard and picked up her mobile. 'Liz?'

Liz was asking if it was a bad time. Juliet Beak was rapping on the other side of the glass partition with her heavy rings and calling out, 'Has that call been transferred or not?'

'Liz, I'll call you back.' Luc glanced at the switchboard. All the lights were dead. Shit. 'They've gone.' She cringed.

Mrs Beak advanced towards Luc like a Panzer tank with big hair. 'Miss James, is it necessary to remind you that you are being paid to act professionally?'

'Sorry.'

'Kindly confine your social calls to your time, not mine. I suggest you take an early lunch and deal with whatever was so urgent.'

Feeling crushed, Luc skulked off to the sandwich bar. Blowing at the froth on her cappuccino, she wondered why she wasn't a lady who lunched. Why wasn't she toying with sushi?

As she munched on her cheese and pickle sandwich, picking at the button on her cableknit cardigan, she decided it was for the same reason that she didn't have a groovy loft apartment, a slim briefcase which screamed brilliant career and La Perla knickers that hinted at her sexual prowess. She was one of lifestyle's losers.

At least the mobile gave her some small stake in the twenty-first century, even if her hair and clothes seemed stuck in the nineteenth. Eyes scanning *The Times*' flatshare column, she rang Liz.

Luc rolled her eyes as Liz told her to get on to the bank, now. 'Remember, Luc, procrastination is the thief of time.'

Switching off from the scolding, Luc realised her motto must be never do today what you can put off until tomorrow.

'In the meantime, think about house-sitting.'

'House-sitting?'

'Owners often need people to keep an eye on their places if they're away. You're ideal. Responsible, female, non-smoker. You don't smoke, do you?'

'Hardly ever.'

'Make that never. Register with one of the agencies. I'll ask around, see if my clients need anyone. Ella can give you a reference. How is she?'

'Well. Yannick's arrived.' Luc felt the stabs of disquiet again.

'Is she doing that Master's or not?'

'Don't know.' Luc frowned, realising that Ella hadn't mentioned anything since Greece. She didn't want to get drawn into any arguments. 'Have Marina and Alex really split up?'

'I hope so. Marina doesn't want the real-life workaholic Alex. They were living in a dreamworld. As soon as she began moaning about his flat, I told Tim it wouldn't last.'

'It sounded horrible,' said Luc. 'She was frightened.'

'She was probably more frightened of giving up five bedrooms and seven figures' worth of mock Georgian close to Wimbledon Common. Are you calling from your mobile?' demanded Liz suddenly. 'Not from work? Get off the line. It's costing you a fortune. Now, sort out the bank and get on to those house-sitters.'

'Bully.'

'It's good for you.' Liz hung up.

Luc realised she'd spilt pickle down her cardigan.

Dark because of its frosted windows, the pub's carpet reeked of old beer. The usual sad old bores were sitting on their usual stools at the bar. Luc was glad to get out into the walled garden. It seemed depressingly typical that her local was a traditional boozer, rather than somewhere chi-chied up with a stripped wooden floor and a wine list.

Ella was sitting in the remotest corner, her mineral water

untouched. She smiled wanly. 'Another fine mess I've got myself into.'

'You've told him?' said Luc. 'Hang on, I'll get a drink.' Coming back from the bar with a whisky and a wet cuff, she sat down at the rickety table. 'Where is he?'

'Don't know. He walked out. Probably to pick up a together thirty-something who'd never forget to take the Pill.' She scowled. 'Perhaps he got lucky and is sneaking back into the house to get his stuff before scarpering for ever.'

'What happened?'

'We were having brunch in bed and he went on about me putting on weight. Fattist pig. Then I explained.'

'And?'

Ella's brown eyes watered. 'The *merde* hit the fan. He almost punched a hole in the bedroom wall. Went ballistic. How dare I try and trap him? Why can't I get rid of it?'

'He was in shock,' said Luc soothingly.

'I know, but . . .' Ella's face crumpled.

Luc scowled at a pair of jowly suits at the next table who were gawping. 'Give him time to get used to the idea.'

'It was like being with Jekyll and Hyde.' Ella dug a tissue out of her combats' pocket. 'He's so nice, you saw the other night. Making me that silly crown of flowers. I've never felt so easy with anyone, I honestly thought he might be my long-lost twin. And then today . . .' she swallowed.

Luc froze. 'He didn't hurt you, did he?'

She shook her head. 'Hurt the wall instead. And my Sooty and Sweep eggcups. Can't think what all that adrenaline in my system did to Chelsea.'

'You're not really calling it Chelsea?'

'Better than Stamford Bridge.' Ella sighed. 'What am I going to do?'

'Go it alone. You planned to, anyway.'

'I've got doubts again.' She screwed up her face. 'I don't think I'll be able to cope all by myself.'

'Of course you will. You're young, strong, healthy. Besides, as you said, you don't need a man around.'

'Need? No. Need is different from want. I had what I wanted over the past few days. Until this morning.'

Luc studied her glass. 'You hardly know Yannick, do you? Perhaps he was only meant to be a holiday fling.'

'Like Lorenzo was only meant to be a holiday fling? You hardly know him.'

'That's different . . .'

'Why? How?'

'Guess.' Sighing, Luc glanced at Ella's tummy. 'It's a huge step. The biggest you'll ever take. I can't see how resenting the father is the best start.'

'Resent?' Ella was puzzled. 'Resent? I don't. Why should I? I'm confused, that's all. I had this stupid fantasy that he'd want to play Happy Families with me.'

'You're bonkers.'

'I'm not.'

'You meet a stranger in Greece, you get yourself pregnant, you never expect to see him again. But when he turns up out of the blue you expect this stranger to fall in with your plans.' Luc shook her head. 'For a start, he might not want to live in London.'

'I can move.'

'Or be a father.'

Ella scowled. 'Tough.'

'Or be with you.'

'Thanks, Luc.'

'Be realistic. You don't know him. He could be anything. Feckless, unfaithful, a user . . .'

'Bullshit,' protested Ella. 'You don't know Lorenzo. But that doesn't stop you from knowing that he's one hundred per cent perfect.'

'No one's perfect,' blurted out Luc.

'I thought Lorenzo was.' Ella finished her mineral water. 'By the way, how is he?'

'Great.'

'Next time I suggest a holiday, say you're staying in and washing your hair, will you? Can we go? My back aches.'

Following her past the crowded tables, Luc noticed that Ella's walk was no longer an easy, long-legged stride. Her trainers seemed to be worn for necessity and comfort, not fashion, making her look dowdy.

Turning into the Fulham Road, Luc caught sight of her own reflection in a shop window. 'The past-it girls.' She sighed. 'I want to burn everything in my wardrobe.'

'Good idea.' Ella was massaging her lower back.

'You're not meant to say that.'

'Clothes talk. Yours say you're up for a visit to a mosque. Or, on a good day, take me to matins.'

'I'm not that much of a frump.' Luc scowled down at her skirt, almost skimming her ankles. 'Am I?'

'You must keep Laura Ashley in business. My back.' Ella rubbed harder. 'Why worry? You can get away with it. Yannick thinks you're stunning.'

'What?'

'He told me.' Ella yawned. 'You're not his type in a million years, but you're stunning. That's what he said.'

Hearing Ella sound so unconcerned, Luc's pulse quietened.

'Wake up, Luc. Nabbing Lord Snooty must finally convince you that you've got something going for you.'

'I haven't nabbed him. Far from it.'

Ella slowed in front of an antiques shop. 'Presents, Prague, flowers, hours of calls. What more do you want?'

'Him. To be with him. Every second of the day.'

'As long as you both shall live,' said Ella absentmindedly, peering at a chaise longue. 'I could recline on that and read improving literature. Chatterton . . .' Voice fading, she stared at Luc. 'You'd really get married? You'd marry Lorenzo?'

'If he asked, yes. But he won't, will he?' Luc kept her eyes on the pavement. 'You play with them, you don't marry them. No one wants to trade down.'

All the awkwardness between them returned; a shadow fell. It deepened the closer they got to the Doll's House. If Ella had admitted she'd been too hasty and asked Luc to stay on, Luc would-'ve accepted. If Luc had asked to stay, Ella would've immediately said yes. Neither referred to the subject and the moment passed.

A smell of garlic and herbs was wafting from the kitchen. The table was covered with a heavy white linen cloth and gleaming silver. 'Ella?' called Yannick, rushing out of the kitchen with a tea-towel over his shoulder.

'What's going on?'

'I'm cooking dinner. I had no idea France had colonised South Kensington. Fromagerie, boulangerie. Luc, you're joining us? Good.'

'I thought you'd scarpered.' Ella was bewildered.

'Scarpered? What's that?'

'Disappeared. Fled. Run away. After this morning.'

'I was shocked.' He appealed to Luc. 'You know what's happening, of course. You must've been shocked when Ella told you. Imagine this news for me.'

Luc hesitated, not wanting to get involved.

'Wonderful news.' He put his arm round Ella's shoulders and laughed joyously. 'The most wonderful, wonderful news. Me. A father.'

'You mean it?' gulped Ella, weeping again.

Gently he wiped away her tears with a corner of the tea-towel and kissed her nose. 'Of course. Some champagne to celebrate, eh, Luc?' His smile was so sweet, she wondered if she hadn't imagined that morning's scene in the kitchen. 'No, you're not intruding. Sit down.'

He brought the heavy silver wine cooler from the kitchen and three crystal glasses. Ella frowned. 'All that stuff's been packed away for years.'

'I know. From the date on the newspapers.'

'How did you find it?'

'I was looking for the fuse-box.'

'Oh. Why?'

'To mend the light on the landing.' The bottle opened with a pop. 'Which I did.'

'But that hasn't worked since I moved in,' exclaimed Luc.

'And all the kitchen cupboards now close properly. You two never heard of a screwdriver?'

'It's a drink, isn't it?' said Ella, refusing the champagne. 'Vodka and orange.'

'It's not funny, Ella,' he reproved. 'You have a beautiful house and you should take care of it. Instead, half the electrics don't work, there's damp everywhere and your guttering is a mess.'

'It is?' She sounded alarmed. 'I was always useless at DIY. Prefer GSR.'

'Get Someone Round,' explained Luc. 'Except it's hard to find that someone.'

Yannick smiled. 'That someone's me. I'm very practical.'

'And a good cook by the smell of it,' said Ella.

'Of course. I'm French.' He raised his glass. 'To the four of us.' He turned to Luc. 'And not forgetting Lorenzo.'

'No chance of that.'

For the briefest moment he met Luc's eyes, causing a prickling of unease. 'So, Ella, tomorrow we'll go through the house and make a list of what I have to do.'

'You're really not scarpering?' she asked.

'I'm staying. Let me check my crème caramel.'

He went back to the kitchen. Ella sat on the sofa looking like the cat with the crème. 'Gorgeous, practical, a cook,' she whispered. 'Blimey. It's too good to be true.'

Luc remembered being told by Ella that things that were too good to be true usually were. 'Are you still doing that Master's?'

Ella frowned. 'Don't know. Last thing I heard I'm still weight-listed for a place. What makes you ask?'

'Liz, actually. She called me today.'

'Oh. Why?'

Luc wriggled, wishing she'd kept quiet. 'She suggested I find out about mortgages. And house-sitting.' Luc took a deep breath. 'I know how you feel, but she's being kind.'

'Makes a change. What does she think about Chelsea?'

'I haven't told her. You must. Very soon.'

The temperature in the room seemed to be plummeting by the second. 'Well, well, well.' Ella scowled. 'Liz the Miz, Timid . . .'

'There's nothing wrong with Liz and Tim . . .'

'. . . Alex Bleeding Heart Ireland.'

'He's one of the good guys.'

'The Chippy Chappie. Ever thought you'd have made a good collaborator?'

'Ella, they're your quarrels, not mine.'

'Music. Some Berlioz, I think.' Shaking a jar, Yannick went over to the stereo. 'Hey, you two look very serious.'

'It is serious. I can't believe that Luc can be such an under-hand snake.'

'And I can't believe that you can be such a childish control freak,' retorted Luc. 'Ella's got a problem with me talking to her sister.'

'Half-sister.'

'Hush, both of you,' ordered Yannick.

'Ever thought I might need all the help and advice I can get?' demanded Luc.

Ella huhed. 'Why run to Liz of all people? You know our history.'

'Your history. Not mine,' shrieked back Luc.

'Ella, Luc,' pleaded Yannick.

'How can you be so fucking insensitive?' Ella ignored him.

'And how can you be so fucking selfish? Your favourite song, Ella. "Me, Myself, I".'

'Please. I feel like the United Nations,' said Yannick. 'Calm down. Will someone explain?'

'I've got to find somewhere else to live and I need help,' said Luc. 'And one of the people who's helping me is Liz, Ella's half-sister. But despite making me homeless, Ella doesn't want Liz to help me find another home. Right, Ella?'

Ella was obviously groping for words, then gave up the struggle. Her head hung in defeat, her face hidden by a curtain of blonde hair. 'Yes,' she admitted finally. 'But if our situations were reversed, you'd feel uncomfortable too.'

'Maybe,' conceded Luc.

Yannick stared at Ella. 'It's that bad between you and your sister?'

'Half-sister.' She scowled.

'Half, full, quarter, what difference? Bury the past, move on.'

'Why? What for?'

'Because resentment makes you ugly. Luc's right. Grow up.' Ella became as open-mouthed as if she'd been slapped. 'If she's friends with Liz, that's her decision. Stop blaming her because you're so insecure.'

Insecure? Ella? Luc couldn't believe her ears.

'Thanks, Yannick.' Ella gave a long, despairing sigh. 'And tonight, ladies and gentlemen, our specials are crème caramel and food for thought.'

Throughout dinner, Ella was so subdued that Luc and Yannick could've been alone. Yannick urged her to have some champagne, then some claret, but she stuck to mineral water; most of her coq au vin was uneaten, the cheese ignored. Listening to Yannick's tales of scummy jobs he'd done before he started his Civil Service studies, Luc was comforted. Sorting out Casey's plumbing problems wasn't that much of a hardship compared to being a *plongeur* or working in a morgue.

'What are you going to do next?' she asked, knife cutting into a perfect Brie.

He smiled. 'Be a father. Look after a mother.'

Overnight, London seemed almost deserted. The streets were empty, the shops emptier still. Those who hadn't joined the August exodus had an air of belonging to an unofficial urban survivors' club. As they sweltered in the mugginess, trying not to think about beaches, they consoled themselves with being able to find parking spaces more easily, emptier buses and Tubes, and the chance to go to the Proms.

No rain had fallen for weeks. The newspaper headlines screamed drought, the inside pages were full of explanations about global warning. The grass in the parks was strawlike, the pavements gritty. Everything looked in need of a rinse to wash away the dust.

One Thursday evening, Luc stood outside a terrace house in Battersea. It was the third flat-share she'd been to see. Every letting agent had been as snooty as Marina's, all implying that Luc should be selling the *Big Issue*. Liz had tried to get her house-sitting, but had failed. 'Bad time of year. You've missed the boat. Has Marina called you?'

'No. Not for ages.'

Luc had called friends who said they'd call friends and get back to her. She was sick of hearing that it was a bad time of year to be looking, that she'd never get anywhere as good as the Doll's House, followed by the inevitable roundabout probing as to why she and Ella had fallen out.

'We haven't. I feel like a change,' she'd answer evasively.

She wished it were true. She didn't feel like a change at all. She hated change, which was being thrust upon her. She wanted her old life, which she'd easily dismissed as being so predictable that she thought she ought to be getting one.

Instead she was facing being torn out of the familiar ground where she'd planted herself for years. She was frightened that she'd find herself transplanted to the wrong part of the garden where she'd wither away and die.

The first room she'd seen had been so promising. It was in a terrace house in Hammersmith owned by a cousin of Jamie's who worked at the BBC. Kate was away a lot, needed someone to keep an eye on the place and feed the cats. The only drawback was the litter tray in the bathroom, which Luc had tried not to gag at. Kate was waiting to hear from her sister, who had first choice. Two days later Kate had heard, the sister was moving in.

The second, in Earl's Court, had been described as a Chelsea penthouse by its owner, Gerard Double-Barrelled. It was on the fifth floor of a liftless building. Gerard had a signet ring, boozy breath and a leer in his bloodshot blue eyes. 'Your first task,' he'd joked, pointing to a dirty Everest of washing-up in the sink of the grimy kitchen. He'd waved at the sofa in the sitting room. 'Yes, you can fuck on it. You can even fuck me on it.' Luc had fled.

The Battersea room had been taken an hour before. Angela was sorry that Luc had wasted her time, she'd invite her in for a drink, except she had to feed Jake and read Jodie a story. Luc could hear a bawling Jake and a whining Jodie in the background. Knowing that she'd be roped into baby-sitting, Luc wasn't nearly as sorry as Angela, who had baby sick down her shoulder.

Waiting at the bus stop, footsore and fed up, Luc wondered if she should start sleeping on the sofa in the Julian Group offices. Every time she went back to the Doll's House, the more unsettled she became. It was no longer home. It felt temporary, hotel-like. She was a guest who mustn't make herself too comfortable because she'd be moving on soon.

Ella wasn't hostile, just remote. Not that they'd seen each other much; Luc had filled her evenings as much as possible. She'd even endured a dinner with Quentin the Zit, trying to laugh at the whoopie cushion on the Golf passenger seat. She'd gone to the Proms. Alone. She'd started reading Kafka. She was keeping herself busy with pointless and not particularly enjoyable activity as if to prove something to Ella. Prove what? That she could survive without her? That she wasn't hurt about being made homeless? Or that she wasn't jealous that Ella had a mane of long golden hair, a platinum credit card, the love of a good man and soon, a child? A child who, like Ella, would only have the good fairies at its christening?

Yannick's devotion seemed limitless. He shopped, he cooked, he mended. He touched Ella non-stop as if she were his good luck charm, he said he'd like to chop her up and eat her, or put her in his backpack so he could take her everywhere.

If Luc ever caught his eyes on her, she'd always meet them and smile unreservedly. If she ever thought about what happened that morning in the kitchen, she'd either laugh at herself or shrivel with shame about being so foolish.

His warmth, his tactility, his presence contrasted horribly with Lorenzo, who'd scarcely called. He was away again, in Kazakhstan. But his absence filled Luc's world.

All the talk of heat and humidity was exhausting. Luc woke up feeling drained, as if she needed a turbo booster to get her through the coming day.

On her way to work she made an appointment to see Steve at the Agency. At lunchtime she turned up with her updated CV, typed in snatched bursts between trying to chivvy Casey's plumber and doing a spreadsheet for Juliet Beak.

On the corkboard next to Steve's desk was a collage, mostly of George Clooney and Prince William. 'Nice cuff-links,' he oohed.

'Nice tie,' said Luc.

'Ta. Hours old.' He patted his hair. Luc wondered how much his highlights cost. 'Let's get down to it, shall we?'

Less than ten minutes later, Luc was out the door. Steve was catching the late afternoon flight to Mykonos where he'd arrive in time to go clubbing. He travelled light, taking just the necessities — drugs and his mobile. He'd try for her on return, but, Luc love, bad time of year to be looking.

Walking back across Green Park, now more Yellow Park, Luc sank into a deck-chair and turned to the flatshare columns. It was obviously a bad time of year to be looking for a new place to live, too. She threw aside the paper and gazed up at the sky. Thinking of Steve going off to Greece, she rebelled at the thought of an afternoon's incarceration in the office. Why didn't she have the guts just to get on a plane and get out? Spend the summer on somewhere like Ia selling ice cream?

Alex's home phone and mobile were both switched to voice mail. Perhaps he was still away. Having hung up, she called his mobile again. 'It's Luc. Hope you're well. I owe you a giant grovel. And I need some advice about changing my life. Call me sometime. Thanks.'

She sat back, surprised by her cheek. Why feel compelled to talk to someone who wasn't even sure he liked her?

Retrieving the paper, she fanned herself. Her clothes felt sticky, her hair a lead weight. She had no energy to get up and buy an ice cream, let alone change her life. When her phone rang, she stiffened. Remembering his anger and hurt on Brighton beach, she wanted to chicken out of answering.

'Lucasta.'

'Hello.' She braced herself for an ear-bashing, then gasped. 'Lorenzo?'

'Are you free for lunch tomorrow? Yes? Good. I'll call in the morning and pick you up. *Ciao, bella.*'

The line went dead, Luc leaped to her feet, screamed in ecstatic triumph and kissed her mobile. 'Yes.'

'A man about the Doll's House,' said Ella the following morning, squatting down and cuddling Yannick from behind. She grinned at Luc. Screwdriver between his teeth, he was lying on the floor peering at a socket near the fireplace. 'Sure I shouldn't call an electrician?'

He frowned. 'Go and wash the mussels.'

'Rather look at yours.' Ella kissed his brown shoulder, shown off by his singlet. 'Go run a marathon or something, Luc. You're making me nervous.'

'Sorry. I can't bear this. Supposing he cancels?' Luc stopped pacing and checked that her mobile was fully charged. 'Oh God.' She threw herself down on the sofa only to get up again.

'Call him,' suggested Ella.

'Tried. His phone's switched off.'

'Have some breakfast.'

Luc shook her head. 'Feel sick.'

'Tidy your room. Change the sheets just in case.'

'Did that last night.'

'Hidden your vibrator?'

'Ella,' protested Luc as Yannick laughed. 'I haven't got one.'

'Borrow Ella's,' said Yannick, who got a sharp pinch from a blushing Ella. 'Ow.'

Luc gazed wide-eyed. 'Ella . . .?'

She shrugged. ''Tas got it in Amsterdam. Remember all that grass we brought back? That's where it was hidden. Inside. He figured Customs wouldn't check.'

'My God.' Yannick shook his head. 'The mother of my child.' He fastened some screws, got up and plugged in a lamp. 'It works. Now what?'

They stood side by side studying Ella's list, his arm round her shoulder. Luc was struck by how they seemed made for one another and remembered the picnic at the cove in Ia. Opening the sea urchins, Henri had told her to make a wish. If only she could've deferred it, she would've asked for Lorenzo to turn up that morning.

'Don't look so worried.' Yannick smiled. 'He'll come. What are you going to wear?'

'Virginal white shirt, nun-like black pinafore dress, dykey flats,' intoned Ella before Luc could speak.

'I haven't got anything else.' Luc was defensive. 'Shit, why can't I afford to be a fashionable label queen?'

'Fashion is for people without style,' said Yannick, lighting a Gitanes.

'It is?' Luc cheered up momentarily, then panicked. 'But my style is virginal nun dyke. I've become Sister Joseph.'

Ella rolled her eyes. 'Are you always this hysterical before you see him?' Luc nodded. 'And he really lives up to this advance billing?' Luc nodded again. 'Must be quite something.'

'He is. You'll see. Please God, you'll see.'

Luc went down to her immaculately tidy bedroom which she'd mucked out the night before in between washing her hair, putting on a face-pack in the bath and giving herself a manicure. Worrying about garlic breath, she'd picked round Yannick's delicious fish stew. Later, as the three of them had settled down to watch a video, Luc studied his Apollo profile and thought how seamlessly he'd melded into life at the Doll's House. It was almost as if he'd always been there. Perhaps it was working on yachts that had made him so adaptable and easy-going?

Outside, Yannick was saying good morning. Luc heard Dolly Tilling booming something French in an appalling accent, before a hasty and very uncharacteristic apology for her appearance. Luc peered out. Dolly was wearing a mac over stripy pyjamas and odd slippers. 'Trotsky's done a bunk. You haven't seen the bugger?'

Nerves in shreds, Luc half wished she could have vanished with him.

'I'm actually on my way out. Sorry.' An hour later, Luc was hopping from foot to foot, as if she were desperate to go to the loo. Why did Alex have to call just when Lorenzo was about to arrive?

'Hot date?' he asked.

'Sort of.'

'Not with a German-Italian spelling mistake?'

'Call you later?' begged Luc. 'Please.'

'Tell me I'm wrong.' She couldn't. Alex sighed. 'OK, Lucasta, I'll have my heart transplant kit on standby.'

'What? Why?'

'To replace your broken one.'

Before Luc could reply, the line went dead. She was about to go and wash the stress sweat off her hands, when the phone rang again. 'Shit.'

'Luc, can you get that?' called out Ella from the front door, where she was holding a rickety ladder. 'Yannick, be careful.'

'Hello.' The receiver felt sticky.

'Luc, Liz. How are you?'

'Bit rushed.' A Jaguar was pulling into the Mews. Her pulse went into meltdown. 'Just on my way out.'

'We know it's very short notice but Tim and I were wondering if you could come to dinner tonight.'

He was getting out of the car and glancing round. Behind his sunglasses, she knew he was taking stock. Assessing. It reminded her of when his helicopter had landed in Ia. The feline cool was intact.

'Sorry?' murmured Luc.

Liz sounded put out that she had to waste time repeating herself. 'Tim and I . . .'

A piercing wolf whistle echoed round the Mews.

Ella. Ella outside by the front door. Luc froze, could've murdered her. How could she? Cringing, she peeked down. All the feline reserve gone, Lorenzo was throwing back his head and laughing. 'Ella? You must be Ella.'

'Tonight?' said Luc, edging closer to the window, trying to keep him in sight. Tugged too far, the phone was yanked out of its socket. 'Shit.' She sprinted across to the other side of the room, stabbing her fingers and breaking nails as she reconnected Liz.

'What happened there?' demanded Liz. 'Tonight? Yes or no? Timmy would really like to see you.'

'I'd love to, but I can't.' The laughter downstairs was disconcerting. She'd never sparked such amusement in him, didn't know he was capable of it. 'Sorry, I must go.'

'Don't let me detain you. Is Ella there?' asked Liz frostily. 'I need a word.'

'She's holding a ladder.'

The laughter grew louder, provoking further disquiet. Luc had felt the same way when she'd been about to chuck out a cableknit sweater, appropriate for a WI meeting. Ella had grabbed it, put it on and looked like something in *i-D* Magazine, making Luc feel oddly cheated every time she'd seen it since.

'Are you having a party or something?' demanded Liz.

'No.'

'Luc,' called Ella. 'Lorenzo's here.'

'Lorenzo?' said Liz. 'Lorenzo?'

Luc froze, feeling sick. She knew it was one of those moments when she'd wish afterwards that she could've pressed the delete button, erasing the previous few seconds. 'I'd better go.'

'Lorenzo von Retzen? What the hell is he . . .'

An avalanche of fury had started and was gathering speed. In her panic to escape it, Luc did the only thing she could. Hung up.

'Luc,' repeated Ella.

Heart hammering, blushing beetroot, she galloped down the stairs and out into the Mews.

Lorenzo smiled, but if she'd expected him to throw his arms round her in uncontrollable joy, she was disappointed. Yannick was speaking French at machine-gun speed while playing with Ella's fingers.

'Hello, Lucasta.' Lorenzo kissed her cheek, nodding to Yannick to continue. Standing mutely at his side, she caught Ella's wink and prayed he'd not see her thumbs-up.

'Liz wants a word.'

'What about?'

'She didn't say. How's the light? Need an electrician?' Why wasn't she enjoying a long lingering kiss as Lorenzo waltzed her round the Mews, instead of blurting out banalities? Out of the corner of her eye she could see he was wearing a blue-black linen suit, excessively formal compared to Yannick's bare feet, singlet and track-pants. Catching the word 'Atlantique', she guessed they were talking about *Les Voiles Blanches*.

Ella glanced over to the black Jaguar and its waiting driver. 'Perhaps I should write to Father Christmas.'

'He'd never understand your writing,' smiled Yannick, squeezing her tight. His arm muscles bulged like Popeye's after the spinach. '*Vous prenez du café?*'

Lorenzo shook his head. 'Thank you, but we should go.'

'Anywhere nice?' asked Ella.

'I hope so. Ready, Luc? One thing. Who's Lord Snooty?'

'A character in a comic.' Luc glared at Ella. 'Like Minnie the Minx. Or Fat Slags.'

'*Touché*.' Ella was taken aback. 'Might see you later then. If not, keep sending the flowers.'

'Ella,' protested Luc. Lorenzo was smiling, a smile that broadened as Ella let out another wolf whistle in farewell.

'She's fun. So warm,' said Lorenzo as the car pulled away. 'Great tattoo.' Luc was astounded. 'That's her house? And the bum arrived when?'

'Bum?'

'Drifter.'

'You mean Yannick? A few days ago.' Slightly miffed by his reaction to Ella, she said, 'He's really nice. Great cook.'

'And looks like a young Marlon Brando. Lucky Lucasta.'

'Lucky Ella,' said Luc.

'Is she? Is that why you're moving out? Because of him?'

'No. It's just time for a change, I guess.' She sighed. 'It's probably for the best. I don't want to live in a crèche.' Seeing him frown, she added, 'Ella's pregnant.'

'His? I see. Nice for him.'

Before Luc could ask what he meant, he pulled her to him and kissed her. The driver watched them in the rear-view mirror. A long, lingering kiss, worthy of the sonnets, the symphonies and the waves crashing on the beach.

They were sitting beside the Thames, out in the gentle Oxfordshire countryside. Barges drifted alongside the meadows and the fields awaiting harvest. Like Narcissus, wild flowers seemed to be gazing at their reflection in the water. Bees, birds, even the wind were having a siesta.

Luc's heart had sunk when they arrived at the restaurant, a converted country house. Deeply carpeted, richly wallpapered, hushed, swagged and ruched, it bore no resemblance to a real house. Its gardens had all the depressing municipal formality of the grounds surrounding a crematorium. As they were taken to their table outside on the terrace, she felt herself being smothered by a cushion of opulence.

She looked at the novel-length menu without much enthusiasm. 'Can you choose for me?'

Three Michelin stars; she'd end up looking like three Michelin men. She'd prefer to be lying in a field eating cheese and pickle sandwiches with him than fussed over by the regiment of waiters who were hovering. It had taken three of them to arrange the umbrella ensuring that there was enough shade. The wine list Lorenzo was studying was as long as *War and Peace*, which was still in the bottom of her bag in the wardrobe. Unread.

Her irritation grew at the mâitre d's grovelling appreciation of whatever Lorenzo had chosen. For God's sake, he'd picked two courses, not painted the Sistine Chapel. 'You came to England for lunch?'

'Shouldn't I? This place closes for a month tonight.'

'Getting bored with your beautiful house?'

'No.'

Luc gazed at a motor-cruiser chug-chugging past. 'When can I see it?'

He flinched so minutely that she almost missed it. 'It's featured in some newspaper supplement next week.'

'Great.' She forced a smile, glaring at the sommelier, whose forehead was almost on his knees as he took Lorenzo's order. 'All this deference.'

She'd been just as guilty. Awestruck, lovestruck, she'd given him an easy ride.

'What's wrong?' He stubbed out his cigarette.

She was about to explain, but a waiter sprinted across to take the ashtray. Then the sommelier returned, carrying a bottle of white wine as if it were a relic of the True Cross. Luc ordered herself not to be such a crosspatch misery guts. She was about to have lunch at one of the best restaurants in Europe, the sun was shining and she was with the man of her dreams whose eyes were the colour of lapis lazuli. On paper, it couldn't get much better than this. Ever.

'I'm wrong,' said Luc, sipping the wine. 'Or I have been.'

'How?' He was still, the way cats can be for hours.

Luc was unable to put it into words. She couldn't explain how ever since they'd met in Greece, she'd tiptoed round him, frightened of frightening him off. That when she'd heard Ella take the mickey and make him laugh and treat him normally, it had shown up her own deference, as abject and grovelling as any of the waiters'. At least they were getting paid to pretend to be servile. She wasn't being paid and she wasn't pretending.

'Because being with you is like being in a place like this. I have to sit up straight and dress up and be on my best behaviour. When I'm with you, I'm as artificial as any of the staff here.'

'And what would you rather do?'

'Lie in a meadow and have a picnic. And be able to talk.'

'About your hopes and wishes and dreams and heart's desires?'

'And *your* heart's desires,' snapped back Luc. 'If you've got one. The jury's still out.'

She watched three ducks make such a synchronised landing on the water they should've been part of the Red Arrows. When she looked again, the lapis lazuli gaze was still on her. It stayed on her as he fished the mobile out of his pocket and rang the driver. 'Harry. I need a small-scale map and a rug.'

They lay on the rug spread out on the edge of a meadow. Not much more than a stream, and in no great hurry to meet up with the Thames, the river eddied lazily around stones. Sunlight was filtered by the cool green of the overhanging trees. The peace was total.

'Sandwich?' said Luc, who'd scraped the *parfait de fois gras aux truffes noires* off the plate and shoved it between two slices of brioche. Lying on her back, sharing his jacket as a pillow, she gazed up at the sky, munching happily. 'Have some. It's like you.'

Stretched out beside her, he smiled. 'Delicious?'

'That too. I meant incredibly rich. More wine?'

'We're depriving the sommelier of his glass,' said Lorenzo. 'The poor man looked heartbroken.'

'But not furious like the mâitre d'.' Who'd spat frigidly that Monsieur le Chef would never permit his food to be served as a picnic. Lorenzo had insisted on seeing M. le Chef, a ferocious Cockney, who'd at first been incredulous, then roared with laughter, saying that he wouldn't want to sit in a fucking mausoleum surrounded by a bunch of tossers either.

Luc had another sip of the wine, certain she'd just spotted a kingfisher. 'It tastes even better now.'

'Thank you,' said Lorenzo, kissing her cheek. 'For bringing me here.'

'Thank Harry.' The chauffeur had studied the Ordnance

Survey and suggested the spot, about half a mile off a winding hedgerowed track.

'You should've brought your sketchbook. Why didn't you go to art college?'

'I explained. Because I had to earn a living.'

'What about grants?'

Luc shrugged. 'It was all a complicated mess. I took the easiest option. Learnt to type and do shorthand. You're told that thousands of girls start off as secretaries and end up as TV stars or in the boardroom. I fell for it. But I've ended up tracking down plumbers.'

'Sort out the mess. Get a grant. Go to college.'

'How can I? Right now, I need a home and a home means a salary and a salary means a job.'

'Be a free spirit. Travel the world.'

'Free spirit?' Luc sat up, staring at him, her jaw dropping. 'Free spirit? Coming from a Swiss banker? A Swiss banker in Gucci loafers whose life is as organised as the Swiss railways.'

He pulled her back down to him. 'Perhaps I want you to have what I'll never have for myself.'

'Such as?'

'The chance to escape the stultifying boredom of a life as organised as the Swiss railways. To enjoy, not to endure.'

'I don't believe it.' Luc yanked herself away. 'You've got everything, Lorenzo. Brains, looks, money, even a title. You're blessed. And you've got the cheek to whinge about your lot. I'd swap with you right now.'

'If you knew . . .'

'If I knew what?' She was furious. 'About driving an Aston Martin and having a house so beautiful it gets photographed? You're as bad as Ella. In fact, you two would make a stunning couple. You're so spoilt.'

'Money doesn't buy . . .'

'Happiness? Fuck right off.' She scrambled to her feet. 'Try seeing how much poverty buys you.'

Blinded by fury, she began tearing up the dusty rutted path, ignoring his calls to come back. Not looking, she caught her little toe on a stone and stumbled. Into a nettle patch.

'Ow.' Her bare feet and ankles were on fire. She hopped from foot to foot, her face screwed up. 'Ow. Ow. Ow.'

'What's the English I'm looking for?'

'Dock leaf,' gasped Luc.

'Kiss them better?' he offered, smiling.

'Dock leaf,' she repeated, alarmed. Supposing her feet, now filthy, also smelt?

After he had pressed the leaves on the red blotches, he gave her his arm and led her back to the rug where he poured out more wine and gave her a forkful of fish salad. 'So, I'm heartless and spoilt.'

She tried to place the flavour. 'Sage?'

'Sorrel.'

'I don't want to be a free spirit, if such a thing exists. I want what you've got, Lorenzo.'

'An Aston Martin and a house beautiful enough to be photographed?'

'No. Security. That's why I was so pissed off the other night when you called. I'm jobless and about to be homeless. The future looks a bit bleak and scary.'

'Or exciting and full of endless opportunities. You don't realise how young you still are.'

'Not that again,' said Luc. She lay back, closing her eyes against the sunlight, feeling its warmth on her face. The world was suddenly too good a place to have problems in. She smiled lazily. 'Lorenzo Methuselah von Retzen, the oldest man in the universe.'

'You've plenty of time to fulfil your dreams and wishes and heart's desires.'

'What about your heart's desires, Lorenzo?'

Somewhere, perhaps three fields away, a tractor was being

driven. Its faint rumble joined the softest breeze and the gentle splash of water.

'Right now?' He reached over and began to unfasten her cufflinks.

As the car sped back along the motorway towards London, Luc was curled up in the car beside Lorenzo. She felt woozy from all the wine and the sun. Her bare feet were itchy from the nettles. Not wanting to be like something in the Ape House at London Zoo, she'd wriggled and winced trying not to scratch.

She kissed the underside of his jaw. 'Go back tomorrow.'

'I can't. Meetings.'

'Have a holiday. It's August. Everyone else is.'

He leaned forward. 'Terminal Two, please, Harry.'

'Take me with you,' pleaded Luc. 'Let me see your beautiful house.'

'I'll fax you the article.' He ruffled her hair, making her feel like a dog being patted. 'A perfect day.'

'End it with a perfect night,' she wheedled, as they turned off towards the lights of Heathrow. He shook his head. 'Please, Lorenzo. Please.' Realising that kissing his ear wasn't going to make him change his mind, she gave up and pouted. 'God, anyone would think you've got a wife to go back to or something.'

'Or someone.'

'Are you correcting my grammar? You're as bad as Alex.' Luc's voice trailed off. She sat up, her insides turning to ice. How ugly the orange road lights were, making the world look shoddy and denying the infinity of the heavens. 'Someone. Is that who your meetings are with?'

'Not all of them. I have to take some boys sailing tomorrow afternoon.'

'Boys?'

'Freddie and Max. They're ten. Twins.'

Luc's heart had stopped. 'Your nephews or something?'

'Not mine. My fiancée's.' Lorenzo lit a cigarette and opened the window. 'I'm sorry, Luc. I should've told you before.'

The air rushing in was so very cold. It couldn't be happening. Not to her. A jet screamed overhead. All those billboards advertising phones, faxes, Internet services. The planet would be deafened with all this talking. Ceaseless communication. A tower of babble.

'Your fiancée's . . .' Luc felt as if she were in the middle of an earthquake. Her whole world was out of control, smashing into pieces. 'Your fiancée . . .' She was going to be sick. 'Get a window seat. Otherwise it's a waste of a plane trip . . . like, like missing out on . . . a room with a view . . .' She didn't know what she was saying, didn't care. Nothing mattered, nothing would ever matter again. Shock was pulverising her. 'Fiancée.'

They had gone into a tunnel. Luc bit the inside of her cheek. Hard. 'Fiancée . . . You made love to me, sorry, fucked me three times this afternoon. Something biblical about a three-times denial. Or am I being sacrilegious. I'll ask Ella's priest.'

In the front, Harry coughed. 'Terminal Two up ahead, sir.'

'Can you take Miss James back to Chelsea?'

'I'll get a taxi,' said Luc. It was as if she were having an out-of-body experience. So much of her denied it, yet there was a cold, rational core that denied those denials. Her cold, rational core made her eyes sharper, so she noticed the orange lights, the tunnel walls, all those happy couples on billboards made happier by their mobile phones.

The car stopped outside the terminal building. Numb, frigid, she got out.

'I'm sorry, Luc.' He picked up a lock of her cinnamon hair and curled it round his fingers. 'I'll call you and explain.'

She looked up into his eyes. 'You know I'm in love with you.'

He nodded. 'I know.'

'Love at first sight.'

'Just like a fairy-tale.'

'Yes.'

'Suits you. You look like a fairy-tale princess.'

'Prince Charming.' Luc spotted a cab rank up ahead and began to walk in her bare feet. Turning, she called back, 'So where the fuck is my happily ever after?'

Chapter Thirteen

Luc was bleeding grief.

Up on the roof terrace the following morning, Ella and Yannick had been trying to calm her down. She buried her head in Yannick's shoulder as Ella held her hand.

'Tea?' offered Ella. 'Brandy? Grass? I think I've got some somewhere.'

'All three,' said Yannick. 'Luc, this must stop. You'll make yourself ill.'

'I am ill. My fucking heart's been ripped out.'

'It hasn't. It will mend.' He gave her an encouraging squeeze. 'There'll be others.'

'Quentin the Zit called yesterday,' said Ella, trying to be helpful, but provoking another howl. She backed away. 'We'll skip the tea, shall we?'

'Why couldn't he have been honest?' demanded Luc, eyes swollen like gnocchi.

'Found it.' Ella came back with the brandy bottle and chucked Yannick a bundle of grass. 'We've been through this. Because he's a perfidious, spineless, heartless, selfish shit. We know that. What I can't fathom is why you didn't get the dirt on her. The fiancée. Now she's always going to be Rebecca.'

'Rebecca Hill, the head girl?' Luc frowned. 'What's she got to do with it?'

'No. Rebecca, Rebecca. Daphne du Maurier.' Ella sighed. 'The first Mrs de Winter. The one who had the lot. Beauty, brains and breeding. Whose image tortured the second wife.' Yannick was looking bewildered. 'Girls' book. We all fall in love with Max, like Luc fell in love with Lorenzo.' Luc choked back a sob. 'Drink, will you?' ordered Ella.

'It's not even eleven o'clock.'

'So?'

Luc swigged from the brandy bottle. She hadn't slept, hadn't eaten. Spent the night weaving, unpicking and reweaving her times with Lorenzo. 'When's he going to call to explain?'

'He won't.' Ella was blunt. 'He's getting married.'

'He must,' bleated Luc. That he said he would, was all she had left.

'Why? To be given a hard time? He knew you were hurt and that you loved him and he let you walk off barefoot into the night. Sorry, Luc, it's not going to happen. Forget him.'

'I can't,' said Luc, dissolving.

Yannick shook his head. 'Let's do something. Ella, call your sister and get your car back. Please.'

'I've told you, she won't give it back until I get my licence back. We made an agreement.'

'Please, Ella. We can all go for a nice picnic.'

'Oh God.' Luc began to sob again.

Having a broken heart was like Christmas falling on a Tuesday, everything was out of kilter. Luc stumbled downstairs. She closed the curtains and managed to doze off in the half-light, stoned on skunk grass and misery.

The Doll's House was silent. Ella and Yannick had gone out. Luc ran a bath. Her head ached, her red-rimmed eyes were itchy. As she lay in the steaming water, she wondered when Lorenzo was going to call. He'd said he would, hadn't he? He owed her that much.

What was She like? Luc decided She was called something impossible, like Cosima. A poised Euro aristo, tall and clever and elegant? Beautiful, naturally. Multilingual, of course. Rich, definitely. Perhaps working at one of the grander auction houses. Or a serious-minded physician with cool, immaculate hands? She'd be able to fly a plane and drive an Aston Martin with calm competence and be at home in his beautiful house.

The water grew tepid. Luc sobbed silently. It couldn't be The End, could it? The thought of never seeing Lorenzo again was too awful to pursue. Surely he wasn't simply going to cut her out of his life, as if she'd never existed? Rewrite his history, press the delete button in his memory bank, wiping her out for ever?

Didn't he have a conscience? How could he tear her apart like this, cause such pain? What was he doing now? Sailing on Lake Geneva with that cool, clever Cosima and her twin nephews? Were they having a picnic, or reading the Sunday papers in his beautiful house? A house which She'd see and share, something which Lorenzo had denied Luc.

Luc clung to the side of the bath, crying her eyes and her heart out. She was in mourning, grieving for her destroyed dreams.

'I looked in but you were asleep,' said Ella, later that evening. 'You should've come. Better than sitting here moping all day.'

'I was fine,' croaked Luc.

'Walk in the sea air. Coronary-on-a-plate cream tea.'

'Glad we got the car?' Yannick gave her a squeeze. 'May I, Luc?' He lifted the whisky bottle off the drinks tray.

'Sure.' Luc never wanted to taste the stuff again. She forced herself to be sociable. 'Liz let you have the car?' It was a 1960s Mercedes convertible, once owned by Janie.

'Not exactly.' Ella squirmed guiltily. 'We liberated it from Kew. Poor thing, out of its comfort zone.'

'It's far happier being back in Chelsea,' said Yannick.

'I remembered I had the spare key.' Ella giggled. 'So we went to Kew, left Miz a note and drove off. Easy peasy.'

'That means she'll be calling.' Luc didn't want to think about Liz, on top of everything else. She buried her head in her hands.

'What's up?' Ella was curious. 'Why's Liz suddenly got halitosis? Luc?'

Luc hesitated. 'Remember that Lorenzo was Tim's client?'

'That's why he was at the villa. They were trying to finalise everything. House, wasn't it? So?'

'A beautiful house. So, the deal wasn't closed. But Lorenzo's gone ahead anyway. Using Tim's plans, but another architect. Who will get the credit.'

'And Tim's percentage of the building fees,' said Ella.

'And Tim's percentage.' Luc swallowed hard. 'I don't think Tim will mind about that so much as not getting the recognition he deserves.'

'He's got paid for the plans for this house, surely?' said Yannick, who'd started rolling a joint. 'It is such a big deal?'

'It is,' said Ella thoughtfully. 'Architects need to do work to get work. And they like to see a project through to the end.' She whistled. 'Shit, Liz will go ballistic that you kept that one quiet, Luc.'

'Luc was put in a difficult position,' offered Yannick.

'I put myself in a difficult position,' said Luc. 'Conflict of loyalties.'

Ella sighed. 'This means Liz will be after two lots of blood. Yours and mine.'

Luc sat staring at the television. She had the dazed look of someone who'd just crawled from the wreckage of a car smash. Yannick made them some omelettes, but she couldn't eat.

'Listen, Luc,' said Ella gruffly, during an ad break. 'Yannick and I were talking today. If you haven't found anywhere else to live, don't feel under pressure. Take your time.'

'Thanks.' Luc nodded, too choked to speak.

Smiling, Yannick reached over to the armchair and squeezed her hand. 'At least you won't be sleeping on the street.'

'True.' Luc sniffed hard.

'Luc needs cheering up.' Yannick winked at Ella. 'I can call Henri for you.'

'Don't,' yelped Luc, horrified. 'It's not funny.'

Grateful as she was to Ella, she knew she'd have to move out soon. Sitting isolated in her armchair, her loneliness was reinforced by the sight of the two of them entwined on the sofa. His hands moved under Ella's singlet, massaging her tummy. Was Lorenzo doing that to Cosima right now? Was everyone in the whole world, apart from sad losers like her, cosily paired off as if they were about to board Noah's Ark?

Luc slept-walked through work the following day, in a haze of grief and pain. Her hands trembled over the keyboard. Everywhere she went, whatever she did, Lorenzo haunted her. Lorenzo with Cosima. It made her feel sick. Mrs Beak, who seemed to come into work merely to finalise her plans for lunch and the hairdresser, asked if she was ill.

'You seem a bit *piano*, Lucasta.'

Piano? Upright? Grand? Fat-ankled? 'I do?'

'Out of sorts. And terribly pale. You're not coming down with anything?'

Luc could've explained that she'd fallen down and down and down into a black abyss of despair. 'I'm fine. Really.'

Mrs Beak looked at her watch. Claridges beckoned. 'Don't let yourself go, my dear. No matter what else is going on. Appearance is a woman's armour.'

Watching her stride out on lizard heels with matching

handbag, Luc wanted to call the Animal Liberation Front. She knew she ought to be confronting Liz, and finding a permanent job and somewhere to live and catching up with her friends and collecting her dry-cleaning and going to the bank . . . Instead she slumped on to a bench in Berkeley Square, trying to swallow a double espresso which made her feel even sicker. A couple of pigeons pecked at the ground near her feet.

Cosima had it all. Luc decided that Cosima was everything that she wasn't. A PhD, who looked like Michelle Pfeiffer, with a brilliant career. She'd probably read *War and Peace* in Russian and Kafka in Czech and could argue cogently about their flaws. But if Cosima was such an Überwoman, why had Lorenzo bothered? Why had he ever called, let alone come to London? When would he call again? Would he ever call again?

Luc's thoughts were the motor that drove the merry-go-round horses of her mood. Up one millisecond, down the next, round and round and round. Desperate optimism, bleak despair, numb acceptance, stubborn denial. Oblivious to the traffic, the passers-by, the pigeons, she sat on the bench weaving, unpicking, reweaving.

'It's a graphic, harrowing depiction of war, according to the paper,' said Ella, who was trying to coax Luc to come to the cinema. 'It'll do you good.'

Luc nodded wearily. 'I must have a shower. Ten minutes?'

'Fine,' called Yannick from the kitchen, where he was kneading pizza dough.

The doorbell rang. 'Not those guys flogging tea-cloths again.' Ella scowled. 'Where's a quid?'

As she ran downstairs, Yannick asked Luc if she'd like a glass of wine.

'I shouldn't, I haven't . . .' Luc broke off. Where could she hide?

'You made an agreement,' Tim was saying.

'How dare you go back on it?' squawked Liz.

'I'd rather you didn't disturb my neighbours,' retorted Ella. 'So you'd better come in.'

'The sister?' hissed Yannick to Luc.

As Ella stomped back up the stairs, truculence was sewn on to her face.

'Been decorating?' asked Tim, looking round the sitting room. He blinked behind his glasses and sketched a smile in Luc's direction. 'Hello, Luc. You well?'

'YesthanksfinehelloLiz.' Her words came out in a rush. Liz was staring at her as if she'd found maggots in a tin of caviar.

Yannick stretched out his hand and smiled disarmingly. 'You must be Tim. And Liz. I remember you from Ia. Sit, please. Would you like some wine?'

'We can't. Thank you. We're driving,' snapped Liz, emphasising the 'We're' and looking at Ella.

'As you're not taking my car, only one of you is driving,' said Ella. 'Tim, wine?'

About to sit, he caught a look from Liz and straightened himself. 'No thanks.'

'Coffee, then?' asked Yannick.

Liz clenched her teeth. 'No wine. No coffee. Just the car.'

'No,' said Ella, plonking herself on the sofa. 'Do sit down, both of you. I explained in my note that I'll reimburse you for the tax and insurance and stuff . . .'

'You've lost your licence, remember?' Liz spoke very slowly, as if explaining something to a three-year-old. 'Banned for drinking and driving. Again.'

'But I'm not,' said Yannick, perching on the arm of the sofa and putting a proprietorial arm around Ella.

'But Ella made a deal,' said Tim. 'Liz would look after the car for a year, rather than let it rust to nothing. It was a perfectly good arrangement all round.'

'You know I reported it stolen,' cut in Liz.

'What?' Ella frowned. 'What for? I explained everything in my note.'

'Which was buried under a pile of junk mail. You can sort it out with the police, I'm taking the car.'

'You're not,' insisted Ella. 'It's mine.'

'This is unacceptable.' Tim was equally insistent. 'You promised, Ella. I'm sorry if it no longer suits you, but a promise is a promise. Isn't it? Luc?'

'Er . . .' Luc had been trying to melt into the wall and sidle off down the stairs.

Liz spun round. 'Ah yes, Luc. Don't even think about sneaking off. Have you been seeing Lorenzo von Retzen?'

'Liz, one thing at a time. Please,' said Tim. 'Ella, you realise we could've played a very silly game of tit for tat. Do what you did. Sneak round and drive off. Quite honestly, I expected better of you.'

'Why?' Liz huhhed. 'It was a typically immature, selfish thing to do.'

Ella took a deep breath, got up and pulled her cheque-book out of her bag. 'Five hundred quid cover things?' She made a quick scribble. 'Take this, give me back my car keys and go.'

Tim frowned, staring down at his polished brogues. 'No, Ella. No.' He sounded quiet and thoughtful. 'I'm not sure what your arrangements are with Yannick, but you're not paying me.'

Yannick stood up, his face like thunder.

'What?' gasped Ella. 'I'm not . . . How could you even . . .?'

'And how could you cause us all this upset and trouble, then think that a cheque will smooth it out?' Tim glared at her. 'You gave an undertaking which you should honour.' He caught Yannick's smirk. 'If that sounds pompous and old-fashioned to you, tough. It's your call, Ella. Either you do the right thing and stand by your commitment or you don't.'

Ella pouted with sullenness, her scowl deepening when her eyes fell on Liz. 'Yes, I should've called and explained in person. But I didn't want the hassle. Yes, we made an agreement, but I want to unmake it. Things have changed.'

'Oh, he's a thing?' asked Liz sarcastically, looking at Yannick.

'Circumstances have changed,' corrected Ella, just holding on to her temper.

'Ours haven't,' said Tim. He peered at Luc. 'Are you in contact with Lorenzo von Retzen?'

'I was,' admitted Luc in a small voice.

'I knew it,' hissed Liz. 'It was him here on Saturday, wasn't it?'

'Yes.' She swallowed hard. 'I've been in contact with him since Greece.'

'Since Greece?' Liz was pole-axed. 'But that was ages ago. Why didn't you mention anything?'

'Because . . .' Luc squirmed inside.

'Perhaps that's Luc's business,' suggested Ella.

'Luc's business happens to be quite pertinent to Tim's future,' snapped Liz. 'Maybe she can shed some light on whether he's going ahead with the project.'

Luc hesitated. Half of her would be relieved to confess, the other half couldn't face the consequences.

'Tell them,' urged Yannick with a yawn.

'Tell them what?' demanded Liz.

'He's gone ahead,' said Luc. 'It's done. The house. He used Tim's plans, but got another architect to oversee the project.'

Tim's face crumpled in dismay.

'Finished? It can't be. He can't have gone ahead without Tim,' spluttered Liz. 'When did you know about this?'

'In Greece, the night I met him,' said Luc. 'Sorry.'

Tim stared at her in disbelief. 'You've accepted our hospitality, got Liz to arrange some work for you, knowing what you knew?'

'Sorry,' gulped Luc. 'I felt rotten about it.'

'And your feeling rotten is like one of Ella's cheques, is it?' Tim was almost shaking with rage. 'It makes everything all right? Christ, what is it about this house that makes everyone act so badly?'

'Janie's spirit lives on,' said Liz.

A moment of silence fell before Ella leaped across the room

like a guard dog against a chain fence. She came to within inches of Liz, then forced her clenched hands down by her sides. 'Go. Now.' Liz stared her out, not moving a muscle. 'Yannick, get them out of here.'

He turned to Tim. 'My friend, it's time you left. Take your wife for a nice dinner or something. Oh. One thing.' He put his arm round Ella. 'The car stays. We need it for the clinic.'

Liz stood up straighter and smoothed the sleeves of her black jacket. 'Clap clinic? Come on, Tim. Keep the car, Ella.' She threw the keys on to the sofa.

'Clap clinic?' Ella looked up. 'Ante-natal clinic, actually.' As Liz flinched, Ella's smile was one of utter triumph. 'I'm expecting a baby.'

Liz turned so white, Luc wondered if she might faint. 'No,' she whispered.

'I'm almost three months pregnant.'

'You can't be.' She clenched Tim's hand. 'You can't be.'

'She is.' Yannick squeezed Ella more tightly. 'It's true, isn't it, Luc?'

Luc nodded and glanced away, unable to bear Tim's look of anguish.

Luc was numb. She could touch, but couldn't feel.

Sometimes she wondered if she'd become nothing but a vessel to carry around grief. Never seeing Lorenzo again was a possibility she refused to accept. Ella and Yannick were telling her to let go, move on.

'Move on where? To what?' she cried in despair. 'To nowhere and nothing. Why can't you understand?' Let go? How? Why? Her future stretched ahead of her, but it was a wasteland. An empty landscape of bleak, hopeless nothing.

Weaving, unpicking, reweaving. Over and over. She relived her times with Lorenzo, hearing again what he'd said, seeing how he'd looked. Her mind was a junkie, addicted to memories. Every night she was woken by nightmares about him with Cosima, the perfect other woman.

Dozens of times she started to dial his number only to chicken out and hang up.

She was unable to make the simplest decisions. Going round the supermarket in a zombied trance, she became overwhelmed halfway round the aisles. All the choice was claustrophobic. All the food stacked up on the shelves made her feel sick. She dropped her empty basket and fled.

She existed on nothing but cigarettes and coffee. Tasks such as washing her lifeless, shineless hair were impossible. She had no energy. By the end of the week, peering at Luc's increasingly wan, spotty face, Juliet Beak was asking if she had scurvy.

'In secret we met, In silence I grieve, That thy heart could forget, Thy spirit deceive.' Reading the poem one lunchtime in a bookshop in Piccadilly, Luc choked back her sobs. That Byron might also have suffered brought her no comfort, couldn't staunch the grief she was still bleeding.

Coming home on Friday night after the worst week of her life, Luc found a note. 'Found this in the Oxfam shop. Hope it helps. See you Monday. Love Ella.'

She picked up the dog-eared copy of *After the End — A positive guide to surviving heartbreak*, and felt even more pissed off, then wondered if she'd be more positive after she'd hit Ella over the head with it. She didn't need to be patronised by someone who'd only had the good fairies at her christening.

Slumped on the sofa, Luc lit up yet another cigarette and stared at the wall. A week before a much younger self had been getting ready to see Lorenzo. Younger, optimistic and happy. Had it really been her?

Had it really been her on Ia, in the Czech Republic? Waltzing on the quayside, lying on the beach, getting on a train with a sugar-mouse pink hat box, ending up in a hotel that could've been a Disney castle? Why couldn't he have told her that night at dinner, when she asked him why he'd never got married? Starting to cry again, unthinkingly she began burning off the ends of her hair with her cigarette.

Why had he let her get in so deep, only to walk away, knowing she'd drown?

He should've told her, she should've asked about all those phone calls and business meetings . . . The ends of Luc's hair singed and crinkled, not that she noticed. Her mind was fixed on that hotel room in Karlovy Vary. That morning before they'd left for Prague. When he'd made love to her. When Cosima had called.

'Bastard,' howled Luc, as another tidal wave of pain hit her. 'Bastard. Bastard. Bastard. Bast . . .'

How could she have been so naive and trusting? Why hadn't she asked him outright? The spell would've been broken, she'd have been thrown out of the paradise she'd constructed in her head. If she'd asked sooner, she would never have had to make the compromises. She might've been working in a proper job, Liz and Tim would still be friends. All the sacrifices she'd made for a fantasy.

You play with them, you don't marry them.

It was the bitter, brutal truth. Alpha men like Lorenzo didn't end up with women like her. She could claim no alphas. None. Not for her job, intelligence, looks, confidence, wit, courage, kind heart, style, integrity or loyalty. On a good day she'd scrape C minus, but usually she was about F. For failure. And alpha men like Lorenzo didn't trade down.

Just then, Luc couldn't see the point of being Luc. There was nothing about herself that she'd recommend to anyone. In fact, she decided, Luc was a complete waste of the world's resources. A pathetic daydreamer who was only good for playing a starring role in her own fairy-tale because she'd made such a disaster of real life.

Lorenzo had said as much, standing at the airport, on his way back to Cosima. He'd played with her hair as he'd always done, telling her that she looked like something out of a fairy-tale. Had he too denied reality because it had made it easier on his conscience to break her heart?

'Bastard.' Luc held the burning cigarette end to a lock of her hair, watching it shrivel and burn.

Taking deep breaths, trying to hold back her sobs, she got up and went to the kitchen. She opened one drawer and then another and another, pulling out the jumble of cutlery and uten-sils and rolls of foil. Finding the scissors, still crying, she headed for the bathroom.

She stared back at her reflection in the mirror with a stranger's detachment. A face that was a mess of red, wet blotch-iness and tears, streaked mascara and green, green eyes. The face of a daydreamer who'd been woken to reality with a slap. The fairy-tale was over.

She watched herself, one hand pulling up a fistful of hair, the other holding the scissors. Studying herself, she might've been preparing to sketch. Drawing was the one talent she had, but typically lacked the confidence to pursue. As she thought about the story of her diffident, shy life, she wept in mourning for the opportunities that her gutlessness had caused her to miss.

The blades of the scissors opened and closed. A fistful of long cinnamon-coloured strands fell on the floor.

Why look like something out of a fairy-tale if there was never going to be a happy ever after?

> '*Lorenzo,*
>   *Something for you to remember me by. You were so easy to fall in love with, getting over you is impossible*
>   *Luc*'

'Hearing that you're in the dog-house, I've brought a tin of Pedigree Chum.' Alex stood at the door the following morning. Open-mouthed, he snatched off his sunglasses. 'Fuck.'

Luc tugged at the remains of her hair, now scarcely an inch long.

'Been in a fight with a lawnmower?'

'Kitchen scissors,' sighed Luc. 'Come in. Tea? Coffee?'

'Got anything for shock?' He followed her up the stairs. 'You've got a neck. And ears.'

'They feel cold.' She tried to smile. 'Coffee?'

'Great.' As she went to the kitchen, he studied the bookshelves. 'Surprisingly well read, aren't you?'

'Ella is,' called back Luc.

'Who's expecting a baby fathered by some French deckie, according to my sources.'

'The same sources who told you I'm in the dog-house? How are they?'

'Tim I'm-usually-so-laid-back-check-that-I-have-a-pulse is unusually agitated. Furious, in fact. I got the tour. Ella's car to Ella's baby via your treachery.'

In the kitchen, Luc winced. 'Milk?'

'Black. Liz was foaming at the mouth so much, I wondered if I should call a vet and get her checked for rabies.'

'Don't joke,' groaned Luc, managing a small smile. She handed him a mug. 'And?'

'And I got it in the neck for not telling them about your liaison with Lorenzo. Never mind that my life seems to have hit black ice and skidded out of control.'

Luc took him up to the roof terrace. As he saw the view of the rooftops and church steeples, he whistled. 'Be quite a wrench to leave, won't it?'

'I've got a reprieve for a bit,' said Luc, fiddling with what was left of her hair. 'Shit, it's almost as short as yours.'

'We could be twins.'

'The ugly sisters.' She stared up at him, horrified. 'What the fuck have I done, mutilating myself like this?'

'Oh thanks, sweets.'

'I didn't mean . . . You're not ugly.' Misery overwhelmed Luc.

She started tugging at the spikes. 'I am. Look at me.'

'You'll get used to it.'

'I won't. What have I done?'

'Collaborated? You look like a candidate for being tarred and feathered.'

'Shit. Shit, shit, shit.'

'Please don't cry,' begged Alex. 'I was joking. Just think how practical it is, you'll save a fortune of time and money on shampoo and blowdrying.'

'Practical?' shrieked Luc hysterically. 'I don't want to be practical, I don't want to be your twin, I'm not a butch muscly Aussie, or a collaborator. I want . . . I want to be pretty.' Sniffing, she frowned. 'Where are you going?'

'Phone book. You need a hairdresser.'

A bit later, Luc had calmed down. 'Your black ice first.'

'Marina? *Finito, cara*. She's back with Gordon the Golfer. I'm just wondering if I should join your remedial class for relationships.'

'You finished with her, didn't you?'

'There should've been nothing to finish. It should never have started.' Alex shrugged. 'She'll be happier in Surrey than in Sydney. How many times did she say she was seeing you or Liz or her sister but was in fact meeting Gordon the Golfer on the sly? Must be interesting to cheat on your lover with your husband.'

'Is she really back with him? She said he'd finished with her.'

Alex stretched out his long legs. 'If he had, she would've come grovelling back to me. She's back all right.'

'That's good.'

'Is it?'

'Of course.'

'Have you been taking long-distance lessons in being judgemental from Liz?'

'Long distance?'

'London to Coventry. Where you've been sent.'

'Don't.' Luc flinched. 'Any news on the book?'

'Nothing. Nada. Niet. Zero. Zip. Zilch. My agent's still swanning about in Umbria.' He sounded bitter. 'Why worry about the planet being poisoned when you've got the comforts of Chiantishire?' He looked at his watch. 'Hairdresser's.'

'You don't have to come,' said Luc.

'If I don't, how else are you going to buy me lunch?'

'She was drunk,' said Alex to a horrified Bryan, who was picking up Luc's spikes between finger and thumb and tut-tutting.

'Paralytic, were we, dearie?' said Bryan, all ginger highlights, bondage pants and mauve nail polish. 'Whoops, missed a bit. It was that long?'

'Yes,' admitted Luc miserably, staring at her reflection. She looked like someone who'd escaped from Alcatraz. Added to ugliness was the feeling, as soon as she entered the salon, of being terminally unhip. Definitely without it, not with it. Why hadn't she taken the scissors to her cableknit cardigans and her frumpy skirts instead?

'Do you buy hair?' Alex asked as Bryan tilted Luc's head this way and that. 'You can sell it, Luc, like one of those sisters in *Little Women*.'

'I can't.' Luc squirmed. 'I posted it last night. It's on its way to Lorenzo's office in Geneva. Farewell present.' She wondered what Madame Royer would make of it.

'Drama queen?' Alex whistled. 'You're Melrose and Macbeth rolled into one. You tied it up in a red ribbon, I suppose?'

'Black.' Off the hat he'd given her. Yet another hysterical act of desecration. 'Know any good psychiatrists?'

'*Moi*,' trilled Bryan. 'Ooh, this sounds right up my *strasse*. You vamousse, honey,' he told Alex. 'And Luc and I can have a lovely broken heart-to-heart after she's been shampooed.'

*

An hour later Alex came back, as Bryan was admiring his handiwork. 'We've given it a bit of oomphy height. And by taking it back, it shows off the eyes and bones. Very gamine. Very Jean Seberg.'

'Who's he?' asked Luc, alarmed. She frowned at herself. She'd never get used to it. How long would it take to grow back? Years?

'He? She.' Bryan tutted. 'So beautiful, so tragic.'

'I don't want to be tragic,' yelped Luc. She met Alex's eyes in the mirror. 'Don't stare. Verdict? It's really awful, isn't it?'

'It most certainly is not,' bristled Bryan.

Alex was staring and staring. 'It's absolutely stunning.'

She pulled a face. He was just being nice, wasn't he?

'She'll wear it,' Alex told the shop assistant. He held open a carrier bag for Luc's T-shirt, cardigan and skirt. 'Come on. Dump the frump.'

The dress was pretty, but far, far shorter and more clinging than Luc was used to. She looked in the mirror. 'Doesn't it make me look fat?' she asked automatically, then did a double-take. She'd actually lost weight.

'A size ten can't be fat.'

Luc hesitated. 'It's really nice, but it's not very, very . . .'

'Very chic and expensive enough looking to compete with the wardrobe you imagine Lorenzo's girlfriend having.'

Luc coloured. He could read her like a copy of *Little Women*. 'That's not what I meant.'

'It is, sweetheart.' He turned to the assistant. 'She's taking it.'

The carrier bag of dumped frump joined the others piled next to the counter. Luc couldn't believe she was handing over her credit card yet again. Thank God the sales had started. 'Haven't you got things to do?' she asked Alex.

'I enjoy playing Pygmalion. New look for a new Luc. Now

all you have to do is get the rest of your life sorted out. And buy me a beer.'

'He deserves it,' said the assistant pointing to where Luc should sign. 'Not many blokes enjoy shopping, do they? How did you find him?'

'She got lucky.' Alex picked up the bags.

Following him out, Luc realised she had. As Lorenzo's image returned to haunt her, she realised that Alex could make her forget about him for at least two minutes.

Luc returned from the bar with two lagers. Two butch women drinking pints of bitter stared at her as she went past. 'Think you've broadened your fan base,' muttered Alex.

'Dyke target. Last thing I need.' She had to pick her way amongst the mountain of bags to sit down. 'Thanks for everything. I know you wish you were playing cricket.'

'It was cancelled. Typical Pom apathy.' He stretched out his long legs. 'Come and watch sometime. It's a nice afternoon out. Beautiful village green. You can just sit under a tree with the papers, you don't have to understand what's going on.'

'I know the game,' protested Luc. 'We had to play at school. Ella and I were always in the outfield, so we could sneak off for a fag.'

'You'd really come and watch?'

'Love to,' said Luc.

He was surprised. 'Marina came once and moaned non-stop. It was dreary. She was bored. Another row.'

'She's Italian. Perhaps she didn't have a clue what was going on.'

'Probably couldn't bear not being the centre of attention. Silly mid-on cow.' He downed his lager. 'The more I think about it, the more I wonder if I haven't had a lucky escape. Another?'

'No. Thanks.' Touching her hair, as if to reassure herself she wasn't entirely bald, she watched him stride to the bar. Other women glanced up at him. His height got him the attention, she decided. Must be useful if he were in a scrum of other reporters trying to get an interview. Would she ever say that she'd had a lucky escape from Lorenzo?

'Where are you?' Alex waved his hand in front of her face.

Luc jumped. 'Nowhere.' Then she admitted, 'Miles away. Geneva. Should I call him?'

'No. It's over. Deal with it.'

It wasn't what she wanted to hear. 'Why did he bother with me? There must be hundreds of women in Geneva and wherever else he travels. Who've got loads to offer. Why me? All that trouble of coming to London.'

'It's not such a big deal. Few hundred miles.'

'And back in Australia you'd drive that far for a packet of fags,' mocked Luc.

'He wanted a novelty fuck.'

Luc scowled. 'Must you be so brutal?'

'Must you obsess?'

'Can't help it.' She sighed. 'He's with me. In my head all the time. I take him everywhere I go. Like my heartbeat.'

Alex stared at her, puzzled. 'You didn't lose your virginity to him or something, did you?'

Luc was startled. 'Are you always so personal? No, I didn't. Why? What difference does it make?'

'If he were your first, I could understand your going a bit nuts.'

'I'm not nuts.'

'Poppet, hacking off your hair and putting it in the mail is sane?'

Luc scowled down at her lager. Then she said, 'Lorenzo was the first. First real love. It's never happened before, you see.' Her voice started to tremble. 'Being that happy. The sonnets and the symphonies and the waves . . .' She choked back a sob. 'I just can't bear losing . . .'

'Come here. Hug.' Alex put his arms round her. 'Fragile, aren't you?'

His arms were so comforting, his warmth so soothing, it was like being wrapped in a cashmere blanket after hours in the freezing cold. She relaxed, suddenly feeling as if she could sleep for a week. Right then. Like that. Wrapped up in Alex.

He suddenly stopped stroking her head. 'Calmed down? I must take you home.'

'Oh.' Luc reluctantly disentangled herself. 'Why?'

'Dinner. With an editor. Not the sort of thing I can take you to. Sorry.'

'Doesn't matter.' She smiled, but felt a prickle of disappointment.

The battered BMW stopped outside the Doll's House. 'Wait,' said Alex, as Luc reached to open the door. 'I've got something for you. Where is it?' He started ferreting around in the back seat among the jumble and found a tiny paper bag. 'Hold out your wrist.'

A strip of multicoloured braid. A friendship bracelet.

'I got it in the shop in Brighton. Before we went to the beach.'

'Before I was such a bitch. Sorry about that.'

'So was I.' Alex held it round her wrist, was about to tie it, but hesitated. 'This is weird. We're not meant to like one another.'

'We do, though, don't we?' Luc was anxious. 'Mates?'

Alex tied the threads. 'Mates.'

'He thought I must be arty, in a band or a writer or a painter or something.'

'And?' Ella was riveted. 'Another hot date?'

'If he calls, maybe.' Luc shrugged. 'Nice lunch yesterday. Nice guy, but.'

'But what?'

'But he's not Lorenzo. He's Nick the Nerd. Ben's brother.'

'But he's the owner of the coolest, hottest record label in New York,' cried Ella. 'Flattering.'

'It was so obvious I was the C-list guest scraped up at the last minute because I was the only person in London free on a Saturday night.' Luc pulled a face. 'Anyway, he's only here for a few days. Then he's off to Ibiza.'

'Must be interested though, taking you to lunch.' She stared at Luc. 'This is unbelievable. I go away for the weekend and you re-invent yourself. A total rebrand. New look, new man.'

'No new man.' Luc was insistent. 'And I hate my new look. Alex is right. I must be nuts.' She glanced at Ella's tummy. 'How's Chelsea?'

'Great. Doctor's tomorrow. Check-up.'

'Yannick?'

'Fine.'

Hearing a sigh, Luc was curious. 'Nothing's wrong?'

'No. Not really.' Ella played with her sleeve. 'It's just I guess we've been together for days without a break.'

'Need an evening off? Some space?' suggested Luc.

'Think so. I started to notice things. You know. Things. Things that get on your nerves. Like how he always has to clear up the moment we've eaten. And how he can't get jokes. And how he hates me reading in bed because of the light. And doesn't know about Ealing comedies.'

'He's French.'

'I know. I can't believe the Channel is only twenty-two miles. The differences. He can't see the point of Marmite. Or cricket. Or Hattie Jacques and Carry Ons. And I hate the racket his bloody skateboard makes.'

'Small stuff.'

'I know, I know. But . . .' Wincing, Ella shifted on the sofa, then undid the top button of her skirt. 'Then there's the big stuff. Like what are his plans? He can't work on yachts living here. If that's what he wants to do.'

'Don't you know?'

'He doesn't know. He seems happy enough to coast around here.'

'So?' asked Luc.

'So if he's not working, what's he going to do for money?'

'Perhaps he's got a huge Trust fund or something.' Luc was dry.

Ella looked at her crossly. 'No, he hasn't. He's skint. Church mouse.' She stood up. 'Those potatoes must be done by now.'

'Something's wrong, isn't it?' said Luc. 'Ella?'

'Not really. Small stuff. The rest I'm just imagining.'

'Like what?'

'Like catching him going through my papers. Bank accounts, Trust statements, deeds, tax returns. He said he was looking for some sandpaper.'

Despite the reassurances from Ella and Alex, Luc was convinced she'd done a Delilah on herself. Instead of strength, she'd hacked off her femininity, her fears reinforced when a bus conductor called her laddie.

A startled Mrs Beak asked her if she'd had an accident requiring brain surgery. 'Then why rob yourself of your crowning glory, Lucasta?'

'Felt like a change,' fibbed Luc. 'It's more, er, practical.'

'Oven gloves are practical, but they're not exactly pretty, are they?'

Put out, Luc called the Agency. Back from Mykonos, Steve's mind was still at the nudists' beach rather than finding her a new job. 'Difficult time of year. Take yourself off to Greece for a couple of weeks, do you good.'

She hung up, her mind immediately jumping from Greece to Lorenzo. The tiniest of triggers did it; the word Geneva, a glimpse of an Aston Martin. Her head kept playing Monopoly, sending her back to a gaol called Lorenzo. Sometimes she thought she was going mad with unhappiness.

Who could she turn to? Ella was preoccupied. They could spend evenings together like the night before, but ever since Greece their friendship had changed. It was no longer unconditional. The unusual tensions, Yannick's arrival, Luc's moving out. The biggest barrier of all, one which neither of them had properly acknowledged, was Ella's baby.

Luc knew that she wasn't jealous of the baby, or even resentful. What she couldn't deny, she realised as she stared at her computer screen, was that she was unsettled by it.

THE ONLY CERTAINTY IS CHANGE. THE ONLY CERTA . . . Instead of typing out pathetic crackerbarrel philosophy she ought to be arranging Casey's ticket to Bristol and tracking down his tailor so he could get a pair of trousers altered. As she pressed the delete key, she wished she could wipe out the whole of that summer so easily.

'My God, *cara*. What has happened to you?' Marina choked on her champagne as Luc walked into the department store bar. 'Incrrredible.'

Luc was almost asphyxiated by Marina's heavy scent and blinded by the dazzle of diamonds on her earrings. Her hair was up and she was wearing a scarlet suit which was half a size too small. Her feet were swollen in her high heels. There was too much gold, from her charm bracelet to her watch to the chain on her quilted bag.

'Been shopping?' asked Luc. A juggernaut would be needed to carry the bags back to Wimbledon.

'A few things for the holiday.' Marina smiled. She called over the waiter and asked for another glass and the bill. 'Gordon and I are going to Cap Ferrat tomorrow. Second honeymoon. This time he prrromise, he leaves his golf clubs behind. I can't stay long, I have to get home. You needed to talk, so talk. Here.'

Luc took the champagne. Luc had wanted to talk about Lorenzo, about Liz and Tim, about the whole smoking rubble that was her life, but guessed that Marina would rather not be bothered. Noticing Marina's credit card, she guessed that Gordon would eventually be picking up the tab. It made her feel uneasy.

'To our good health, though you look so different, *cara*. The hair. The clothes. And you've lost weight. Very much the angelic choirboy.'

Hearing the boy in choirboy, Luc felt depressed. 'It wasn't wrong of me to call you, was it?'

'Wrong? No, of course not.' If the speed of Marina's denial hadn't given her away, then the slight blush would have. 'Lovely to hear from you. And to see the new Luc.' As she patted Luc's hand, she glanced surreptitiously at her watch.

'Sorry, I didn't realise you were going away.' Luc doubted that Marina would again be playing at being the hippy chick with flowers in her hair. 'You've patched things up with Gordon?'

'Please God, *cara*. We agree, what's past is past. No more Alex, no more Valerie, that bitch from the golf club. Forgotten. Fresh start.'

'But how can it be that easy?' blurted out Luc. 'You can't just forget.'

Marina shrugged. 'You must. I must. I don't want my marriage to end. Gordon doesn't want it either. So we forgive.'

'But . . .'

'When you're married you'll understand. Divorce is not like splitting up with one of your boyfriends.'

Luc fiddled with her friendship band. 'What about Alex?'

Marina gave Luc the smallest of glares. Pouting, she studied her long polished nails. 'Alex. A wonderful body but married to his work. All he cares about is his silly book and getting hi reports in the papers. I thank God I never have to go back to tha dump of a flat again. It wasn't me, Luc. I was uncomfortable and unhappy and in fear of my life.'

'But Alex is such a good man,' protested Luc.

'*Cara*, Alex was my mistake, but a necessary mistake. He made me realise how much my marriage really meant to me.'

'She means Valerie made her realise how much her marriage meant to her,' scoffed Ella later.

After showing Luc all her new clothes, wafts of Giorgio almost provoking an asthma attack in Luc, Marina had scampered away as fast as the bags and her four-inch heels allowed. '*Cara*, lovely to see you. Mwah.' The air kiss came with a huge, false smile. 'Listen, I call you perhaps. In a few months. When the dust has calmed. Come to the 'ouse one day, but never mention Alex. We think up 'ow we met so as not to 'urt Gordon's feelings.'

'She's going to learn to play golf,' said Luc. 'Poor Alex, to be written out of the script so fast.' Had Lorenzo done the same to her? Had she been a necessary mistake to make him realise how much Cosima meant to him?

'Come back from Geneva,' ordered Ella, glancing up from the travel section of the Sunday paper. 'Stop obsessing about Lorenzo.'

'I wasn't.'

'You were. You go into these trances.' She ringed something and reached for the phone.

'Going away?' asked Luc.

'Trying to. Maybe Amsterdam or the south of France. Bank Holiday weekend. You should get away, do you good.'

'Can't afford it,' said Luc. 'Besides, I don't really want to go on my own.' She could think of absolutely nothing worse than being alone on holiday. Brooding and miserable, she'd be surrounded by couples all rediscovering the joys of sex and doing it in the afternoon.

'You might have a holiday romance,' said Ella, then cringed. 'Tactless. Sorry.'

'What did the doctor say?'

'Mother and baby doing brilliantly. Keep up the good work and just sit it out growing like a space hopper until the middle of March.'

'Hello,' Yannick called up from the front door. He puffed up the stairs laden down with groceries and his skateboard. 'The house boy returns.'

'I didn't mean . . .' Ella sighed impatiently. 'For God's sake.'

'Hello, Luc. Ella thinks I'm a servant. Called me house boy.' He dropped the bags. 'Here's your change, madame.' He pushed aside Ella's hand, trying to hold his own. The topaz eyes were without a hint of warmth. 'I must have a shower.'

'Where are you going?' called out Ella.

'Out. Get Luc to cook your dinner.'

Ella leaped to her feet. 'Yannick.'

He charged up the stairs, Ella following him. Hearing her banging on the locked bathroom door, answered only by the torrent of water, Luc felt uneasy. She didn't want to witness their rows and knew her presence as a spectator was equally unwelcome. She must find somewhere else to live.

'Yannick. Yannick. Where are you going?' Ella was demanding.

'Somewhere where there's life and people enjoying themselves. With beautiful thin girls who want a good time.'

'You bastard.'

'Not this tomb where all I hear about is books and babies and what I'm going to cook.'

The following morning Luc's head was pounding so hard she thought it would explode. She'd come home at four, but was still so wired she'd been unable to sleep. Feeling like an intruder at the Doll's House, she'd immediately accepted Nick the Nerd's offer of meeting up. She'd trailed round what seemed like dozens of bars and clubs, her progress helped along by tequila and toots of charlie.

If Nick were the epicentre of hip, Luc decided at around midnight that she'd rather be out than in. If he had a good ear for music, it was definitely a sticky-out one. His black spectacles made him look like Joe 90, he dressed like a trainspotter. His clothes might be Prada but they could've come from Millets. And he was weedy, with non-existent sloping shoulders and a concave chest.

She couldn't believe the hatchet-faced door vetters treated him as if he were an apparition of the Archangel Gabriel. His name, one look at their clipboards, and ropes were whisked aside, doors opened, VIP passes handed out. It was rather like being with the Queen on a state visit. The strangest thing to Luc was that a week before, with her hair and her frump, she would've looked and felt as out of place as Mrs Beak at a vegan conference. Now she felt she was accepted. When Nick said she was his latest signing, everyone believed him.

With Casey in Bristol, the office was even duller than usual. Luc dropped another two Alka Seltzer into a glass, wishing she could crawl back into bed and quietly die. Juliet Beak caught her mid-swallow. 'The post hasn't been sorted?'

Luc shuddered. 'Not quite.' She sniffed, certain she felt more of last night's cocaine hitting the back of her throat. Half of Colombia's annual crop must be still lodged in her nostrils.

The headache-bravely-borne look appeared. 'If you're ill, Lucasta, I suggest you go home. You're neither use nor, may I say after that dreadful haircut, ornament.' Luc stared at her open-mouthed. 'If I could see my mail today, it would be appreciated. I'll trouble you to remember the meeting is at eleven. Coffee and biscuits for four.'

Even though she was anaesthetised by her hangover, and probably sweating tequila, Luc was stung to the quick. She sorted the post, tempted to use the letter opener to cut off her porridgey painful head. Drink, drugs, no sleep; her life seemed to be spiralling out of control. Everything was as muddled as that horrible khaki painting in Juliet Beak's office. Had she gone out with Nick, nerdy but with gold stars for hipdom, to prove something to Lorenzo? Would she ever get out of the habit of mentally trying to impress him? Having her actions governed by how she imagined he'd react?

She was nuts. There was no Lorenzo any more. No Lorenzo, no hair, awful job, homeless future. Instead of trying to show off to someone who had deleted her from his memory bank, why hadn't she stayed in, gone to bed early and been in a fit state to try to get her life vaguely in order?

'Alex. I can't talk,' she hissed into her mobile, which rang just as she'd sorted the post. 'Call you later.' She wasn't quick enough to cut him off before Juliet Beak caught her through the glass partition and gave her a turning-to-stone glare.

'Lucasta, personal calls in your time, not mine,' snapped Mrs Beak as Luc handed her a bundle of letters. 'I need a hairdressing appointment. Sometime after three.'

'But you went on Monday,' said Luc without thinking.

Mrs Beak put down her fountain pen. 'A criticism?'

'No, er, sorry. An observation.' She backed away hurriedly. Big hair required big effort. Mrs Beak seemed to be shampooed and set three times a week. Monsieur André should have a camp bed in the office.

'Coffee and biscuits, please.'

While the coffee drip, drip, dripped through the machine, Luc phoned the salon. At that moment she was absolutely and thoroughly pissed off with the personal in personal assistant. If she'd had any hair left, she would've pulled it out. No wonder she hadn't chased round the agencies or scoured the jobs columns. She was sick of temping. No matter how hard she worked there was no reward. If things went wrong the temp was always blamed.

Luc knew she never wanted to type another letter, send

another fax, or unjam another photocopier ever again in her whole life. She didn't want to address another invitation to a lecture to which she wasn't invited, or help to arrange another corporate jolly from which she was excluded. She didn't want fingers clicked at her, she didn't want to be told that her first duty in the morning when her employer walked through the door was to inquire about his health, she didn't want to take out her revenge on another office's potted plants. And she never wanted to remind another up-his-own-arse executive shackled to a corporation by a three-series BMW that it was his wife's birthday or their anniversary.

She was sick of helping to organise the ball and not going to it herself.

Even if she were offered a permanent job, she didn't want to be a PA or a secretary. She'd rather be a prostitute, at least they could choose their hours.

She stacked the cups and saucers on to a tray, slammed on the sugar bowl and gobbled down five of the best biscuits from the tin before arranging the dullest-looking wafers on a plate. She poured the coffee into a Thermos pot, had three more chocolate digestives and sniffed again. She felt as rough as industrial sandpaper.

Taking a deep breath, she picked up the cluttered tray and went into Mrs Beak's office. Juliet Beak glanced up over her half-moon spectacles and let out a slow, hissing sigh which sounded like air coming out of a punctured tyre. 'Lucasta, you have forgotten the milk.'

Luc glanced down at the tray. 'I have?'

'Has that unbecoming haircut addled your senses?'

'Actually, I'm coming to my senses.' Luc glared back. 'And I quit.'

'You can't leave,' screeched Mrs Beak. 'You've got a job to do and that includes getting the milk.'

'Kindly get it yourself.' Luc threw the tray up into the air, snatched her bag from her desk and walked out.

*

Luc thought her mobile would melt in the heat of Carole's rage. How dare she act so unprofessionally, how could she just walk out, and walk out without getting her timesheet signed?

'We're breaking up,' said Luc distractedly, peering into a gallery window in Cork Street.

'Now listen here, Lucasta James . . .'

'We're breaking up.' Luc turned off her phone and felt an enormous sense of liberation.

The gallery was as quiet as the Julian Group offices and probably as awful to work in. If she hadn't been given a look of blood-freezing hauteur, Luc would've sympathised with the girl sitting behind the desk. Instead of scuttling out, she followed Lorenzo's example and immediately asked for a catalogue, turning the pages to the artist's biography.

'Vivacity with luminous depth,' said the assistant, catching Luc's gaze at *Penelope, vicarious warrior*, which was made up of a spinning wheel and some eggs sitting on what looked like used Tampax.

'Fifteen thousand?' Luc did a double-take at the price list. 'Is that a misprint?'

She spent the rest of the day scouring Mayfair and St James's, going from one gallery to the next, studying biography after biography. The Slade, St Martin's, Chelsea, Goldsmiths. Was there any chance that her long neglected skill could be nurtured at an art college?

'It's a great idea,' said Ella. She was sitting at the table studying a copy of the *Wall Street Journal*. A sheaf of company reports were at her elbow.

'I probably don't have enough talent. There must be so much competition. Besides, could I get a student loan?' Luc was filled with despondency.

'Don't dwell on the obstacles.'

'They seem so daunting. Anyway, I've asked for prospectuses to be sent, so I guess I've made a start.'

'You should've gone years ago. You got a brilliant A-level.'

'I know, but I allowed myself to get pushed around. Story of my life. My fault for being so feeble.'

Ella scowled. 'We don't need men, we need mentors.'

'Where's Yannick?'

'At the gym. It's all right, no need for you to make a tactful disappearance tonight. We've had today's row.'

'What happened?'

'We'd made up and he'd even started to fix the damp by the window in your room, despite my saying that I'd find a builder. Then some bitch called Isabel rang, asking me why had he stood her up at lunchtime. She said they'd met in some bar last night. I went ballistic.' Ella doodled on the *Journal*. 'Anyway, he claims it was innocent. Said that she said she could get him some work.' She cringed. 'As a model.'

'So?'

'Male model? Himbo? Yuck. He'll end up starring in knitting patterns or porno films. No. No. No.'

'What's wrong?'

'It's so bloody nancy, that's what's wrong. It feels wrong.'

'Ella, aren't you being unreasonable? He's amazing looking. His face might be his fortune.'

'It's hardly a job for a grown man.'

'Well, it's a job. More than you've got.'

Ella's brown eyes narrowed.

'More than I've got,' added Luc hastily. 'You said he needed to work. He can't crew yachts in London.'

'I know. It's just . . .' Ella searched for words. 'As soon as I put the phone down on Isabel, I could see him coming out of Madame's cabin that morning.'

*

Luc was so worn out that she almost dozed off standing up as she made bolognese sauce. Ella continued to study company reports. Luc assumed she'd visited her stockbroker that afternoon. By the time Yannick came back however, the table was cleared and Ella said she'd been to a yoga class.

He tenderly kissed her forehead, then her eyes, then her tummy, and handed her a single bird of paradise flower. 'It reminded me of you.'

'Poisonous?' Ella laughed.

'Spiky, colourful, beautiful. How's Luc?'

'More dead than alive,' she called from the kitchen.

'Chucked in her job and is planning to go to art college,' said Ella.

'That's wonderful.' Yannick whistled. 'Some wine to celebrate.'

Luc shuddered. 'No booze for me tonight.'

As they sat round the table, he reached across and playfully touched her hair. 'It gets better each time I see it. Henri would hate it. No more shy English rose.'

'I haven't changed,' said Luc forlornly. 'I'm still pathetic.'

'You no longer look as if you're hiding away from the world.'

'Should I stop hiding away from Lorenzo and call him?'

Ella and Yannick looked at one another, then at Luc. 'No,' they cried in exasperated unison.

Luc's sleep was broken by two nightmares about Lorenzo. She'd woken at five and spent the next few hours trying to read but instead reliving every moment of their time together and wondering if she should call him. Every minute that went by that she didn't was a victory. She longed to capitulate and admit total defeat.

At nine, absolutely exhausted, she set off for the library to read up about applying for a college place. She'd do some research, then go for a swim at the baths next door. Promising he'd try not to make too much mess, Yannick had taken down the curtains in her room and was hacking away at the bubbling plaster around the window. Ella was busy trying to find out about flights to Nice.

With the Bank Holiday approaching, London felt as if it was already winding down for the weekend. Ben had invited Luc round to his place in Notting Hill for a Carnival barbecue, but she knew she must get a portfolio together, dig out her A-level stuff, do some drawing and painting. Her mind drifted back to the sketches of the villa she'd done sitting on the terrace, then inevitably to Liz pouring Pimms and introducing her. And how he'd stood against a backdrop of sea and sky the colour of lapis lazuli.

Luc squeezed her eyes shut, telling herself she wouldn't cry again today, at least not in public. She ought to carry a jumbo box of Kleenex instead of a bag and swap her mascara for permanent dark glasses in case she got caught out. Walking up the steps to the library, she remembered how she'd borrowed all those books on flying and banking.

Instead of heading for Reference, she went to the Self Help section. She needed a book on broken heart surgery.

'You're really going?' asked Luc, catching sight of the backpacks in the middle of the sitting-room floor. Ella was out doing some last-minute shopping.

'We'll be in Nice at eight,' said Yannick, who was adjusting his skateboard wheels with a screwdriver. 'If Ella decides something, it's done.'

'Amazing you could get a flight.'

'If you pay enough, you can get anything. Ella was prepared to pay.'

'Have credit card, will travel.' Luc remembered the platinum plastic being handed over at Mathi's airport.

'I've some friends in St Tropez, so if I can get hold of them, we'll stay there.'

'Perhaps *Les Voiles Blanches* will be in the neighbourhood,' teased Luc.

'Then I can get my wages off Henri, though I doubt if Ella would touch Madame's money. She lives in a different globe.'

'World,' corrected Luc. 'Who? Madame?'

'Ella. You wouldn't think it if you didn't know her.' Yannick looked up from the skateboard. 'Just how rich is she?'

Luc stared at him, feeling uncomfortable. 'I don't know. I don't want to know.' She yawned. The swim had finished her. 'Have you finished in my room? I must have a snooze.'

She plodded downstairs and kicked off her shoes. The curtains were still folded on her bed. Not having the energy to rehang them, she dumped them on the floor. At least Yannick had cleared up as he'd promised, although her decorating was ruined. Collapsing into bed, she pulled the sheet over her head to block out the light.

She was stoned on exhaustion, but still her mind wouldn't switch off. Lorenzo invaded every cell of her brain. She was suddenly transported to Prague, to Charles Bridge. Where they'd kissed and kissed and kissed. Where he'd been furious about the possibility of them being filmed. No wonder. Cosima might see it. Perhaps he was taking her away this weekend. Lorenzo and Cosima. Ella and Yannick. Marina and Gordon. The world was full of happy couples jetting round it . . .

Luc felt her control wash away as a desperate loneliness flooded her. She'd be like Miss Haversham. Imprisoned by rejection. Year after empty, lonely year would pass with her becoming more embittered and mad. 'Oh, God help me.'

'Luc,' called Yannick tentatively and opened the door. 'Luc?'

She burrowed deeper down the bed. 'I'm all right.'

'This must stop.' He crouched beside her and gently pulled the sheet back. 'No one should be as unhappy as you.'

'I'm all right.' She turned over, curled up and faced the wall.

'You're not. You must get over this.'

'I can't. I want to be with Lorenzo so much.'

'You've got to forget about him.'

'I know I should. He's getting married. But I can't,' sobbed Luc. 'No one will ever be as perfect . . .'

'No one is perfect,' sighed Yannick.

'Lorenzo is, for me.' Her body was convulsing as she cried and cried.

'Sssh.' Yannick put his arms round hers and gently pulled her upright. 'Sssh. Sssh.'

Rocked by Yannick's arms as if she were in a cradle, Luc swallowed back her sobs, almost tasting the Sachertorte Lorenzo had brought her in its wooden box. She saw him smiling in the passenger seat of the Aston Martin, touched his blond hair and smelt his aftershave. When Yannick began stroking her back, Lorenzo was stroking it when they were lying under the tree having the picnic. Luc's eyes were shut, but Lorenzo filled her sight.

She was still crying, but Lorenzo's touch was warm, so comforting. Lorenzo's fingers were on her neck, Lorenzo was gently kissing away her tears, Lorenzo was holding her closer. Lorenzo's low voice was saying how much he wanted her, Lorenzo's lips on hers, Lorenzo who she was clinging to, Lorenzo she was kissing and kissing and kissing.

'A going away present?' Ella stood at the door to the bedroom. Yannick and Luc sprang apart, he leapt to his feet. Ella's eyes flashed. 'You bitch, Luc.'

Paralysed by shock, Luc couldn't speak.

'Ella . . .' pleaded Yannick.

'Don't even think of telling me it's not how it looked.' Ella's expression was murderous. 'I looked. I saw it. Serendipity, I guess. You taking down the curtains.'

'Ella, listen, will you?' He clutched her arm. 'Luc was very upset about Lorenzo, and, and . . .'

'And needed a fuck to make her feel better.' Ella wrenched herself away from Yannick. 'That's right, Luc. Best way to get over one man is to get under another.'

Luc screwed up her face. 'No,' she whispered.

'You slag.'

Luc shook her head. 'No. Please, Ella . . .'

'Ella, please,' said Yannick desperately. 'Just calm down.'

'I'm calm enough considering. Considering you both must think I'm a cunt, up for being fucked over.' She was shaking as she surveyed the pair of them. 'I've got a plane to catch. You'll be gone by the time I get back, won't you, Luc? Post the keys through the letter-box.'

Immobilised by shell-shock, Luc stared at the ceiling for what could have been hours. The Doll's House was silent. Wordlessly, Ella had gathered up her stuff and left, ignoring Yannick begging her to let him explain. A few minutes later he had knocked on Luc's door. 'I'm going to the airport.'

She had been unable to meet his eyes.

'Pity Ella came back.' Yannick had smiled. 'I've been waiting since Greece. Some other time, maybe?' Luc had gasped in horror as his words had sunk in. 'Leave me your new number and I'll be . . .' He'd paused. Then his grin had broadened. 'In touch. Very soon.'

Luc had heard Ella's car start up, reverse and squeal out of the Mews.

Chapter Fourteen

'Another fine mess you've got yourself into.' It was almost midnight when Alex turned up. 'I should hand in my Press pass. Occupation, mate to Luc James. It's a full-time job.' Seeing her misery deepen, he quickly added, 'Joke. Is this all your stuff?' Luc nodded. 'Haven't got much, have you? Thank God for that.'

'I travel light,' said Luc, trying to sound it.

After they'd loaded up his car, Luc double-locked the front door of the Doll's House and posted the keys through the letter-box, as Ella had told her to do. She couldn't believe she was leaving the place she'd called home for three years.

'Aren't you reaching for your passport?' said Alex, as they approached Chelsea Bridge. 'We're crossing the river.' He glanced at her, then sighed. 'I want to get this straight. I'm used to living alone, I like living alone, so it's just until you sort out somewhere else. To which you will apply all your energies.'

Luc nodded. Alex suddenly seemed as prickly as he'd been in Greece.

'House rules. We recycle. No battery eggs or you're out.' Luc nodded again. 'I don't want you slagging off the area or my neighbours. I had enough of that from Marina. And if we can keep the daily Lorenzo count to single figures I'd be grateful.'

'He is a Count,' said Luc, puzzled.

'That's a typo. I meant the number of times I have to hear his name.'

Fifteen minutes after leaving Chelsea they pulled up in a side street. Luc was completely lost. Seeing her glance round apprehensively, Alex snapped, 'For Christ's sake, we're only just in Zone Two. By the way, the Tube's about five minutes' walk.'

From what Luc could make out, the litter-strewn street was tree-lined, the terrace of houses Regency. Their paint was peeling and their windows dirty. A rusting Toyota had been abandoned, its windows bashed out. The corner shop's metal grilles were covered in graffiti. An estate was a road away, its concrete tower blocks obliterating the night sky. Her heart sank.

'All your worldly goods you me endow,' said Alex, piling up Luc's two bags and six boxes outside the front door down in the basement. He unlocked the door. 'Welcome. Shit, the hall light's gone again.'

Remembering Marina's description of a hovel, and knowing that some men seem to live as if they'd just been burgled, Luc wondered what she'd let herself in for. As she followed him through the hall, she remembered the state of his car and braced herself. When he turned on the light, she was astonished. 'It's really nice.'

'There's no need to sound so surprised.'

The living room was huge and open-plan with painted floorboards and high ceilings. White wooden shutters covered the windows. A kitchen and dining table were at the far end. French doors opened on to a walled garden.

'Sit down,' offered Alex, sorting through his mail and pointing to the two sofas next to the fireplace.

'Can't I see upstairs?' Upstairs was a bathroom and two bedrooms, one of which Alex used as a study. Floor to ceiling shelves lined two of the walls and were full of books and files.

'Sofa bed,' said Alex. 'Sheets are in the cupboard. Where you can store your stuff.'

'I thought . . .' began Luc.

'You thought I was a slob and the flat would be a sty.'

'It's huge,' said Luc, gazing at the enormous windows.

'And light and airy. And a quarter of the price you'd pay for a shoebox in your postcodes of preference. I must eat.'

At half past twelve, she and Alex were sitting on the sofas. He was munching bagels and drinking the brandy she'd bought him as a present. 'So you led him on.'

'I didn't,' protested Luc. 'I promise. I was just really upset and . . .'

'And you thought you could swoon into his arms. In your bed. And snog him.' He sounded exasperated. 'And be caught red-handed. And Ella would somehow overlook this? You're a fuckwit, sweets.'

'I didn't kiss him. Not consciously,' insisted Luc.

'Why not? He's an Adonis from what I can remember.'

'Because he's Ella's.'

'So?'

'So? So?' shrieked Luc, incredulous. 'So, Ella and I are best friends, have been for more than ten years.'

'And you don't cheat on your mates,' said Alex.

'No, you don't. Ever. It's worse than cheating on your husband.'

'Well, why did you do it?'

'I didn't. I was distraught. I didn't realise what was happening. Oh God, if you don't believe me, Ella won't, will she?' Luc began pulling at her hair.

'I just might believe he took advantage of your grief.' Alex poured himself more brandy. 'She won't.'

'She must.' Luc was aghast.

'She won't. You two will always be stuck in the remedial class when it comes to judging men. Yannick sounds as much of a shit as Lorenzo. But Yannick is the father of Ella's child. Of course she's going to believe him when he says you're to blame.'

*

Alex helped her make up the sofa bed. Luc collapsed into it, but half an hour later, she got up and began reading an old copy of *Private Eye*. Unable to concentrate, she turned off the light again.

Lucasta? Like Lovelace? Do with my life? Look like Julie Christie in Darling. Not Mrs, Miss. Besides, she's Janie. You'll love her, Luc, everyone does. Green tea? You twit, don't you know, it's grass. If I were Princess Elizabeth, I'd have fallen madly in love with Protector Somerset. How could anyone not fall for Moshe Dayan? For Alexander the Great. For Byron. For Max de Winter. Come on, Lukewarm. Prince Charlie must have been bonnie, but not from his portrait on the shortbread tin. Fuck lacrosse, let's go to the pub. How do we know, Sister Joseph, that Jeanne d'Arc wasn't hallucinating when she heard those voices? Half of medieval Europe was stoned on bread. I just know that I'll never need differential equations. He's called Tas, short for Tasmania, because he's so wild. Twice over the limit and a gram of charlie in my pocket when they stopped me. What's the Greek for fur coat and no knickers? Help me, Luc, p-p-please. Jolly boating weather, hail harvest home. An epiphany, outside Chelsea football ground. We need mentors, not men.

A car blaring dub was cruising down the street. Luc looked at her watch. It had gone three and she still couldn't sleep.

Alex glugged from a bottle of water, emptied it and threw it on the back seat on top of his cricket gear. It was midday and they'd crossed the Sussex border. Fields stretched to a horizon of hills, misty in the heat. Acid greenery had long since softened. The mellowing was a reminder that autumn was only a few weeks away.

Suddenly Luc sat bolt upright. 'Tim's not playing, is he?'

'Don't think so. Someone mentioned he was going away.' He glanced at her. 'Don't tell me I should be getting in some Winalot. Haven't you made amends yet?'

'Still in the dog-house,' sighed Luc.

'Have you made any effort to grovel your way out?'

She shook her head. 'Too chicken.'

He turned into a B road. They were on the outskirts of a

village. Up ahead beyond some trees was a church spire. They passed rows of cottages, gardens as colourful as paint palettes, before Alex stopped in front of a squat, thatched pub which overlooked the cricket pitch.

A group of about a dozen, some of them in whites, were gathered outside round a table groaning with pitchers of beer. 'Alex, *mon brave*,' called one of the men. Before Luc realised what was happening, a glass of Pimms was shoved in her hand and she was being introduced.

'Where's the signorina?' one of them asked Alex quietly, but loud enough for Luc to hear.

'The signora. Back where she belongs.'

'Found a replacement smartish, haven't you?'

'She's a mate, mate.'

'Not for long with your form.'

As Luc was pondering over what she was hearing, a beautiful willowy blonde came over to her. She was in her mid-forties and wearing faded jeans which matched her twinkling eyes, plimsolls and a white rugger shirt. 'Katie. And you're Luc. You're coming to supper tonight.'

'I am?'

'If there's anything left to eat. The boys have just got back from their French exchange. All they learnt was "La France est merde".'

She picked the orange out of her Pimms and sucked on it. 'Known Alex long?'

'About three months.'

'One of the best, isn't he? Where's the signorina?'

'Marina?' asked Luc. 'I think that's all over.'

'Really? Excellent.' Katie looked round to Alex, who was still talking to the same man. 'Bill and I thought she was yuck. Bill,' she hissed. 'Rector's arriving. Stop fratting with the enemy and look after your team.'

'The enemy had better change,' said Alex, who wasn't in whites.

'Can I watch?' Katie's eyes twinkled more brightly. 'I should've emigrated. You Aussies have the most gorgeous bodies.'

Before he joined the teams outside a tiny pavilion, Alex threw his car keys at Luc. 'Good catch. Perhaps you ought to play.'

'Absolutely not,' said Katie. 'She's sitting next to me for a gas and a goss. Come on Luc, bench.'

As she followed Katie carrying a jug of Pimms, Luc felt irrational tears prick her eyes. A bitch like her didn't deserve such kindness. Ella, Tim, Liz. Nigel Mann and the Wise Men. Even Juliet Beak and Carole at the Agency. They all knew what she was really like. If Katie knew, she would be avoiding her like a bacillus. Terrified of screwing up again, Luc wanted to escape.

Out on the field the umpire was tossing a coin, just as a man in whites began running from the direction of the pub waving his bat.

'Alex is batting,' said Katie, shielding her eyes. 'Let's hope God's on the Rector's side and Bill doesn't get another duck. Shaming.' She poured some more Pimms. 'So, another journo?'

Luc shook her head and explained about her dismal lack of career.

Katie clapped Alex's four. 'You know it's actually very nice to meet someone who's normal. All these terrifyingly high-powered women make me feel inadequate that I just want to live in the country and look after my children, my husband and my house. But I feel blessed.'

'Aren't you meant to feel unfulfilled?'

'A downtrodden slave, I've been told. But there's only a certain number of chiefs out there and I was always going to be an Indian. You and Alex are just good friends?'

'Yes. Hope so. I mean about the friends,' said Luc. 'I've asked a lot of him recently, so he might be getting fed up with me.' Soon Alex would decide that she was worthless, beyond redemption. Like Ella had. And Lorenzo and Tim and Liz and . . .

'You look a bit fragile. Been through the mill?'

'Hungover,' fibbed Luc. Part of her longed to confide in the serene woman beside her, but she was overcome with too much shame and self-disgust to say a word. She gazed at the field, only seeing Ella standing at her bedroom door. As Alex made another run, Yannick was grinning, saying he'd been waiting since Greece. She shuddered and closed her eyes.

'Hard cheese, Alex,' said Katie, standing up. 'You're here. And looking very chic, showing up us country bumps as usual.' Luc stared up, horrified. 'Liz, this is Luc,' added Katie. 'A very nice chum of Alex's. Luc, meet . . .'

'What's happened to your hair?' demanded Liz. She could've been a member of the Inquisition in a white linen dress.

Luc cringed.

'You two know one another?' asked Katie. 'Small world. Luc, budge up.'

'Luc shares a house with my half-sister,' said Liz, glaring. 'And gatecrashes villas in Greece. How is Lorenzo von Retzen?' Luc bit her lip. 'Isn't his house beautiful?'

'I never went there.' Luc's voice was cracking. 'I wouldn't know.'

'Tim knows. He designed it. The readers of some Euro glossy know. A five-page feature, but no mention of Tim.'

Luc hung her head.

'According to the spread, the architect was one Amelia Schennen. A real-life princess from one of those obscure places in Germany.' Liz looked at Luc as if she were an avocado bathroom suite with gold taps. 'We know you have no career to speak of, Luc. Is that why you wanted to undermine Tim's?'

There was a horrible silence while Luc studied her flip-flops. Liz's dainty brown feet were ensconsed in Manolo Blahnik sandals, her toenails perfectly polished.

A triumphant cry went up from the field. 'Bugger,' said Katie. 'A six. And Bill's bowling.' She clapped, then shielded her eyes again. 'Luc, how about a trip to the pub for some more Pimms? Do sit down, Liz. Or move to where you can do something useful like being my sunshade.' Handing the jug to Luc, she winked. 'Lots of ice. Cooling for Liz.'

Luc seized the chance to escape. In as much of a hurry to return to Liz as to go into a burning building, she mooched towards the cottage-loaf pub to the sound of the ball being lazily thwacked. The church spire seemed to be stretching to the sunny sky. The scene was so perfect, it seemed to belong on a jigsaw puzzle box. When her mobile rang in her bag, she jumped, as guilty as if she were taking a chainsaw to the trees.

'Lucasta? Thank God.'

Luc stopped, the world around her imploding until there was nothing but him. Her heart began to race.

'Your present arrived safely.'

Shock was tightening her throat.

'If you wanted to make me feel any worse, you succeeded.'

She couldn't speak.

'Have you any hair left?'

'Not much,' whispered Luc.

'Are you mad?'

'Probably.' Her hands were shaking. 'Why are you bothering to call?'

'Because I was worried you might have done something worse than cut off your hair.' He sounded furious. 'I've been away and that's what I find on my desk when I get back. Emotional blackmail is ugly.'

'Well, so am I now.'

'That's impossible,' snapped Lorenzo.

'Sorry if my broken heart troubled your conscience. Actually, I didn't think you had one to trouble.' Luc looked at the cricketers, white against green. Alex had just hit another four. 'Or a heart, come to that.'

'Meaning?'

Alex was talking to Tim, who she now realised was the player who'd arrived late. 'You wouldn't know anything about cricket, would you?'

'It's boring baseball. Meaning?'

'Straight bats. For a start you should have been straight with Tim. Been honest.'

'A long story.'

'And been straight with me. If you had, I might not have got in so deep.' Only to drown.

'Another long story.' He sighed. The silence that followed was so long, she wondered if he'd hung up. 'I must see you. Can I?'

'What?' Luc was stunned. 'Why?'

'Can I?'

'When?'

'Today. There's a plane in an hour. Please.'

He was so beseeching that she was unnerved. Lorenzo didn't plead and beg. That was her job. 'What about your fiancée?' Her trembling worsened. 'Or is she another long story?'

'If you've got plans, please cancel them. Please, Luc.'

'I'm not in London.'

'You're not? Where are you?'

'About sixty miles away.'

'Meet me at the Chester Hotel at six. Please, Luc.' Again, need made his voice alien. 'Please.'

Half an hour later on the road to London, Luc wondered if she should turn back to the village. Alex would be furious that she'd done a bunk. And stolen his car to make her getaway. She'd be homeless again.

The minutes had ticked past as she'd stood outside the pub paralysed by indecision. Overwhelmed, she couldn't think straight. Alex had looked set to remain at the crease until the next millennium. She'd been too shy to cross the pitch and interrupt the game. Especially to be given grief.

Seeing Lorenzo would only deepen her wounds. Why should she go running just because he called? Crossing Europe for one of his smiles had been like lighting the fuse that had led to the smouldering rubble that was her life. It was pointless, he was engaged. He was already playing Happy Families with Cosima's nephews.

Lorenzo was a cheating, lying, spineless bastard who had treated her appallingly, letting her get in so deep that she'd almost drowned.

Luc had abandoned the empty jug on an outside table and sprinted to the car.

'Has Count von Retzen arrived yet?'

'No, madam. We're expecting him shortly.'

'I'll wait for him in the bar.' Luc strode purposefully into the bar, as she'd strode up the steps. Thinking of her previous diffidence, her fear of being told to use the tradesmen's entrance, she described herself as pathetic. She ordered some coffee. 'And biscuits, please. Lots.' The waiter said he'd see what he could do.

She got out her mobile. 'Hello, Alex. You're going to be cross with me. Again. I'm in London thanks to your car. Something came up, or rather someone's coming over from Geneva.'

Luc was about to reach for something Lorenzo-impressing like the *Financial Times* but instead picked up a copy of a woman's magazine, and settled herself on the sofa.

Ten minutes later, engrossed in the horoscope, mouth full of shortbread, she sensed someone approach. 'Mwellob Mwrenzo.' Luc swallowed. 'Sorry. Hello, Lorenzo. Biscuit?' She held out the plate. 'Apparently I'm going to have a good month for travel. But I guess it won't be to Geneva for your wedding.'

He stared and stared at her. 'It's not just the hair, is it? You seem so different.'

Luc shrugged. 'How are you?'

'Tired.' He sank into the armchair beside her. 'So tired, Luc.'

He was still feline, but the cat had spent the night in the freezing rain. His clothes were the same expensive tailored shell, but he was different. The lapis lazuli was deadened, the suntan had faded into sallowness. For the first time she noticed the lines on his face and a slight slackening around his jaw heralding middle age.

'Coffee? Whisky? Both?' Luc summoned the waiter.

He pulled out his cigarettes and the lighter she'd held up to the newly risen sun on the beach. 'How are Ella and the drifter? Well?'

Luc froze. 'Away. In France.'

'Tim and Liz?'

'Furious with me. And with you.'

He sighed wearily. 'Tim got his fee. A very large fee.'

'Perhaps the money's not the issue. Perhaps he wanted to see the project through to the end.'

Lorenzo tssked irritably. 'Well, why didn't he make an effort?'

'And get the recognition for it. It was his work, he should get the credit, not Amelia whatever her name is.'

'You've seen the article?'

'Heard about it.'

'The journalist screwed up.' Lorenzo buried his head in his hands. 'I should never have agreed to it.'

'You should've been honest with Tim from the start,' said Luc. 'But I guess being honest isn't one of your strengths.'

Lorenzo winced at her sarcasm. 'As Tim should have been with me. If he couldn't give me the commitment, he should've said. Instead I had Liz, putting me on hold. Stalling. Arranging meetings in Geneva only to cancel.'

'But . . .'

'Tim was trying to juggle too many projects. I told him at our first meeting that I wanted the work done quickly.'

'You're not his only client . . .' began Luc.

'He's a great architect but a lousy time manager. And my time, if you haven't noticed, is limited. I didn't appreciate waiting around to fit into his schedule.'

'Perhaps you should've explained that to him.'

'I did. I called him. A few days after I last saw you. He said he was disappointed, but would take what I was saying on board for the future. He understood I was trying to be constructive. As for the article, the reporter got it wrong. Amelia knows she doesn't deserve the credit. She only supervised the final stages.'

'Amelia. A real-life princess from one of those obscure German places,' murmured Luc. She stared at him, the biscuit turning to ashes in her mouth.

He asked her where she'd like to have dinner. Distracted, she answered she didn't care. He said he needed a shower and had to go up to his room. Was she coming?

'I'll wait for you here.' Luc picked up the magazine.

'But . . .'

'I'll wait for you here.'

It didn't register when he momentarily squeezed her hand. The bar was filling up around her, but she didn't notice, her head was invaded by images of Amelia. Amelia, not Cosima. Amelia, a real-life princess, who was an architect. Perhaps she was a princess like one of the mad Hapsburgs of history; so deformed by inbreeding that her huge warty nose met her moose jaw like a tin-opener. Momentarily cheered up, Luc thought of Michelle Pfeiffer's double and was plunged into jealous rage.

'A walk?' suggested Lorenzo.

Luc was startled out of her reverie. 'A walk?' She realised she didn't want to be cooped up in an expensive restaurant, waiters fussing, other tables too close. She was finding his presence claustrophobic, all her pent-up recrimination stifling. 'Let's go to the park.'

She suggested they walk round the Serpentine to the Peter Pan statue. It was still warm, but in just a matter of weeks the light had changed. Luc could almost smell the autumnal woodsmoke. She and Ella had made jam last year.

'You didn't like Yannick much, did you?'

'I didn't trust him,' said Lorenzo. 'A user. Within a minute he was asking if I had a ski chalet and inviting himself to stay.'

'You've got a chalet?'

'In Gstaad.'

'Oh.' She and Ella had made chutney too, stinking out the Doll's House and burning saucepans. The result had looked like sewage sludge and had smelt worse. Laughing and laughing, they had to chuck it out. 'You were right. Not to trust him.'

Lorenzo glanced at her. 'Luc? What's wrong?'

'Nothing.' The memory was so shaming, so painful. She gazed up at the treetops and then beyond. 'Ella's been my best friend for ten years.' Luc could hardly get the words out. 'And I've messed it all up.'

'What happened?'

Luc didn't reply.

'It's retrievable, surely?'

'Easily said,' spat Luc. 'What would you know?' Abruptly she stopped. 'What the fuck would you know, Lorenzo?'

A roller-blader turned round and stared. Lorenzo raised an eyebrow. 'Does screaming hysterically help?'

'Yes. Yes, as a matter of fact it does.' Luc was shaking with rage. 'It helps. It might help you understand that I'm in such a mess that I'm frightened of ending up being certified. That my life used to be dull, so dull I thought I ought to get one. And then you come along and suddenly everything's changed without my realising it. Because I was so in love, so completely in love with you.'

'I'm sorry, Luc. So very sorry.'

'Nothing else mattered. And what was the point, Lorenzo?' Luc didn't realise she was crying. 'Tell me, what good did falling in love with you do me? Falling in love, only to drown.'

He flinched. 'I suppose making me feel guilty makes you feel better.'

'You don't feel anything,' screamed Luc.

'Don't shout. I can't bear it.' Glaring at her, he took a deep breath. 'Let's sit down. On the chairs over there. Have this.' He reached into his pocket and gave her a handkerchief.

They crossed the scrubby remains of grass and sank into the uncomfortable green canvas. Luc watched a pair of ducks skimming to a stop across the flat sheet of water. Ella had once wondered if the Canada geese ever got fed up with the assumption they must be American. It was the day after she'd run out of clean knickers, quickly washed a pair and tried to dry them in the toaster. Distracted by the phone, Ella had forgotten about them and the toaster had caught fire. Luc remembered how she and Ella had collapsed on the sofa, how laughing had hurt and hurt.

Lorenzo was smoking, playing with his lighter. 'I should've told you that first night. On the beach.'

'Yes. But you didn't. You somehow managed to forget that you were planning to be married all those other times as well.'

'I couldn't forget. Why do you think I tried to stay away from you?'

Luc gazed at him. 'That's why you didn't call? After Greece?'

'That's why.'

'And that's why you wanted me to be discreet. And that's why you made such a fuss on the bridge in Prague.' Luc's eyes flashed. 'What are you doing, Lorenzo? Surely I'm not the best start to married life. I could almost feel sorry for Amelia. If I wasn't so pissed off with you. Amelia, the real-life princess. It is her, isn't it?' Luc didn't wait for him to answer, not needing confirmation. 'Any relation to the Hapsburgs?'

'Why do you ask?'

'Deformed by inbreeding?'

'As you ask, Amelia is very clever and rather beautiful.'

Luc cringed as if she'd been slapped. She gazed down at her feet in their flip-flops, grubby and probably smelly. A real-life princess who was very clever and rather beautiful. She felt sick. 'Then why bother with me?'

'I don't know.' He lit another cigarette. 'Perhaps because you wore silly hats and fell into harbours looking at the stars. Perhaps because you reminded me of a girl I once knew a long time ago. I tried not to bother with you.'

'Thanks.'

'I didn't realise you cared so much. Until that Saturday. You were always so aloof, so distant. Nothing was ever good enough. I arrange lunch and you want a picnic. I show you Prague and you complain about being tired. I go out of my way to get you a cake and you say you'll get fat. Whenever I called, were you ever interested in me? Or did you just want to show off about all the concerts and parties you'd been to?'

Luc stared at him open-mouthed.

'You say you fell in love with me, Luc. You don't know me, you've never tried to get to know me.'

'Maybe you're so cold you're impossible to get to know. You shut everyone out. Maybe you're so privileged that you should be up on Mount Olympus, not down here among ordinary people who get hurt.'

'Privileged?'

'Born on a golden escalator and one smooth gilded ride up ever since.'

Lorenzo threw away his cigarette and stared at her. 'You don't know anything about me, do you?'

They began walking again. '*Es war einmal*,' began Lorenzo. 'Once upon a time there was an only son. He grew up in Berlin in a small, dark, dirty flat in a large dark, dirty tenement, where the hall smelt of cabbage water. His mother was a very bad cook but each night the tiny kitchen table would be laid with silver. His father was very proud of that silver. Instead of working like a normal man, he would spend hours cleaning it. The mother and father cared nothing about the food, which was disgusting. What mattered was the silver, the family silver.

'There were some large, dark pictures in that small, dark, dirty flat. The son was beaten once for letting his forbidden football bounce against one. A portrait. Of an ancestor, a general who fought at Blenheim. The pictures were the family portraits. The wooden carving was of the family coat of arms.

'There was a photograph album. Green leather. Instead of working, the father would sit in his dusty chair in his shabby suit and study the pages. The photographs were old family photographs of the family's confiscated castle and the family's confiscated estates and the family's horses and dogs and the family's army of servants.

'Being a dutiful son, the boy never questioned why he wasn't allowed to play with the other children in the tenement. He believed, because parents always tell you the truth, that one day soon he'd return to the castle. It was his birthright, his inheritance. The castle was so real that the grime and the poverty and the cabbage smells were imaginary.

'Denied the company of other children, the boy would read and magically leave the dark, dirty flat much as his father would be transported back to his estates by the silver and the paintings and the photographs. He was a solitary, proud, clever little boy, but it took him years to realise that his parents were cankered with bitterness.

'The journey from privilege to poverty is a hard one. They were poor, but they kept reminding themselves they weren't like everyone else. They were better. Noblemen whose ancestors were cousins to princes and had fought at Blenheim and with Gustavus Adophus don't go to offices. It was only a matter of time, the Communists would go, the estates would be the family's again.

'There were always letters. Letters to the Government, letters to distant relatives, letters demanding compensation, letters begging for money, letters to newspapers. More shrill, more hysterical, all with the family crest.

'The food was even worse when the writing paper was running out. It was expensive. They'd rather starve than compromise, they'd rather the boy's shoes hurt than sell the portraits or the silver. They'd rather live on a pittance of a pension and dreams of past glory. Daughters like the boy's mother aren't brought up to clean and cook. Blinded by memories, she couldn't see the squalor, the grime on the windows. Perhaps she didn't want a clear sight of the real world outside. Perhaps she didn't want to see how poor they really were.

'The air in the flat was full of unhappiness and thwarted dreams and apathy, as real as the cabbage smell. The parents would argue. Shouting and shouting and shouting. The boy hated shouting, the man still hates it. The boy shut himself away with his books, with his school work. He was a brilliant student. Brilliant, but disliked. The boy had grown up cold and proud, he was the heir to great estates, the descendant of generals and princes. Warped by his family past, his vision was as opaque as the grimy windows.'

Lorenzo slowed down to a stop to light another cigarette. The sun had gone. When Luc rubbed her goose-pimpled arms, he offered her his jacket. Putting it on, she remembered that first night on Ia.

'When he was twenty-two, he met a girl and, despite everything . . .'

Luc frowned. 'What was everything?'

'A young man like him doesn't fall for a girl like that. A daughter of Turkish *Gastarbeiter* living in Kreutzberg.'

'You don't trade down. You play with them, you don't marry them,' intoned Luc. 'What was she like, apart from being broke and from the wrong background? I assume she was, most of us are. We can't all be princesses.'

'Good and kind. Beautiful. Long black hair.'

'Nothing like me then. Why did I remind you of her?'

'The same lost look. A waif.'

'That's creepy.' Luc shuddered. 'Laying her ghost, were you?'

'Meaning?'

'Meaning she broke your heart. Back then, I guess you had one to break. What happened to her?'

'She went to Paris and disappeared. In Berlin she'd been waitressing, trying to break into singing. Opera. I spent months searching for her. Before I went to Boston.'

'She didn't die tragically after rejection, did she? Like Anna Karenina or Emma Bovary?'

'No, Luc, she didn't.' He scowled. 'She got married. Is very happily married to her manager.'

'You're in contact?'

He shook his head. 'I read about her. See programmes. I saw her once, at Verona. She's become very successful, as she told me she would all those years ago. She warned me to keep faith with her, to free myself from my background, to ignore my parents. That she'd prove them wrong. You must have heard of her. Yasmina Bois.'

'La Divina?' Luc gasped.

'It must have been five years ago that I saw her perform. I'd achieved what I'd set out to do. Workaholics are as bad as any other addicts. They escape life, they let it pass them by. I realised I'd done that. I suddenly knew then that the most valuable things are what money can't buy. That's when I went to Mount Athos.'

Luc walked around the statue of Peter Pan. 'And your parents?'

'Dead. I hope they're happier and finally at peace.'

'Mats and rice.' Smiling sadly, Luc crouched down and studied the animals carved into the bronze. 'Ella couldn't decide if they were mice or rats. So she said they were a mix of both. You haven't had a smooth glide up a golden escalator?'

'What?'

'Alex . . .' Luc corrected herself. 'It's assumed you must've had it so easy.'

'You mean Alex assumed. He was wrong. Like him, I've had to work for it.' He gazed at the statue. 'Are we revisiting your childhood?'

'Ella's.'

'Have you and Yannick ended up in bed together?'

'No,' yelped Luc. 'Not exactly.' She hesitated. 'It's not what you think. It's not what Ella thought either.'

'What happened, Luc?'

Straightening, she winced as her knees cracked. 'I'm growing old before I've grown up. Let's go.' She began striding towards the road as if she were trying to beat a personal best.

'What happened?' repeated Lorenzo, sounding breathless.

'Hasn't the princess told you to stop smoking?' mocked Luc.

'What happened?'

'Perhaps you should go jogging with her.'

'Stop it.'

'Or is sex a good enough work-out? Especially when you're called by her as you're doing it with me.' Luc lengthened her stride, was almost running. 'That must've really raised your heart rate.'

'Luc.' He clasped her arm, holding her still. 'What are you talking about?'

She wrenched herself free. 'In wherever we were. Karlovy Vary. That morning. You took a phone call in the middle of, of, of . . . from her.'

'What?'

'Her. Amelia.'

'. . . The call was from a fund manager . . .'

'. . . A fucking princess . . .' screamed Luc.

'About a statement from the chairman of the Federal Reserve.' Lorenzo shouted her down. 'The markets were expecting a rate cut.'

'What? The markets? As if I give a shit about the markets.' Luc was beside herself. 'Keep them for pillow talk with Amelia. The princess who's very clever and rather beautiful.'

'You're getting hysterical again.'

'Oh. Oh, I'm so very sorry. Sorry for being upset for being cheated on and hurt and made to look such an idiot. I suppose

Princess Amelia is as cool and poised as Grace Kelly. As well as being very clever and rather beautiful. I guess you make a perfect couple.'

'On paper. Yes. Yes, we do.'

'Which bit of paper? The marriage certificate? The announcement in *The Times*?'

Lorenzo sighed. 'There's been no announcement, it's not official yet. Yes, I admit Amelia is ideal . . .'

'If she's so fucking ideal, Lorenzo, what are you doing here? Stop torturing me and go back to her.'

'Will you calm down and discuss things reason—'

'No. There's nothing more to say.' Suddenly all the fight left her as Luc stared at Lorenzo. She gazed into the depths of lapis lazuli blue and recognised defeat. 'Nothing. Is there?'

She had lost, not that she'd ever been in with a chance of winning. She couldn't compete with real-life princesses who were very clever and rather beautiful. Another Ella, who'd only had the good fairies at her christening.

'Luc, don't.'

Ignoring Lorenzo's pleas, she bolted towards the road and almost threw herself in front of a passing cab, forcing it to squeal to a halt. As she scrambled inside, she refused to allow herself to look back.

Chapter Fifteen

'Smells good.' Alex slung his laptop, mobile, a pile of newspapers and notebooks on to the sofa.

'Nice day at the office, dear?' teased Luc. It had become part of their ritual. 'Wine or beer?'

'Beer.' Alex went to the fridge. 'Actually, shite day. What's that?'

'Green curry. The man at the Asian shop gave me the recipe.'

'And you went to the Portuguese deli.' Alex peered at the custard tarts.

'Signora Mendosa's a grandmother again. Insisted I have them.'

'Apart from gossiping with all the local shopkeepers, what else have you done today?'

'Sent off two more applications. St Martin's and Chelsea. Went to an interview about some bar work. Weeded the garden. Did some drawing.'

'Bar work? As in judges and lawyers?'

'As in booze. A champagne bar in the City.'

'The Shitty?' Alex was dismayed. 'It'll be full of loudmouths earning telephone numbers and going on about speccing up their Porsches.'

Luc shrugged. 'So? The tips are supposed to be brilliant.'

'Most of those City boys are animals. Work at a proper zoo.'

'Not qualified.'

'Temp.'

'No. I've told you, I'm never unjamming another photocopier for as long as I live.' Luc reached into the cupboard for the rice and a cup. 'At least at the bar there'll be a variety of animals. Some might even say thank you. Unlike most of my previous bosses. Anyway, it's not for ever.'

'Haven't you had enough of international financiers?'

Luc pulled a face. 'What about your day? Why shite?'

Alex took a long glug of beer. 'Book got turned down.'

Rice spilled out of the cup as his words sank in. 'Oh, Alex. I'm sorry.'

'Not as sorry as me.' He scowled at his beer bottle. 'Almost a whole year of my life wasted. All that research. All those hours of sitting cooped up indoors staring at a computer screen while the sun shone outside.'

'I remember. In Greece.'

'It's like having a baby. Only to find out it's born dead.'

He was so forlorn, Luc couldn't bear it. It was as if a giant oak tree had been felled. 'There must be loads of publishers. Don't give up.'

'It's like being a boxer. A bad one. Getting punched to the mat again and again. The time comes when you just don't want to get up.'

'What does your agent say?'

'Perhaps there just isn't the market for it. Perhaps it's only worth a page on the Internet.'

'Rubbish,' protested Luc. 'It's brilliant.' She'd read the manuscript. Alex had turned the unpromising material of the agri-chemical industry into pure gold. It had read like a thriller. Even a science dummy like herself had been enthralled. 'Change your agent. Take it to America.'

'Perhaps I should take it to the dump. Build a bonfire.'

'You can't give up.'

'I'm fed up with living to fight another day. I've battled enough. I want to savour the sweet taste of success right now. The book's good enough. I'm good enough.'

His yearning was so fierce it could've burned him. If wishing made it so, he'd be carried to the top of the bestseller lists and win the Pulitzer prize. 'You'll do it.' She knew he would one day. She handed him some cutlery and mats. 'After you've laid the table.'

They enjoyed a lazy evening of supper then television. Alex was addicted to the news, and could watch one bulletin after another every evening. Luc secretly wished he was as hooked on *EastEnders* which she never got a chance to watch any more. Otherwise, living at Alex's was far easier than she'd expected.

Too easy. She had to remind herself that it was only short-term. The flat was so comfortable. Late summer light poured in through oversized windows. She enjoyed pottering around in the garden, weeding and pruning. Grateful that Alex had given her sanctuary, she did her best to thank him in small ways such as cooking him dinner. It was when she was washing the windows at the front that she got talking to the neighbours. With Bertha from Trinidad and Dr Lal from Delhi and Carrie from Auckland, the street was like an outpost of the United Nations headquarters. It was a world away from leafy suburban Wimbledon, but Luc couldn't understand why Marina had hated it so much.

'It was just an excuse.' Alex had been impatient. 'She didn't want to admit she'd made the most awful mistake and really wanted to be back with Gordon the Golfer.'

Watching the box, Alex usually commented vociferously, scoffing at Government ministers' pomposity or tut-tutting over an interviewer's technique. That night he was silent, dejected. When she announced she was going to bed, he grunted a good-night, but only after she was halfway up the stairs.

As she brushed her teeth, for once Luc wasn't fixated on the mirror and the state of her hair. She wanted so desperately to cheer Alex up, to reassure him that he'd come good one day. What could she do?

'Don't want a mercy fuck, do you?' she offered as he passed the bathroom door.

His jaw dropped. 'Did I just hear what I heard?'

Luc nodded. 'Thought it might brighten your day.'

'Lucasta, you're insane.' He started to smile. 'It's tempting.' Their eyes met in the reflection of the mirror. 'It's the nicest offer I've had in ages.'

Luc was wondering if she were insane. She started to blush. What had possessed her?

'Thanks,' said Alex. 'But no thanks.'

'The hair? It's growing.'

'Will you stop going on about your hair? It's got nothing to do with it. We're mates, remember? You're in remission, but still healing. I'm not mucking up your recovery from a broken heart.'

'I've recovered,' protested Luc. 'No more hysteria. No more car stealing.' She cringed at the memory.

'I should hope not.' When he'd returned to the flat after the cricket match, his terrifying anger had been off the Richter scale. Luc had felt pummelled as if his list of her failings had been body blows. She'd had no defence. Ordered out at once, told to collect her stuff some other time, she'd gone. It was only when she was halfway up the street on her way to Ben's, Maggie's, anyone's, that Alex had relented and let her stay on. 'Why I didn't throw you out, I don't know. Your big blue eyes perhaps.'

'They're green.' She smiled. 'I have recovered, Alex. It's all history.'

'Then why do that magazine quiz? Is he a love cat or a love rat? Bet you had Lorenzo in mind. And I'd put my overdraft on the fact that you read his horoscope.'

'Not necessarily,' spluttered Luc.

'I rest my case.' He came over and ruffled her hair, kissing her forehead. 'Night, Luc. Great offer, but I'm not going to mess up a beautiful mateship.'

Three weeks had passed since Luc had last seen Ella, who was back at the Doll's House. Luc knew that much. She'd called on the Tuesday, a week after the Bank Holiday weekend. Ella had immediately slammed down the phone as if Luc's tentative greeting would give her the plague. Luc had called again, only to be rebuffed again. Close to tears, she had left it for a few minutes then got the answering-machine. 'If that's a medium from the late Lucasta James, I never, ever want to speak to her again. Anyone else, please leave a message.'

The late Lucasta James. Luc was shaken to the core, had sat staring at the phone. To Ella, she was dead. Ella had read the rites and buried their friendship.

The consequences were too horrible to contemplate, of such magnitude that Luc had been unable immediately to grasp them.

For years, ever since she had turned up at school Ella had been there. A rock, a fixed anchorage. For almost as long as Luc could remember, Ella and Janie and the Doll's House were the nearest to home and family she'd known. With Ella gone, Luc was floundering.

As she undressed, Luc felt a bleakness descend and wrap itself around her. She told herself to be positive, that she had other friends, knew lots of people, would meet more. Kind, good-hearted people like Alex. That right now, her life was in a turmoil of change, which must be better than being stuck in a rut. That she'd never have to unjam another photocopier for as long as she lived.

What she didn't have to convince herself of was that she missed Ella terribly. That without Ella, the world seemed a more impermanent place, that she was adrift, that all the fun seemed to have gone out of life.

The Ella and Luc roadshow. They were one another's better

halves. Ella's confidence and brains, Luc's imperative to work and common sense. Blended together, they could have made an almost perfect person, although one that was completely useless when it came to dealing with electricity.

Alex had urged her to call again, but Luc knew she would be wasting her breath, because she knew Ella. Better than anyone else in the world. If Ella had decided, that was it. Stupid, wilful stubbornness, he'd suggested. Maybe, replied Luc. Maybe someone who had the courage of their convictions.

'The only convictions Ella knows about are drink-drive related.'

Luc had managed to smile. 'She was also arrested for breach of the peace. On the bypass protest.'

Ella had a good memory for poetry and didn't forget much else. She wouldn't forget catching Luc and Yannick, or forgive Luc. 'Women are much harder on women, aren't they?' she'd said on their last orphans' Easter Sunday when they'd cooked lunch for Ben. 'Because we expect more of them than we do of men.' Like what? 'Like the through-thick-and-thin stuff. Loyalty. Trust.'

Luc imagined Ella at the Doll's House, hardening her heart still further as she repainted Luc's old room in readiness for the inevitable nanny. She'd be wiping away any traces of her. Ella knew her course and plotted her chart towards destination motherhood. Certain of her goal and with Yannick at her side, it was even easier to cast Luc adrift.

Yannick was forgivable. Ella was in love with him, and even if love weren't blind, he was the father of her child. Ella's allegiance would be his, automatically. He was as plausible as his looks were beguiling. 'Luc's mad. You know it, Ella. Look what she did to herself, cutting off her hair. One minute I thought she'd be cutting her wrists, the next she's trying to seduce me.'

Ella would want to believe Yannick, until the next time. Alex was certain there'd be a next time. 'He's a serial cheat,' Alex had said. 'He won't change.'

And if it didn't work out with Yannick, Ella would shrug her shoulders and cast him adrift too. If she wanted one, she'd find another frog to kiss. She'd never have any romantic fantasies that he'd turn into Prince Charming. Ella was like Janie and Ella's daughter would be like her. Their pot of gold wasn't at the end of a rainbow, but in house deeds and Trust documents and the tiny print columns of the *Financial Times*. They'd be their own fairy godmothers. They didn't need Prince Charming.

Luc was probably too late, the college administrators had warned her. Someone might drop out but generally all the places were assigned. Besides, she might not get a student loan organised in time. Her A-Level results showed she had the talent, but did she have the dedication? Perhaps she ought to apply for the following academic year.

Undaunted, Luc continued reading prospectuses and filling in forms, while trying to bone up on champagne, keep an eye on the accommodation columns and immersing herself in art books.

Working at the bar was frenetic. 'Teeth and tits,' ordered the manager, Sim, a dour Kiwi teetotaller, whose other life was spent at the gym body-building. He undid a button on Luc's white staff shirt which was a size too small. 'Remember, Cristal or Krug if you're asked your favourite.' They were the two most expensive on the list.

The bar was always packed with raucous men whose mobiles went off constantly. After the first night, her arms ached from opening bottles, her legs from standing and her face from forcing it to smile. Her dreams were full of pin-stripes and chalk-stripes and the sound of explosions. At first she felt as embarrassed as if she'd wandered into the gents or a rugger club locker room by mistake. Luc learned fast to turn a blind eye to the leers at her cleavage and backside, and a deaf ear to some disgustingly sexist jokes.

429

'The tips are amazing,' she marvelled at the end of the first week, collapsing on to the sofa.

'Bet that's almost what your punters say.' Alex raised an eyebrow. 'Buttons fallen off your shirt?' Luc looked down and blushed peony. 'The titbit.'

'I'm not.'

'Sure. How many propositions tonight?'

'Three.' She took out the business cards that had been pressed into her hand. 'Thank God I'm not stuck in an office with any of them. All equally repulsive. House meths, not Krug.'

'So, they'd be in with a chance if they were Krug?'

'No,' she protested.

'Sounds like it. That place is corrupting you.'

'It's a job.'

'It's a job dependent on your tits and ass oiling up to letches earning obscene amounts of money.'

Luc got up and made herself a cheese sandwich. It did seem almost immoral that she could earn so much just by opening bottles, wearing a tight shirt and being smiley. It didn't even feel much like work, she'd been too busy to be bored. Surely you were meant to study and train for years at something to get this sort of money?

'What's that?'

'Yeats.' Alex held up his book.

'One of Ella's favourites.' Luc felt a shadow of unease cloud her. It always happened whenever she thought of Ella. Ella had had a Yeats fest in February, curled up in front of the fire, sipping Bushmills. She'd told Luc to stop moaning about her lack of Valentine cards, and get reading. 'How would I go about getting an article in a paper or magazine?'

'Writing it would be helpful.' Alex put aside his anthology.

'I can't write it,' she yelped. 'Besides, it's more for publicity.'

'You're talking about a Press release. On?'

Luc hesitated. 'An artist.' Close enough.

'News or feature?'

'Feature, I suppose.'

'Out with it, Luc.' After she had explained, he sat back, studying her. 'So there's hope for you yet. For a moment back there I thought you were turning into a money-grabbing slut.'

Luc threw a cushion at him.

'Well, stop getting your tits out for the lads. Nice as they are.'

'The lads?'

'What else?' He picked up his book.

On Sunday evening Alex flew to Berne to cover a conference about a strip of disputed territory in the Balkans. After driving him to the airport, Luc let herself into the empty flat and went upstairs to his study. Turning on the computer, her eyes stared at the blank screen. What had Alex said? Short sentences, short paragraphs. The important stuff at the start. Besides, the photographs would speak for themselves.

Thinking of who might end up reading her writing, her brain seized up with fear. She was like a novice, recipeless cook making a soufflé for Delia Smith.

Dear Applicant,
I regret to inform you that . . .

Luc read and re-read the rejection letter. It was the third she'd opened that morning. Over the past weeks the images in her head of her new life as an art college student had been so real that she had never properly considered the possibility that she might not get in. She had been the star in her own movie, *Educating Luc.*

Screwing up the letter into a ball, she threw it against the hall wall. The film should've been *Fantasia.*

All the buoyant optimism she'd felt for weeks about her future seeped out of her. As flat as a punctured tyre, she was back on the hard shoulder, while everyone else was speeding past her in the fast lane knowing exactly where they were headed.

'Shit. Shit, shit, shit.'

Tears of misery and self-pity pricked her eyes. She tugged at her hair, which made her feel worse. Would nothing ever come right? Was she only good for unjamming photocopiers and falling in love with bastards who were as good as married?

A bulky envelope was still wedged in the letter-box. It was addressed to Alex and Luc guessed it might be a copy of the magazine. Suddenly, her plan seemed futile, silly. As futile as everything else she'd attempted.

She was no good at anything or for anyone. Perhaps she was cursed? Everyone she met only seemed to have bad luck as soon as they set eyes on her. Alex and his book, Tim and his projects. Even that day in the kitchen department of Peter Jones, Quentin the Zit had been complaining that his golf had gone off the boil.

She tore off the brown wrapping. The magazine was so glossy it seemed varnished. On the cover was a bathroom, looking like something out of a film set. It was chalky white and huge, empty apart from an old-fashioned claw-footed bath and a classical fireplace. A minimalist's interpretation of a corner of delapidated Venetian palazzo. The only colour were the flowers, the colour of lapis lazuli.

'If you don't mind.' Luc edged sideways to escape the hand feeling her backside. She opened the champagne bottle and poured out three glasses. She knew the trio of suits were eyeing her up and down as they dragged on their torpedo-sized cigars. Two glasses and the lowliest currency dealer had delusions he was Sir James Goldsmith. This lot were sweating their way to their fourth bottle.

'Size matters,' said the Hand, winking at Luc, while waving his cigar suggestively. His tie was as askew as his focus.

'Really,' said Luc, plonking the bottle into the ice bucket. 'Then I'd better get you some more peanuts.'

Pressing her way through the raucous throng to the bar, she rolled her eyes. Since her shift had started, she'd been asked how she liked her eggs, 'So I know what to cook you for breakfast,' and told that it was her lucky decade. 'Why? Because you've met me.' Her smile was as fixed and unreal as if she'd been caught out when the wind changed.

'A bottle of the Widow,' brayed a midget in chalkstripes, clicking his fingers at Luc. 'Chop chop.'

'And I'd like to chop, chop your dick off,' murmured Luc through her smile.

Five minutes later she was aware that a fleshy fifty-year-old was staring at her over his glass. He stood alone at the bar. His pudgy, sweaty hands matched his fat, wet lips. He beckoned her over and pointed at the drinks list. He smiled confidingly. 'I fancy something else.'

Luc reached for a list. 'Your choice, sir. By the glass, we have . . .'

His finger ran up and down the prices on the list. 'Where would you be? How about here?' He'd stopped at £100. 'Or here?' £150. 'Not here, surely?' £350. 'Don't flatter yourself. Settle on this, shall we? Cash.'

As his words sank in, Luc gasped in outrage. Smile broadening, she leaned forward. 'Fuck right off, right now. Sir. Or shall I call security?'

Alex was unsympathetic. He glowered over a copy of the *Economist*. 'If you work in a zoo, expect to have trouble with the animals.'

'Which would you be? The bear with the sore head?' snarled back Luc. 'What's wrong?'

'Book. Another rejection.'

'And two more for me today.'

'The losers' trifecta. Great. By the way, you stink of cigar smoke.'

Luc stomped upstairs to have a shower. Her ears were still ringing from the noise at the bar, the smell of smoke seemed to be oozing from her pores. She told herself that every job had its off days, that it had to be better than unjamming photocopiers, that the tips were great. That it wasn't a dead end . . .

Her dreams of art college had given her a mental safety net. She was a student, really, not a bottle-opener hired for her looks and ability to smile non-stop. Rejection by every single college that she'd applied to had ended those illusions. She was being slapped awake to reality, which included repulsive creeps wanting to buy her.

Ella would've been able to empathise with her sense of disgust, then cheered her up. 'Look on the bright side. It's character-building. Two hundred and fifty quid. And that's without lowering yourself to haggle.' They'd have ended up by having a laugh.

Luc imagined Ella entwined on the sofa with Yannick, both glowing with companionable contentment. By now, she'd be speaking French all the time, he'd be amazed by her progress, but Ella was clever, quick. There'd be nothing in the Doll's House to remind her that Luc had ever lived there. Anything Luc had mistakenly left behind would've been thrown out. Even the spices in the kitchen. Ella had always hated cinnamon. Perhaps she'd move to the country, fulfilling Janie's wishes for a family house packed with children and dogs. Perhaps not.

Wherever Ella was going, Luc knew there was no place for her any more. She was as good as dead.

In mourning for their friendship, there hadn't been much grief left over for Lorenzo. Even the photographs of his house in the magazine had left her oddly unmoved. She knew Tim the architect, not Lorenzo the client. Lorenzo was as much a stranger to her as any Fifth Avenue socialite whose penthouse was featured in *World of Interiors*. A stranger she'd thought of as so perfect that somehow after meeting him she'd lost a job, her home, her best friend and even her hair, all as casually as if she'd mislaid a thimble.

She'd had colour copies of the photographs of Lorenzo's house made at a print shop. After she'd sent off the eight sets, Luc had chucked the magazine into a litter bin on the street outside the post office. In trying to make reparation to Tim, she was tying the last loose end left hanging from her disastrous liaison with Lorenzo.

'Chain yourself to the railings, take the principals hostage, bomb the colleges, anything. Just do something.' Alex took his exasperation out on his Sugar Puffs which he chewed with unnecessary force.

'They've turned me down.'

'Someone might drop out. There's a couple of weeks left before term starts. Talk to them, inspire them with your fervour. It's worth a try.' He stared at Luc, slumped on the sofa in abject misery. 'It's better than your backside wearing out my upholstery.'

Half an hour later, Luc found herself at the Tube station buying a one-day travel pass. She planned her zig-zag across London. First stop, Goldsmiths.

Footsore and thirsty, it was almost four-thirty when she trudged up Ladbroke Grove. The Notting Art School was ugly, a grey concrete slab of sixties brutalism. The administration office was down a dingy corridor. Luc wondered if she ought to bother.

'We're closing,' announced the girl emerging from the office behind the desk. Despite the magenta spiked hair, her tone was as jobsworth as a doctor's receptionist in blue crimplene.

'You close at four forty-five. It's only four thirty-nine,' pleaded Luc.

'That clock's three minutes slow.'

'Then you're not closing for another three minutes. Please.'

'Come back tomorrow.'

'It will only take . . .' Luc shook her head in despair. 'Fine.' Why get into a row when she knew the answer? She'd heard it repeatedly from every office she'd visited. According to the records, the tutors had seen her work. No, they hadn't given any feedback. Waste of their time and hers. There were no places. Try next year.

'An expenses form, please.' A short woman with a blonde bob and giant pink-framed glasses bustled up to the desk. She was weighed down with a pile of books and folders.

'Too late.'

'I beg your pardon?'

'We're closed.'

'You can't manage the five paces to the filing cabinet?'

'Come back tomorrow.' The magenta spikes turned off the light and disappeared back into the office, slamming the door behind her in triumph.

Luc and the blonde stood blinking in the half-light, staring in disbelief at the closed door. 'They get worse, don't they?' A book fell off her precarious pile. Luc picked it up, then two more fell off. A few minutes later Anna Klein was inviting her into her study for a cup of tea.

Dr Klein had seen Luc's work and said she should sail through the application process for the next academic year. Luc explained that she wanted to start now and was gently reproved for being unreasonable.

'So, twelve months,' she told Alex later. 'I guess it's nice to know I'm so promising.'

'Her words?' He whistled. 'That's great. Glad you got off the sofa?'

'Very. Thanks.'

'I was about to get out the cattle prod. Tomorrow, the travel agents.'

Luc frowned. 'What for?'

'A Round-the-World ticket. You've got a year, use it productively.'

'Me? Go round the world? Who with?'

Alex rolled his eyes. 'By yourself, of course.'

'Alone? Go round the world on my own?' Luc was horror-struck. 'You're joking. I couldn't. I can't even go to the cinema alone.'

'That's pathetic. Worried that everyone will think sad fuck, no friends?'

'No,' she protested, then nodded sheepishly. 'Round the world? I couldn't. Look at the mess Ella and I got ourselves into in Greece. And that's Europe.' Luc knew she'd end up in a cooking pot or being sacrificed in a pagan ceremony. Or in that prison, the Bangkok Hilton. There'd be no Liz and Tim renting nice villas halfway up the Congo, not unless Condé Nast *Traveller* magazine had recommended one. 'Besides, I'm too broke to take a year out travelling.'

'How old are you?'

'Twenty-five.'

'Easy. You can get a working visa for Australia.'

'Australia?' Where people got boiled in the heat on the sides of the roads, or taken by sharks, or eaten by crocodiles. Red deserts and a brutal history and melancholy gum trees and bush-fires. And jambucks and coolabahs, whatever they were. And nice men like Alex and great wine and a city on the world's most beautiful harbour . . . 'Australia?'

That night Luc found it hard to sleep. The more she thought of going away, the more appealing the idea became. What did she have to stay in London for? To kill a year in a series of scummy jobs? Summer was over, in a matter of weeks it would be dark at four o'clock. Why not escape that never-ending grey gloom of the English winter when the clouds are so low they squash everyone's spirits?

She couldn't stay with Alex indefinitely, she'd be flat hunting again. Bar work? She could do that anywhere. Even un-jamming photocopiers might be more tolerable 12,000 miles away. Why not be homeless and jobless in the sunshine where the living was easy and the natives, Alex assured her, were friendly?

Were her roots so deep that it was impossible to transplant herself? What was there to keep her in London? A home? A career? A best friend? A lover?

It would soon be summer in Sydney, where the light bounced off the harbour water and she could travel to work by ferry, passing the Opera House with its sea-shell roof.

The following morning, passport in her bag, Luc headed for the Aldwych and the Australian High Commission.

On Sunday, Alex told Luc to get ready, she was coming to brunch.

'Can't afford it.' Engrossed in yet another soap star scandal, she didn't look up. With all the newspapers scattered around, the sitting room looked like a recycling depot.

'My shout. Stop reading that rubbish.'

'You bought it.'

'Duty, not necessity. Come on, Luc.'

'Must I?' The rain was beating hard against the window. Luc felt as if she were snug inside Alex's BMW while it was going through a car-wash machine. She was planning a lazy day of doing the chores, watching the matinee and trying to sort out her wardrobe to see if anything was worth selling. She had a sinking feeling that even the charity shop might be sniffy about taking her stuff. 'Where?'

'Somewhere very stylish that does a brilliant cappuccino.'

'I need to wash my hair . . .'

'Stand outside with the shampoo. Come on.'

'Is this a set-up?' Luc wiped away the condensation and peered out into the drenched Kew street. Soggy leaves filled the gutters and splattered against the windscreen. 'No, Alex. No. I can't face them. Take me home.'

Too late. Tim was waving from the front door.

'You'll wear out your shoe leather,' said Alex, as Luc mumbled her greetings and wiped and rewiped her feet on the mat, even doing the twist to get off the water. She was frightened of leaving muddy footprints on the pristine wooden floor.

'Gosh, Luc, that haircut really suits you.' Tim smiled and gave her a hug.

'*Très gamine*,' said Liz. 'Next time try Michel, my man. Mention me and he'll do something about the price. Let's go through.'

Perched on the orange-cream sofa, Luc gulped back a Bloody Mary and peered about her, while Alex gave an update on his book. Although the *Observer* had been read and folded with origami precision, the lit fire in the sitting room and the smell of coffee and baking muffins lent a semblance of cosiness.

Liz bustled in and out of the kitchen, picking out a faded lily from the vase, putting on more Mozart, laying the dining table. She wasn't wearing her black polo neck sweater and faded black 501s, so much as stating 'design classics'.

'And your news, Luc?' Tim refilled her glass. 'Alex mentioned that you're going to art college.'

'Next year. Probably. I left it too late for this one.'

'Luc's off to Oz,' said Alex. 'Aren't you?'

She nodded. 'In November. For nine months or so.'

'Australia? Marvellous,' exclaimed Tim. 'Hear that, Liz?'

Liz smiled. 'Just in time for summer. Lucky thing. Can you put me in your suitcase?'

'Backpack.' Luc had bought one the day before. She'd sell anything that didn't fit in it. Everything she had in the world would be in it to start again on the other side of the world.

'Won't you get homesick?' asked Tim.

'No. I don't have a home to get sick about.' Luc sounded cool, matter of fact, but Liz and Tim exchanged uneasy glances.

'Change of scene does everyone good,' said Tim.

'Hope so.' Luc shrugged. Often, thinking of how she was putting herself into voluntary exile 12,000 miles away because she'd reached such a complete dead end was depressing. She stood up. 'Can I help?'

'You have helped. Sit down,' said Tim. 'We were going to do this later, weren't we, Liz? Where is it?'

'I'll get it.' Liz went to the kitchen and came back with a beautifully wrapped parcel. 'For you, Luc. To say thank you.'

'Me? Thank you? For what?' She was bewildered.

Tim smiled. 'For writing the most bizarre Press release that features editors have been sent in ages. Wednesday morning the phone didn't stop ringing.'

'Two interviews on Friday. Two more next week,' said Liz. 'And photographs of this place as well as Lorenzo's. Who's been incredibly nice about it. Most clients refuse point-blank.'

'*Home Beautiful* today, burglars tomorrow,' said Alex.

'An unhelpful myth.' Liz tssked. 'Anyway, Lorenzo couldn't have been more accommodating. He said he felt awful about the original article, how Tim hadn't been mentioned. Your work too, Luc?'

She shook her head, unable to speak. She didn't want to hear about a nice Lorenzo with a conscience, putting himself out to help Tim. He was a cold, rich bastard who'd broken her heart. Who'd wrapped her in magic, then left her to drown in sorrow. Who was getting married to Amelia, a very clever and rather beautiful real-life princess.

'Open it,' urged Alex.

Luc tried to smile as she undid the ribbon with fumbling fingers, remembering the last present she'd opened. A ring? A tiara perhaps? It had been the best chocolate cake she'd ever tasted. He was used to the best, men like him didn't trade down. 'It's gorgeous,' she gasped, pulling out the violet cashmere. A pashmina. She stroked it like a cat. Ella had a drawer full of them, a silky rainbow.

'Put it on then,' said Alex. He whistled. 'That colour's amazing on you.'

'Liz is so clever,' said Tim. 'Her choice, of course.'

Luc felt overwhelmed. It was the nicest gesture anyone had made in a long time. 'I don't deserve it,' she protested.

'Luc, you might've turned my career around,' said Tim. 'I should've done what you did ages ago, but my confidence was shot to pieces.' He raised his glass. 'Here's to keeping the faith.'

The brunch was delicious, homemade blueberry muffins, waffles, scrambled eggs, coffee. Luc was miles away. Like picking at a chickenpox scab despite being warned not to, she wanted to ask about Lorenzo. Had he mentioned her? Was he married yet? Perhaps Tim and Liz were invited to the wedding . . . The muffin turned to sand in her mouth.

'Ghost gone over your grave?' Tim squeezed her hand.

'Sorry.' Luc was suddenly scared. Lorenzo had suddenly been as real as if he were sitting beside her. Was she always going to be haunted by him? Was her mind never going to be hers again?

'She hasn't called you, has she?' asked Liz.

'Who?'

'Wake up, Luc. Marina. No?'

'It's not like you to turn down business,' said Alex. 'Don't on my account.'

'It's inappropriate. As I told her.' Liz began to gather up plates. 'I wouldn't be able to look the husband in the face. And he'd be the one writing the cheques. I'd feel grubby.'

'How's her golf?' asked Alex.

'Improving. She's going out every afternoon. It was like talking to Nick Faldo. Golf?' Liz shuddered. 'The clothes are so naff.'

'Diamond-patterned sweaters, Jag in the car-park, and a G and T for the lady wife.' Alex pulled a face at Luc. 'Is my love life always going to be as much of a disaster zone as yours?'

After everything had been cleared away, Liz asked Luc to come upstairs to her study. The thank-you letter for her sketches of the villa was somewhere. As Liz closed the door, Luc wondered what she wanted.

Ella.

Liz was desperately worried. As soon as Ella had called the day before, Liz had known something was very wrong. The whole terrible story had come out, Ella sounding strangely calm as if she were sedated. Liz had gone straight to the Doll's House but Ella had refused to let her in. She'd looked dreadful, as if she'd been crying for a month. Her hair hadn't been washed, she was terribly thin in her dirty track-pants and a vest that looked as if she'd spilt wine down it weeks before.

'We all know that Ella has always been a lousy housekeeper, but she always had plenty of zest. Yesterday, when I saw her, her batteries had run out, all her life had gone.'

Ella had begged Liz to take the car back. When Liz had refused, the door had been slammed in her face.

'What terrible story? What about Yannick? What about the baby?' Luc asked.

Liz was horrorstruck. Didn't Luc know? When was the last time she'd seen Ella for goodness sake? She'd known that there was some sort of falling out, that's why Luc had moved in with Alex, but she assumed she and Ella were still in contact.

'You haven't spoken? For more than a month? Before she went to France? You don't know what happened?'

Ella had miscarried.

Liz became almost hysterical. 'She spent almost a week on her own in hospital in Nice. She had some sort of fever, blood poisoning. At one point the doctors were wondering if she'd pull through.'

'A miscarriage?' Luc repeated in a whisper. The rain was beating down so hard it seemed to be trying to force its way in.

'No. It couldn't . . . Not to Ella.' Healthy, strong, vibrant Ella, so full of life. Luc's eyes narrowed. 'On her own? Why was she on her own in hospital? Where was Yannick?'

'Vanished. Sailed away on that yacht. You know. The one from Greece. That's right, *Les Voiles Blanches*.'

After arriving in St Tropez, Ella had been dumped on Yannick's friend, Mimi, who was far from pleased by the pair of them turning up uninvited on her doorstep like unwanted strays. Mimi had entertained Ella while Yannick disappeared. He hadn't come back until five in the morning, then went off again immediately after breakfast. Ella assumed he'd gone to find a hotel . . .

'Madame?' Luc interrupted, her memory straining. Hadn't Henri said Madame lived in St Tropez? 'She owns *Les Voiles Blanches*. He'd seen her, hadn't he?'

Had Luc spoken to Yannick or something? How did she know?

'Just guessing.'

When he'd come back to the flat to collect his stuff, Ella and he had an enormous row. 'He said some truly vile things to her, then just disappeared. It was the last she saw of him. She was still dazed when she left the flat and the stupid girl was walking down the stairs as she was trying to put on her backpack. She slipped. That's what she thinks caused it. An hour later she was bleeding . . .'

It was only three o'clock but it already seemed to be getting dark. The wipers couldn't clear away the water from the windscreen fast enough. The car radio reported flooding. Luc asked Alex to drop her off at the entrance to the Mews. Ella was in, she'd answered the phone, although she'd immediately hung up on Luc.

Luc walked into the Mews feeling like a sightseer. A gawper on a tour of where the rich lived. She could almost hear a guide saying it. 'As you can see, ladies and gentlemen, in this particular part of London you don't get much square footage for your seven-figure investment.'

She'd forgotten its peace, its serenity. No litter, no graffiti, no abandoned old cars. Just two rows of pastel-coloured houses set either side of the cobblestones. And an unhappy girl called Ella with her million-pound Doll's House to play in.

Luc went up to the front door and rang the bell. She waited, listening for footsteps on the stairs. Instead there was silence. She rang again, then stepped backwards and peered up at the sitting-room windows. She was certain she caught a glimpse of Ella, but the rain was pouring into her eyes.

She rang again, only to be answered once more by silence. She hammered on the door with her fists, then called through the letter-box. What should she do? She had to see Ella, but she couldn't smash the door down. Standing in the pouring rain, Luc wondered if she should break a window, then got out her phone. She was answered by the machine. 'Ella. I know you're there. And I'm going to wait out here until I see you.'

She went to the middle of the shiny cobblestones, right in Ella's line of sight if she looked outside.

Eyes fixed on the window, Luc stood sentry. The rain was falling hard, beating like shrapnel on her bare head. Water was seeping through her mac and was trickling down the back of her neck. She didn't move a muscle except to blink away the drops.

After ten minutes Luc called and spoke to the machine again. 'Look out of the window, Ella. I'll stay here all night if I have to.'

Ella finally opened the door. She threw a towel at Luc then stomped back up the stairs.

Sneezing, Luc struggled out of her sopping mac and kicked off her shoes. The dye had run into her feet. She wiped the water off her face and rubbed at her hair. Her fingers were crinkly, waterlogged. Her clothes must have shrunk after more than twenty minutes of drenching. Feeling achy, she climbed the stairs.

Ella was on the sofa, huddled under a duvet. She looked dreadful, gaunt and hollow-eyed. She stared at Luc, as if she were trying to work out where she knew her from. 'You're leaving puddles on the floor.'

'Sorry. Can I borrow some clothes?' Ella nodded and Luc went up to her bedroom. It was a chaotic jumble of clothes, books, cassettes and half-empty mugs. Mouldy apple cores, peach stones and strawberry stalks were scattered across the bedside table. Luc went to the cupboard and found a pair of track pants, some socks and a sweater. She gathered up as many mugs as she could carry and took them down to the kitchen. 'Coffee?'

'Have some, then go.'

As the coffee dripped through the machine, Luc tried to clear up some of the mess. The kitchen stank. She hauled the overflowing rubbish sack out of the bin, took it downstairs, and threw it outside. Opening the window, she began loading the dishwasher with dirty crockery. The milk, like almost everything else in the fridge, was way past its sell-by date.

Placing a mug beside Ella, she caught sight of the drinks tray. Her whisky was still there, Lorenzo's brand. She splashed some into her coffee. 'Want some?' Shaking her head, Ella shrank back, like a vampire seeing a cross. Luc sat cross-legged on the floor beside the fire. 'Liz told me what happened. Have you seen a doctor since you got back?'

'I'm fine. Ex-mother doing well. A1. No long-term problems.'

'Physically.' Luc sipped. 'What about the rest?'

'Fine.'

'Really? Then how come you look so awful? You should see a counsellor.'

'Really?' Ella sounded mocking. Her eyes finally met Luc's.

'And your life is so wonderful, Luc, that you can blithely hand out advice like Smarties? How is Lorenzo?'

Luc looked into the black of her coffee. 'He's still the sonnets, the symphonies and the waves crashing on the beach.'

'The one great true love of your life then.'

'That's Lorenzo.' Luc sighed. 'He's getting married. To Amelia. A real-life princess.'

'Shit happens.'

Luc recoiled as if she'd been slapped. Why was she bothering? Ella had read the rites and buried their friendship. They were like strangers to one another. She might as well say her farewells. 'What happened with me and Yannick was the worst mistake . . .'

'Actually, Luc, what happened with *me* and Yannick was the worst mistake of my life.' Ella pulled the duvet around her more tightly, her fingernails were bitten down to the quick. 'He was only after the money. I guess I suspected the afternoon I saw my broker, when I said I was at a yoga class. For him it must have been over when he was snooping, pretending to look for fuse wires and screwdrivers. He found the Trust stuff.'

'So?' Surely exact knowledge of Ella's wealth would be an added attraction for most men? She caught Ella looking at her as if she were a half-wit. 'Sorry, I don't have a Trust fund to know about.'

'Alex's chippiness must be contagious.' Ella pulled a face. 'My grandfather might have been rich, but he wasn't stupid. Yannick thought he could marry me and then get half. Like Liz's mother thought Pa might have some claim on Janie's estate. The Trust is watertight. No court in the world can break it. No outsiders or ex-husbands can get their hands on a penny. Or, in Yannick's case, a centime.'

'He really went off with Madame?'

'The sixty-four-million-dollar question. In fact, he claimed that's less than she's worth. I can't compete with that. I don't want to. She's welcome to him. She's got a new skipper, Henri's in the Bahamas somewhere.'

'How do you know?'

'Yannick called the yacht. The moment we got to St Tropez. Pretending to try and get his wages. He just wanted to find out if she was in town.' Ella scowled at Luc. 'He admitted he took advantage of you. *Carpe diem*. Seized the day. Or rather, seized Lucasta.' Ella's eyes were as cold as flint. 'I'll never forgive you for letting him.'

Luc swallowed hard. 'He was a bastard . . .'

'And you were a bitch. You can't be trusted. You blew it, Luc.' She stared with revulsion, as if she'd just come across a corpse in the undergrowth. 'Why are you here? To feel my pain, or something? You can't, so just fuck off.'

'Ella, please . . .'

'In fact, you're just making it worse. I don't need you here to remind me how I messed up. Large.'

'A miscarriage isn't messing up. It was a terrible, terrible accident.'

In the silence, Luc got up to refill her coffee mug. When she squeezed Ella's shoulder, Ella flinched and shied away. In the kitchen she began hunting through the cupboards. Ella ordered her to stop. 'I was going to cook something. You look as if you haven't eaten properly for days.'

'Luc, piss off. Why pretend?'

'Pretend?'

'You act as if nothing has happened, but you're worse, far worse, than Yannick. You committed the biggest act of treachery, the biggest betrayal. Trying to screw your best friend's man, even if he was a shit. You should live in a trailer park and go on Jerry Springer.'

Luc's ears smarted from the assault. Her hands shook as she poured more whisky into her coffee. 'What are your plans?'

'Plans?' Ella sounded as if Luc was mad.

'For the future. You've got to move forward. What about this Master's degree?'

Ella sprang to her feet. 'Are you going now?'

'I'm trying to help you.'

'Then leave. Shouldn't you think about helping yourself? Or are you going to spend the rest of your life moaning about temping and pining for Lorenzo?'

Luc slammed down her mug. 'Actually, Ella, since you ask — which is very rare for someone as completely self-obsessed as you — I'm not temping any more. I'm going to Australia and then I'm going to art college. At the moment I'm working in a bar where I earn a huge amount of money just by smiling. Remember that? Smiling? You should try it again one day.'

For the briefest moment Ella looked stunned. 'My, my. Hasn't a lot happened in the last month?'

'Maybe it comes from sharing a flat with someone ambitious who actually has to work and wants to achieve something in life.' Luc snatched up her bag. 'I'm very sorry about your miscarriage, but you're right. I should be going. This is getting us nowhere.'

'We've got nowhere to go, Luc. We reached the end about a month ago.'

The next morning the rain had died to drizzle. Alex amazed Luc by being completely on Ella's side. 'She's been through hell, you helped start her journey. And you thought you could just waltz in dishing out tea and sympathy and be forgiven?'

'I went to help. God, she can be monstrous and vile and hurtful when she wants.'

'No one who loves Yeats can be vile.' He finished his Sugar Puffs. 'What's her number? I'll give her a call.'

Luc was dumbfounded. 'What are you, Alex? A one-man emotional clear-up operation?'

'What's the problem? Tim and Liz are very worried. They

can't get through to her, not with all that ancient baggage in the way. He suggested I offer a shoulder.'

A magnificent shoulder, as Ella had once said. Luc raised an eyebrow, gazing at Alex afresh. A tall, broad, very attractive man, who was bright and well read, whose personality was as strong as Ella's. 'Thought you couldn't stand one another.'

'I once found you a complete pain in the whatsits too, titbit.'

'My shirt is done up to my collar these days. Well, almost.'

The skies matched Luc's mood. She would spend the morning going through her bank statements as well as her clothes. If the account looked healthily black rather than merely grey, she'd bring her departure date forward.

The horrible showdown with Ella, the rain, the fact that almost half an hour of daylight was being lost each week and the hideously depressing thought of two more months of being smiley was making up her mind: she wanted to get to Sydney as fast as possible. She didn't plan to send Ella a postcard.

'Shit.' Yesterday's dress and cardigan were still at Ella's. She had Ella's stuff. What could they do? Arrange for neutral observers to be there as they did a swap in the middle of Chelsea Bridge? It was worse than getting a divorce. She gazed down at the pile of clothes, hating each garment.

The only thing that she might possibly be able to sell was the hat Lorenzo had given her. When they'd walked across the park and into Bond Street. And gone to the gallery. 'Dollars or sterling?' Before they'd fled from the restaurant because . . . Luc willed herself to stop. He was getting married. To Amelia. The princess. And the hat was probably worthless after she'd hacked off its ribbons.

She was crying because she'd destroyed something so beautiful, wasn't she? Not for the man who gave it to her. Swiping away her tears, she heard the second post dropping on the mat downstairs.

*

449

'What do I do?' wailed Luc.

'Accept, of course.'

'But what about Australia?'

Alex rolled his eyes. 'Sweets, it's been there for hundreds of millions of years. It's not going to go away, is it? Go in the Christmas holidays.'

'But . . .'

'You never know what's going on in education. Courses get scrapped. Grants get cut. Tuition fees might go up. You've been offered a place. Take it. When do you start?'

'Two weeks.'

'Where's the champagne?'

'Back at the bar. Where it stays.' Luc shuddered. 'I've gone off the stuff. It must be like working at a chocolate factory.' She cleared her throat and twisted her hands. 'The thing is, one of the reasons I . . . er . . . can I stay on here? Tell me I can't and let's get it over with.'

'You want to?'

'Sure. If I can.'

'You can.' Alex hesitated. 'For now. I've sort of promised your room to a guy from back home.' He scowled. 'I've got used to the rent. I need the rent, especially with a book deal looking as elusive as the Scarlet Pimpernel.'

'When's he arriving?' Luc's heart was sinking. But she'd meet people at college, wouldn't she?

'November. Don't worry. We'll work something out before then. Maybe you and Ella will work something out before then.'

'Did you call her?'

'Only to be snubbed. At first, anyway. She asked if I were a recusant in my previous life, harbouring traitor priests who deserve to be burnt at the stake. Reference to you, by any chance? God, she can be crushing.'

'Told you.'

'When Ella gave me a dissertation on Yeats this afternoon, brutally highlighting my ignorance, I thought, what am I doing?

Why am I bothering? Why are Tim and Liz bothering? Chasing round after some spoilt slacker. Let her rot in her own self-pity.'

'Harsh.'

'I know. But I hate seeing waste. She needs to channel all that energy, all that intelligence. She's the original lost girl, isn't she?'

Luc looked at him, bemused. 'She once said we needed mentors, not men.' She added drily, 'Perhaps you can be Ella's.'

'Perhaps she can be mine.'

'Really?' Not exactly pleased by his suggestion, Luc tried to sound neutral.

'She said she wanted to read my manuscript.'

'You fell for that?'

'Of course. I was completely charmed.'

Luc raised an eyebrow. 'Did you send it?'

'She sent a bike to collect it.'

Work was sending Alex to Belfast for a few days. After he arranged the ticket, he left a message for his agent. When he rang off, he was in such a foul, grumpy mood that Luc wished he was leaving that very minute.

The more she thought about Ella and Alex being in contact, the more it unsettled her. Ella was clearly happy to pretend that Luc had never existed, but was equally content that their lives should continue to overlap. Luc felt out in the cold. She was getting divorced only to find the ex moving in next door and inviting all the joint friends to the house-warming.

She told herself to be more charitable, be more Alexy. Ella had been through hell, had suffered terribly. A miscarriage, falling for a gold-digging bastard like Yannick. Money didn't cushion blows like that. And even Ella's money, as Alex pointed out, had only come to her from a terrible loss.

Luc wondered if she should call Ella, but it would be a waste of ten pence and her breath. The unquestioning trust between them had gone when she had started to make love to an imaginary Lorenzo.

Their friendship couldn't be put back together, it was as

smashed as a crystal glass dropped on granite. Ella had read the rites and buried it. Luc was the one in mourning, Luc was bereft.

Luc hesitated before signing the acceptance form for college, then rushed off to post it, only to hesitate again in front of the red pillar box. As the traffic rushed past, buffeting her, drizzle began to fall. In her agitation she didn't notice.

Was she doing the right thing? Perhaps she should ask if she could defer her entry and go to Australia after all? Perhaps the only solution was to run away?

But Lorenzo would be on the other side of the world too. He'd be in her mind for ever. He was her shadow, except he was there in the dark as well. In her sleep, controlling her dreams. The sonnets and the symphonies and the waves crashing on the beach. And every chocolate cake and every piece by Mozart and every hat and every walk in the park.

No matter how hard she tried to shut it out, Lorenzo's image returned to haunt her. She was too scared to admit to anyone that she was still obsessed with someone who'd caused so much destruction, who was lost to her for ever. Alex would send for the men in white coats. Sometimes Luc felt like calling them herself.

A Royal Mail van pulled up and the driver jumped out, startling her. He opened the box.

'In here or not?' he demanded, holding out the sack to her.

Luc looked down at the letter in her hand. She'd call the college and ask if she could defer. Lorenzo would melt away in the Sydney sunshine. She shook her head. 'Not.'

'Dear John, is it? Telling the boyfriend to sling his hook?'

'He's slung it.' Luc sighed.

The postman looked Luc up and down. 'Bonkers.'

'Probably.'

'Not you. Him.'

She looked down at the letter. She'd walk a million miles for one of his smiles. She'd pass up the chance of a lifetime to cross the world in her desperation to be rid of a ghost. Someone who was lost to her for ever anyway.

'Here,' said Luc, and dropped the envelope into the mailbag.

A note from Alex greeted Luc on her return from work. 'Quentin – is he for real? – called. Been yonks, vair, vair eager to see you. Fumigate the house when he leaves. Back Saturday.'

Luc crumpled up the paper and grimaced. 'Thanks, Ella.' Ella must've given her number to Quentin, the most boring estate agent in the world, whose jumbo insensitivity matched his jumbo cords.

Quentin, coming back. Luc froze in horror. Quentin coming back into her life like a she-elephant, trampling all over her with his bullying good nature and Monty Python quotes and devotion to rugby and the Tories.

In the middle of the night, Luc woke up. She was certain the phone had rung but there was silence. If anyone had called at two o'clock in the morning, they too had decided it could wait.

'Do you want, Lucasta?'

It was four o'clock the following afternoon. The garden with its eddies of dead leaves looked bedraggled after another drenching. Luc had spent the day hanging around trying to sort out a student loan. She'd got soaked on the walk home, where she had five minutes to change before dashing out into the rain again to get to work.

Luc's heart stopped. She sank on to the sofa, feeling giddy. Clutching the mobile, her hands shook. 'Wh-wh-what?' she whispered. 'Lorenzo?'

'Are you busy?'

Luc shook herself out of her daze. 'I'm leaving for work and I've got to change and . . . Are you in London?'

'Yes. Can we meet? Work? Are you on a night shift?'

'I'm working at a bar,' croaked Luc. She could almost hear her heart thumping. 'In the City and I'm going to be late . . .'

'Which bar? I'll pick you up from there when you've finished.'

'Charlie's . . . As in a Champagne Charlie.' Anger suddenly flashed through her like an electric shock. 'Aren't you married?'

'Not yet. No.'

He sounded infuriatingly amused.

'And how is Amelia?' spat Luc. 'The princess.'

'Very well, thank you. I'd prefer to have this conversation when I see you.'

'Suppose I don't want to see you?'

'But you do, don't you?'

Luc gasped, outraged. 'No. No I don't.'

'Cross your heart?'

'Fuck off, Lorenzo . . .'

'Cross your heart.' He repeated, laughing.

'It's not funny,' screamed Luc. 'You walk away and leave me to drown and just as I've saved myself you call up and, and, and . . .'

'Do you want?' he interrupted.

'Want what? Oh shit.' The other phone was ringing. 'Hold on.' Luc threw down the mobile and dashed to answer it. A minute later she was gasping that she'd call him back.

In the cab, Luc huddled forward on her seat willing the driver to go faster. Up ahead he was moaning about the rain, saying it always made the traffic ten times worse. She wished he'd shut up and concentrate. The sky was battleship-grey, the Thames sludgy. All colour seemed to have abandoned the world. As they were forced to a halt by a jam on Chelsea bridge, Luc was silently screaming with frustration.

Liz had been so panic-stricken, she'd hardly been able to speak. She was in Glasgow, with Tim. Ella had just called her. A sobbing Ella, sobbing so hard she could hardly get the words out, asking what was the point, she was so useless and worthless. And that she was sorry about being such a bitch for all these years.

'Then she hung up. She was saying goodbye, Luc. It was as if she's planning to do something terrible . . .'

Luc's insides had turned to ice. All thoughts of Lorenzo forgotten, she told Liz she was on her way round to Ella's. Grabbing her bag, dashing back for her mobile, she headed out into the street and sprinted up to the main road. Her eyes scoured the traffic for a taxi as she tried to calm down Liz.

'Here's a cab. I'll be there in fifteen minutes. No, don't call the police . . . Positive . . . I'm sure Ella's fine . . .'

'Something's very wrong. Oh God, she's not going to take an overdose, is she? She was so desperate. Why am I here? I feel so helpless.'

That the normally cool, composed Liz sounded it unnerved Luc still more. Promising she'd call back, Luc then tried to ring Ella but there was no reply. Not even the machine. Luc let the phone ring and ring and ring, imagining it echoing round the Doll's House, too late for Ella to hear. Panic made it hard for Luc to breathe. She could picture Ella taking pill after pill or lying in a bath with a razor at her wrists. Ella comforted by poetry which made the terrible sublime. Ella looking so gaunt and unhappy and dead-eyed on that Sunday afternoon.

Chapter Sixteen

'Prison, Luc. They might send me to prison.'

Ella was shivering, huddled in a sopping deck-chair on the roof terrace, her blonde hair in rat's tails. The honeysuckle was battered, forlorn.

'Is that what your solicitor said?'

Ella nodded. 'It's a possibility. He gave the impression it would be justified. The bastard's a constipated, starchy Scot. Very wee free and proper. He rather regrets having me as a client.'

Luc was horrified. 'He's going to do his best for you tomorrow, isn't he?'

'Miss Parr.' Ella mimicked a Morningside accent. 'If you are questioning my professional competence perhaps you ought to find someone else to represent you.' She shivered again. 'It's too late to find anyone else. My life's in his hands.'

'Inside. Now,' ordered Luc. 'I'm running you a bath. I'll get some food organised. And call a glazier.' She had smashed the downstairs bedroom window to get in.

Ella looked up at Luc, her eyes pleading. 'Will you come with me tomorrow?'

'Of course I'm coming with you. And I'm staying here tonight.'

Ella clutched Luc's hand, tears running down her face.

'Thanks, Luc. Thanks. I tried to call you last night, but I thought you'd never want to speak to me again . . .'

'Sssh.' She pulled Ella to her feet. 'Let's think about what you're going to wear.'

As the bath was running, down in Ella's bedroom they examined her overflowing wardrobe, full of combats and fleeces and long, urban hippy dresses. 'I need some of your old frump. What's happened to it?'

'Dumped. Charity shop. Take out that nose ring.' Luc pulled out a garment bag. 'What's in here?'

'Some stuff of Janie's. She always said a good classic suit will get a woman through anything.'

'You're about the same size, aren't you?' Luc unzipped the bag and gasped. 'It's Chanel. Try it.' Ella hesitated. 'You can't go to court in combats and flip-flops.'

Ella kicked off her trainers. As she wriggled out of her trackpants and baggy sweater, Luc saw how horribly thin she'd got. Her ribs and shoulder blades stood out like a famine victim's.

'Blimey,' exclaimed Luc as Ella did up the black jacket's gilt buttons. 'It's perfect. Shoes and tights and you're going to look a million dollars.'

'Is that all?' said Ella wryly.

'Look in the mirror. The socks aren't ideal.' The black skirt came just above the knee, looking absurd next to Ella's fishermen's socks which concertinaed round her shins like a schoolboy's.

Ella turned round and gawped at her reflection. She stood one way and then the other, then peeled off her socks. 'I can't believe it's me.' She rummaged around the wardrobe and pulled out some black pumps and a leather box. Inside was a three-string choker. 'I could be in *Country Life*. The gel in pearls.'

'If you take out the nose ring.'

Ella suddenly seemed a touch more optimistic. While she was in the bath, Luc called a glazier, then rang Liz again. She'd called the first time as soon as she'd found Ella alive if far from well on the roof terrace.

'She's been arrested for drink-driving and driving while banned. She's in court tomorrow.'

'What?' Liz's shriek was so loud that Luc's ear hurt. 'When?'

'The day she came back from France.' Luc tried to keep her voice as matter of fact as possible. 'She drove the car back from the airport. Its back light was out. The police did a check, remember it was reported stolen? They were obviously suspicious and followed her into the Mews, breathalysed her and arrested her.'

'Has she got a solicitor?'

'Yes.'

'What's he told her?'

'That she could be sent to prison. Six months.'

'Prison? Ella in gaol? Stay there. Let me get a pen. You find the solicitor's number. She's not still using that Mr MacLeod is she? A son of the manse Scot. Teetotaller.'

'Sounds like it.'

'The very worst type to be defending something like this.'

'That's what Ella said.'

'I'm going to talk to him. If he doesn't do his best for Ella, I'll get him struck off.'

Luc wished she could eavesdrop. She tidied up the newspapers, emptied ashtrays. The dining table was littered with unpaid bills. The gas, water and electricity were about to be cut off. Calling Sim at the bar, fibbing about an attack of food poisoning, Luc shivered.

The Doll's House was a forlorn mess, made worse by damp, dismal chill. Going into the kitchen to turn on the central heating, she saw a beautiful bouquet of flowers in the sink among the chaos of crockery and dirty scrambled egg pans. It was as unexpected as a diamond in a sea of mud. Luc read the tiny card attached to the ribboned wrapping paper, *'Je reviens, si tu veux.'*

Luc jumped as if she'd seen a snake. Yannick. The man who'd come close to destroying them both. The rat who looked like Apollo, whose beautiful face masked his cynical, gold-digging soul. If she had poison, she would have given it to him.

'Madame must have made him walk the plank.' Gazing at the flowers, Ella looked as if she were about to be sick. 'Throw them out?'

'Yes.' They heard a knock on the door downstairs. 'Glazier.'

Luc sorted him out, vacuumed, cleaned the kitchen, ordered a pizza delivery and chivvied Ella into getting her paperwork in order and paying some bills. It was a relief to keep busy. She didn't want to think about tomorrow.

As they munched on pizza, the last supper as Ella called it, she said her place on the Master's course was confirmed. 'It was you. Coming round that Sunday. All your plans, how you were moving forward. Australia, art college. Gave me the kick up the backside I needed. Then I got the summons.'

'Liz is giving your solicitor what for.'

'Poor MacLeod. She's quite a star, isn't she? When I think of what she's put up with from me over the years. And despite it, she's there for me.'

'Sisters,' said Luc.

'She'll probably bake a cake with a file in it. If the *River Café Cookbook* has the recipe.'

'You won't be sent to prison,' said Luc, trying to sound convinced.

'Drink-driving while banned.' Ella shook her head in despair. 'MacLeod said they might make an example of me. I was so knocked out, I couldn't think straight. I hadn't had a drink for months. That mixed with the pills the hospital had given me. I got off the plane and just wanted to get home. Fast. And there was a mile-long queue for a cab.'

'You'd had a miscarriage. The court will be sympathetic.'

'No mitigating circumstances for drink-driving, apparently.' Ella sighed wearily. 'Oh God, the Press. If I'm sent down, they'll have a field day.'

'They can't . . .' began Luc, although she was clueless. Chelsea heiress in drink-drive shame. It sounded more than probable.

'What are you doing?' asked Ella as Luc got up.

'Calling Alex.' Infuriatingly, his mobile went straight to voice mail. Luc asked him to ring back, it was urgent. 'He's away. Belfast.'

'Nice, isn't he?' said Ella. 'No wonder Marina swapped golf clubs for a surfboard.'

'She's back with the golf clubs for good.'

'More fool her. The book's brilliant.'

Luc raised an eyebrow and suppressed a smile.

Ella mirrored her. 'Have you and he . . .?'

'No. Never.'

'Why not? He's got the most amazing body.'

'And heart,' said Luc. 'Alex and I missed our chance. It would now be like incest.'

'Is he seeing anyone?'

Ella sounded so off-hand it couldn't be natural. Luc smiled. 'Not at the moment.'

They spent the rest of the evening playing Scrabble. Ella was so jumpy that the tiles shook in her hands. 'Remember one of the last times we played? The beach on Praxos.'

'When we got stoned. Before getting into the jeep.'

'Before going to Ia. Before Yannick.' Ella shivered.

'Before Lorenzo.' Luc yelped. 'Shit. I've forgotten. He wanted to see me.'

'When?'

'Tonight. Now. He's in London. He called earlier.'

'Jesus, Luc, what are you doing? Go and see him. Right now,' exclaimed Ella. 'He's the sonnets and the symphonies and the waves crashing on the beach. Go.'

Luc pictured herself arriving at his hotel room and throwing her arms round him and holding him closer and closer. Feeling the peace of utter contentment, of safe arrival after a long, arduous journey.

'You're still in love with him, aren't you?' demanded Ella. Luc nodded. 'Go.'

For the briefest moment Luc was tempted. She looked at Ella, who needed her that night more than anyone had ever needed her. Men came and went. There'd be another Lorenzo one day. There could only ever be one Ella. One best friend.

'The condemned woman ate a hearty breakfast, and threw up.' Ella was pacing the sitting room. Luc couldn't believe the transformation. In her black suit, black tights, pearls and with her hair up, Ella looked as if she should be sitting with the magistrates rather than in the dock. Only the paleness of her face gave her away.

'If I'm sent down, will you move back in and look after the house? Actually, will you move back in anyway?'

Luc was taken aback. 'Are you sure?'

'Sure I'm sure. The Doll's House isn't home without you.'

In the cab to Victoria, Ella took deep breaths, staring out of the window as if it were her last ever sight of the streets she'd taken for granted. She clutched Luc's hand. The cabbie kept on staring at them in the rear-view mirror. They pulled up in front of the courthouse. 'Wish my brief looked like yours,' he said, glancing at Ella admiringly as Luc paid him. 'What are you up for?'

Luc scowled; he obviously mistook her for an accused. 'Assault.'

'On an impertinent taxi driver,' added Ella.

Their giggles died as they climbed the steps into the courthouse. Ella glanced around her apprehensively. Holding Luc's hand tight, she swallowed hard. 'I can't do it. I can't.'

'Come on. It's like the dentist. Thinking makes it worse.'

She yanked Ella inside like a stubborn dog on a lead. Having seen enough courtroom dramas on TV, she expected dignified calm, bewigged barristers and judges asking what are the Rolling Stones. However, the place had all the formality of a DSS office and was twice as dismal. Ella was told to go along a dingy corridor and wait outside Court Three until her case was called.

'Didn't realise we'd have to queue,' she muttered. All the vending machines they passed were out of order.

'Luc, thank God.' Liz was sitting on a bench with Tim. 'Where's Ella?'

'Here.'

'Ella?' Liz blinked. 'Ella? That's Chanel.' She made it sound as if it were Joseph's Amazing Technicolour Dreamcoat.

'I told you not to fret, Lizzy,' said Tim, kissing Ella's cheek. 'Very respectable.'

'If I were, I wouldn't be in this mess.'

'You'll be fine, sweets.' They all spun round and saw Alex. He looked as if he'd slept in his crumpled suit.

'Aren't you in Belfast?' exclaimed Luc.

'Liz called me last night. I got the first plane this morning.' He clutched Ella's shoulder. 'Where's your solicitor?'

'God knows.' Ella looked as if she were about to cry.

'Plenty of time yet. You're fifth. I'll get him paged. What's his name?'

'MacLeod. What do you mean I'm fifth?'

Alex opened a computer print out. 'Today's Press briefing. Four cases before yours. All drink-driving. Unfortunately you stand out because you're female with a very swank address. But there's something interesting in Court Two. Or so I'll tell my esteemed sheep-like colleagues.'

'What?' Ella was as bewildered as the rest.

'What's a brilliant reporter like me doing in a poxy magistrates' court, they'll ask themselves. And fear they're missing out on the scoop of the century. It might work. I'm going to schmooze around the Press Room. Cheer up, everyone. And switch off your phones.'

Mr MacLeod walked straight past until Ella called him. A dried-up stick in pinstripes, he was a walking gentleman's club committee and unimpeachably respectable. Ella's appearance passed muster, because he lost his bad-smell-under-his-nose look and actually bared his teeth in an almost smile. 'Don't worry, Miss Parr. We'll sort out this little difficulty.'

Tim coughed. 'Prison has been mentioned.'

'A possibility. About which I had to warn my client.'

Ella looked as if she were about to faint.

They waited in silence for what seemed like hours, then suddenly Ella was called. 'At least I'm not going in handcuffed. Coming out, who knows?' She stood up and took a deep breath. Mr MacLeod held the courtroom door open for her. Somewhere a clock struck eleven. ' "And therefore never send to know for whom the bell tolls; it tolls for thee." ' She straightened her shoulders and walked in.

Sitting in the public gallery, Luc couldn't see anyone scribbling. Alex must have been as good as his word. Standing in front of the three magistrates, Ella looked white but composed. She took the oath and pleaded guilty in a quiet, firm voice.

As the prosecuting counsel outlined the case, Liz and Luc glanced at one another. When he said the Bench had the power to impose a custodial sentence, Liz stifled a cry of dismay. Ella's back was ramrod-straight, she didn't move a muscle.

'Damning,' muttered Liz. 'How could that stupid man tell me last night he's got everything in hand?'

Whatever was in hand turned out to be in MacLeod's black briefcase. He handed the usher a medical report from the Nice hospital, 'translation attached, if required'; a second report from a pharmacist, 'the smallest quantity of alcohol with this drug has a deleterious effect on the system'; and a letter confirming Ella's place at the LSE.

'My client is an intelligent young woman who will be the first to admit she has transgressed in the past. She had learnt from her mistake and was looking to the future. The loss of the child she was bearing is a tragic misfortune. That misfortune brought her to this courtroom. A prison sentence is within your powers to bestow, but justice would not be served.'

The magistrates' chairman, a young woman in a dazzling turquoise sari, said they would retire to consider their verdict. As they left, Ella could be heard gasping for breath as if she'd been drowning.

On the courthouse steps Mr MacLeod declined the offer of lunch as if the suggestion were most unseemly. 'A satisfactory result, Miss Parr. I'll bid you good day and trust we'll meet under happier circumstances next time.' He briefly held out a desiccated hand, as if Ella's touch might be corrupting.

'Thank God.' Ella gazed up into the sky as if for the first time. She was so elated she seemed about to take flight. 'Six months more ban and a fine. Not bad.'

'Not bad? Brilliant,' said Alex. He nodded towards MacLeod's disappearing cab. 'Portia did her stuff.' Ella giggled. 'Where did you find him?'

'Inherited. Like everything else I possess. He hasn't done criminal work in years, apparently. I'm a bit of a come-down for the firm.'

'Not dressed like that,' said Tim.

'You in Chanel,' marvelled Liz.

'There's about a dozen in the wardrobe. Come round and take your pick.'

'What?' Liz was flabbergasted.

'You of all people must have a dressmaker,' said Ella. 'Get them altered. I'll keep this one, it's obviously lucky. And take the car, will you? Who's got the mobile?'

Luc handed over hers. She noticed it needed recharging. Ella booked a table. For five. Overlooking the park. Then she started singing 'Puttin' on the Ritz'.

Before they entered the Grill Room, Alex was handed a tie which he scowled at. 'If I wear the suit, you wear the tie,' said Ella.

'Remember, I wear the trousers,' said Alex.

'Promises, promises.'

'I mean it.'

Luc caught Liz and Tim glancing at one another, intrigued. 'I thought you two didn't get on,' said Liz.

'We don't,' they answered simultaneously.

'I can't bear spoilt little rich girls,' said Alex.

'I loathe chippy Aussies.' Ella ordered a bottle of champagne. She raised her glass. 'Thanks, everyone. Especially Luc. To freedom.'

'I must thank Luc too,' said Tim. 'I should have two features around November and a third in December. Perfect timing for August, eh, Lizzy?'

Liz glared, causing him to wince.

'What do you mean?' demanded Ella.

'Nothing.' Tim blushed tomato-red.

Liz put down her glass, unsmeared despite her lipstick. She shot him a furious look. 'What Tim means is that we're going to have a baby. Sorry, Ella, Tim's being tactless. After what you've gone through I'm sure you don't want to hear.'

'Oh yes I do.' Ella stared at them open-mouthed. 'It's brilliant news. What do you mean, August?'

'Tim should have enough work by then for us to get by on just one and a third incomes. And it's better for a child to be the youngest in the class. The academic year starts in September, so a birthday has to be as close as possible to the end of August.' She took another sip. 'I'll be conceiving in November.'

'What?' Ella burst out laughing. 'Liz, you're incorrigible. You mean . . . you've planned . . .'

'I really don't see what's so funny about giving a child the best possible start.'

'No. It's great.' Ella squeezed her hand. 'For both of you. It'll be a Virgo. Organised, meticulous, like you, Liz. Apparently Virgos make the best Nazis.' Alex laughed as she cringed. 'Forget I said that.'

Luc stared out at Green Park, where maintenance men were battling against the leaves. Swept into rust-coloured pyramids, gusts of wind would scatter them . . .

Liz was talking about another of Tim's new projects, a Jacobean manor whose owner wanted to build an indoor pool. Something ultra-contemporary. Refreshing to find a visionary client. If architecture had always emulated its history, the manor would never have been built.

Luc tried to imagine people sunbathing on deck-chairs, as unreal as her walking arm-in-arm with Lorenzo.

'I must send a *cadeau* to Amelia,' said Liz. 'The client called her when he saw the Geneva article, but she immediately put him in touch with Tim.'

'Integrity. All too rare, unfortunately,' sighed Tim.

'Is any envelope long enough for her name?' asked Liz. 'It goes on and on. Von this, zu that, bei the other. And the title, of course. A princess.'

'Lizzy, Amelia Schennen will do,' said Tim. 'She hates all that, wants to be taken on merit. She's very unassuming. Sweet.'

Uneasy, Alex and Ella looked at Luc, whose eyes were in her lap as she folded and refolded her napkin.

'How's the book, Alex?' asked Ella desperately. 'Have you two read it?'

Luc looked up. 'I guess she won't be changing her name when she's married.'

'Who?' Liz was puzzled.

'Amelia Schennen. The princess.'

'She's getting married? To who?'

'Whom,' corrected Ella and Alex under their breath.

Luc could hardly speak, the lump in her throat was so ginormous. 'Lorenzo von Retzen.'

'Lorenzo? Really?' squeaked Liz, then beamed ecstatically. 'We'll be invited to the wedding, won't we, Tim?' Her face fell. 'What shall I wear? It's bound to be incredibly grand. If I could look over that Chanel, Ella . . .'

Luc fled from the table.

In the ladies' loo, Luc took a deep breath and scrubbed away the mascara streaks under her eyes. She felt wretched, guilty about spoiling Ella's lunch. She tried to count her blessings — art college, moving back to the Doll's House, Ella — but she was as defeated as when she'd tried to grapple with trigonometry in double maths. And her hair was having the very worst day.

Reaching in her bag for a comb, she noticed her mobile flashing up 'Message'. Idly she pressed 'Play'. Why had she cut off her hair? Why was she getting a zit at an age when she should be investing in anti-wrinkle cream, not Clearasil?

'This is Lorenzo. I waited and waited. You didn't want. Now it's my turn to drown. Lake Geneva is more beautiful than the Thames. A consolation.'

Luc was statue-still. She gazed blankly at the mirror, seeing only lapis lazuli. The message had been left almost two hours earlier. She returned to the table in a trance. They were studying menus, Liz smugly giving her order in French to the Parisian waiter.

'What will you have? Luc?' asked Ella.

'Decide for me . . .' She frowned as if trying to work out a puzzle. 'Back in a minute.'

She leaped up and sprinted across the dining room, almost slaloming into a cheese trolley before richocheting off a party of elderly Americans. Hurtling along the mirrored corridor, she threw herself down the steps and out into Piccadilly. The traffic was deafening. Please God, he hadn't gone. Her fingers stabbed at her phone.

'Lorenzo. Lorenzo.' She was screaming to make herself heard. 'Luc?'

'Where are you?'

'Heathrow. About to get on a plane. Where are you?'

'The Ritz. About to have lunch.' A bus pulled up in a squeal of brakes. She wanted to scream at it to shut up. 'What? What did you say?'

'I've got to go. It's the last call. Too late, Luc.'

'Don't drown, come back, I do want . . .'

The phone was dead.

'Lorenzo?' asked Ella. She looked round the table. 'Told you so.'

'Sweets, no. It's not true.' Alex sighed despairingly. 'You'll ruin Ella's carpets. All that weeping.'

Luc looked at Ella. 'He sent the flowers. Not Yannick. He didn't know I'd moved out. *Je reviens, si tu veux.*'

'I'm coming back if you want me to,' said Liz. Her eyes widened. 'Lorenzo von Retzen said that?'

'Is he for you, Luc? Really?' asked Tim gently. 'Wasn't he just a holiday fling that got out of control? You girls do get into muddles. Look what happened . . .'

'To me?' Ella scoffed. 'Lorenzo's different. He's the sonnets and the symphonies and the waves crashing on the beach.'

'Precisely. An endearing, but rather immature attitude. Concentrate on college, Luc. Don't let that talent get distracted.'

'You'll make a great father,' said Ella. 'Cheer up, Luke-warm.'

Luc gazed down at her plate of smoked salmon. 'He was probably joking and is back with Amelia. I've left it too late. Besides, I can't compete with a princess.'

'You can,' said Alex. 'Get a plane to Geneva. Walk if you

must. Hunt him down.' She was bewildered. 'Life will be a misery for you and everyone around you if you don't.'

'You loathe him.'

'I loathed you. And Ella. I can be wrong. The only time I've seen you properly happy was that last morning in Greece. Follow that dream, sweets.'

'Like you and your book.'

'You don't have to keep updating your research every week.'

'Luc did,' said Ella. 'What about the Lorenzo homework? She's not still reading up on aeronautics, is she, Alex?'

'Shut up,' hissed Luc.

'Aeronautics? Luc?' Liz and Tim were incredulous.

'It was love,' said Alex.

'Still is,' said Ella.

Urged on by the four, Luc decided she'd call Lorenzo in a few hours once he was back in Geneva. She had nothing to lose. He wasn't married. Not yet, anyway. Ella, Alex, Liz, Tim. Looking round the table, she felt as she had in double maths when she'd finally understood the beautiful logic of equations. Even if she was still hopeless at calculus and would never see the point of logarithms, she could suddenly count her blessings.

As the final glass of champagne was poured and coffee ordered, Luc almost jumped out of her seat in alarm. How could she completely forget about work? 'I'd better find out if I still have a job. Can I borrow your mobile, Alex?'

'Have mine,' said a voice behind her.

Luc froze, then turned round as if in slow motion. Speechless, she gazed up. A hush fell around the table. 'You're meant . . .' she could hardly speak. 'Why aren't you in Geneva?'

'*Je reviens, si tu veux.*' He was grave, unsmiling. Another black-suited defendant who was waiting to hear his fate. 'Do you want, Luc?'

She dived into the depths of lapis lazuli. 'More than anything else in the whole world.'

*

Lorenzo broke off from gazing at Luc to glance around the gilded dining room. He smiled at Liz. 'A long way from the taverna on Ia.'

'No fuss about ties there,' said Alex. 'I'm being strangled.'

'Use it as a gag,' suggested Ella.

'Then he couldn't read you poetry,' said Tim, causing her to blush scarlet. As he watched Lorenzo kiss Luc's fingers, he motioned to Liz that they should go. 'Are you sure about this, Ella? It's very generous.'

'My pleasure.' She called for the bill. As Liz got up, they hugged one another. ' 'Bye, big sis.'

'Less of the big,' reproved Liz. 'I know I've got to lose a kilo but life's been . . .'

'Take her away, Tim,' begged Ella. 'And force-feed her *marrons glacés* and violet creams and chocolate truffles.'

Luc and Lorenzo were staring at one another, enraptured. Mesmerised, they could hardly say their goodbyes. He touched her face as if to make sure she was real. 'A long way,' he murmured.

'It's the same, wherever.'

Sounding ultra-casual, Ella was suggesting that Alex came to the Doll's House to borrow a Yeats biography. Even more casually, she asked where Luc was staying that night. 'Mine or Alex's?'

Luc looked up at the pair of them. For some reason Alex avoided her eyes and Ella was concentrating hard on the gilt buttons on her jacket cuff. Luc raised an eyebrow and suppressed a smile.

'Neither,' said Lorenzo. 'We're staying here.'

It was dark outside, Green Park an expanse of inky black. Luc snuggled closer to Lorenzo and tried to untangle the bedclothes at the same time. She didn't want to let him go. 'What about Amelia?' A wave of anxiety broke over her. 'The real-life princess? You're sure you're not getting married?'

'Keep still.'

'I'm trying to get closer.'

'Good.' Smiling, his grip round her tightened. 'Once upon a time there was a beautiful princess living in a white castle. She had a mane of long golden hair . . .'

'Like Ella,' said Luc.

'Just like Ella. Although younger. She was spoilt and indulged by her parents, the king and queen, and allowed to do almost whatever she liked. Only one thing was forbidden to her. She must never kiss a frog.'

'But they turn into princes.'

'Sssh. One day the princess with her mane of golden hair was all alone in her enchanting garden. There, perched on a rock beside a waterfall, she saw a little frog. He was the most beautiful emerald-green. Very gently, she picked him up. Furtively, she glanced around her. No one would ever know. And very quickly the beautiful princess kissed this beautiful little emerald-green frog.'

'And . . .?'

'And . . . suddenly there were two beautiful little emerald-green frogs in the enchanting garden.'

'Hang up the suit,' said Alex the following morning. 'It's lucky. Or do you always use the floor as a wardrobe?'

Ella tipped a bundle of newspapers on to the bed. 'Do you always need a rain forest to be cut down for your morning's amusement?'

'Work,' said Alex. 'Something you don't know much about.'

'Will soon.' She had told him the night before that once the Masters was out of the way, she wanted to do a PhD. She kissed his shoulder and gazed and gazed at his bare chest. 'You've got the most amazing . . .' she paused, grinning at her good fortune, 'heart.'

'Can I wear you?' He pulled her down, rolling her across the bed until she was underneath him. 'You're not as classic, but definitely lucky.'

'Close the deal first. If you're offered one.'

'I will be.' He smiled down at Ella. His agent had called him late the previous afternoon. Two American publishers were interested in his book. She was busy exploiting the cut-throat rivalry between them and expected a definite offer within days.

Later, Ella went downstairs to make breakfast. For the hundredth time she silently thanked Luc for clearing up the Doll's House, otherwise Alex might have fled and reported her to the environmental health police. Instead of going through the books on her shelves and talking and talking and laughing until . . . She grinned again.

'No,' cried Alex from upstairs.

'What is it?'

'Quickly.'

'What?' Ella rushed back into the bedroom.

'Look.'

Ella's eyes widened as she read the forty-odd words. 'Better call the Ritz.'

'What are you doing today?' Luc munched on a jammy croissant. She must go back to Alex's and get some clean clothes.

'That's up to you.'

Luc had woken to find him showered, shaved and dressed. Apparently he'd been up for hours. The *Wall Street Journal* and the *Financial Times* were unread. His laptop was shut, his phone silent. He seemed distracted, a cat prowling around unable to settle. 'I might be viewing some property. Very close to Ella's house.'

'In London? As an investment?' Luc told herself off for being lazy, remembering Liz's advice about buying somewhere. Not that it was an option for another three years. He came and sat beside her on the bed. 'You got up too early.'

'Perhaps I'm too old. For a student.'

'Perhaps I'm too old to be a student. Most people will have just left school.'

He looked strained. But smelt glorious. Luc reached out to touch him, but realised her fingers were covered in jam and butter grease and crumbs. And yesterday's eye make-up which wasn't on the white linen pillowcase was probably somewhere round her chin.

'Lucasta, Luc . . .'

'I must have a shower.'

He tried to stop her but she wriggled away. As she stood under the gush of shower water, she was certain she heard the telephone ring. Amelia? A chill ran through her. It couldn't be. He said it was over, finished the moment the helicopter had landed on Ia. Luc wrapped herself in a bathrobe.

Lorenzo was holding a paper, smiling as he read something.

'Good cartoon?' asked Luc. 'Show me.'

'Ella called. I said you'd call back later. Can you sit down? Luc? Please?'

'Only if you show me the cartoon.' Smiling, she sat beside him. As she caught sight of what he was reading, her smile faded. Forthcoming Marriages.

She gazed up into the blue depths of his eyes. 'Is this a misprint? A joke?'

'I hope not.' He smiled a smile of heartbreaking joy.

Speechlessly Luc read and re-read the announcement. 'The engagement is announced between Lorenzo Leopold Heinrich . . .'

Gently Lorenzo took her left hand.

Luc gazed down at the ring he had placed on her third finger. In a setting of lapis lazuli was a diamond as big as the Ritz.

SARAH INGHAM

PARALLEL TURNS

Skiing? Forget it!

The thought of hurtling down a mountainside on two pieces of fibreglass fills Flora Rose with horror. How could she ever have let her fiancé Jamie cajole her into sharing an Alpine chalet with his motley crew of friends!

So begins an extraordinary week of drama, danger, thrills and spills, passion, violence, tears, tantrums, sordid secrets – and unexpected romance.

Nothing will ever be quite the same again.

> 'Even the snow-laden atmosphere does nothing to cool the passions in this steamy story of sex, snowploughing and chalet girls'
> *Marie Claire*

> 'Jauntily entertaining . . . A very well-written romp with more twists and turns than an off-piste run'
> *Ms London*

HODDER AND STOUGHTON PAPERBACKS

A selection of bestsellers from
Hodder & Stoughton

Parallel Turns	Sarah Ingham	0 340 74843 5	£5.99 ☐
Lizzie Jordan's Secret Life	Chris Manby	0 340 76918 1	£5.99 ☐
Deep Heat	Chris Manby	0 340 71761 0	£5.99 ☐
Snap Happy	Fiona Walker	0 340 68227 2	£5.99 ☐
Well Groomed	Fiona Walker	0 340 66049 X	£5.99 ☐

All Hodder & Stoughton books are available at your local bookshop or newsagent, or can be ordered direct from the publisher. Just tick the titles you want and fill in the form below. Prices and availability subject to change without notice.

Hodder & Stoughton Books, Cash Sales Department, Bookpoint, 39 Milton Park, Abingdon, OXON, OX14 4TD, UK. E-mail address: order@bookpoint.co.uk. If you have a credit card you may order by telephone – (01235) 400414.

Please enclose a cheque or postal order made payable to Bookpoint Ltd to the value of the cover price and allow the following for postage and packing:

UK & BFPO – £1.00 for the first book, 50p for the second book, and 30p for each additional book ordered up to a maximum charge of £3.00.

OVERSEAS & EIRE – £2.00 for the first book, £1.00 for the second book, and 50p for each additional book

Name _____

Address _____

_____

_____

If you would prefer to pay by credit card, please complete:
Please debit my Visa/Access/Diner's Card/American Express (delete as applicable) card no:

Signature _____

Expiry Date _____

If you would NOT like to receive further information on our products please tick the box. ☐